John Gilbert, John Frederick Smith

Stanfield Hall

Vol. 1

John Gilbert, John Frederick Smith

Stanfield Hall
Vol. 1

ISBN/EAN: 9783337347383

Printed in Europe, USA, Canada, Australia, Japan

Cover: Foto ©Andreas Hilbeck / pixelio.de

More available books at **www.hansebooks.com**

STANFIELD HALL:

AN

HISTORICAL ROMANCE.

By J. F. SMITH,

AUTHOR OF

"MINNIGREY," "WOMAN AND HER MASTER,"
"WILL AND THE WAY," Etc.

VOL. I.

Illustrated by SIR JOHN GILBERT, R.A.,
AND OTHER EMINENT ARTISTS.

LONDON :

BRADLEY & CO., 12 AND 13, FETTER LANE, E.C.

MDCCCLXXXVIII.

LONDON:
PRINTED BY C. W. BRADLEY AND CO,
12 AND 13, FETTER LANE, E.C.

CONTENTS.

~~~~~~

ILLUSTRATIONS.

~~~~~~~

STANFIELD HALL.

CHAPTER I.

STANFIELD HALL, the scene of so many remarkable events and fearful crimes, is one of the oldest manors in England. It is called in the Norman register, known by the name of "Doomsday-book," Stainsfields, and sometimes Stanfells. It seems to have been erected into a lordship as early as the Heptarchy, having probably been held at that remote period by one of the powerful franklins of the East Angles.

In the reign of Edward the Confessor it was possessed by the rich and ancient family of Hale, or Held, as they are denominated in the chronicles of Walter of Cotessy, a monkish writer of the twelfth century, whose quaint histories and obscure Latin will well repay the labour of those who have either time or patience to pore over his dusty manuscripts.

At the period at which our tale commences—the year preceding the fatal battle of Hastings—it was the chief residence of Herwald de Hale, so called by all the Norman writers—the distinctive particle *de* marking their acknowledgment of the nobility of the powerful Saxon, who was more familiarly known to those of his own race as Herwald of Stanfells, or Herwald of the Tower.

Stanfield, in the age of which we write, presented a far different appearance from the present comparatively modern pile, which offers a fair specimen of the mixed domestic architecture which characterised the reign of Elizabeth ; a low range of buildings, built of sunburnt bricks and rough stones, inclosed a large quadrangular court, capable, in case of need, of containing the herds of cattle which formed no inconsiderable portion of the wealth of the Saxon proprietor. The windows—if the unglazed apertures might be so designated—were all to the interior, a few narrow loopholes only being left in the outward walls for the purpose of reconnoitring or defence. The place, or holm, as the buildings were called, was still further strengthened by irregular towers at its respective angles.

B 2

The principal tower, from which the Saxons gave to the lord of Stanfells his distinctive appellation, was a lofty building, with more pretension to architectural ornament than the rest. Over the low, circular arched door was a rudely-sculptured shield, displaying a bittern in the centre of a cross engrailed—the arms, doubtless, of its founder ; but how obtained, or by whom bestowed, it might puzzle the Heralds' College to decide. A corresponding door on the opposite side of the tower admitted into the interior of the quadrangle, of which it formed the principal object and defence. The lands surrounding the edifice were rich pasture, well drained by irregular channels, cut to convey the water to the extensive moat, which said moat was crossed by a rude drawbridge of wood, which partially extended over the stream, and rested on an irregular bridge of stone, whose arches reached to the middle only of the moat. The drawbridge was capable of being either removed or destroyed upon the first approach of danger. Low, thick woods extended from the clear pasture lands even to the limits of the town of Wynmondham, or Wyndham, as the inhabitants now call it, then celebrated as the residence of a sainted anchorite, upon the ruins of whose cell the present church is built. These woods served as the retreat of vast herds of swine, which lived in a half-savage state within its almost impervious recesses, and served as shelter to the deer and game for which that part of England has so long been celebrated.

Herwald of the Tower, the owner of the edifice we have endeavoured to describe, was a true Saxon, generous, fierce, and impetuous —a mixture of the good and evil qualities of his unhappy race. Passionately addicted to war, and its mimic pastime the chase, his character naturally bore the impress of his pursuits. He was proud of his wealth and lineage, but still prouder of the object in which they were both to centre—his only child, Edith, the heiress of Stanfield, and many a fair broad land beside. Resolute as the franklin was, he had seldom been known to resist the slightest wish of his daughter, who might without impropriety have been called Our Lady of *Bon Secours* by all who stood in fear of her impetuous father's resentment. As good as she was beautiful, even the extravagant indulgence of her sire had failed to spoil her—an indulgence more frequently forced upon her than sought. Edith possessed neither the blue eyes nor fair hair so characteristic of her race ; on the contrary, her tresses might have vied with the raven's wing in blackness ; her eyes, of the same colour, were chastened in their brilliancy by a melancholy expression, which seemed to foreshadow some impending doom ; but the maiden's complexion was fair as e'en the fairest of her race—so pure, so transparent, and so clear, that her rising thoughts might be read in roseate changes, as clouds are seen reflected on the bosom of some tranquil lake. To the advantage of personal beauty, Edith added that of simple as well as rich attire.

It is true the arms and neck of the noble Saxon maiden were circled with jewelled bracelets and a collar of gold—ornaments indispensable to her birth and station ; but her robes were made in the simplest form, and generally of white ; the girdle which bound them to her slender waist being of needlework, and matching with the embroidered hem of the ample veil which floated round her.

It was in a costume much like the one we have attempted to describe that Edith, surrounded by her handmaidens and two or three officers of her father's household, stood, at the close of a cold autumnal day, within the narrow entrance of the principal tower of Stanfield, to await the franklin's return. Darkness already obscured the horizon, and a shower of sleet began to fall.

" I wish," exclaimed Judith, Edith's favourite attendant and foster sister, shivering, and drawing her wimple closer round her shoulders, " our master would return, or that you, noble lady, would retire to your chamber : the sleet reaches you even here ; and it is not so long," she added, in a lower tone, " since your illness, that you should unnecessarily brave it. Be persuaded, dear lady, and let us in."

" Not so," mildly replied Edith, whom the whispered allusion to her illness had evidently disconcerted, but not angered. " Thou knowest, Judith, that my father is displeased if his daughter's step fail to meet him at the threshold on his return ; and I must not anger him. Disobedience in a child is a sin ; in me it would, I ween, be a fearful one," she added, tears suffusing her eyes as she spoke, " having so kind a parent."

" The kindest are sometimes unreasonable," thought Judith, who, however, was far too prudent to give utterance to her imagination, certain that it would be disapproved by her young mistress. Perhaps her knowledge of her lady's secret cause of uneasiness was present to her ideas, for she knew that Edith loved, and that her love was not blessed with her father's smile.

" Our master will soon be here," exclaimed old Hubert, the nominal seneschal of the holm—we say nominal, for, on account of his great age and blindness, the duties of his office were performed by his nephew, Huon, a sturdy man-at-arms, whose tender assiduities had, it was supposed by the gossips of the household, at length found favour with the pretty Judith.

" Soon be here, indeed ! " he repeated ; " why, uncle, do you pretend to the gift of second sight ? Our eyes are young, and keen enough, yet we can discover no traces of our lord's approach."

" If my eyes are dim, boy," answered the old man, " praise to St. Cuthbert, my ears are as true as ever. Hark ! " he added, forming a hollow with his hand to his ear, to aid the sense as he spoke, " black Hubert is giving tongue right merrily. There are other dogs than our lord's," he added, after a pause, during which the rest of the attendants, who had more faith in his perception than his ungracious nephew, had vainly listened for the distant sounds ; "some stranger of note is with our master. In, knaves, in, and prepare for the reception of an honoured guest."

"By Hengist, lady, but old Hubert is right," said Judith, who at last caught the distant baying of the deep-mouthed hounds ; "your honoured father approaches.; but whether accompanied by guests or no is more than I can guess or tell, though any guest were welcome, provided he were young and handsome, to these old towers."

"Peace, Judith," answered her mistress, with a smile, "thy tongue outruns discretion. See !" she added, as the hunting party appeared in sight, emerging from the thick umbrageous wood, "my honoured father comes ; let us forth to meet him."

Scarcely had the expecting party, who followed their young mistress, gained the drawbridge, than the hunters reached it. The franklin, a hale, powerful man of fifty, was the first to cross it. Leaping from his horse, which he left to his numerous attendants to catch, he hastily approached his lovely child.

"Why, how now, Edith, bird !" he exclaimed. "Why have you quitted your tapestried nook to expose your cheek to the keen blast ? This is no night for maidens to be abroad in. Come," he added, throwing his mantle round her shoulders, after kissing her on the forehead, "let us in. I must see you with your brightest eyes and sweetest smile to-night—we have a guest at Stanfield." Her father indicated with a glance at the conclusion of his speech a man about five-and-twenty, who was in the act of dismounting, that he might in a more seemly manner pay his homage to the Lady Edith.

"My uncle said we should have guests," muttered Huon, aside ; "but little did I dream that it would be our lord's nephew. What brings him here ? The old scent, I suppose."

"Whatever brings him," whispered Judith, who had overheard the observation, "it bodes our lady no good. Why, the two years accorded by her father are not yet expired ! "

"Perhaps," answered Huon, "he comes to renounce his claim to the Lady Edith's hand, seeing that she hath scant love for him."

"He renounce his claim to her hand ! " answered Judith, her lips curling with scorn. "No, no ; you know him too well to think or hope it. .He will never renounce it while she is the heiress of broad lands, or his craven heart thirsts for gold. He resign her ! As well ask thy hawk, Master Huon, to forego its prey, when poised to make the deadly swoop, or lure the bloodhound from the track it hath followed for days, as expect Herman of the Burg to forego the prize which he believes to be within his reach."

"Believes within his reach ! If our lord's will does not alter, he is sure it is within his reach."

"Perhaps," replied the damsel, with a smile of intelligence ;

" but wills as stern as the franklin's have ere now been thwarted, and by a thing as weak as woman's resolution."

The effect produced by the appearance of Herman of the Burg upon the lovely Edith was most distressing ; the blood forsook her lips and cheeks, and her mild eyes were cast hopelessly round, as if to seek a refuge from some impending evil. Her wily suitor either did not or would not notice her distress ; with a high-bred courtesy, whose refinement was a mockery, he half-bent the knee as he saluted his cousin's hand ; his triumphant glance gave the lie to the humility of the action—the latter was for his uncle, the former for his intended victim.

" Come, my children," uttered Herwald, who at last perceived his daughter's agitation, " this is no place for greeting. You, Herman, go and change your rough riding gear—women love not to look upon soiled garments and stained plumes ; and you, Edith," he added, " to your tire-women. Remember," he whispered, in reply to her glance of supplication, " your brightest smiles and gayest robes to-night."

The passionate fondness of the Saxon franklin for his daughter will at first, perhaps, appear to our readers incompatible with the violence which he evidently placed upon her inclinations. A few words will explain the seeming incongruity. Herman of the Burg was the heir of his name, and consequently preferred by him as a suitor for his daughter's hand.

In Herwald the love for his child, deep and indulgent as was the sentiment, was second only to his pride of ancestry. No other Saxon, no matter how noble his lineage, how valiant his achievements, could perpetuate to his race the name which he himself so proudly bore, and to this vain pride the happiness of his child was to be coldly sacrificed.

Indulgent to excess in every other matter, he would listen to no remonstrance to this. Two years previous to the commencement of our history he had quarrelled violently with his oldest friend and brother in arms, Edda, the Saxon, because his son Edward had presumed to love his daughter. In birth, disposition, and fortune they were equal. As children they were reared together. The gentle disposition of the gallant boy had won the maiden's heart, and they mutually loved, in the confiding innocence of their natures, before they were aware that the fatal passion had found an entrance to their souls. Time at length revealed to Edward the nature of his hopes and wishes.

His high sense of honour told him how to act. He sought his father, confessed his passion, and besought him to demand the hand of Edith of the franklin. The result of their interview has been already stated. The two fathers, who had so long been sworn friends, parted declared enemies ; each commanding their offspring never to think of such a marriage more.

How easy it is for parents to utter commands which the heart finds it impossible to obey! Edith, who till that moment had found her chief happiness in fulfilling her father's wishes, for the first time in her life found them harsh and difficult. Edward, till then all submission to his venerable parent, declared obedience impossible. Vainly they strove to forget each other—memory had too fondly treasured each loved image in its shrine for mere commands to part them. In short, aided by the faithful Judith, whose indignation at her master's cruelty was often loudly and vehemently expressed, the lovers contrived to meet. Eloquence is doubly persuasive when uttered by those we love. Edward succeeded; and the unhappy Edith was, at the period of which we write, in secret both a wife and mother.

"Now, may the Mother of Heaven aid me!" exclaimed the unhappy Edith, as soon as she had reached her chamber, throwing herself at the same time on the neck of the faithful Judith. "The hour I have so long dreaded has arrived—the hour when I must brave a father's curse. Oh, the sin," she added, wringing her hands as she spoke, "the bitter sin of disobedience!"

"Be comforted, dear lady," soothingly uttered her attendant, alarmed at the despair of her mistress. "Your noble father loves you dearer than aught on earth. He will never resist your prayers and tears. Besides, you have an advocate in your fair boy. Think you, that when he sees the heir of his proud name, the son of his loved Edith, his iron nature will not at last give way? Besides," she added, with a half-smile, "at the worst, it is but running away. Your lord hath a fair castle to receive and brave friends to protect you. Things are never so bad but that they may be mended, or but they might be worse."

"This visit, this ill-omened visit!" murmured Edith, scarcely conscious of the utterance of her thoughts. "This very night, too, I was to have seen my Edward."

"And your boy, your fair, sweet boy!" interrupted Judith, willing to change the current of her thoughts. "You must think of him, act for him. I would that black Herman had met the foul fiend in his path ere he had crossed yours. But since it is so, let's meet him bravely. At ten to-night your lord and infant will arrive at my mother's cottage. The little rogue, how I do long to kiss him! You must contrive to see him, and consult what is to be done."

"Impossible! I must remain within the banquet hall. You heard my father's words? And even supposing I could contrive to escape the feast, how quit the manor?"

"Leave that to me," answered Judith. "Huon keeps the keys, and never more shall he have smile or fair word of me unless he do my bidding. And now," she continued, "dear lady, let me arrange your hair. Your veil is damp with the night dew and the sleet.

The bell will soon sound, and your noble father is impatient of being kept waiting."

Edith, seating herself upon a faldstool, resigned herself into the busy hand of her attendant, who, removing the veil and fastening from her mistress's head, suffered her long tresses to flow for a few seconds over her shoulders, while she sought in a small, quaintly-carved ivory cabinet a rich circlet of gems to replace the simple bandeau which she had removed.

While so occupied Edith sat like a statue of Grief, fair in its pensive loveliness, her long hair, like a sable veil, shading her pallid features ; her pure heart torn by the agony of conflicting emotions ; her mind absorbed, calmed by the intenseness of its agonies.

The hall was illuminated by pine torches, and huge candles of coarse tallow placed in iron. sconces at irregular distances on the wall. The logs of wood burned briskly in the wide chimney ; their dancing flames and crackling embers sent forth a genial heat, and gave an almost comfortable appearance to the desolate apartment.

The broad-chested staghounds were lying at their ease before the fire, fatigued by the day's protracted chase. A careless observer would, from their half-closed eyes, have pronounced them sleeping ; but whenever a fresh footstep fell on the rough stone pavement the open eye and pricked ear showed that they were wakefully attentive to all that passed.

The numerous domestics had already placed the manchet bread and spiced cover, when Herwald entered the hall, accompanied by Herman and others of his guests. His pet hound rose lazily to meet him, and with the familiarity of an admitted favourite, thrust his long nose into the franklin's hand, in order to attract his attention and obtain the customary caress.

" Down, Odin, down ! " cried his master, peevishly, his displeasure excited at the absence of his daughter Edith, who had not yet made her appearance. " What do the hounds do here ? Is there no chenery at Stanfield, that we must have them in our very chambers ? See to it, knaves, for the future, and force me not to look to it."

The faithful animal was not to be repulsed by words, but continued to press his claim to notice, the canine courtier not knowing, like his human brother, that there are moments of *ennui* in the lives of despots when even flattery offends and homage fatigues—a truth of which poor Odin soon received a practical illustration. An impatient kick sent him howling to a distant corner of the apartment.

" Come," continued Herwald, " let us to the feast, and you, Huon, must serve my cup to-night. It seems my child hath forgot it is her father's hour of service."

" Not for lack of being reminded," said Herman. " For 'tis not so long since you bade her to the feast."

" Humph ! " muttered the franklin ; " that speech were better from her father's lips. Thou hast scant courtesy. Herman, in that rugged heart of thine, and I sometimes wish that thou wert other than my brother's son. What right hast thou to blame her?"

The wily nephew perceived that he had gone too far. Herwald's parental love and pride took the alarm that another should presume to blame his child. Herman knew that his uncle loved him not for himself, but as the heritor of his name, and that, if provoked, he was capable of sacrificing even the fixed purpose of his life to Edith's tears and his own resentment.

"You deal not fairly with me, noble franklin," he replied. "You first cut short my speech, then blame me for its harshness. I was about to express my fear that the keen blast and sleet which blanched my cousin's cheek had chilled her blood. That illness might——"

"Illness!" interrupted Herwald, his love to Edith changing the current of his thoughts. "What a churl am I to blame her! It must be so. I marked her pallid cheek and clouded eye, and thought they both proceeded from a different cause. Now, knaves, can ye not stir? Haste to your lady's chamber; tell her——"

His further words were cut short by the entrance of Edith, who at last had mustered sufficient courage to meet her father's glance—to endure her cousin's detested assiduities.

"Why, this is well," cried the franklin, kindly taking her by the hand to lead her to a seat, his eye glancing in approbation on her improved attire. "Our feast were dull, Edith, without thy presence. To your places," he added, turning to his guests. "Our worthy chaplain will ask the blessing, and my daughter speak her father's welcome."

The portly ecclesiastic spoke the hurried benediction, and the flowing wine cup soon began to circle in the hall of Stanfield.

In a distant chamber of the holm a different scene was passing. Hubert, the aged seneschal, was sleeping in a rough settle lined with deer-skin, beside a smouldering fire, whose red, flickering blaze, as it alternately rose and fell, gave a Rembrandt-like expression to his features. His bunch of ponderous keys hung on a hook within reach of his shrivelled hand; the doors had all been fastened for the night, and the faithful servitor, conscious that he had fulfilled his duty, was indulging in repose.

The sounds of revelry came louder and louder, when Huon, followed by Judith, appeared cautiously at the door of the chamber in which his uncle sat; and, after reconnoitring awhile, slowly, and with the stealthy pace of a cat, approached the old man's chair. His manner would have seemed suspicious, had not the open, manly expression on his rough, handsome face, and the half-laughing, half-anxious countenance of the damsel, who was watching him, precluded all idea of any sinister design.

Comparatively noiseless as were the steps of Huon, they fell upon the sleeper's ear, or perchance his breath fell upon his aged face as he leant over him to reach the keys ; for at the very moment he grasped them, Hubert awoke, and caught the culprit's receding arm.

"Eh ! what ? " exclaimed the seneschal, " have we thieves in Stanfield ? What, ho ! help ! knaves ! Help, I say ! "

Fortunately at that moment a fresh burst from the banquet chamber covered the speaker's voice.

· Silence, uncle, silence ! " whispered Huon, " 'tis I, your nephew. Have you been dreaming ? or do you suppose that I am come to rob you ? "

· I don't know," replied the old man, suspiciously, " the world has grown so changed and wicked. What want you with the keys ? The gates are all made fast ; and without the franklin's order, none may enter or have egress to-night."

"Pshaw, uncle, our master carouses ; would you have me disturb him for a trifle like this ? It is only for Judith, who is anxious to visit her mother's cottage to-night ; her young lady hath given her permission to be absent, and—here, Judith," he added, "come and speak for yourself."

The maiden advanced and laid her hand upon the arm of the valiant guardian, half-smiling and half-pouting as she did so.

"Come, Hubert, you surely won't refuse me," she said ; "my poor mother is ill, and tards to see her child."

"Well, well," replied the old man, gradually relaxing his grasp upon the keys, for Judith was a favourite with him, " I am glad it is no worse. Thou art a duteous child," he added ; "unlike my roystering scapegrace ; thou canst honour grey hairs. There, take the key ; but who is to go with thee ? True, the land is quiet, and there is little fear of robbers, but still it is not seemly that my old cummer's daughter should cross the wold like a wayfarer or run-away serf."

"I shall accompany her, uncle ; under my care it must be a bold arm that would do her wrong."

Huon's glance of affection as he spoke was answered by Judith with a corresponding one of innocent confidence

"Ho, ho ! " laughingly exclaimed the old man, "what ! is my dainty springer caught at last ? Huon," he added, checking his tone and speaking in a more serious voice, "this must be no light of love."

"Uncle——"

"Well, well—there now, I'll trust thee—I'll trust to thee," and the aged man sank chuckling in his warm seat by the fire, his thoughts gradually becoming confused, wandering from Huon and Judith to the recollection of his own all but forgotten boyish passion.

"In an hour meet me at the gate," whispered Judith to her

lover. "By that time the household will have retired to rest, and I may pass forth unperceived."

"But my guerdon," replied the squire, not willing to be baulked of his promised reward.

"Out on thee for an unreasonable creditor!" said his mistress. "Wouldst have me pay thy service before it is performed? It were poor wisdom that."

Huon, expecting that he should have a fair opportunity of urging his suit during their walk to the cottage, grumblingly submitted to the postponement of the kiss, the bribe for which he had been tempted to steal the keys from his uncle, to whose charge, after the fastening of the doors, they were invariably given.

On reaching her chamber, Judith found her young mistress, who, under the plea of indisposition, had contrived to withdraw from the banquet, awaiting her return. The triumphant confidence of Herman terrified her; her father's open allusion, when warmed with wine, to her approaching union too plainly told her how fixed was his resolution, how hopeless the chance of moving him from his long-settled purpose; and the timid girl, with a firmness springing from desperation, almost rejoiced at the insuperable bar which her secret marriage placed to the intended union.

A few moments under the hand of her nimble confidante served to remove the jewels and gay attire, which, in obedience to the franklin, she had assumed. A dark dress and linen wimple supplied their place; and as they passed forth together the heiress of Stanfield might have been taken by any straggling domestic for a fellow servant passing to perform some household duty.

"How now?" whispered Huon, as they reached the gate where, by appointment, he waited the arrival of Judith; "a companion! This is more than I bargained for, surely," he added, in a tone of reproach, "you cannot mistrust me?"

"And surely," said his mistress, in a corresponding voice, "you cannot judge so lightly of me as to suppose that I would quit the holm at such an hour alone with any man. No, Huon, no. Evil tongues are too often busy with a maiden's fame. They may say I have a careless laugh and a light word, but none shall say my acts were not of honesty and virtue."

"Tell me, at least, who is to be our companion," he replied, at the same time opening the great door.

Edith, who overheard the words, passed hastily through.

"Humph! it can't be old Alice," he continued; "her step is too nimble for her."

"Perhaps," said Judith, "it is deaf Ann. But no matter who it is. Give us your arm, make fast the tower, and Heaven and St. Cuthbert guide us on our way."

The astonishment of Huon on his arrival at the cottage may be imagined when he found that he had been instrumental in the absence of his young lady. His fair tempter's smile and kiss reassured him, and the visions of punishment and terror of his master, which the discovery at first conjured up, gradually gave way to the smile of Judith and the iterated thanks of Edward and his lady.

The jest and song had long ceased in the hall of Stanfield, and its inmates retired to rest, when a phantom-like figure might be seen approaching the walls. With the utmost deliberation he counted the loopholes, commencing with the left of the principal tower, and paused at the twelfth. Looking carefully round, he threw himself into a crouching position beneath the shade of an aged pollard, and placing his fingers to his lips imitated the peculiar cry of the bittern, paused for a few moments twice, and after each pause renewed it.

At the end of the third signal Herman and his confidant, Unolff, appeared upon the walls, their usual costume hid by the close leathern shirt usually worn by the superior vassals and ecclesiastical serfs. A cord, which the squire fixed to one of the rough projecting stones of the tower, enabled them to descend, and in a few moments from their first appearance on the walls they stood before the holm. At a signal from Herman the crouching man approached.

"Speak," whispered the Saxon, repressing passion, causing the words to whistle through his close set teeth ; "have you dogged him to the lair?"

"I have, noble franklin," replied the man. "I followed him for many a weary mile, often burying myself in the bog to the shoulders to avoid recognition ; sometimes trailing my limbs like a serpent through the woods ; and I housed him safely at last in the cottage."

"Thou art the best of bloodhounds!" exclaimed his master, a gleam of ferocious joy lighting up his pale and agitated features. "Are your fellows posted? 'Tis well," he continued, in answer to a sign of assent. "Now, then, follow me. Let your hearts be firm and your hands sure. You know the recompense."

His two companions inclined their heads in token of obedience, and the doomed murderer sullenly pursued his path, bent on his cruel purpose, reckless alike of human or divine retribution, which, sooner or later, with its iron hand, crushes the mail of guilt, lays bare the sinner's breast, and vindicates the eternal laws of justice unto man.

How sweet, how ennobling, are the sentiments of maternity ! how vast the courage inspired by a pure and virtuous love ! In the caresses of her child and husband, the sorrows, the wild despair of Edith became calm, and she viewed the inevitable *eclaircissement* no longer with the sullen stupor of a hopeless heart, but with the calmness of reason and the trustfulness of religion.

It was finally arranged that Edith should disclose her marriage to her father, trusting to his extreme affection and the impression likely to be produced by the sight of his infant grandson, who was consigned to the faithful Judith's care, to effect a reconciliation.

"Trust me, dearest Edith," said her husband, as the parting moment arrived, "that all will yet be well. Stern as is the frauklin's heart, it hath a stream of tenderness for thee too deep for anger to freeze, too pure to be sullied by unreasonable resentment. At first, I doubt not but his rage will be fearful ; fortunately, violent emotions soon exhaust themselves. Would," he added, "that I could be the first to bear the brunt of his indignation, to turn his wrath from thy dear head ! Remember, it is for our boy you plead : a mother's eloquence is ever irresistible. Take courage, Edith ; and many a joyous hour in Stanfield's halls shall well repay thee for each sorrow past."

With this and similar arguments did Edward sustain the courage of his trembling wife, whose resolution rose and fell as hope or fear alternately prevailed. The hour of parting at last arrived. The iron tongue of night had long told the birth of morning when Edith and her attendants set forth to return to the hall.

"I must to my father," said Edward ; "I can trust his generous nature for forgiveness. His anger, like a summer's storm, is fierce, but quickly dies away. With the morning, I am sure he will be at Stanfield to calm your father's wrath, or, at the worst, protect his child."

The parting kiss was given—the last that cruel destiny permitted them on earth. A serpent envious of their happiness was in their path, and Edward's guardian angel slept. Agreeable to his intention of seeking his parent, he directed his steps towards the distant village, where his horses and attendants waited him, chewing, as he walked along, the cud of many a sweet and bitter fancy, hope and confidence alternately giving way to the gloomy forebodings of despair.

Just as the first streak of ruddy day, piercing the veil of night, appeared above the horizon, he reached a rising knoll, where rustic piety had erected a rude cross and seat, to invite the traveller to prayer or repose. Just as he gained the spot the distant matin bell fell upon his ear. Kneeling on the turf-raised altar, he commended his wife and child to the protection of that Being whose arm can sustain the weak, whose wisdom guide them through the storms of life.

While absorbed in prayer he might be seen suddenly to spring from the earth : one convulsive bound, and all was over. The being lately all life, intelligence, and animation lay a senseless corpse—a bolt winged from an arbalist had pierced his manly heart ; sent him in the moment of prayer, his pure soul raised to God, strong in the hopefulness of youth, in the confidence of a happy future, to meet the Judge whose ear was even then mercifully inclined to his supplication. A few moments afterwards, and Herman, together with his companions, stood by the dead man's side.

As the hour drew nigh in which Edith was to meet her father and confess the secret of her marriage, her high-wrought courage began to fail her. It needed all the encouragement of her faithful Judith, and the contemplation of her slumbering child, to nerve her for the task. She was in the act of rising from her knees, which had been bent in prayer, when the franklin entered the room. Despite her resolution, she trembled at the sight of him.

" Edith, my child," he said, kindly taking her hand, "why start? A daughter's prayer should ever be fitted for a parent's ear; and thine, I doubt not, has been to bend thy unreasonable objections to my will. Is it not so, my child ? "

Edith remained silent.

" Listen to me," resumed her father. " When thy mother died there was left a tender, gentle flower ; so fragile, that the slightest breath of coldness or unkindness would have cut the slender thread of its existence. Edith, thou hast known me only as the rough hunter, the successful soldier, or stern franklin."

" More," interrupted his hearer, weeping, and passionately kissing his hand, "as the father—the kind, the generous, too indulgent father."

" Somewhat, perhaps, too much so," he resumed. " It was my nature, and I cannot change it. But I have been thy nurse, Edith —watched night after night the little cot where slept my motherless treasure ; schooled my rough voice to woman's softness not to disturb thy slumbers ; tended thee with more than a father's fondness —with almost the yearning tenderness of a mother's love. Say, have I not the right to demand some recompense ? "

His daughter clasped her hands in silence.

" For thy sake I have sought to rear no other heritor to my proud name. Must, then, that name, which is dear to me as my own existence, be transmitted through another? Must the long-cherished hope of years be disappointed ? Will the child whom I have so blindly loved blight the one hope of my existence, or by an effort worthy of herself assure her father's happiness ? Think what will be your feelings when, standing by my grave, you are enabled to say, ' I have done my duty—I have closed my father's eyes in peace.' "

During the franklin's last address the agitation of Edith had visibly increased. The tone of affectionate entreaty pierced her very soul ; and had the sacrifice been possible, at that very moment gladly would his child have submitted to become its victim.

" Would—would that it were possible," she replied ; " in this bitter hour I feel the sin, the curse of disobedience."

" What mean you ? " uttered the franklin : " what fearful mystery is this ? Speak ! Have I still a child ? "

" You have ! you have ! " frantically exclaimed his daughter, " but know that child is——"

" What ? "

"A wife and mother!"

Edith, exhausted by the effort, remained gazing in speechless agony upon her father's face—life, hope, happiness, all seemed to hang upon his lips.

Had a thunderbolt fallen at the feet of Herwald he could not have been more astonished.

"Married!" he exclaimed, "and a mother! Well, well, I have no child now."

"Do not say that," sobbed Edith. "Do not say that; speak to me —look upon me—call me daughter—for Heaven's sake, call me daughter!"

"No," sternly answered the franklin, shaking himself from her grasp. "My curse pursue thee! Hear it in the arms of thy husband! tremble at it when the tempest rages! and when the sun shines upon thy father's grave, remember whose disobedience laid him there! When the thunder roars, mayst thou fancy thou heardst thy father's curse! If thou hast children——"

At this moment Judith, who had been a trembling spectator of the interview, with one of those sudden acts of inspiration to which only woman's heart can aspire, and which no philosophy can teach, placed his infant grandson at his enraged grandfather's feet. The shock was electrical. Vainly he struggled to continue his malediction; nature was too powerful for passion, pity too strong for anger. The kneeling mother and the helpless infant formed an appeal he could not resist.

"No, no!" he murmured in a broken voice, "I cannot, dare not curse thy child—Edith's child," he added, gazing almost with love upon the little stranger who lay smiling at his feet. "Edith," he added, after a short struggle with his better nature, "'tis past—this boy hath made thy peace. Come to thy father's heart—once more his child!"

With a cry of joy, which burst from the deepest recesses of her heart, Edith threw herself into the arms of her forgiving father.

The words of parental forgiveness—the caress of parental love— were the last rays of happiness the unfortunate Edith was destined to taste on earth. Scarcely had the reconciled Saxon and his child recovered from the agitation of the scene which we have so faintly endeavoured to describe, than the Recluse of Wynmondham entered the apartment unannounced, the universal reverence in which he was held rendering his visits everywhere a welcome honour.

"Franklin," he exclaimed, "to horse! Blood hath been shed upon thy land! the blood of the noble and the good! Edward, the son of thy oldest friend Edda, the Saxon, lies murdered at the foot of the cross!"

A piercing shriek burst from the lips of Edith—a shriek fearful as the despairing agony of a departing soul; and the heiress of Stanfield lay a senseless maniac at the feet of her agonised father.

[DISCOVERY OF THE BODY OF HUGH DE BIGOD.]

C

CHAPTER II.

IT would be impossible to describe the rage and confusion of Herman when his uncle informed him not only of Edith's marriage, but of the birth of an heir to Stanfield; the prize for which he had imbrued his hands in blood, and yielded his soul to the dark fiend, seemed for ever to have escaped him. 'Tis true the melancholy state of Edith gave but little hope of recovery; but the boy lived—Edward's boy—to become the inheritor of the broad lands for which his cupidity panted, and perhaps the avenger of his father's assassination. This last consideration, or both combined, determined him on attempting to remove the infant heir. Open force, guarded as was the holm, he knew to be hopeless: he determined, therefore, to seek by other means the accomplishment of his detested purpose. As prompt in execution as in thought, he mounted his horse and, attended only by the easy confidant of his crimes and pleasures, directed his head towards the thick wood of Wynmondham, where he trusted to find a fit agent for the crime he meditated. In the deepest recesses of the wood in question stood a rude hut partially formed of unhewn stones and logs of wood; strength, more than convenience, seemed to have been the builder's object, not less in choice of material than situation. A thick stagnant pool cut off all access to the back part of the building, where the only apertures for admitting light were situated. The stout oaken door was thickly studded with nails, and, from its solidity and strength, seemed to defy intrusion; the danger of which was still further lessened by the absence of all regular road, and the thick, low, stunted pollards, which prevented the traveller or hunter from seeing the edifice until close upon it. When by accident any such approached, they hastily crossed themselves, and fled, casting furtive glances in their flight, to assure themselves that they were not followed by its mysterious inmate, Haga, or the dark man of the wold, as the occupant was called. He bore a most equivocal character for miles around; none knew his place of birth, or the history of his past life. Deeply skilled in medicine, and in the knowledge of all healing plants, his wisdom was seldom taxed by the superstitious boors or neighbouring franklins, and then only in extreme cases, when all other remedies had failed. In his intercourse with such rare visitors, his words were few, but to the purpose; his manners cold, stern, and dignified; added to which, he invariably rejected all gifts or proffers of remuneration. In person Haga was tall, though bent with age; a long beard fell over his ample dark tunic, reaching the silver girdle which bound it to his waist; on it were engraved certain Runic characters, the meaning of which were

c 2

known only to the Druids, and bards of the Saxon nation ; indeed,
by some he was considered as belonging to the all but extinct order
of the former sacerdotal race—a supposition in some measure confirmed by his never having been seen, within the memory of man,
in any building dedicated to Christian worship. From whatever
source he obtained his means, they were ample ; indeed, he had
been frequently known to bestow on the wayfarer or the unfortunate
an alms which many a noble and wealthy franklin would have
grudged. Still he was not beloved ; but fear served him as a
more efficient protection, for the wretch who would have plundered
and fired the roof which sheltered him, trembled as he passed the
rude hut of Haga of the Wold. The fact of several children having
been missed from the neighbouring villages still further tended to
increase the superstitious dread in which he was universally held ;
for although few tongues ventured to accuse, there were many who
doubted not but that Haga was in some way connected with their
disappearance ; some, more charitably inclined, suggested that they
had probably wandered too far into the woods, and either perished
of hunger, or from the attacks of the wolves, at that period so
plentiful in England. When Herman had approached within bow-
shot of the hut, he reined in his steed, and, dismounting, took from
his attendant a dark hunting cloak, in which he enveloped his
person so as effectually to prevent recognition, and directed his
steps towards the unhallowed spot, leaving his squire lost in
admiration at his master's hardy courage.

"Enter ! " exclaimed the deep voice of the inmate, as the third
blow of Herman's dagger fell on the iron-studded door of the hut ;
" be thou poor or wretched, rich or noble, weak or strong, craven or
brave, enter the hut of the recluse."

The visitor did as he was commanded, and found himself for the
first time in his life face to face with the being whose name was
seldom pronounced without awe, and even whose benefits were
received with a secret malediction.

The interior of the cottage presented a far more comfortable
appearance than its exterior seemed to promise. A long carved
oaken settle extended on one side of the wall ; over it was hung
several antique bronze instruments, such as are still occasionally
found in cairns and Druid mounds, and which modern antiquaries
have alternately decided to be instruments of sacrifice or divination ;
a withered leaf of ivy lay upon the huge block of wood which
served as a table, and whose roots, still deeply embedded in the earth,
showed that it retained its primeval position.

Haga was occupied in sorting a collection of herbs gathered in
the neighbouring woods, when Herman entered, and seated himself opposite to him. For a few moments they gazed on each other
without speaking. The recluse was the first to break the silence.

" What brings the franklin to my secluded dwelling ? " he demanded ; "his cheek seems flushed with health. Why comes he disguised ?" he added, a shade of displeasure passing over his haughty brow ; "it was not thus his fathers of yore sought the wise men of their race."

"The wisdom of the sage," replied his guest, "is medicine alike unto the body and the mind : if my cheek is flushed with health, and my limbs are strong, my heart is sick——"

"For vengeance!" interrupted the old man ; "for vengeance! I read it in thy knitted brow—the paleness of thy lip, which shames thy cheek's deep red. Thou wouldst remove a rival from thy path of love, or of ambition ! Begone !—I cannot aid thee."

"Will not, rather," answered his guest. "Come, let us understand each other ; although I give not credence to the idle tongues of superstitious fools, I have not now to learn that thou art skilled in herbs—that nature, like one vast book, is opened to thy gaze— and that thy wisdom may be turned to good or evil. Come, sell me a draught, the slightest drop of which shall stop life's current at its very spring, yet leave no tell-tale evidence behind. I'll pay thy price in gold."

"Gold !" replied Haga, with a scornful laugh ; "were a mine of the pale yellow dross beneath my feet, I would not raise the soil which covers it. Gold ! I loathe it more than I loathe humanity, for 'tis its worst weapon. Go, man, go : the outcast of the world— the condemned of men's opinion—will not justify their judgment by participating in a crime like this."

"This is cant !" exclaimed Herman, starting to his feet with ill-suppressed rage, "mere cant, to enhance the value of the service I demand. Fear not to tax my purse—it shall pay thee both for thy conscience and thy nostrum. Why, man," he added, "if what men say of thee be true, thou art already damned beyond the reach of mercy ; earth hath no absolution, holy Church no prayer for crimes so black as thine."

"Such is thy Christian creed," retorted Haga ; "I trust not in it —it binds not me ; I worship not in temples made with hands—the umbrageous forest is my tabernacle—primeval rocks my altar—my matin hymn the feathered minstrel's song—my oracles the running stream or brook."

"Thou art a Druid," observed Herman, "one of a race proscribed."

"The last of a race proscribed, thou mightest have said," proudly answered the old man. Cruel hath been our persecution, and cruel vengeance follows it! The Norman is at hand—the avenger of our sacred race ! Odin and Thor no longer guard a land where their altars are deserted and their priests unhonoured ! Soon, soon will their judgments be accomplished."

"Pagan," said the Saxon franklin at the same time devoutly crossing himself—for, like most of the nobles of his age, his character

formed a strange mixture of cruelty and superstition—" darest thou
avow such heresies to me ?   Although the sainted Edward no
longer wears a mortal crown, the Church is powerful still."

"And who will be my denouncer ?" demanded the Druid with
a sneer—" the noble franklin who came to solicit a poison at my
hands, to remove from his path a rival whom he fears, perchance,
to meet in open fight ?   I have no fear of such an accuser."

" No man have I ever feared to meet on equal terms, or against
such sought the aid of ministry like thine," said Herman ; " it is
an opening flower I would close, not uproot an oak—I would efface
the stain upon an ancient house, without, if possible, steeping my
hand in an infant's blood."

"An infant ?" eagerly demanded Haga ; " hath it been baptised ?"
He fixed his eyes keenly on Herman, as if he would read his very
soul.   There was a pause, during which the latter weighed in his
mind the import of the question.

" It hath," he slowly answered.

The old man rose and paced the narrow limits of the chamber, as
if communing with himself.   His mind seemed at last made up.
Laying his hand upon the arm of the franklin, which trembled beneath his touch, he whispered—

" I'll make a compact with thee.   I'll give thee means to steep
the child in sleep, but not in death—in sleep so deep and calm that
not one pulse shall indicate that life remains within its secret
sanctuary ; the mother's kiss shall not detect the lingering breath
upon its lips—the eye of hate discover the latent bloom upon its
cheek.   I will do this on one condition."

" Condition," faltered Herman, whose superstition recoiled from
the Druid's words.   " What condition ? "

" That when he sleeps his sleep of seeming death," replied the
old man, " you shall convey him here to me ; that I shall remain
sole master of his fate—no question asked—no future count demanded."

" Horror !" exclaimed the Saxon ; " wouldst have me barter the
infant to the fiend ?   Never, never !   Though criminal, I am a
Christian."

" Begone then at once," said the tempter ; " thou knowest the only
terms on which my services are to be bought.   The child here,
living at my absolute disposal, what is't to thee whether his blood
bedew the shrine of Odin, or that I rear him to serve his neglected
altars ?   Thy conscience," he added with a sneer, " will be free."

" True," muttered Herman ; " and holy Church may yet absolve
me."

" It may be," sarcastically resumed the Druid.   " Gold will buy
pardon for a heavier sin.   Is it a compact ? "

" It is," after a struggle, answered the wretched man.   " There is
no other way."

The Druid, without further word, went to a dark recess, and after searching for some time amongst its contents drew a small crystal phial from it, and placed it in the hands of the trembling homicide.

"There is the drug you seek," he exclaimed. "One drop, and the drinker will for hours appear as dead. Once in its death-like trance, it will be easy to remove the body here. In five days I shall expect you. Beware," he added, "how you break faith with me! None ever did so with impunity; and Herman of the Burg shall not be the first."

His hearer started at the ominous manner in which the speaker pronounced his name.

"You know me, then?" he murmured, his countenance changing with fear and passion.

"Well," resumed the old man. "Know thee as the murderer of Edward, heir to the Saxon Edda; know thee as the betrothed of a bride thou never shalt possess—as the heir of a name which, if thou keep not faith with me, never shall be thine! Farewell! Pass on thy way, and till the deed is accomplished darken my door no more."

That very night Herman, under pretence of leaving the franklin to indulge in his natural grief and watch over his unhappy child, started from Stanfield on his way to Burg—a strong fortress which he possessed, built on the ruins of the Garionorum of Cæsar, the Roman remains of which have survived the more modern structure, and still attract the attention of the antiquary and traveller as he passes over the shallow waters of Braidon, which wash their base. But although he left the home of his destined victim, instruments worthy of their master remained behind to work his will. Before the five days were elapsed a fire broke out in that part of the holm where the infant heir reposed. His attendants had been drugged with the Druid's fatal gift, and slept when they should have watched. The unfortunate wretches perished in the flames, in which the infant was also supposed to have found an untimely grave. It was long ere Edith and her repentant father recovered this second blow.

Eighteen years had elapsed since the fire at Stanfield, in which so many persons perished; the base contriver of the deed remained unsuspected; but the vast political changes which had placed the Norman Conqueror on the throne prevented his profiting, as he anticipated, by the deed. It was the policy both of William and his successors to amalgamate as far as possible the still hostile races. In many instances confiscation was avoided by the Saxon heiress marrying some Norman knight, who thus became an inheritor of the soil. The wealthy franklin purchased the peaceable possession of his ancestral domains by allying himself with some powerful noble of the invader's blood, whose dowerless daughter bestowed at least security with the possession of her hand.

Stanfield, as may be supposed, was too rich a prize to escape the Conqueror's cupidity. Had her own safety only been at stake, Edith would have defied the utmost malice of her fate ; but when she reflected that her father, her indulgent father, even if his life were spared, must wander forth unhonoured and defenceless, exposed not only to the reverse of fortune, but to the conquerors' unpitying scoffs, her last resolve gave way, and she bestowed her hand on Hugh de Bigod, created for his services at the battle of Hastings Earl of Norwich, and marshal of the king in that portion of his dominions formerly comprised under the name of the East Angles. Fortunately for Edith, she met with no ungenerous wooer or stern lord. Love, it was not in her power to bestow ; but as the manly qualities of the earl's nature developed themselves, her friendship gradually became his. Like herself, he had mourned the loss of the object of his first affections—two infant pledges of which, a boy and a girl, remained to him. The spirited Norman and his sister Matilda gazed at first with fear upon the pale cheek and gloomy brow of their new mother—whose gentleness, however, gradually won their hearts, and on whom she soon bestowed some portion of that love which her heart still treasured for the memory of her lost boy. The franklin, full of years, had long since slumbered at peace. Even the deeply guilty Herman shared in the protection which the union of Edith with the powerful favourite of the Conqueror extended to her race. He was a frequent visitor at the castle of Norwich, where the earl and countess generally resided ; and, if not a welcome, was, at least, a tolerated guest. Age had not taught him penitence, or cured him of his ambitious dreams—the murderer plotted still.

The sun was shining cheerfully on a fine morning in September, gilding the lofty tower of the cathedral, which still remains the pride and admiration of the ancient city of Norwich ; its rays, after striking the lofty pinnacle and fretted niches, rich in many a quaint device and sculptured saint, fell in quiet repose upon the emerald turf inclosed by the cloisters of the sacred edifice; causing the shadows from the western windows to fall upon the pavement. The last chant of the matin hymn was fading through the aisles, when an ecclesiastic, whose chain and cross indicated his episcopal rank, entered from one of the side doors of the church, and began to pace the cloister ; his rich purple soutan fell in graceful folds around his stately form, which seemed bent less by age than sorrow. The arched brow, piercing eye, and aquiline nose of the individual sufficiently indicated his Norman blood. To a casual observer, the general expression of his countenance would have been taken for pride : to those who examined closer, a decided character of benevolence redeemed it. Such, as we have endeavoured to describe him, was Herbert de Lozenga, Bishop of Norwich and Chancellor to William the Conqueror—a man of whom even his enemies said much good, and whose friends were enthusiastic in his praise. Born of high rank, and elevated to ecclesiastical dignities, he possessed some of the prejudices of his birth, and many of the virtues of his state. Those who saw in him only the noble and the prelate, envied him ; the few who knew the man, wondered that he was unhappy ; a subdued melancholy seemed to be the prevailing feature of his disposition. Perhaps in the priest he had not learnt to subdue all the recollections of the man. The general companion of this solitary morning walk within the cloisters was a young orphan named Ulrick, whom he had reared from infancy, and to whom scandal assigned a nearer claim upon his bounty than mere charity.

" How keen and freshly blows the mountain breeze ! " muttered the prelate to himself, as he paced the cloister, his eye glancing alternately from the fretted roof to the inclosed space before him. " Where can Ulrick linger ?—the matin song fell harshly on my ear, wanting his voice to give it melody. 'Tis strange," he added, " how the boy hath twined himself round my heart ; I should remember that the hour will arrive when we must part—when he must mingle in the world, and seek to win by gallant deeds the name which cruel fate denies him."

The speaker continued his walk with the same languid step, sometimes lingering to catch some new point of view, as the tower and spires of the cathedral were seen through the deep fretwork of the cloister windows—sometimes to listen to the echo of some distant step, as it either receded or drew near the spot where he was meditating. At last the sound of a footfall lighter than the tread of the sandalled monks drew near, and in a few seconds the object of his thoughts presented himself.

Ulrick the Orphan, as he was generally called, was formed in a mould where symmetry and manly strength were blended. Although generally supposed to be, if not the son, at least in some way connected by blood with his patron, his features bore the impress of the Saxon rather than the Norman race—blue eyes, a fair complexion, and light chestnut curls ; the first down of manhood shaded his lip and chin, redeeming the almost womanish character of his beauty. Although mildness seemed to be the general expression of his countenance, there was great determination in the mouth and nostrils, the chiselled lines of which generally indicate courage, firmness, and perseverance. His step, though light, was stately, like the young fawn's, when sauntering from its evening lair, it snuffs the breath of morning with an air in which affection and reverence are mingled. The youth approached the spot where Herbert de Lozenga awaited him ; and, silently bending the knee, he asked the usual benediction, which the prelate bestowed upon him by making the sign of the cross above his head.

" Forgive me, reverend father," said Ulrick, as he rose from his knee ; " but I have been detained beyond my usual hour. I encountered the noble Mirvan in my walks, and "—here the speaker hesitated.

"With him one," interrupted the prelate, with a melancholy smile, "whose charms, I fear, endanger Ulrick's peace—his gentle sister."

The youth blushed, and was silent.

"Hear me, boy!" resumed Herbert. "I have long wished to speak with you on the subject, but weakly hesitated, knowing how sad it is to be sternly wakened from those blissful dreams in which youthful confidence too often plunges us. You love!"

His hearer started as the gentle voice of his patron pronounced the fatal words which tore from his soul its sweet delusion; still, as drowning wretches cling to the last plank, he struggled to avoid confessing even to himself the folly of his passion, the madness of his hopes. Matilda, the daughter of one of the most powerful nobles of the Norman race—and he an orphan, a being without a name—the stain of doubt, perchance of infamy, upon his birth—and he to dare to raise his eyes so high! No, no! He had mistaken friend-ship for love; it could be nothing else!

"Think not, my lord," he replied, as soon as he recovered from the confusion in which the unexpected accusation had thrown him, "that such arrogance and pride e'er harboured here; the Lady Matilda can ne'er be viewed by me but with such awe and reverence as the shrine of some bright saint enthroned in bliss might claim. Chance, you are aware, led me to preserve her brother's life; the grateful maid hath deigned to call me friend. Think, father—friend! That," he added, fixing his eyes almost imploringly upon his interrogator, "is a name distinct from love."

An expression of sadness clouded the usually calm, clear brow of the priest. For years the page of human life had been his study. Perhaps some recollection of his own youthful dreams came over him, when he, too, had struggled to blind his reason to the true nature of his heart—its weakness, passions. Perhaps his natural sympathy with humanity interested him in the struggle between truth and delusion which was evidently taking place in Ulrick's soul—a struggle which, for its victim's happiness, he was resolved at any risk to end.

"Your sentiments towards Matilda are, then, merely those of friendship—nothing more?" Ulrick remained silent; the precipice was becoming gradually defined before him. "Could you," continued Herbert, "with joy be present, see her wed, and her rich beauties grace another's arms? You tremble, Ulrick, at the thought. Why is this?"

"Yes 'tis not love!" passionately iterated Ulrick; "for I should be content could I but live for ever in her sight, nor frame one wish beyond. But never more to hear the music of her voice, or catch the expression of her dark blue eye when mirth illumes it, or when sorrow's tale hath gemmed its fringes with a pitying tear, would give my heart a pang."

The vehemence of the speaker betrayed too clearly, even to himself, the state of his affections. Like a child attracted by the pleasing colours of the snake, he had played with the reptile till its venom had infused itself into his soul.

" We have both been to blame," exclaimed the prelate, rising from the rough stone on which he had been seated, and pacing the cloister with a firmer step than usual ; " we have been dreamers both. You must to the world, boy ; my selfish love hath too long detained thee here. Action is the best cure for sorrow and for ill. Our monarch prosecutes the war in France : honours and lands may be won by gallant deeds : if fate denies a name, thy sword must win one."

" Honours and lands the sword indeed may win, but what deed can efface the stain of infamy upon my birth ? "

Ulrick's voice trembled with emotion as he spoke. The general opinion of his being the son of the bishop had at times struck him with a sad foreboding ; he feared to find in the author of his being the man whom he most loved and reverenced on earth, the term " son of a priest " being at that time the most bitter reproach an insulting enemy could bestow.

" Infamy ! " repeated Herbert ; " and who shall dare pronounce it so, when I, who have reared thee from thy tenderest years—I, who received thee a smiling infant in these arms—believe thee noble ? "

Never before had Herbert de Lozenga been so explicit with his orphan _protégé_, whom respect, and perhaps a nameless dread, had hitherto prevented from demanding an explanation of the tie between them. The words of his protector fell like a precious balm upon his soul ; they conveyed to him the assurance that he was not the wretched being he suspected.

" You, then ! " he exclaimed, " are not——"

The blush upon the brow of his guardian arrested Ulrick's words ; he paused, and bent his eyes to earth in silence.

" No, Ulrick," replied the prelate to the half-uttered interrogation, " I am not thy father ; no offspring's tear," he added, in a voice of deep emotion, " will fall upon my grave. Thinkest thou, had I so far forgot the laws of God—my priestly vow—I could have ever gazed without a blush upon thee ? "

" Pardon, pardon ! " sobbed Ulrick, prostrating himself at his feet, half choked with emotion ; " I am indeed a wretch to have formed one doubt of purity like thine. Tell me, I entreat thee, all that thou knowest touching my wretched state."

The bishop in his turn seemed confused at his request; for the required explanation recalled the most painful moments of his existence—the struggles of passions which had left their scars upon his very soul. Feeling, however, how necessary it was to make the effort, he resolved to subdue the natural hesitation which he felt, and add another to the long list of pangs he had endured.

"Be it so, Ulrick," he replied ; "but not now, not now. I lack courage for the task—firmness to bring my mind to part with thee. I must seek them both in prayer. In three days thy letters shall be prepared for William's camp—all things arranged for thy departure ; but ere thou leavest the solitary man whose heart has been thy home, thou shalt learn the sorrows of his life, and how thou first wert cast a helpless infant on his care. Go," he added ; "take leave of thy friends at the castle, of the noble Mirvan and his gentle sister ; but remember, Ulrick, not one word of love ; plant not a thorn where thou wouldst place a rose. Since 'tis the lot of man to suffer—to feel his heart consume beneath the serpent-tooth of deathless passions —suffer alone—and, like the wounded eagle on the rock, pine in solitude away."

On the evening of the same day, Ulrick directed his steps towards the castle, to announce to his two friends his intended departure for the camp. With the peculiar sensitiveness of his nature, he had refused, on several occasions, to partake of the almost regal hospitality of the earl, whose residence emulated the splendours of the Court, and who had frequently expressed a wish to meet the preserver of his son. As he crossed the open space which divided the cathedral precincts from the city, now known by the name of Tombland, his heart beat with contending emotions ; he was going, for the last time, perhaps, to listen to the voice whose tone found so deep an echo in his soul—to gaze upon the eyes whose light to him was as twin stars to guide him to his destiny ; was going to part— the words of love which glowed upon his tongue unspoken—the wishes, passions, and regrets which burnt within him as closely sealed as in a sepulchre. Still, despite of the barriers which reason presented to his passion, his step was buoyant ; hope held possession of a corner of his heart, even as she lay hid at the bottom of Pandora's box ; and that which was only not impossible seemed half-achieved.

"Yes," he exclaimed, apostrophising the object of his adoration ; "her name shall be my beacon in the path of honour ; if I fall, she shall feel I was not altogether unworthy of her love ; if I return with fame, that love may crown me."

Ulrick had crossed about half the distance which separated the city gate from the castle, when he was surrounded by a gay and laughing band of youthful nobles, who, headed by Mirvan and Herman of the Burg, had been indulging in the pleasures of the chase ; his sister and her fair cousin, Isabel of Bayeux, had accompanied them.

"So ho !" exclaimed Mirvan, dismounting from his horse, and placing his arm in Ulrick's, "I have caught the sage at last. No refusal now ; not e'en my sister's word shall set you free ; for once we'll have philosophy at our gay banquet, that when beauty's smiles lead our hearts astray, wisdom, in time, may pull the reins of our understandings to check us. Wouldst believe it, my fair coz," he added, turning to Isabel, "although Matilda and myself, time out of mind, have tried to tempt him, this is the first time we have lured the hermit from his cell ?"

"And not soon again to return to it," said Ulrick, bowing lowly to the two lovely girls, who had reined in their stately palfreys on first perceiving him. "I am bound to the country of the Lady Isabel, to try my humble fortunes in the wars."

At the concluding words a close observer might have seen the cheek of Matilda turn pale. Herman observed it, and his heart overflowed with bitterness and gall.

"You are right, young man," he haughtily and loudly answered ; "Normandy is the land of those who have neither country nor nation, birth nor name ; it is a land for adventurers. You will do well to cast your fortunes there."

To most of the young men the bitter sarcastic humour of the speaker was well known ; they passed his observations therefore with a laugh. Not so Isabel, who with the penetration of a woman's wit had detected the desire of the franklin to humiliate Ulrick in the presence of Matilda, whose love, despite the disparity of years, he ridiculously aspired to.

"Sir Saxon," she exclaimed, "it is the land at least of courtesy, since it permits those whom it has conquered to rail. unpunished against their masters. It is the land of the brave," she added, proudly, "and worthy to become the home of those who have true hearts and loyal weapons."

"By my faith, fair cousin," interrupted Mirvan, secretly annoyed at the turn the conversation had taken, "if their swords are but half as keen as thy tongue, I had rather be friends than quarrel with thy brave countrymen. Our kinsman meant not to offend thee,— do not quarrel with him."

"Quarrel with Herman !" iterated the haughty beauty, perfectly aware of her power over Mirvan's heart ; "quarrel with the spleen ! no, no ; he is to be endured, not quarrelled with."

"Kinsman," exclaimed the young noble, who read in the glowing cheek and flashing eye of his young friend a coming storm, "pleasure me by riding with our friends on to the castle. The ladies will accept of mine and Ulrick's escort."

The grave tone in which the request was made implied a command to the haughty Saxon. But Mirvan was too important a person for him to offend ; besides he felt that he had already lost ground in his favour by his churlish speech to one to whom he was not only sincerely attached, but deeply indebted.

"Willing, cousin," he brought himself to answer. "My absence shall be my punishment ; the fair Isabel, I doubt not, will feel it more than sufficient for the crime. At least we part as friends," he added, raising his plumed cap as he spoke, and bowing to the very saddle-bow of his fair enemy.

"Friends!" carelessly repeated Isabel; "oh, yes; friends as much as ever."

The franklin either would not or did not see the irony of the last words of the speaker, but turned his horse's head towards the castle, attended by all but Mirvan, Ulrick, and the two ladies.

"You are too hard, Isabel," said the former, "on our kinsman; he hath a heart!"

"Heart!" interrupted the maiden, "so hath the tomb its tenant. Heart! 'tis a cold and frozen spectre; love, friendship, confidence, the ties which bind us to our fellow-creatures, the gushing sympathies of love, all that ennobles man, and lights this dull earth with gleams of Eden's sunshine, are his scoffs."

"I cannot argue with you," said Mirvan. Then turning to Ulrick, he continued, "and so you leave us for the wars? The cloister then, it seems, has lost its charm—is Mars or Venus now in the ascendant?"

"Neither, I trust," answered the conscience-stricken youth; "but I am sick of dreaming out my life in cloistered ease. 'Tis time I see the world, and mate myself with men. My guardian's influence hath ope'd the path of honour—I were a sluggard did I not pursue it. If I have neither name nor birth, country nor station, who shall blame me that I strive to win one?"

"Blame!" said Isabel; "thou shalt have one Christian maiden's prayers at least for thy success! Nay, I think I may venture to promise thee my pensive cousin's too?"

"You may, indeed," softly uttered Matilda, thus directly appealed to; "they are due not less to his own merits than to the preserver of my brother's life."

The quiet tone of the speaker's voice told to her cousin that her calmness was assumed; indeed, she had long suspected a mutual passion, not the less ardent for being unconfessed, between Matilda and the unknown orphan.

"Happy Ulrick!" exclaimed Mirvan, who, in the blindness of his own passion for the volatile Isabel, did not suspect his sister's; "did not a dearer tie withhold me, gladly would I share thy perils and behold thy triumphs; as it is, although I may not witness, perchance I can assist them. My father, as thou well knowest, stands in high favour with our valiant monarch, and I am sure will gladly stretch his utmost influence to serve thee; he will doubtless furnish thee with letters to those who can place thee foremost in the path of danger and of honour."

"I ask no more," replied Ulrick. "If I fall, it matters little; few will mourn me, and none know the wild ambitious aspirations which perish with me. Should I survive, those who interest themselves

in my wretched fate shall not blush for the favour they have shown
me."

On his arrival at the castle, Ulrick was presented to the earl and
countess, the former of whom thanked him with stately kindness
for the service he had rendered Mirvan, whose life our hero had
preserved from the attack of a ferocious wolf, when, wounded and
unhorsed, he lay exposed to the savage monster's fury. Edith.
whose remarkable beauty time and sorrow had mellowed, but not
destroyed, sighed as she gazed upon the gallant youth, who modestly
knelt to kiss her extended hand ; perhaps some feature jarred the
chords of memory, or some mysterious sympathy formed a link between them. The pressure of his lips upon her hand thrilled to her
matron heart.

"Such," she mentally uttered, with a sigh,—"such might have
been my gallant Edward's boy, had cruel fortune spared him to my
widowed heart."

The modesty with which Ulrick listened to the counsel of the
earl, the extreme grace of his person and purity of mind, made a
favourable impression upon that powerful nobleman. His guests
and officers perceived the entrainment of their host and chief, and
vied with each other in courtesies. All who listened to the eager
hopes and noble aspirations of the gallant youth wished him success
in his career of arms ; all but one—the jealous, disappointed Herman, who sat listening to his rival's praise in gloomy silence—for
rivals he already felt they were. At length, unable longer to endure
the gnawings of his envious heart, he quietly withdrew from the hall,
to indulge in gloomy meditation.

"Bring Ulrick to the chapel," whispered Isabel to her cousin
Mirvan, as. leaning on the arm of Matilda, they followed the countess
from the banquet ; "although we cannot dub him knight, at least
we may arm him for the battle in which he is to win his spurs. I
owe him," she added, " no less a debt of gratitude than Matilda, and
am impatient till the debt be paid."

The last part of the maiden's speech was too flattering to Mirvan
to make him wonder at the unusual request. As soon, therefore, as
the feast was ended, and the principal guests retired from the hall.
he took the arm of Ulrick, and led his wondering friend towards the
chapel.

The two fair cousins were standing near the altar when the young
men entered the sacred edifice. The light from the ever-burning
silver lamp before the shrine gave a religious, mellow tone to the
scene ; the segment-formed arches dimly receding till they were
lost in darkness. Four purer hearts, or more devoted to each other.
were seldom met than those assembled there. It is true that between
Matilda and Ulrick no vow had e'er been spoken ; each seemed instinctively to feel it would be wrong that it should be so : the youth
felt that the idol of his worship could receive no clandestine homage ;

the maiden, that the favoured of her choice would fall from the high place he held within her breast by any rash avowal ; and yet they loved—loved with all the pure confiding innocence of youth—the confidence of humanity ere sin or the world's treachery had blighted them.   Confident in the sinlessness of her passion, Matilda advanced to meet them ; her voice was firm, as her heart was pure and holy.

" Ulrick," she said, " the sister cannot permit the preserver of her brother's life to go unarmed into the battle.   The sword is a strange gift from a woman's hand ; but when grasped by honour, 'tis the best —in thine 'twill ne'er be drawn but in the cause of virtue and of truth."

" To virtue and justice I devote it ! " exclaimed Ulrick, sinking on one knee, as he received the weapon from her hand.   " Lady, this moment shall be graven in the cell where memory treasures up its deepest joys—round it entwines the thread of my existence.   It fortune smiles upon the soldier's arm, thy virtues will have been the inspiring cause ; if death should call me on the field of honour, thy image shall console me."

For a few moments the lovers gazed on each other in silence, drinking, in that brief space, a draught for years, a happiness for ages.

" Though far less prized," exclaimed Isabel, willing to end the scene, the excitement of which she feared, " do not refuse my gift."

She passed a silken scarf, embroidered by her own fair hands, over the shoulders of Ulrick, as she spoke.

" It was intended for another, but not more worthy object."

" Less worthy far to wear it," said Mirvan, who understood that it was for himself that the prize had originally been destined.

" Beggar that I am, in all but thanks," sighed Ulrick, as he kissed the embroidered hem of the maiden's gift ; " how have I merited such goodness ? "

" By prudence," replied Isabel, in a marked tone ; " by courage, not in its brute contests with man to man, but in its loftier struggles. We have performed our task—farewell ! "

" Farewell ! " exclaimed Ulrick, kneeling, and passionately kissing the extended hands of the fair cousins ; " you have lit my soul with energies—armed me to brave all that the wildest fortune can wreak on me.   I will return worthy of such angelic goodness, or return no more."

The excited youth rushed from the chapel as he spoke.   Isabel and Matilda retired in silence to their chambers.

That night Mirvan had much for study and reflection.

How delicious is the moment when the youthful heart first feels that it is loved !   The soul expands, merges in a new existence, and all around partakes of Eden's bliss.

[ERNULF DEMANDING THE PERSON OF ULRICK.]

D

"Yes," exclaimed Ulrick, as he left the bridge which crossed the castle moat, "I now am armed to meet adversity; armed against all the terrors of impending fate. Matilda wills that I should gain a name; others alone, by vile ambition led, have for high deeds been raised to greatness and to honour; and can I fail when her voice bids me on? No, her name shall prove a beacon-light to guide me o'er life's waves."

"Say rather an *ignis fatuus*, to lure thee to thy ruin," interrupted Herman, whose unsocial temper had driven him from the banquet, and who, unfortunately, overheard our hero's meditation.

The moon was shining brightly, and Ulrick recognised the voice as well as the person of the speaker. The recollection of their previous meeting galled him, and he answered, in a tone as haughty as his own—

"When I require counsel, it is not of Herman of the Burg that I shall seek it. When I desire a confidant, it is not Herman of the Burg that I shall choose. Pass on, Sir Saxon; meddle in that which concerns you, and our Lady speed you on your way."

"It doth concern me, boy," retorted Herman, "that my kinswoman's name should not be sullied by every peasant's breath."

"Peasant," iterated Ulrick, his eye flashing fire, and his hand instinctively grasping the sword, Matilda's gift.

Herman beheld the action, but, confident in his strength and presumed superior skill, determined to provoke him. His heart was overflowing with pent-up bitterness and gall. Ulrick appeared to be a subject on whom he might vent them safely.

"Ay! peasant!" he repeated; "or, if thou likest it better, bastard of a Norman priest."

"Liar!" thundered Ulrick; "I thank thee for that word; it nerves my arm and justifies my hate. Draw, and defend thy life; be yon bright moon the witness of our quarrel. Strike at the breast that never did thee wrong—aim at the heart whose manhood thou wouldst trample—strike at the life whose current thou wouldst taint, but Saxon, guard thine own."

So impetuous was the attack of Ulrick that his opponent must have succumbed, despite his cunning fence and giant strength, had not the combat been interrupted by a voice all were accustomed to obey,—by the earl, whose attention, in the course of his evening walk round the ramparts, had been attracted by the clashing of their weapons, and who, in his haste to separate them, had sought the spot unattended and unarmed.

"How is this?" he cried; "my kinsman and my guest at mortal strife! Put up your swords, tell me your cause of quarrel, and let me judge between you."

Ulrick dropped the upraised weapon from his hand. How explain, without compromising Matilda's name, the cause of their dispute? He bowed his head in silence.

D 2

"Well may he be silent," exclaimed Herman, with a coarse sneer of triumph. "Wouldst thou believe it, noble earl, this peasant knave, this serf in blood as well as nature, dares raise his eyes where mine have feared to gaze—e'en to your daughter's love?"

"Young man," demanded the earl, sternly, his brow so deeply flushed with indignation that it was perceptible even in the pale moonlight, "can this be true?"

"An hour since, my lord, I had answered No," replied, Ulrick, "for I knew not then the nature of the fire which threatens to consume me. Hear me, sir earl," he added. "If to have loved your daughter as mortals love some distant star, as pilgrims worship the virgin saint before whose shrine they bow, be criminal, I am most guilty; but never have these lips breathed words of passion, uttered one thought of earth. I have adored as spirits worship—in the heart, in silence! Farewell, my lord. When men shall speak of the poor orphan boy who dared to love your peerless child, their tongues shall say, 'Proud was his sin, as proud was his atonement!'—For you," he continued, with a contemptuous glance to Herman, "this time you have escaped me—beware the next!"

Bowing with deep reverence to the earl, the excited youth turned his hasty steps towards the episcopal palace.

"Poor boy!" said the earl, touched by the noble frankness of his manner, and perhaps viewing his passion more in the light of that chivalrous devotion which the manners of the age permitted, than positive love—"were thy birth but noble as thy heart, I would not turn thee hopeless from my door."

"Perhaps, my lord," said Herman, "this moment may be suited to the words I have to offer; at least, I'll seek no other. Thou knowest the wars in which our Norman sovereign is engaged have given courage to the Saxon chiefs to attempt one blow for freedom, to cast off the yoke that for long years has galled them; it is the time to knit still closer the bond of unity between us, or weaken it for ever."

"What meanest thou?" demanded the earl, his attention deeply interested by the words which the excited Herman, contrary to his usual caution, had let drop.

"It means," said Herman, "that I love your daughter: her hand once mine, your interests are mine, your nation mine; the moment which bestows it sees the conspiracy unravelled, the traitors at your feet."

The earl, though deeply attached to the interests of his sovereign, was too generous a father to sacrifice his child to a being so base, so utterly void of honour. The hint at a conspiracy alarmed him, for well he knew the uncertain tenure by which the Normans held the land. He determined, therefore, to keep an eye upon his dangerous kinsman. With respect to the proposed alliance, he refused to entertain it for a moment.

"Franklin," he replied, "my life hath been one of honour; so shall be my speech. The difference of your years renders your union with my child impossible. Besides, while I am resolved never to yield her but to one of equal birth, her heart must be consulted. Well I know it never can be yours. Speak of it no more. With respect to the complots of your Saxon friends, we will speak more before the council; there may be other means of recompense. Come, let us to the castle."

"No," sternly answered the Saxon, "my path is taken; to the castle I return no more. I have had enough of Norman justice, of Norman hospitality. Farewell!"

"Not so," said the earl; "you must return with me. You have said too much or too little to be further trusted."

"Must go with you!" repeated Herman, who saw too late that he had betrayed himself. "And why must?"

"Because it is my will," replied the earl; "and I have power to enforce it. What, ho! warder!" he cried, elevating his voice so as to be heard by the officer who kept watch upon the distant keep, "a guard! De Bigod to the rescue!"

Scarcely had the words passed the noble lips than Herman sprang upon him, and a short struggle ensued. The earl, though unarmed, was strong, and succeeded in dragging his assailant towards the moat, when the sword which Ulrick had lately dropped, and left behind him in his excitement, struck against the Saxon's foot. In an instant he raised it, and plunged it into the body of the earl, who, uttering a deep groan, expired at his feet.

The alarm had been given, and Mirvan, with the knights and guests, followed by the castle guard, were seen hastily approaching over the bridge. The alarm bell pealed forth its deep loud notes—flight was impossible: but the assassin's presence of mind did not forsake him; he first threw from his grasp the blood-stained sword, then raising the dead body, he placed it across his knee, and called loudly for help. In a few moments he was surrounded by Mirvan and the soldiery.

"Heavens!" exclaimed Mirvan, "my noble father murdered! Who hath done this?"

"Alas! I know not," replied the hypocrite. "I came too late to save him. On my approach the assassin fled. Somewhere he dropped his sword."

A hundred torches were in an instant bent to earth—the fatal weapon was found—blood upon it. The knight who raised it held it to the light. It bore the name of Ulrick.

CHAPTER III.

NIGHT had spread her mantle o'er the twilight world, and found Herbert de Lozenga seated in an apartment of his episcopal palace; on a table near him were two antique mitres, one pertaining to him as Bishop of Norwich, the other as Abbot of Hulm, by which latter dignity his successors in the bishopric still sit in the House of Peers; before him lay a steel-clasped casket, containing various papers and memoranda, together with a ruby ring and richly mounted dagger, upon whose hilt some Saxon artist had sculptured a rude crest. The prelate had evidently prepared himself for his promised interview with Ulrick by prayer and stern control; all trace of the agitation of the morning had disappeared; his brow was calm as though passion's tempests had never ruffled it, or human sorrows ploughed one furrow on its polished surface.

The prelate wondered at his self-possession, and regretted that he had so long delayed an explanation, which would have prevented many a painful impression to the disadvantage of his youthful *protégé.*

"How strange," he murmured to himself, "is the human heart! how inexplicable in its strength and in its weakness! Philosophy cannot sound its depths. The angels who stand before the throne of Heaven cannot pierce its mysteries! He who framed, alone can read it!"

His reflections were interrupted by the entrance of Ulrick, whose flushed brow and hurried step were but the outward signs of the agitation of his soul. For a few moments his benefactor gazed on him in silence, at a loss to account for his unusual manner. The idea that he had been indulging in the wine-cup at the castle, naturally presented itself, and created a painful impression in his mind.

"Ulrick," he exclaimed, for the first time perhaps in his life using the accent of reproof, "whence this flushed brow and flashing eye? A step like that might suit the battle-field, but not my peaceful halls. Is this a mood to seek my presence in?"

In an instant the words recalled the young man to himself. The fear of giving pain to one whom he so deeply venerated, enabled him to check the passionate impulse of his heart, and control the bitterness of its emotions. Never before had he been exposed to scorn and contumely; the iron had entered his soul, and he felt it deeply.

"Forgive me, father," replied Ulrick, bending the knee; "forgive the boy your charity has reared, if he forgets the lowness of his state, and dares to act and feel himself a man. Scorn have I met from one I never wronged—foul-mouthed reproach, and biting, bitter taunts. Why—why," he added, passionately, "did I ever for a moment quit this calm retreat, to mingle with a world which mocks my wretchedness ? "

The cold, reproving manner of the prelate immediately changed. He saw that Ulrick had been wounded where youth is most sensitive. In his mind he rejoiced that his first suspicions were unfounded, and sought, by even more than his usual kindness of manner, to atone for the involuntary wrong.

"The world, 'tis true," he said, "is thickly spread with briars and foul weeds; but trust my word, sweet flowers may still be found. What! Ulrick, foiled in thy first encounter with the world ! Be more thyself—answer its injustice with high deeds—pursue life's path wherever honour leads ; and even if happiness escape thy search, believe me, boy, thou'lt stumble on content."

"I feel that I have a heart to bear its dangers manfully," answered the young man ; "but not to endure its sneers, its heartless falsehoods, and its slanderous tongues. If the world, indeed, be such as schoolmen paint it, and as priests believe, I could, with scarce one sigh, renounce its charms, and seek a refuge here."

The despondent tone of Ulrick alarmed his benefactor, who well knew the impressionable nature of his character, and the advantage which might be taken from it.

" Seek not within the cloister's shade for happiness," he exclaimed, "or shelter from the world ; its jealousies, its slanders and deceits may reach thee even here. The man who wastes his spring of life, unloving and unloved, leaving unfilled the ends of his creation, casting aside the tender ties of parent, lover, friend, may reach indifference, but rarely happiness. I will relate to thee some passages of the history of my life," he added—" a life chequered by passions such as sear the heart—by hopes as bright as those which angels dream."

The prelate motioned Ulrick to seat himself beside him, and was about to commence his tale, when he was interrupted by the entrance of Father Oswald, a Saxon monk, whose frightened mien indicated that some unusual occurrence had taken place.

"Now, son," mildly demanded the bishop; "what means this untimely visit ?".

" Our sanctuary is invaded," answered the intruder ; "armed men are in the cloisters, and the tramp of war disturbs the voice of prayer. A pursuivant and a party of men-at-arms, in the name of the Earl of Norwich, demand an audience, venerable father."

" A pursuivant and men-at-arms," exclaimed Herbert de Lozenga, hastily quitting the seat he had assumed ; "and at an hour like this !—surely you dream. Follow me, Ulrick," he added ; "but remember, boy, whatever may ensue, mine is the only voice to find an echo here."

When Herbert and his *protégé* entered the cloisters they found a number of the brothers, like frightened sheep, gathered together, gazing on a compact body of men-at-arms, headed by Ernulf, the reckless squire of Herman of the Burg, who wore over his steel hauberk a tabard blazoned with the arms of the house of Bigod. Insolent as he generally was, his eye quailed before the firm step and indignant glance of the Norman prelate, who, casting a look of reproof upon his alarmed brethren, boldly fronted him. Ulrick and Father Oswald closely followed him.

"Now, Sir Squire," exclaimed Herbert, "what means your presence here? Why are these aisles, the house of prayer and peace, invaded in the hour of night by armed men in such discourteous guise? Was he drunk or mad who sent you here upon this valiant expedition?"

"Neither, my lord," replied Ernulf, "but sorrowful at the stern duty others' crimes impose."

"Sorrow and duty—others' crimes! Speak not in riddles, man. Art really sent by Hugh de Bigod, or is this some jest, ill placed, to try our patience?"

"Noble prelate, the Earl of Norwich, Hugh de Bigod, is dead."

"Dead!" interrupted Ulrick; "impossible! Not two hours since I left him full of health and vigour, giving the promise of long years of life."

"The noble earl," continued the squire, addressing himself to Herbert, "has been murdered; and I am here in the fulfilment of mine office to arrest his murderer! Behold him there!"

The speaker slowly raised the silver staff of his office; all eyes followed its direction, till it pointed full at Ulrick. For an instant the proud glance of the prelate failed. His recollection of the agitation of his *protégé*—his flushed cheek and quivering lip, drove the blood fearfully to his heart.

"Murderer!" he slowly repeated, fixing his eyes at the same time on Ulrick; "murderer!"

The calm confidence with which the youth met his gaze restored in an instant his benefactor's confidence. Guilt ne'er wore a look so pure, so clear as that. A fearful weight fell from the good man's heart.

"And who," he demanded, with cold dignity, "is his accuser?"

"My noble master, Herman of the Burg," answered Ernulf, beginning, he knew not why, to feel uneasy at the tone of the priest, and the cold, statue-like self-possession of the accused.

"Anathema maranatha!" shrieked Father Oswald; "be his name accursed! Herman of the Burg hath guilt upon his soul would damn his race—his path hath been of blood and human tears!—be his accuser! the wolf accuse the lamb! the kite arraign the innocent dove!—crime assume the judgment-seat on virtue! No," he added, "there is yet a bolt in heaven, and a red arm to wing it." All were appalled at the vehemence of the speaker, whose vast age, majestic appearance, and fearful penitence had procured him a high character for sanctity. Seldom he spoke but to demand the prayers of his confrères—his days were passed in the most rigid abstinence—his nights in fearful vigils. There was a silence of some minutes after his denunciations. The bishop was the first to break it. "Say to your master that Sir Ulrick is prepared to meet all accusations; he will remain within these walls until the hour of trial. I grant him sanctuary, and will answer for his appearance."

"It may not be," insolently interrupted Ernulf, whose orders were at all risks to secure possession of Ulrick's person. "The murderer may escape. Advance—secure him!"

The men-at-arms, in obedience to the order of their chief, made one step to advance towards arresting the accused, when Herbert de Lozenga interposed between them. His manner was unruffled and dignified as when seated upon his episcopal throne, in the exercise of his spiritual office—his voice as firm and calm.

"None may arrest within these sacred walls," he exclaimed. "Have you not heard I grant him sanctuary? Advance one step, and on each- one I breathe the curse, which, in its wrath, has shattered crowns—broken the sceptres of earth's mightiest kings— the awful curse of Rome!"

The soldiers shrank at the prelate's voice as at the presence of a destroying angel, so profound was their dread of excommunication, the most tremendous engine ever yet wielded by priestly power; even Ernulf, their bold and reckless leader, was prepared to resign a contest in which he saw that defeat was certain; for not one man-at-arms, it was clear, would second him after that fearful threat, when Ulrick, for the first time, broke silence.

"No, father, not for me this contest; I were indeed unworthy of thy love, could I consent to shield my honour 'neath thy sacred mantle. Let craven guilt crouch 'neath the voice of accusation— innocence fears not the lightning, but defies the storm. If Hugh de Bigod hath indeed been murdered, I owe it to his son," he added, "to Mirvan's friendship, as well as my own truth, to lay my heart before him. Sir Squire, I am your prisoner."

In vain did his more cautious protector struggle against the resolution of the noble youth; he well knew that innocence is not always a protection, and would have preferred to guard his *protégé* within the peaceful walls of his own palace. But even his entreaties were useless. The thought that Matilda had heard the fearful calumny stung Ulrick to desperation; he imagined that to prove his innocence, it was but necessary to assert it; nor dreamt that there were beings in the world so practised in the wiles of crime, that e'en from virtue's self they could weave the net that should entangle it.

"Be it so!" exclaimed the prelate, won, but not convinced, by his arguments; "give thyself, in the generous confidence of thy nature, blindly to those now plotting thy destruction: despite thyself, I'll save thee. Our royal master's confidence gives me a voice in every tribunal in the realm; at the hour of judgment, thy enemies shall hear it."

Ulrick, unwilling to prolong a scene as painful to his own heart as to the prelate's, tore himself from his embrace, and surrendered his person to the men-at-arms, who, overjoyed at the unexpected turn the affair had taken, immediately surrounded him, and bore him from the cloisters. The monks watched his departure with regret, for he had been reared from infancy amongst them, and like some graceful tendril, had twined himself around their rugged natures. With pensive steps they retired to their cells, leaving their superior and father Oswald alone.

"He is innocent!" exclaimed Herbert to himself; "I feel he is innocent; guilt never bore a brow so clear as that. Murder scowls; in its restless eye you read the page of guilt. Yet, how to prove it? This Saxon, Herman, bears an evil name. Could he? I know not what to think. I'll seek the earl. The cause of quarrel —all must be explained; the accursed author of the deed made plain, or Ulrick's life is lost."

"It will be," solemnly answered the monk, "unless we help to save him."

Herbert started at the deep tone of the speaker's voice; so absorbed had been his feelings by his favourite's danger, that he had been unconscious of the old man's presence.

"What mean'st thou, brother Oswald?" he demanded; a ray of hope, from certain recollections of the past, dawning on his mind.

"To the confessional, father," answered the speaker; there, and there only, dare I breathe the fearful tale of guilt within thy ears! —a tale," he added, clasping his brow in agony, which fiends might laugh to hear—a tale which, uttered but in penitence, would rend this massive pile above my head, and make the very saints themselves turn pale."

"Follow me, son," exclaimed Herbert de Lozenga, in a tone of mild authority: "and remember that there is no sin so dark beyond the Church's power to pardon; no stain so deep that tears of penitence cannot efface it." Long and fearful was the conference which ensued: the midnight hour found the horror-stricken prelate still seated, pale as some monumental statue, in his confessional, and the guilty penitent prostrate at his feet.

Morning had just begun to dawn as Ulrick was led by his guards to the great hall of the castle, where the nobles and petty vavasours —a species of landed gentry, dependents on the late earl—were assembled. Unfortunately for the accused, Mirvan was not present; he had even a more sacred duty to perform than to avenge his

father's memory—to dry the despairing tears of his sister and
doubly-widowed mother ; for such the gentle Edith had ever
proved to him. Besides, gratitude to the preserver of his life, to
say nothing of his natural sense of justice, prevented his assuming
the jugment-seat, where his feelings were so deeply interested. He
had, therefore, despite the remonstrance of Isabel, and the silent
tears of Matilda, delegated to Herman the authority so fatally
become his ; equally determined, neither by his influence to strain
the course of justice, nor to suffer his friendship for the accused to
impede it.

The hall, so late the scene of mirth and generous hospitality, still
retained some traces of the banquet which had lately graced it.
Side-tables, covered with huge flagons and silver cups, had been
removed into the arched recesses on either side. The gallery,
where lately rang the sound of the minstrel's harp, was crowded
with the sunburnt visages of men-at-arms ; old Norman followers
of the house of Bigod, men who had served in many a gallant field
with the murdered noble, and whose stern visages bespoke a
sombre resolution to avenge him. On the daïs at the upper end of
the hall was seated Herman de Burg. No outward indication
marked his internal struggles for composure ; his eye was clouded
as from grief, not restless as through fear. Indeed, so completely
had his sense of danger schooled him that even his squire, Ernulf,
the minister of his many crimes—the instrument of his will—the
companion of his thoughts—suspected him not in this. The other
nobles were either seated or standing round him, conversing in low
whispers ; that involuntary respect which death inspires restraining
even the tongues of the more youthful. The body of the deceased
earl, covered with his marshal's mantle, lay extended on a bier in
the centre of the apartment ; two kneeling priests beside it, repeating the litanies of the dead.

" They are long upon their errand," observed an aged knight,
alluding to the expedition sent to secure the person of the accused.
" Surely the monks would never dream of offering resistance."

" Their superior may," replied Herman, not altogether easy at
the idea the words suggested ; " he hath ever shown great love for
this same Ulrick. Evil tongues are busy with his name ; men say
the orphan is his son."

No one offered a reply ; the name of Herbert de Lozenga was too
much reverenced by every Norman to be lightly spoken ; to be
even discourteously glanced at by a Saxon's lips was offensive in
the extreme. Herman perceived the ill effect his words had produced, and endeavoured to dissipate it.

" Doubtless," he resumed, " the noble prelate deemed such idle
rumours unworthy of his notice. Slander's weapons strike alike,"
he added, " the noble and the clown, nor stay to ask the difference
of degree."

At this moment the confusion and bustle at the lower end of the hall announced the arrival of the prisoner ; all eyes were fixed upon him as he advanced with a firm step towards the daïs where his judges and accuser both were seated. As he passed the bier he bent his head in reverence to the dead ; the only passages in life between them had been of kindness, and deeply he regretted his untimely end.

As he glanced towards the table his eye fell upon a sword stained with blood ; for an instant he started, and his cheek became flushed ; it was Matilda's gift to him. His judges noted his confusion, but were silent. Ulrick was the first to speak.

" Of what am I accused ? " he demanded, " and by what authority dragged from my peaceful home before this secret, strange tribunal ? "

" Of murder ! " solemnly answered the aged seneschal of the late earl. The slumbering echoes of the old hall were awakened at the sound, and the word " murder " was repeated as if whispered by invisible voices. A chill ran through the assembly, whose silence was again broken by the firm, manly voice of the prisoner.

" By whom am I accused ? "

" By the noble Saxon Franklin, Herman of the Burg, kinsman to your victim," again answered the same officer.

For a moment the accuser and accused gazed upon each other. In the glance of the former might be read the dastard triumph of vindictive passion ; in the calm, steady gaze of the latter, scorn of its baseness ; bitter, proud contempt.

" I do refuse him for my judge. Hear me, noble Normans," exclaimed Ulrick ; " 'tis but a few hours since I sat beside you in this festive hall, the guest of him whose murderer I am called. Returning home I was assailed by Herman ; not as man should meet his foe—with unsheathed sword—but with woman's weapons—base taunts, vile slanders, poisonous words which drink the lifeblood of the noble heart by poisoning its existence, the coward's courage and the base mind's vengeance. I had chastised him then but for the interference of the man of whose blood he would accuse me."

" 'Tis false ! " retorted Herman, stung by the keen tone of contempt which his victim evinced.

" 'Tis true as thou art false," said Ulrick. " Noble knights, did you not hear him, when first we met, this very day, breathe forth the natural venom of his leprous nature ? sneer at my unknown birth, my orphan state, and mock the heart which never did him wrong ? "

" We did ! " exclaimed several of the younger nobles, who began to feel interested by the high courage of the prisoner, and to suspect his accuser's disinterestedness in the affair.

" I claim the trial by battle," resumed Ulrick ; " noble knights, you will not refuse me this ! Give me the chance to meet yon craven dastard on the list. Heaven will uphold the righteous weapon and decide between us."

The nobles and knights at the upper end of the hall consulted amongst themselves ; several of the younger were for granting the prisoner's demand, the elder and more influential were against it. Their advice prevailed over the more generous sentiments of their confrères. Odo of Caen announced their decision.

" It may not be," he said ; " the right you invoke unfortunately belongs only to the noble and the free-born."

Ulrick bowed his head in shame and silence. The unfortunate mystery of his birth precluded him from meeting his enemy in the list of honour—from appealing from the judgment of his foe to battle.

" Ulrick is noble and free-born ! " exclaimed a stern voice at the end of the hall ; " the mate of any here."

" Who dare utter that monstrous lie ? " demanded Herman.

A stately figure, dressed in the habit of a monk, advanced from the crowd to the higher end of the daïs, and steadily confronted him ; slowly he raised the cowl from his still pale features, and discovered the person of Father Oswald. Ulrick's heart beat high within him.

" I dare ! " he said.

There was nothing in the features of the monk which spoke to Herman's recollection ; he deemed him a mere emissary of the bishop, sent to watch the proceedings, and whose zeal in the behalf of the prisoner had outrun discretion ; still the boldness of the assertion slightly staggered him.

" And on what proof are we to believe thee ? " inquired Odo.

" On the word of a noble Saxon," firmly answered the old man. Then, as if regretting the momentary pride of human life, he added, in deep humility, " on the faith of an unworthy priest of the Most High."

The firmness of Father Oswald's manner carried weight with it ; and a fresh consultation ensued, in which Herman, who now began to be seriously alarmed at the idea of being compelled to meet his victim on the list, actively joined, and decided the matter by his influence. Odo of Caen announced it :—

" We neither question, father," he said, " the nobility of thy birth nor the sincerity of thy heart ; but this is a matter of knightly judgement, and requires a knightly guarantee. We do again refuse the combat, unless some noble or some knight confirms by his testimony the nobility of Ulrick's birth."

The prisoner, agitated by hope and fear, turned from the haughty speaker to the extraordinary witness who had strangely testified in his favour. The old man met his glance with a smile of encouragement and benevolence, but was silent.

" You hear ? " said Herman, with a sneer ; " a noble and a knight."

"He must be noble?" demanded the monk, with hesitation; but under which a closer observer than Herman might have perceived a cold smile of conscious triumph.

"He must," impatiently iterated Herman; "as noble as myself."

"And a knight?" coolly continued Oswald.

"Like myself, he must wear upon his heels the golden spurs of chivalry," haughtily replied the Saxon; "if thou canst find such a witness."

"He is found already," interrupted the monk; "thou art that witness."

All started at the firmness with which the aged man pronounced the words, and Herman himself turned pale. Ulrick, as our readers may naturally suppose, was not the least excited at the scene. The clouds, the dark clouds of mystery which had so long obscured his birth, seemed for the first time about to clear. To him, who knew the sombre character of the speaker—the holiness of his life, his rigid love of truth, his fasts and fearful penance—the words of the monk were as oracles. He feared to speak, lest his voice should break the spell—lest he should find his glimpse of happiness was but a dream.

"What should I know of the craven bastard's birth?" faintly muttered Herman, in a hoarse voice. "What jugglery is this?"

Father Oswald advanced to the wretched man, and slowly raised to his view a ruby ring, the same which Ulrick had previously noticed lying on the table of the bishop at the interview which had been interrupted by his arrest. The effect on Herman was electrical. Had an accusing angel risen before him and displayed the record of his secret crimes, he could not have been more appalled; indeed, his agitation was so visible that all remarked and commented on it. Could the agony of mind which he endured have effaced a life of crime, in that bitter moment Herman had atoned for all.

"Dost recognise the token?" demanded the monk, still holding the ring before his eyes.

"I do," faintly answered the conscience-stricken man.

"And Ulrick's birth is noble?" he continued.

There was a pause—involuntarily the astounded criminal's hand rested on the hilt of his dagger, and then fell motionless beside him. The cold, stony glance of his pitiless questioner seemed to have deprived him of all power of resistance, as birds are supposed to be fascinated by the eye of the rattlesnake; the struggle between hate and terror was intense, but terror conquered.

"It is," he faintly murmured.

"As noble as thine own?" added the monk.

"As noble as my own!" frantically exclaimed Herman.

Unable longer to endure the recollections and terrors which the sight of the mysterious token conjured up, he rushed from the hall, leaving his brother nobles to make their comments on his conduct, and arrange for the combat which he now felt to be inevitable.

Surprise and consternation were on the countenances of all ; men felt that they had assisted at a scene whose mystery was yet to be unravelled. The unexpected testimony borne to the nobility of Ulrick's birth by his bitterest enemy, and through the agency of the monk, excited the imagination, and caused a more favourable sentiment towards the prisoner. Many a half-forgotten tale to the prejudice of his accuser was revived ; most began to doubt the truth of the accuser, and it was finally settled that the trial by battle should take place in three days, Ulrick in the interim remaining in close ward, under the custody of Herman.

Vainly both the prisoner and the monk protested against a decision which placed the former in the power of his deadliest enemy ; their resolution was not to be revoked. In vain Ulrick intreated to be allowed to converse in private with the mysterious being who seemed to possess the clue to his wretched destiny. His judges were inexorable. The youth was conducted to his dungeon, and Father Oswald slowly pursued his pathway to the monastery.

Thrice was Ernulf summoned by his impatient master, who rushed from the hall, where he had been so singularly confronted, more with the air of a raving maniac than a Christian knight. After long years of fancied security and peace, a clue seemed found to his disgrace ; the baseless fabric of his honour already tottered ; and conscience presented to his tortured imagination the rabble's curse, his brother nobles' scorn. He was pacing his chamber, a prey to these and similar reflections, when the ready instrument of so many of his crimes appeared before him.

"Hast thou beheld yon cursed monk ? " he exclaimed. "Didst recognise the token by which he mastered me ? Can this Ulrick be indeed the being whom I most fear to name, whose image haunts me in my dreams, the certainty of whose existence would poison all my joys, e'en were they those of Paradise ? "

"Impossible, my lord," replied Ernulf ; "this stripling is of Norman, not of Saxon blood. The pampered prelate brought him a child to England. Why, I remember him ere he could lisp a word of Saxon tongue. Your fears betray you."

"But the ring—the ring—the father's ancient crest," interrupted Herman, "lost on that night when my arm failed me. Cursed be the tempest's terrors which unmanned me, and doubly cursed the meddling fiend who foiled me in my purpose ! "

"My lord," exclaimed Ernulf, after a few moments' reflection, "I think I can explain this seeming mystery. Some dying penitent gave the ring to yonder monk—perhaps made him the depositor of his suspicions, for proofs he had none ; and the cunning churchman hath used the knowledge to his purposes—it can be nothing more."

" Perchance," muttered Herman, but half satisfied at the suggestion, yet still grasping at it like some drowning man ; " yet I would make assurance more than sure. This monk—this being who, like Providence enveloped in a thundercloud, unseen can strike me : he must die ! "

" Die ! " repeated the squire, recoiling with superstitious horror at the idea of steeping his hands in a churchman's blood—" not by my hands, my lord ! 'Tis true they are stained enough already, but not with priestly blood. Oh, never, never ! "

" Churl ! is it redder than a noble's ? " said his master, with a sneer ; " beside, thy life is in the noose. Should this mad priest possess the key to my past crimes, thinkest thou they would hesitate to place thee on the rack to wring confession of them ? As a noble, I might perish by the sword ; but think, Ernulf, how fearful a destiny would then be thine ! "

The argument was artfully used, and not without its due effect upon his hearer, who well knew how little their Norman rulers hesitated to employ the torture upon men of far higher lineage than his own. Herman watched his hesitation.

" Besides," he added, " in a distant land I will enable thee to live in safety and in honour. Thou knowest I am no churlish master ; restore to me my signet-ring, no matter by what means ; and let me hear the only being whom I dread on earth is dead, I'll count thee down a thousand silver marks."

" Faith ! 'tis a tempting sum ! " exclaimed the ruffian, his eyes sparkling with cupidity.

" And for what ? " continued the tempter ; " for cutting the exhausted thread of an old man's life—extinguishing a dying lamp. Decide thee, man ; the tithe part of the sum I offer thee would buy thee pardon for a dozen murders."

" It will be difficult," said Ernulf musingly ; " Father Oswald seldom leaves the cloister's shelter. 'Tis true he sometimes sits in the confessional, shriving such penitents as speak no Norman tongue ; but then it would be sacrilege ; and that——"

" Too, shall be paid for," interrupted his master ; " 'Tis just that every crime should have its price—are we agreed ? "

" We are," rejoined the squire, chuckling at the anticipation of the promised gold ; " be he priest or fiend, I'll drive my weapon to his heart. Within two days you shall have news of me."

Thus did Herman, and his too willing minister, continue to plot fresh crime. The forbearance of Heaven they regarded as impunity, and in the fancied security of their cunning defied its vengeance. They knew not that if the steps of Divine Justice are sometimes slow, they are sure—that her hand is iron, and her blow is death.

" What was the decision in the hall below ? " demanded the franklin, " after the monk—curse on my weakness—drove me from the hall ? "

[THE OLD SENESCHAL DESCRIBING THE SECRET PASSAGE.]

E

"The combat was decided on."

"I know—I know!" muttered Herman—"they could not well refuse it. Where is the Norman bastard?"

"Safe in a dungeon of the castle, in your custody."

"In my custody!" repeated his master; "humph!—that was kind at least—and in how many days the combat?"

"Three days, my lord!" said the squire; and a look of peculiar intelligence passed between them.

"Three days," muttered Herman, as he quitted the apartment; "the time is short, but, well employed, much may be done by then."

At a later period of the day a cavalcade might be seen approaching the castle from the episcopal palace; heralds with their tabards blazoned with the arms of the Church led the way, then followed a party of priests and men-at-arms, who preceded the litter in which rode Herbert de Lozenga, the ensigns of his office as Chancellor of England being borne before him. Several of the nobles beheld his arrival with dissatisfaction; they felt indignant at the idea of his lending the sanction of his name and influence to shield the assassin of one of his own order. The greeting between them was, therefore, more of sullen respect than cordial welcome. The prelate marked their manner, but disregarded it; his courage was too high, his purpose too holy, to be influenced by the opinion of his fellow-men. Just as he passed the bridge Herman appeared, and in tho name of the young earl bade him welcome, at the same time bending his knee so as to receive the Apostolic benediction; but no upraised hand, no air-drawn cross, followed the act—the piety of the bishop was too sincere to permit his lips to speak the blessing his heart could not bestow. The disappointed man rose from his knee in bitter mortification, and leading the way preceded his unwelcome guest to the late earl's private apartment, where their conversation could be carried on without interruption. Each was on his guard; the guilty one felt that a searching eye was upon him, the priest that he had to do with one a master in the art of crime, an adept in dissimulation. Herman was the first to break the silence.

"Forgive me, reverend father," he exclaimed, "if in the reception you have met with here aught has been lacking to your honour. The hand of grief is on my kinsman's house; he mourns his father lost, his friendship stained, his confidence abused, else had he shown the reverences it is my lot to offer."

"'Tis well," replied the prelate; "the cloister's shade I quitted not for the sake of man's observance or the world's vain honours, but at the call of justice and of truth. By what right have you profaned with ruffian violence our holy church, and torn the youth I cherish as a son from me, his guardian and protector? Speak."

E 2

There was a firmness, a conscious power, in the speaker's voice which grated on the listener's ear. Still he determined to yield no inch of vantage ground—the guardianship of Ulrick's person. The ring which the monk had presented to his view opened to his mind a fearful doubt ; and he determined at any sacrifice to rid himself of one whom conscience clothed in the character of an avenger.

"Is it possible, my lord !" he answered with well-feigned astonishment ; "would you lend the sanction of your high name to shield a murderer ? The indignant earth, which drank the victim's blood, groans 'neath the homicide's polluted tread, and calls for Ulrick's life."

"I deem him innocent ; men do not fall at once from virtue into the extreme of vice. I demand that he be committed to my care ; my palace walls will better answer for his safety than can a dungeon here."

"You deem him innocent," iterated the franklin ; "surely, my lord, you have not heard the proofs ; his quarrel with the earl—his sword found near the spot."

"Something I heard of taunts and bitter jests, unmanly sneers, which sting the generous soul," gravely answered Herbert ; "but nothing of a quarrel with the earl. The hour of combat is appointed. You yourself," he added with peculiar emphasis, "are witness of the nobility of Ulrick's birth. I again demand that till that hour he be committed to my care."

"Impossible," said Herman ; "the proposition wounds my honour."

"And would defeat your purpose."

"Can you suspect, my lord ?"

"Everything," replied the bishop, drawing himself proudly up ; "Herman of the Burg, I am not one whom thou mayst trifle with ; Ulrick, or thou, must with me."

"I !" faltered the astonished franklin.

"Thou ! If I cannot release your victim, I can at least enchain his captor."

"This is madness !" said Herman, rising with a pride equal to the prelate's, and throwing open the doors of the apartment. "Enter, my lords," he cried, "and judge between us. Our reverend father hath declared that Ulrick must be released, or I become his prisoner."

"Prisoner !" exclaimed the several nobles as they entered ; "and on what pretence ?"

"Sorcery and murder !" exclaimed the deep voice of Father Oswald, who had entered with the crowd, and commenced reading from a parchment : "I cite, in the name of the most reverend Father Herbert de Lozenga, Bishop of Norwich and Abbot of Hulm, Herman of the Burg to appear before the above reverend prelate, to answer to the charge of having sold a Christian child to the Arch-Druid Haga for human sacrifice."

All who heard shrank with horror at the charge. Overwhelmed as Herman was by it, his courage did not quite forsake him.

" Who," he demanded, " is my accuser ? "

" I am ! " thundered the priest ; " I, Haga the Arch-Druid." Then, sinking on his knees at the feet of the bishop, he added, in a voice of deep humility, " I, Oswald the Christian."

CHAPTER IV.

THE consternation of Herman at the unexpected accusation of Father Oswald, or, as he was formally called, Haga the Arch-Druid, may be more easily imagined than portrayed ; the crime of sorcery was, in the eleventh century, the most fearful that could be alleged. Society rejected the supposed criminal with horror—the Church cast him from her bosom—his children deserted him—even the sacred tie of marriage, the bond which mystically united him body and soul with the companion of his life, the mother of his offspring, became dissolved, and the wretched man stood like the genius of desolation in the world—alone.

The Norman nobles who had hitherto supported Herman drew from his side—as superstitious as they were brave, they shrank from an encounter with one whose arms were the spiritual weapons of their mutual faith—and Herbert would have met no difficulty in securing his prisoner had not succour arrived from a quarter where he least expected it. The franklins stepped forward to a man, and guaranteed the appearance of the accused before the ecclesiastical tribunal—a caution which, by the laws of Edward the Confessor, the bishop could not refuse to accept. But this unexpected unanimity on the part of the Saxons gave rise in the prelate's mind to a strange doubt.

Uncertain rumours of an intended revolt of the conquered race had indeed reached him ; but nothing tangible, nothing certain. He was, however, too cautious a statesman to betray his suspicions —too experienced a huntsman to let the ban-wolf know that the hounds were on his track. Had the deceased earl been equally prudent, he might have been living still.

" 'Tis well, sir franklins," he said. " I accept your surety for the appearance of Herman of the Burg ; but it is on one condition, and one condition only ! "

" Name it—name it," cried several voices, impatiently.

" A man accused of sorcery may not be the guardian of a Christian noble ; for noble Ulrick is, even by the testimony of his accuser. Resign him to my care."

" No ! " exclaimed the Normans, unanimously—who, however
submissive in things spiritual, bitterly resented the bishop's interference in their feudal justice—" he is a murderer ! "

" Grant him such ; still he is a Christian, and may not be the
captive of a man o'er whom the Church suspends her awful malediction. Provoke me, and it falls on him and all who aid him in
his crimes."

" Ulrick shall be our captive," replied Odo of Caen. " I will be
answerable for his safe appearance on the day of battle ; will that
content you ? "

" It must," murmured the crowd of nobles. " We will all answer
with our lives and honours for his favourite's safety ; we will keep
faithful ward——"

" And honourable treatment ? " demanded Herbert de Lozenga,
who, finding he could obtain no better terms, was fain to accede.

" My word," answered Odo, " is the pledge of that ; till the day
of battle, Sir Ulrick shall be honourably guarded and well tended ;
nor friends nor foes shall have access to him. I'll hold his life as
sacred as I would the blazon of my shield—the honour of my house.
But his safe keeping touches our feudal privileges : my lord, we will
maintain them."

The decided tone of the speaker told Herbert that all further
discussion would be useless ; and having, as he hoped, secured the
life of his *protégé* against any possible machinations of his enemy,
he resolved to appear satisfied with the concessions he had already
obtained ; but three days were to elapse before the day of battle,
and in that brief space he had much work to do for Ulrick's safety.

" Farewell, my lords," he said ; " let us not part in anger. We
have each our duties to perform ; judge, then, each other kindly.
I leave you with every confidence in your knightly faith ; Heaven
will decide between us if you break it."

Every knee was bent to the earth to receive the parting benediction
of the man whose arrival they had so coldly welcomed, whose
reasonable demand they had so unjustly opposed. Submissive as
were the Norman nobles to the Church in all things spiritual, they
were jealously susceptible when it trenched upon their feudal
rights ; and Ulrick's cause was even slightly prejudiced in their
minds by a churchman's advocacy.

A faint smile of mingled satisfaction and triumph passed Herman's
lips as the train of the bishop crossed the castle bridge ; but a deep
observant eye was upon him, for Father Oswald, who had lingered
behind his superior, read that smile, interpreted its purpose, and
determined to prevent it. Instead of crossing the moat with the
rest of his brethren, the monk hastily drew his cowl over his features,
passed quickly to the western side of the massive keep, nor paused
till he reached the angle which it formed with the chapel, the
entrance to which was by a low-arched door, rich in sculptured

imagery. Satisfied that none observed him, he drew a key from his bosom, applied it to the door, and disappeared within its gloomy shade.

"The meddling churchman," exclaimed Herman, who, surrounded by his brother franklins, stood at the foot of Bigod's tower, watching the departure of the prelate, "to accuse one of my blood of sorcery! The hour is not far distant when dear he may abide it. Noble Odo," he added, addressing the Norman, who was standing near him, "what thinkest thou of yon shaveling's scheme to shield his pampered minion?"

"Each power claims its subjects," coolly answered the knight. "The sorcerer to the stake! the assassin to the block! Although I will not suffer Mother Church to interfere with my justice, I am too dutiful a son not to respect hers; aye, by my crest, and execute it too, let me but see good reason on her side."

There was something in the tone of the speaker's voice which vibrated to the very heart of Herman, and blanched his cheek with fear. He saw that the Normans, while resolute to obtain justice on the presumed murderer of their chief and brother noble, were perfectly indifferent as to his fate; nay, that they would assist, if called upon, to execute any judgment which the ecclesiastical tribunal might pronounce upon him, even though its sentence were the stake. He felt that his only chance of safety lay in the success of the insurrection to which he was so deeply pledged.

"It would require a keener sword than even Odo of Caen's," retorted Herman, "to execute a sentence that touched either my honour or my life."

The brow of the Norman became flushed, and his hand instinctively grasped the hilt of his weapon; but with a violent effort he restrained himself.

"Sir Saxon," he replied, "I will not be tempted; thou art the champion of a sacred cause. Would 'twere in better hands! But thou art its champion, and therefore inviolate."

The speaker turned upon his heel and entered the tower as he spoke, without deigning to cast a second glance on the unworthy franklin.

The first act of Odo on entering the castle was to give orders to his esquire, in whom he placed unlimited confidence, to conduct a party of his immediate followers to the tower where Ulrick was confined, and to keep joint watch with his gaolers; to accompany all who entered the prison, and to guard the life of the prisoner as carefully as he would his master's honour—a precaution, as the sequel will show, not unwisely taken, but which would have been defeated, had not an eye more vigilant, a heart more devoted than his, watched over Ulrick's safety.

Edith, the unhappy Edith, doubly widowed by the death of Hugh de Bigod, had retired to Stanfield on her husband's death.

It is true he was not the object of her early choice. The passionate enthusiasm of her young heart, the dreams which, broken once, we ne'er can dream again, were long since buried in the grave of Edward : but respect, esteem, friendship, all that her blighted feelings could bestow, the earl had long since won, and she mourned his loss—if not as women mourn the being whom they love, at least with honour and respect.

It was on the evening which closed the first day of her widowhood that she was pensively seated in the long unvisited cabinet we formerly described. Judith, her still faithful attendant, and the confidante of her sorrows, was at her side. Many and sad were the thoughts which occupied her mind. In that apartment she had listened to the first vow of love breathed into her virgin ear ! It was there she had so oft received her father's blessing, tasted the thrilling pleasure of her child's caress, and there had mourned them both. Her faithful companion's words of consolation fell on a listless ear when she whispered hopes of future happiness and peace.

"Happiness ! " she exclaimed ; "no, Judith, no ! The world knows not the word for me. All who ever loved the wretched Edith have been blighted by her fatal destiny ! The gentle Edward, my kind old father, and my noble boy—all, all have perished, because they were dear to me. I am a thing accursed—a withered tree without one verdant leaf ! and when I fall a stranger's hand will lay me in the grave—a stranger's foot pace through my father's halls."

The hopeless tone in which the words were spoken silenced even the well-meaning Judith, who, with the tact which affection gives, comprehended that her attempts at consolation were ill-timed.

Sinking on her knees beside her unhappy mistress, she timidly kissed her hand, and as she did so bedewed it with tears—a sympathy more eloquent and grateful to affliction than words, which wake no echo in the heart.

"Now thou art kind," Judith, she continued. " Thou hast given me tears, not hopes. I have hoped and trusted, but now I'll trust no more ! The grave is our only refuge from despair, and death the only hope which ne'er deceives us."

"Religion is a better hope, my child," exclaimed the deep-toned voice of Herbert de Lozenga, who entered the apartment. " Remember, there is no state so wretched—no fate so dark—but one kind ray of mercy yet may cheer it."

At the sight of the prelate, whom a holy and important purpose had brought to Stanfield, the widowed countess cast herself upon her knees to implore his benediction, exclaiming as she did so—

"Your blessing, father, your blessing ! Pour words of peace into my bleeding heart ! Teach rebel nature to submit its tears, its vain regrets, and impious struggles unto His will who chasteneth where He loveth."

"'Tis thine, most noble lady; it is thine!" replied Herbert. "May Heaven endue thy soul with strength to bear the trials in its wisdom laid on it! 'Tis natural," he added, raising her as he spoke, "to mourn for those we love! Life from its cradle to the grave teaches no other lesson! But sorrow never should destroy our usefulness—never should prevent the gentle exercise of charity and mercy."

The slight tone of reproof, mingled with the earnest benevolence of the speaker, excited the attention of Edith, who misconceived, however, its tendency.

"My gold I'll freely give unto the poor. The Church hath not found me, I trust, a niggard, father."

"'Tis not the altar's streaming incense, lady—the costly offering of superfluous wealth—which forms the only sacrifice that Heaven demands! 'Tis the more active exercise of virtue, shielding the innocent, and aiding the oppressed."

"I do not understand you," replied the countess. "Point out the way my services can be of use to any! Fear not my zeal, but tax it to the uttermost."

"Ulrick," said the priest, "is innocent! Designing men conspire against the noble boy—in secret work his ruin! Your voice, lady, must be heard in his defence."

"'Tis powerless, father, here. Herman wields his kinsman's delegated rights—go, plead to him."

"To Herman," iterated the bishop; "no, lady, no! He hates the gallant youth, and with untiring vengeance still pursues him; it burns as fiercely in the villain's breast as when I snatched him first an infant from the dagger's murderous aim."

"An infant!" exclaimed both Judith and the countess, the latter of whom became pale as death at the faint ray of hope which the speaker's words let dawn upon her mind.

"Though now," resumed Herbert, "I wear the mitre on my brow, and rank and empty pomp and state are mine, when first I left the world my path was humble—a hermit's cave was my abode. To thee 'twere useless to repeat the wrongs which drove me from my native land. I was a moody, melancholy man, unloving and unloved! My ties of kindred, my ancestral rank, I cast aside; and in this distant isle sought refuge for myself. Perhaps the recluse in Windham's lonely cell was happier than the prelate in his halls."

"Is't possible?" interrupted Edith, with unfeigned surprise. "Art thou the hermit of St. Mary's cave?"

"E'en so," said Herbert, with a melancholy smile. "He whose first errand was of grief and death—he who announced the murder of thy lord—perchance his second is of peace and hope."

"Hope!" murmured his listener; "what have I on earth to hope or fear?" A glance from the prelate thrilled her very soul.

"Speak, father," she exclaimed; "you have raised thoughts that will either restore or crush me !"

"One stormy night," he continued, resuming his narrative, "a traveller, driven by the unpitying tempest, sought shelter at my cave. Nestled at his breast an infant lay, whose innocent smile had won e'en fiends to mercy. Refreshed, I left him to repose. Returning to perform a midnight penance, I beheld the ruffian aim his dagger at the infant's throat. Heaven lent me courage. I wrenched the weapon from the murderer's grasp. He fled the spot and never more returned."

"When was this?" gasped Edith.

"Twenty years ago, St. Hubert's eve," replied the bishop. "This ring," he continued, at the same time producing the ruby—whose effect upon her unworthy kinsman we have already described— dropped in the struggle, "bears the well-known crest of Herman's ancient house ! Confounded at the sight of it, he hath already owned that Ulrick's birth is noble."

"It is ! it is !" shrieked Edith. "Father, it was my child thy guardian hand preserved. Oh, wretched mother ! to have seen my boy, yet felt no token of his presence ! Had not my heart been cold, seared as the inmate's of a charnel house, it sure had leapt to meet him. Norman," she continued, casting herself at his feet, "swear thou dost not deceive me ! By thine order's' oath, thy mother's blessing, swear that he is mine."

"I do believe it," answered the bishop. "Haga the Arch-Druid, whom Heaven, through its unworthy servant, hath redeemed from the dark errrors of his pagan creed, hath confessed he gave into Herman's hand a drug of power to steep the senses in oblivious sleep, on condition that the child should be consigned to him."

"To him ! To Odin's priest !" exclaimed the excited mother. "No, no ! Better that he had perished in the flames in which I had deemed him lost. It is too horrible. He could not have made a compact for my boy ! Father, what have I done—what deadly crime committed—that Heaven should wreak such cruel vengeance on my sinless child ?" Edith pressed her hands to her flushed brow, as if to repress the wild pulsations of its agony. Fortunately a flood of tears relieved her o'erfraught heart, which else had yielded to its wild emotions. A pause ensued, which Herbert wisely forfore to break. He beheld the mother's tears flow on with pleasure ; for he knew that nature had unsealed their fountain to afford relief.

"My boy—my poor, lost, persecuted boy," at last sobbed Edith, her memory slightly wandering, "could no blood but thine bedew the Druids' stone ? Was there no pitying angel to protect thee ?"

"Heaven hath protected him," said the prelate, in a mild, reproving tone. "Its justice smote the minister of blood. The night before the fearful compact was to be fulfilled, Haga was stretched upon affliction's couch ! Chance led me to his wild retreat, where human footsteps feared to tread. I watched, I tended—saved him. Heaven gave eloquence to my unworthy tongue, and truth prevailed. Ere many days elapsed I poured the regenerating waters of baptism on his repentant head."

"But my boy—my Edward's boy?" demanded Edith.

"Herman, no doubt, would have fulfilled his pledge to Haga, but found him raging on a bed of sickness. Wandering with his burthen in the storm, he sought my cell for shelter. You know the rest."

"I do! I do! Heaven hath heard the widowed mother's prayers."

"And doubtless will preserve him," added the prelate; "but this is the time for action, not for words. Ulrick is accused of Hugh de Bigod's death, and hath appealed unto the battle's test. Herman, his accuser is of giant strength, and skilled in cunning fence. Should his sword prevail, the block and axe will be his victim's doom."

"The block!" exclaimed Edith, starting like a roused lioness at the appalling image. "The headsman's office for my Edward's boy! I will call up the vassals of my house. I still have kindred—friends. Enslaved, enthralled, and humbled as we are, the Saxon courage is not yet so low that Norman axe should fall on a son of mine."

"Be cautious, lady; one false step may ruin all. Edda, the father of your Edward, lives, honoured and loved, the most powerful noble of the Saxon race. Seek his presence; fly to him for aid, tell him the heir of his long line yet lives. His strength will aid thy weakness, his wisdom find a clue to this disastrous maze."

It was arranged that Edith, that very night, should, under the escort of the benevolent prelate, seek the protection of the aged franklin, whose stronghold was but a few hours' ride from Stanfield. Judith was accordingly sent to give orders for the departure of her excited mistress. The faithful attendant soon returned with consternation marked in every feature. It seems that, during the interview, Herman, accompanied by a numerous body of vassals, had arrived at the holm, and learning that the prelate had preceded him, had taken possession of the hall, giving strict orders that no one should be permitted to quit the building without his permission. His conscience told him that all had been discovered; he determined, therefore, to throw off the mask, and by one bold step secure himself, if possible, against the punishment of his many crimes. His followers, as deeply implicated as himself in the conspiracy against the Norman race, applauded, and were the willing instruments of his design. He persuaded them that their schemes were all betrayed, and that if Herbert de Lozenga left the place alive, the cord and axe would be their general doom. "Let them perish!" he exclaimed; "the hunter hath fallen into the lion's lair, and prudence commands that he should die!"

It was secretly resolved that that part of the holm in which the apartments of Edith were situated should be fired, care being taken that none of its inmates escaped.

"Lost! lost!" said Edith, when Judith had concluded her report. "Fortune hath cheated me with a gleam of happiness, to make me feel my misery the stronger."

"Courage, dear lady," replied her faithful friend; "hope hath not yet abandoned us. I have heard that from this very chamber one of your ancestors, pressed by the enemy, once fled through a secret passage."

"Known but to one ancient follower of our house," replied the countess, "who, even if he live, must be so aged that memory's seat is shaken."

"Shaken," said Judith, "but not destroyed. At times flashes will fall from memory's torch, and shed a vivid light on scenes long past."

"Seek him," said the bishop. "I know the man with whom we have to cope. 'Tis our last hope, and should it fail, and death becomes inevitable, remember that the priest is present for his office, and that heaven is near."

Judith required no second command, but hastened to the remote apartment of the venerable servitor, whose vast age had long disqualified him for all active service, but who had been retained to dream away the winter of his life beneath the roof of those whom he had so long and faithfully obeyed. The period of her absence, though short, appeared to the prelate and unhappy mother an age. Slight as was the chance of escape, the return of the faithful attendant, leading the seneschal, long since blind with age, was a relief that seemed to say all hope was not extinct.

"Where, where do you lead me?" fretfully exclaimed the old man, displeased at being taken from his favourite nook. "Why have you dragged me here? I passed the court; where am I? There used to be a step. Yes, yes—there used to be a step."

It was evident that he was endeavouring to recollect the spot to which Judith had conducted him, but that memory was struggling with the infirmities of age.

"Knowest thou where thou art?" demanded Herbert de Lozenga, in a soothing tone.

"No! no!" petulantly replied Hubert. "Who is it that questions me? Thine is no Saxon tongue. Lead me back, I pray. The air blows damp and chill, and my limbs tremble."

"Hopeless! hopeless!" said Edith, sinking on her chair. "His mind is gone—quite gone."

It was curious to mark the effect of Edith's voice. The old man trembled like an aspen leaf; its tone had awoke some long-forgotten echo in his heart. He had half-turned, as if to find his way back from whence he came, when its sound arrested him.

" Speak to him, lady," whispered the prelate. " He knows your voice best."

" Hubert," said the countess, advancing and taking his hand, " hast thou forgotten me ? "

" I know, I know thee ! " he exclaimed : " thou art my master's child. Lady, the oldest vassal of thy house would bend the knee before thee, but 'tis stiff with age."

" Hubert," said his agitated mistress, " danger besets my steps, and I must fly—fly from my father's roof."

The word " danger " seemed to restore the old man's faculties. Twice he endeavoured to erect his curbed limbs, like some worn war-steed, who heard the distant trumpet's clang, and thirsts for the fray.

" Danger ! " he repeated. " What danger can assail our lady here ? Shall I raise the banner of your house ? " There was something affecting in the spirit of the old servitor, whose devotion had so long outlived his strength.

" No, Hubert, no," replied Edith. " Mine is a peril that must be met by flight. The times are changed, old man, and we must meet them. This was my grandsire's chamber," she added, " from whence I have heard there is a secret passage which leads beyond the moat—know'st thou of such ? "

" Hush ! " whispered the aged servitor ; " there is such a passage. It—it—oh, memory, memory, do not desert me now ! "

The speaker passed his thin, attenuated hand over his withered brow, to assist his broken recollections, his hearers gazing on him in anxious expectation.

" Where is it ? " demanded Herbert de Lozenga, no longer able to keep silence.

The seneschal started at the sound of the prelate's voice ; 'twas not the one he recognised. And, with the suspicion natural to the aged, he doggedly refused to answer him. It was some time before even Edith's voice could lead him to the subject.

" No, lady," he repeated, " there is no passage. I am old, but faithful. A stranger must not learn the secrets of your house—I have sworn to keep them—Hubert will guard his oath."

" Hubert ! " exclaimed the countess, excited to desperation by the disappointment of her hopes, " I tell thee that I am beset with dangers—my life is in peril. Thou knowest the secret passage from this chamber ; make one effort—recall one ray of memory to thine aid—do it, and save thy mistress from despair ! " The speaker's tears fell fast upon his hands, which, in her agony she had taken.

" Despair ! " he repeated, almost childishly, " and tears—my lady's tears ! Then I must—I must. Give me a moment—where am I ? "

" In my grandsire's chamber—the one in which he died."

" The panelled one ? "

" The same," said Edith, making a signal that neither of her
companions should speak, as it was evident that every voice but hers
disturbed his recollection and excited his suspicion.

" Tell me, lady," he resumed " what is the hour of day ? "

" 'Tis night, Hubert—alas ! 'tis night ! " exclaimed his mistress,
deeming from the question that his mind was becoming again a
blank, and that the clue was for ever lost—" night, dark as my
destiny ! "

" Night ! ah, true, true ! Does the moon shine upon the oriel
window ? "

" It does—it does ! " she replied, hope once more dawning at his
question.

" When," resumed the old man " the shadow of the cross within
your ancient shield falls on the oak-carved panels, then—then—your
father, lady—but we are Normans now," and so again the old man's
memory failed him, and he was wandering in a disjointed strain.
An expression of childish apathy succeeded to the intelligence he
had so lately displayed, and the last ray of recollection quitted him
for ever.

Fortunately Herbert de Lozenga had caught every word he uttered.
In the centre of the window to which he had alluded was a coat of
arms of stained glass, the red cross in which, when struck by the
rays of either the sun or moon, cast a broad shadow upon one of the
rudely-carved panels in the wall. On a patient examination the
prelate at length succeeded in discovering the spring, which was an
iron leaf curiously concealed amidst the oaken foliage ; it quickly
yielded to the strong pressure of his eager hand, and the path of safety
lay open to their view.

" The path is open," he exclaimed ; " not a moment must be
lost."

Judith hastily enveloped the agitated countess in a dark mantle,
and prepared to follow her, when the heat, which had increased to
a fearful extent in the apartment, and which, from the anxiety
caused by their position, they had scarcely observed, burst into a
flame ; perhaps the current of fresh air which the opening of the
secret passage admitted hastened the calamity.

" Heavens, the holm is in flames ! " said Edith. " We cannot
leave the old man to perish here ; that were poor gratitude for
faithful service : aid me to save him, father."

By their united efforts Hubert was led safe into the recesses of
the passage, whose existence he had so miraculously disclosed, and
there left till aid was sent to remove him. The three fugitives,
after traversing the long, damp passage, emerged into a ruined hut,
situated in the deepest recesses of the forest. The prelate cast his
eyes around and recognised the abode of Haga, the Arch-Druid.
Fortunately, he knew the country well, and a few hours' walk
brought them to one of the numerous convents which owned his

spiritual sway. Shelter was instantly obtained, and a strict injunction for secrecy imposed on all its inmates.

" I can brave the world securely now," thought Herman, as the flames of Stanfield reddened in the night. " Edith, who scorned my love, hath proved at last my hate. The Norman priestling, too, who thought to crush me—I trample on his ashes. World," he added, with a scornful laugh, " we shall soon be quits. My debt is lessening."

The next day the rumour of the accidental destruction of Stanfield, and the death of Edith and Bishop Herbert, spread far and near. The good mourned their loss, and the evil triumphed in their fall.

The next morning Ernulf, the worthy squire of such a master as Herman, doffed his hauberk and helmet for the sober, peaceful dress of one of the lower order of franklins, and directed his steps towards the cathedral, where he was sure at all times to find the monks ready to receive their penitents, or to perform the varied ministry of their office.

Disguising his perfect knowledge of the Norman tongue, he demanded of one of the brotherhood to point out to him a confessional filled by some Saxon priest, and was, as he expected, directed to the one usually occupied by Father Oswald.

It was situated in one of those quiet, gloomy chapels at the back of the high altar, which the vandalism of the modern clergy has long since consigned to neglect ; the light faintly penetrated through the richly-stained glass, softening, with its mellow tone, the harsh outlines of the sculptured saint, to whom its shrine was dedicated. The aged priest was in the act of shriving a penitent when the disguised murderer approached.

Despite his attire, and the hypocritical meekness of his look, Oswald recognised him, and instantly comprehended his purpose ; but his courage did not fail him, or the danger which he ran cause his heart to beat with increased emotion. Sternly, seated on his chair, he seemed like the impersonation of one of those fabled deities worshipped of old, his conscious power marked by his impassibility. Before he dismissed his kneeling penitent, he took from an ebony and silver box which hung beside him a small phial, which he placed under his sandalled foot, so that he could crush it by the slightest pressure, and placed a morsel of some highly-perfumed drug within his mouth.

As soon as they were left alone within the chapel—Ernulf and the priest—the former advanced towards the confessional, his eyes bent in seeming humility to the ground, but in reality to hide the ferocious joy which the anticipation of blood gave to their expression. His knee was sacrilegiously bent to the earth even at the moment his hand secretly grasped the weapon concealed beneath his flowing cloak.

" What brings the parricide and sacrilegious robber to the tribunal of penitence ? " demanded Oswald, his aged eyes flashing with holy indignation on the prostrate man. " Is it to commit some new crime ? Is not his soul stained with blood enough already ? "

Had a thunderbolt fallen at the feet of the detected Ernulf, he could not have been more surprised. The being whom he came to strike seemed armed with omniscience to confound him. The secret terror of his life, the sin which haunted him, his nightly dream— his daily curse—rose, as it were, in evidence against him. His craven heart beat wildly at the words.

" Parricide ! " he murmured, faintly.

" Aye, how else," demanded Oswald, " name ye those who shed a parent's blood ? Have so many years elapsed that thou hast forgot the deed—so many tears of penitence been shed, it has effaced the stain ? Fool ! " he added, " should thy life be long and wearisome as mine, and every minute of it be a prayer or tear, it would not cleanse thy hand. A father's blood is on it—his dying malediction on thy soul ! "

Ernulf, overwhelmed with confusion, could only faintly exclaim— " Mercy ! mercy ! "

" Mercy ! " iterated the priest ; " where was thy mercy when he clung to thee, with his white hair dyed in gore, and his dying eyes, in mingled love and horror, fixed upon thee ? Mercy ! Ask it of the fiends," he continued, " who registered thy crime ; ask it of thy father's bones, which, at the archangel's trumpet's sound, shall rise up in judgment against thee—ask it of the innocent blood which thou hast shed, the purity which thou hast violated, the homes which thou hast rendered desolate, but ask it not of me. Minister of justice, as well as mercy, I close the book of life against thee, and pronounce anathema to thy despairing soul."

The voice of the old man was firm as the denunciating angel's curse when it swept over the Cities of the Plain. The appalled Ernulf, confronted with his crime, knew not which way to flee—terror took possession of his heart—hell seemed yawning beneath him—and the strong ruffian rolled in agony at his accuser's feet.

" And now," continued Oswald, " thou wouldst add sacrilege to murder—for base, filthy hire profane the holy sacrament of Penance, insult the indignant saints before their altars, and strike their minister before their shrine ! "

" Art thou a devil, thus to read men's hearts ? " demanded Ernulf, rage and shame gradually mastering his terror.

" Enough, I can read thine," said Oswald. " Aye, grasp thy weapon," he continued, as he witnessed the movement of the squire's hand beneath his cloak. " I fear it not. Thou art delivered to me —the worm beneath my foot is not more hurtless than thy toothless malice."

" Indeed ! " exclaimed Ernulf, casting a deep glance around, to

[THE PRAYER OF MATILDA AND ISABEL.]

see if he was observed, and springing to his feet, "if thou art mortal, this will reach thee."

He drew the concealed weapon from his cloak, and raised his impious hand to strike ; but ere it could descend, the sandalled foot of the monk had crushed the phial beneath it, and the confessional was instantaneously filled by a thin, subtle vapour, whose effects were electrical. The weapon of the assassin fell, as if struck by lightning, to the ground, while he himself stood nerveless as a new-born infant before his judge and his accuser.

"This is the completion of thy crimes," said Oswald, after a pause ; "thy dark career is run."

A party of monks, summoned by his voice, soon filled the chapel ; to them he recounted the attempt upon his life, and pointed to the criminal, whose person was instantly secured, for he made no resistance—his mind, like his body, seemed to have been stricken by palsy, so extraordinary was the effect produced upon him by the means through which the priest had disarmed him—means perfectly comprehended by the scientific of the present day, but which to Ernulf's superstitious mind seemed like the direct interposition of Providence.

CHAPTER V.

IN consideration of the nobility of Ulrick's birth, the confession of which was so strangely wrung from his accuser, he was not retained in the common dungeons of the castle—a series of subterranean cells which extended far below the level of the moat —but in the loftiest apartment of Bigod's tower, the extreme height of which rendered all escape by external means impossible. The interior was equally well guarded ; for the only staircase which conducted to it was situated in the guard chamber, through which all who either ascended or descended were obliged to pass, and where a faithful troop of men-at-arms, who had grown grey in the service of the murdered earl, kept constant watch.

The high courage and sense of innocence which had sustained our hero in the presence of Herman and the assembled nobles gave way as the last ponderous bolt was drawn upon him by his retiring gaolers. The sound fell upon his ear like earth cast upon a coffin, and mentally he saw written over his prison door the tremendous inscription which Dante read upon the gates of Hell :

"LASCIATE ESPERANZA."

"Where," he exclaimed, "are now the joyous visions of my youth, my thirst of honour—of a life of usefulness, of trustful

F 2

confidence, and hopeful love ? Fled for ever. I have dreamt the dream which idiots dream, but, waking, found my reason. Fool ! " he added bitterly, " even for one moment to suppose this world contained aught of love or happiness for thee ! "

In this gloomy mood he continued to pace the floor of his prison, his heart at times cheered by the knowledge of his innocence, and the assurance that his birth was noble. Father Oswald, it was plain, possessed some key to the mystery of his fate ; and like a chained lion, Ulrick fretted his soul against the bars of his dungeon. How often did he pray but for one hour of freedom to rend the veil which obscured his destiny, and which he never felt so palpably before ! At times fancy would represent him as the victor in the coming fight, his honour cleared, his innocence established ; or seated in some old ancestral hall, Matilda by his side, and offspring who resembled her around him ;—then for a moment he forgot his fate, the fearful accusation which hung over him, and felt a taste of joy.

The walls of Ulrick's prison were formed of huge blocks of stone, which rose to the height of about twelve feet, where they joined the rude groining of the arch, the key-stone of which was the quaintly sculptured head of some Saxon king, whose staring eyes, like those of the evil genius of the place, seemed to mock the prisoner ; the window, narrow and strongly barred, was situated in a deep recess cut in the wall, the massive thickness of which might have withstood even the artillery of the present day. In a corresponding recess in the opposite side of the room was a singular piece of sculpture representing a crucifixion, in which the victim was a boy about twelve years of age. According to a tradition well known in Norwich, a Christian youth had been crucified by the Jews on Good Friday, in mockery of the Saviour. On the miraculous discovery of his body, he was canonised, and his name still appears in the Roman calendar under the name of St. William in the Wood. Similar memorials of the legend were once extremely common in the neighbourhood, and may still be found in some of the old churches and conventual remains, not only in Norfolk, but its adjoining counties.

The prisoner's reflections were interrupted by the entrance of Odo's squire, who, followed by the ordinary keepers of the tower, brought Ulrick his repast, the first he had tasted for four-and-twenty hours. To all his eager questions and entreaties they maintained a dogged silence ; each one felt that he was a spy on the other ; and prudence, if not fidelity, fettered their tongue.

Exhausted as the captive was, he merely broke a morsel of bread, and took a draught of the flask of wine which they had left him, and then resumed his walk, again to indulge in the reveries of his excited imagination ; in dreams of hope, perhaps never to be realised ; or in visions of despair, yet more gloomy than his destiny. For more than an hour he had continued to pace his prison floor ;

his brow gradually becoming more and more flushed, and the fire of fever burning in his cheek and haggard eye. He could no longer conceal from himself that he was ill, perhaps dying ; the recollection of the wine which he had drunk flashed upon him, and fearfully explained the mystery.

"I am poisoned !" he exclaimed. "Oh, cruel treachery ! My name will descend polluted to the grave ! Matilda's curse, perchance, will rest upon it. I'll not die, like the wolf, inglorious in his lair without one effort. Help !" he shrieked, at the same time beating with his hands and feet frantically against the door ; "treachery ! murder !"

Long did the wretched Ulrick continue to awake the echoes of his prison-tower. It was evident that he was doomed to die alone, poisoned—treacherously and cowardly poisoned, by the man who feared to meet his victim in honourable fight.

"I'll strive no more," sighed the exhausted youth, "with a destiny so wretched—lost, as mine ; but, since my hour is come, will meet it like a Christian and a man ; and with a sigh to my love, but without one regret for earth, resign my soul to the keeping of the saints."

Unable longer to retain his feet, Ulrick threw himself upon his rude couch ; and although his mind would wander in his prayer, yet still he prayed, until his senses were absorbed in sleep—a sleep his enemy had doomed to be eternal.

The prisoner had not long been lost to consciousness, when the rude stone, representing the martyrdom of St. William, slowly rolled aside, discovering a niche, through which Father Oswald entered the dungeon. Cautiously he approached the couch, and placed his hand upon the bosom of the expiring youth.

"As I suspected," he murmured. "Poisoned ! poisoned ! Fiend, I will defeat thee yet ! He took from his bosom a flask, which contained some highly balsamic liquid, the exquisite perfume of which filled the prison, and applied it to the sleeper's lips, and as the contents slowly disappeared, breathed many a prayer, made many a holy sign, for Ulrick's safety. Its effects were gradual, but most satisfactory. The burning fever of the prisoner gradually yielded to a soft genial perspiration ; his close-set teeth unclenched themselves, and he breathed freely.

"Saved !" exclaimed the priest, who had stood watching him with breathless anxiety ; "two trials more, and thou art safe. In thine hour of need, boy, I will not fail thee."

Before he left the prison, the venerable priest emptied the rest of the poisoned wine, and refilled it from a basket which he had brought ; and kneeling by the rude couch, offered up to Him who guards the fatherless a heartfelt prayer for Ulrick's safety.

*   *   *   *   *

The great bell of the cathedral tolled the midnight hour as the body of the murdered earl, the second evening after his death, was borne by the officers of his household towards its final resting place, within the hallowed precincts. A party of men-at-arms, every fourth bearing a lighted torch, lined the centre aisle from the west entrance to the high altar, where the black-robed priests were ready to commence the Mass of the Dead. The choir of the magnificent church was hung with solemn draperies, and the highly emblazoned escutcheons of the deceased noble, whose military achievements had endeared him to his soldiers as much as his statesmanlike qualities, princely hospitality, and unblemished honour, had rendered him popular with his brother nobles. The richly carved stalls were filled by the monks ; every dignitary of the order was in his place except the illustrious bishop, over whose episcopal throne a purple veil was thrown—typical of the widowhood of the church, from which many believed him violently removed.

As soon as the coffin was placed upon the dais in the centre of the choir, the low, solemn chanting of the priests began ; and many a prayer was breathed by his brother knights, who, clad in steel, were standing round, for the repose of Hugh de Bigod's soul. Mirvan, as the representative of his house, was seated at the head of the bier —his brain almost stunned at the double blow it had received by the murder of his father and the supposed treachery of his friend. Matilda and Isabel watched and prayed in one of the dimly-lighted galleries above.

Herman, the murderer and the accuser, was there, as calm as though his life had been one of innocence, his hand free from blood. Once or twice he looked anxiously amongst the monks, to see if he could recognise the cowled visage of Father Oswald. It was a relief to his heart that he beheld it not. Doubtless he thought that Ernulf had succeeded in his sacrilegious attempt, and smiled at the triumph of his villainy.

Herbert de Lozenga and the old priest removed, the accusation of sorcery, the only danger which had given him any real uneasiness, fell to the ground, and he stood, as he thought, impenetrable in his crime. His approaching battle with Ulrick he looked forward to with pleasure rather than distrust as the consummation of his triumph ; indeed, he could not doubt the result, for he had secretly contrived that a poison should be administered in his victim's food —poison of so subtle a nature, that while it spared the life of the receiver, it deprived him of all strength and energy, by the slow, undermining fever which it engendered, and which must have insured his success in the contest, but for the watchful energy of Father Oswald.

The conspiracy of the Saxon nobles, of which he was the life and energy, was undertaken under circumstances so peculiarly favourable, that its failure seemed impossible. William the Conqueror had withdrawn the flower of his army to France, to continue the war

which he had undertaken against its monarch, and during which he
eventually terminated his career. The Normans who remained in
England were in many instances divided amongst themselves. The
death of Hugh de Bigod, the most energetic of their leaders, and
William's marshal in England during his absence, still further
augmented the Saxons' chances of success. The day of battle was
the one fixed for the explosion ; and Herman, in the anticipated
triumph of his views, tasted as much of happiness as guilt like his
could know.

The solemn chant of the monks had ceased, and the priests at the
altar were about to commence the Mass, when the prior, who
presided in the absence of the bishop, arose in his stall, and, in a
cold, stern voice, commanded Herman of the Burg to quit the
church, adding, that the sacred mysteries could not be celebrated in
the presence of a man accused of sorcery.

" Sorcery ! " exclaimed Herman, red with passion,—" and where
are my accusers ?—where the guilty prelate who, to shield his
unworthy favourite, contrived the accusation ?—where the mad
monk who witnessed to it ? A fearful death," he added, " has
removed the former—the judgment of Heaven has fallen on the
false judge and the accuser."

The prior was a man cold and passionless as the altar which he
served ; yet even his quiet nature was indignant at the aspersion
cast upon the memory of Herbert de Lozenga, whose supposed death
he had many reasons for knowing had been contrived by his
unblushing accuser. The impious blasphemy of attributing his
own crimes to the judgment of Heaven shocked him, and increased
the ill opinion he already entertained against the Saxon.

" Norman nobles ! " replied the prior, " through you alone I
answer the slanders of that bold, bad man. Whether the venerable
bishop be living or dead, Herman is accused of sorcery. The accuser
and the accused may die—the accusation, never. Either Herman
of the Burg must quit the church, or I suspend the rites ; decide
between ye."

At the close of the speaker's voice, the officiating priests descended
the steps of the altar, and began to remove the vestments peculiar to
the service, and the monks stood up in their stalls, ready at the first
signal to depart.

The frowns which he saw gathering on the brows of the Norman
nobles told Herman that it would be dangerous to remain : he made
a virtue, therefore, of necessity ; and, after bending his knee to the
high altar, left the church with an air as much like that of indignant
virtue as he could assume. Seeing that their enemy had fled, the
priests recommenced the interrupted rites.

For a long time Herman paced the cloister, indulging in dreams
of promised vengeance. Let but the insurrection triumph, and he
would waste their church and convent both with fire and sword—

drive every Norman priest from out the realm. "Better," he
exclaimed, "our father's ancient faith, than this enslaving, this
aspiring priesthood ! " The Norman nobles, whose haughty coldness
stung his pride—they, too, must feel his wrath ; in his mad thirst
for vengeance, he contemplated taking even the lives of those with
whom he lived on terms of intimacy and friendship—whose cup he
often drained—whose pleasures he shared ; contemplated it not with
the regret of a man who offers a necessary sacrifice on the altar of
freedom, but with the delight of a being whose instinct was of
blood.

During his walk, his attention was attracted by the rays of a
strong light which pierced through the crevices of the chapter-house
doors.   Finding them not to be locked, he entered, and saw
preparations for a scene which gave him food for reflection.   The
richly ornamented building was evidently arranged, not merely for
an assembly of the chapter, but the trial of a prisoner.   The bishop's
throne was hung with black, as if he were in person about to preside.
Upon the table, in the centre of the room, upon a cushion, lay an
enormous crucifix, and writing materials were placed at either side
for the examiners.   But what most attracted his attention were the
various instruments of torture scattered on the floor—instruments,
in that barbarous age, too often used to extort confession from
innocence as well as guilt.

"Whose trial," he murmured, "can the monks be about to
proceed with ? Can Ernulf have failed in his design ? Hath the fool
been caught in his own snare ? The confident tone of yon shaveling
in the church has staggered me.   The accuser and the accused," he
added, slowly repeating the words of the prior to himself, "may die
—the accusation, never."

"Never ! " repeated a deep, solemn voice, so near to him that the
word seemed to have been whispered in his very ear.   He started
and looked around, but saw no one—it was evident that he was
alone.   Although he attributed the sound to natural causes, it made
an impression on him.

"This is childish ! " he exclaimed ; "I grow, indeed, infirm of
heart, if a mere echo can unman it.   No matter," he added, drawing
a long breath to relieve himself as he spoke, "let but the next two
days securely pass, and, Fortune, I defy thee ! "

Still, however, the preparation for the midnight trial alarmed
him, and as Herman was one who left nothing to chance, he
advanced to the door by which he entered, intending to quit the
chapter-house, and summon an esquire in whom he could confide,
to conceal himself behind one of the colossal statues of the Four
Evangelists placed in the arched recesses of the walls. To his confusion,
however, the door was locked, whether by accident or design he
could not tell, but conscience made him fear the former, and he was
a prisoner.   In vain he thundered at the massive doors ; the sound

of his blows echoed through the cloisters, and gradually faded away, leaving him in fearful silence to commune with himself.

"It must be accident," he thought : "they would not dare to plot an outrage upon my person." This opinion was the more confirmed as he had not heard the slightest sound of a footstep near the door ; indeed, it was not impossible that the wind had done it, for the portal fastened with a spring ; and he resolved, since accident had made him a prisoner, to avail himself of his position to ascertain the tactics of his enemies. With this view he concealed himself behind the statue of St. John, patiently to await the commencement of the trial.

Meanwhile, a far different scene was passing in the church. As soon as the Mass was ended, Mirvan advanced to the bier and, after kneeling reverently to the dead, respectfully removed from it his father's sword, and pressed it to his lips. Every eye in the vast choir was upon him.

"Bear witness for me, my noble countrymen," he cried, "that I receive it unstained by injustice or by treason ; and that he, who so late was of the first among you, has descended to the grave with honour as bright as his own shield."

"He has !" replied the Normans with one voice ; so universal was their respect for the late earl's memory.

"Amen !" ejaculated the prior from his distant stall ; "peace to Hugh de Bigod's soul."

"As the heir of his name," continued Mirvan, "I am the natural avenger of his blood ; I am told the assassin claims the right of battle—is it so ? "

"It is !" again answered the nobles.

"Then," resumed the speaker, "I claim the right to meet him. I might resign to another the judgment-seat, but not the danger of the listed field. I demand it," he added, laying his hand upon the coffin, "in the name of the dead, by my right of birth, by our brotherhood in knighthood, and the justice of my cause. Speak—is my claim allowed ? "

A low murmur of satisfaction rose amongst the nobles, who had beheld, with secret dissatisfaction, Herman of the Burg, a man whom they despised, elevated to the position of Hugh de Bigod's avenger. It shocked their prejudice and pride that a Saxon lance should vindicate a Norman cause. The young earl's demand, therefore, was most favourably received ; still they decided with that gravity of deliberation with which the nobles of the epoch treated all questions of chivalry, and after a lengthened consultation between themselves, Odo of Caen announced the decision of his brother peers.

"Your claim, brave earl, is allowed : here, in the presence of the noble dead, whom all so truly mourn—here, on our faith as true knights, we declare that Herman of the Burg may, without dishonour, forego the fight on your claiming to be the champion in your house's cause. The seneschal," he added, "shall make known to the prisoner our decree, and God defend the right ! "

" Amen," again responded the prior, in which this time all the ecclesiastics joined.

A faint scream was heard in the gallery above, and Matilda was seen borne insensible in the arms of her attendants from the church, followed by the grieving and compassionate Isabel. Mirvan beheld their departure with a deep-drawn sigh ; for already he read the secret of his sister's heart, and loved her too well not to compassionate its weakness and its sorrows.

The holy water was sprinkled on the descending coffin, the priestly blessing given, and the herald's pompous duty done. As the remains of the once powerful earl, Hugh de Bigod, descended to their final resting place, one by one the priests and nobles slowly retired, leaving Mirvan alone within the church, praying by the side of the dead.

As the vassals of the different chiefs drew up under their respective leaders, and were preparing to return in procession to the castle, their departure was delayed by the arrival of George of Erpingham, the bishop's seneschal, who, at the head of a body of troops, entered the inclosed precincts of the cathedral, and placed a guard at the only gate by which egress was possible. Whatever were the good knight's intentions, resistance was in vain, the force he commanded being sufficient to crush the slightest attempts at opposition.

" What means this, George of Erpingham ? " demanded Odo, who from his rank and influence was generally the interpreter of the sentiments of his peers. " Do we meet as enemies ? "

" Heaven forbid ! " replied the jovial knight. " I am here to do the Church's errand, not to break lance with such worthy sons as you. If the wolf hides itself amidst the flock, the flock must not murmur at being detained until the wolf be found."

As he spoke, an officer of the church approached and whispered something into his ear.

" Pardon me, gentle knights," he resumed ; " but the wolf is found, and further precautions are unnecessary."

With a wave of his hand he motioned to the guard at the gate to fall back, and give egress to the nobles and their followers, who resumed their march, wondering what circumstance could have caused so unusual a proceeding.

As the elder nobles passed the gate, the same officer who had whispered to George of Erpingham placed in their hands a paper, on reading which they resigned the conduct of their men to their esquires, and retired, with thoughtful steps, into the cathedral. It was evident that some strange event either had occurred, or was about to take place, and the curiosity of those who were unsummoned was unbounded. But their patience was doomed to be exercised, as well as that of our readers, while we return to the fair cousins who so lately quitted the church.

"Speak not of consolation," replied Matilda to the tender soothings of Isabel, as soon as they reached the castle, and were retired to the privacy of their own apartment ; "grief succeeds to grief, and each fresh hour brings but fresh sorrow with it. I feel so assured of Ulrick's innocence, that I could pin my life upon his faith. But how to prove it ? To-morrow he meets my brother in the listed field ; and either I must mourn that brother lost, or weep the truest heart that crime and calumny e'er sacrificed at the base shrine of jealous, mean revenge."

"Don't weep, don't weep," sobbed the affectionate hearer, the tears at the same time coursing down her own pale cheeks ; "Heaven and our Lady to our aid ! We are not hopeless ; the fight may be prevented yet. Had Herman been the champion, I would not have given one little sigh to have prevented the meeting in the lists. You are convinced, you say, of Ulrick's innocence ? "

A reproachful glance at the doubt which the question seemed to imply was Matilda's only response.

" Be not angry, pretty coz," continued the fair girl ; "remember I am not in love with him ; and I know that when the heart pleads, the judgment is sometimes silent. Besides, this is not the moment for a shadow of coldness or unkindness to pass between us. Could we but see Ulrick, perhaps we might obtain some clue to this most fearful mystery ; for, like you, I would fain believe him guiltless ; though, unlike you, I sometimes mistrust my heart—it leads my head astray."

"Obtain but that, and fear not that he is saved !" exclaimed Matilda. " Trust me, Isabel," she added, blushing at the warmth she had betrayed, " 'tis not the raving of a senseless love that speaks, but the conviction of my better reason. Men do not fall as the archangel fell ; from purity to the extreme of sin a gradual change succeeds. Ulrick's mind was honour's self ; a mirror so highly polished, that Truth might view her image. I have watched its every phase, and found each thought was pure. And he, the good, the gentle, murder an aged—a defenceless man ! murder my father ! Impossible ! If an angel, trumpet-tongued, pronounced him guilty, Matilda never could believe it."

Could Ulrick, from the depth of his prison, have heard the maiden's eloquent defence, he would have deemed his sorrows overpaid. Firmly she met the searching look of Isabel, as every page of feeling was displayed to invite the reader's gaze. The warm-hearted girl threw her arms around her cousin, and exclaimed :

" I do believe thee ! I read it in thy dark eyes' deep intelligence —those portals of thy soul—when thy pure spirit looks upon the world, and scorns its worthlessness. You love him, coz ?." she added.

" Truth needs no subterfuge : I do," simply answered Matilda.
" Then he must be saved. Rouse thee, coz—we have a game to
play will need our woman's wits. Odo of Caen, you know, is
plighted to my sister Jane ; I have some interest with him ; we
both must try him—use all the artillery of sighs and tears—the
weapons with which mother Nature arms our sex when we contend
'gainst proud, imperious man. Doubt not but we will bend
him to our will. Kneel," added Isabel, " and ask His blessing
on our enterprise who reads our purpose, and who knows 'tis good."

The two fair and innocent creatures, like twin seraphs, bent the
knee, and offered up a prayer as pure as ever fell from angel lips
for suffering innocence. The act poured the balm of both courage
and consolation into their souls. Silently enveloping themselves in
their dark mourning mantles and veils, they left their chamber to
seek the knight whose word alone could gain them admittance to
Ulrick's presence.

*   *   *   *   *

Long and anxiously did Herman remain concealed behind the
statue of the saint in the chapter-house of the cathedral ; at times,
he thought of renewing his frantic efforts for freedom, but prudence,
and the desire of witnessing proceedings in which in all probability
he would find himself deeply interested, restrained him. At last,
the distant steps of the approaching brethren fell upon his ear, and
despite his long habitude in crime, and the confidence which success
bestows, his heart beat wildly as they drew near.

" They come," he whispered to himself ; " courage, patience, and
I triumph ! "

From the position in which he was placed he could see all that
passed, but ran little risk himself of being seen, as nothing could be
more unlikely than that any one would take the trouble to mount
the niche in which he was concealed.

First in the procession were two priests, bearing the abbatial and
episcopal cross ; then the members of the chapter, two and two—the
latter, as they entered, bowed to the crucifix, and took their seats in
their respective stalls ; the prior followed, bearing his staff of office,
and assumed his seat at the head of the table.

" I see no prisoner yet," thought Herman ; " perhaps, after all, it
is but some brother of their order whom they have met to judge for
breach of discipline. No matter ; I will see this mummery out."

His doubts, however, were soon ended by the entrance of several
of the Norman nobles in deep conference with Herbert de Lozenga,
who, in his episcopal robes, the mitre blazing on his brow, and the
crosier in his hand, appeared living before him ; from that moment
Herman felt that he was lost.

" Living ! " he exclaimed, almost loud enough to be heard.
" Have, then, the mouldering ashes of Stanfield given up their dead,
or have the fiends, who so long have served, at last deserted me ? "

"Brothers and nobles," said the bishop, as soon as he was seated upon his chair of state, "believe me that no matter of slight interest has induced me to summon you to this our sacred chapter. Danger threatens not only to your lives, but to the Norman rule throughout the realm. A vast conspiracy is organised to root us from the land. Scarce two days and the Saxons rise upon us. The day of battle is the day appointed for the massacre of all our race. Prudence and firmness may avert the blow which want of unity must render fatal. This is no childish menace, no partial outbreak," he added ; "but the organised offort of a people's strength."

There was a pause as the prelate ceased speaking ; men looked upon each other as men look who have received strange news ; and Herman, in the gall and bitterness of his heart, cursed the lips which uttered it. Odo of Caen was the first to speak among his fellow-nobles.

"Father, this is intelligence to stir the blood within us, and worth even the risk your sacred person ran. Deign to explain the proofs on which it rests ; that, knowing whence the danger comes, we may prepare to meet it. Who is the leader of this enterprise ? "

"Herman of the Burg," solemnly answered the bishop, at the same time striking the ground with his crosier.

"Curse him," muttered the concealed listener ; "Ernulf has betrayed me."

At the signal which the bishop gave, the doors of the chapter-house again opened, and the guilty squire Ernulf was led into the assembly by a party of the bishop's guard. Father Oswald followed him. The prisoner's face was flushed, although his limbs seemed feeble ; even the presence of the Norman nobles was a relief to him ; he knew that they were the inmates of the castle—friends of his master's kinsman—and trusted they might befriend him. The hope, however, was but a brief one ; his eye glanced from their stern visages, and fell upon the instruments of torture lying on the ground ; a cold perspiration bedewed his frame, and the strong man trembled.

"Ernulf," began the bishop. Struck by the voice, the wretched man looked up, and recognised in his judge the being whom, four-and-twenty hours before, he had, as he imagined, consigned to inevitable death. Father Oswald's mysterious knowledge of his crimes, and, to him, miraculous means of subduing him, had excited the latent superstition in his nature ; he looked upon Herbert as one arisen from the dead, and armed with supernatural terrors to confound him. "Well may'st thou tremble, guilty man, to find me living," resumed the prelate, who marked the effect his appearance had produced, and trusted that it would enable him to bend the stubborn nature of the criminal to confession, without having recourse to those means which the rude justice of the age not only tolerated, but approved : "hast thou not heard that it is written, 'the triumph of the wicked shall be short'? Confess thy vile conspiracy, thy master's treason, and enable me and these noble knights to unravel the dark clue of guilt, and mercy, perchance, may be extended to thy forfeited life."

A dead silence followed the speaker's words—all waited to see their effect upon the hardy criminal, who, on discovering that the bishop was really in flesh and life before him, recovered the usual audacity of his nature, and determined in the recesses of his iron mind to endure the extreme of torture rather than betray the scheme on which not only his hopes of aggrandisement, but ultimate safety, depended. He remained therefore sullenly silent.

"Saxon dog," exclaimed Odo, "dost thou not answer to thy judges?"

"What should I answer, noble Odo?" replied Ernulf. "Will the word of a simple esquire weigh against the assertion of a mitred prelate? What should I know of conspiracies, which I believe exist but in the imagination of my accuser, to save his favourite's life? He hath already charged my noble master with the crime of sorcery; finding that insufficient, he now adds the charge of treason to complete his ruin."

The firm tone of the speaker shook the faith of several of his listeners, who were not disinclined to believe that Herbert would have recourse to any measures to assure Ulrick's safety. Herman silently congratulated himself upon the dogged fidelity of his accomplice.

"Have you no other proof than mere assertion, my lord?" demanded Robert of Artois, whose influence Herbert de Lozenga had frequently opposed in the council, and consequently excited his hate. "If not, I, for one, would not hang a dog on such a charge."

"Nor I," exclaimed another, "provided it were Norman. But this is a Saxon cur, and we cannot refuse to put the question, should my lord bishop in his Christian charity demand it."

The sneer with which this was uttered did not deter the prelate from his purpose. 'Tis true he had obtained other and ample information, but from a source he wished at present to conceal. Though mild and gentle in his character, he could assume the tone of stern reproof, and meet the boldest with a front as lofty, a speech as cutting, as their own.

"'Tis well, sir knight," he answered, "you have a churchman to contend with; but remember, if I draw no sword, that thousands are ready to achieve my bidding. That if as a priest I pronounce no sentence by which man's blood is shed, that many a belted earl and landed knight are bound by feudal tenure to pronounce it for me. Robert of Artois," he added, "and you, noble peers, no more I sue for your support—I now command it. Apply the question to you wretched man, unless by confession he avoids the ordeal."

Slowly the nobles present proceeded to give the necessary directions, the Catholic church not permitting any member of its orders in any case to pronounce sentence of death, or to shed human blood. Even in the Inquisition this rule to the last was invariably observed. Its familiars were all laymen, and those who were condemned were given over to the secular power, by whom alone they could be sentenced.

As the executioners now approached the unhappy criminal, Father Oswald drew his cowl still further over his features. Devoutly did Herman, who, from his place of concealment, watched the proceedings, pray that his esquire might expire under the tortures to which he was about to be submitted. Dead men he knew could tell no tales, and willingly would he have cut the thread of life of a being, one of whose greatest crimes was perhaps fidelity to himself; as it was, he awaited the result with nervous impatience.

Ernulf, having been stripped of his jerkin, was first placed by his tormentors upon a frame of iron, and bound by leather thongs; by a peculiar mechanism, the machine was gradually distended till every joint cracked in its socket, and the strained sinews throbbed with agony; still the culprit spoke not, but with scowling brow and firm-clenched teeth gazed, like a maimed wolf, on the circle round him. Suddenly, the bands were let go, the frame returned to its natural size, and the distended joints shot in their sockets; then the first groan issued from Ernulf's breast. Father Oswald trembled, and slowly pronounced the word "Confess!"

"What should I confess?" replied the hardened man; "I know nothing, and can reveal nothing."

Again the tormentors approached their victim. Placing him upon his knees, they gathered up his long hair, and plaited into it the end of a cord which hung suspended from one of the beams. As soon as all was prepared, on a signal from Odo they elevated him so that he hung suspended by the hair of his head. For two minutes did he endure the fearful torture, his temples throbbing in agony, his eye-balls bursting from his head. Still he made no sign—uttered no word of confession. The prelate, unable longer to witness his sufferings, made sign they should release him.

By the laws of the question, three distinct species of torture were to be employed. If at the end of the third the prisoner's courage held out, he was deemed innocent, and consequently aquitted. As may be supposed, the last ordeal was the most fearful, and Herbert would willingly have spared it; but Odo, who trusted that the squire's courage would hold out, or who believed that he had nothing to confess, opposed himself strongly to it.

"We are not children, my good lord," he said; "our justice cannot be trifled with. If the prisoner pass the third question, I shall believe he hath been most foully wronged, and disbelieve this strange conspiracy; so please you, let the executioners proceed."

"Be it so," replied Herbert, "since there is no other way ; and be the crime on him whose obstinacy has left no other course."

Silently did Herman pray that Ernulf's courage might hold out, or nature yield beneath the effort. Again the fearful ministers of justice secured the wretched man, and inclosed his legs in a species of iron case compressible by screws. Ernulf groaned with agony. Still no word of confession passed his lips. The screws were about to be turned to their last extent, when Father Oswald, who stood before the prisoner, suddenly dashed back his cowl, fixed his eyes upon him, and at the same time drew back his long white hair, which hid a crimson scar upon his forehead.

"Parricide !" he exclaimed, "can nothing move thee ? Confess, or perish in thy impious pride."

The sudden change which took place in Ernulf's features was terrific. The blood which forsook his cheeks rushed into his eyes, his jaw dropped, and he seemed stricken with a paralysis of horror.

"Spare me !" he exclaimed ; "spare me, avenging spirit, and I will confess—all—all ! Search in the lining of my breast-piece. The letters — pardon ! Mercy ! mercy ! " exhausted with his sufferings, both of mind and body, he found temporary relief in insensibility.

"Bear him to prison," exclaimed the bishop, "and let his breast-piece be placed upon the table here before us."

The mangled wretch was instantly conveyed from the chapter-house, and the assembly relieved of the presence of the executioners.

As Herbert de Lozenga demanded, the breast-piece was placed upon the table and examined by the nobles present. Between the lining and the fold they found two papers ; the first contained a detailed account of the plot, the names of the franklins and Saxon leaders most compromised, their places of meeting, and number of men-at-arms. As the bishop asserted, the day of battle was fixed for the outbreak, when, under pretence of witnessing the combat, they could assemble unsuspected. In the list of the Norman nobles whose lives were to be sacrificed, were the names of most present : the paper was in the hand-writing of Herman of the Burg, and attested by his seal.

"Traitor !" exclaimed Odo ; "much as I despised him, I little expected this."

"Nor I," added Robert of Artois, whom a sense of their common danger for once rendered just.

"But what are we to do ?" demanded the nobles with one voice.

"Leave that to me," replied the bishop. "Do you, as peers and knights, pronounce the traitor's doom ; I'll find the means to see it executed. Think you," he added, with something like an expression of contempt, "that if, like yours, my hand might grasp the sword, that long ere this I had not reached him ? "

Herman, secure, as he thought, in his concealment, smiled at the

[FATHER OSWALD'S INTERVIEW WITH HIS SON ERNULF.]

G

churchman's threats. "Fool," he murmured, "long ere the signal you expect shall strike, England shall be in flames. As we rush on in triumph through your halls, we will remember well each mocking gibe, and strike the oppressor dead!" and the concealed culprit smiled in anticipation of his triumph.

While the nobles and knights were deliberating upon their sentence, Herbert de Lozenga perused the other paper found in the breast-piece of the squire. With a smile of benevolent satisfaction, he whispered something to one of the attendants, who immediately left the chapter-house.

"'Tis well, my lords," he exclaimed, as Odo of Caen announced that the nobles present found Herman guilty of high treason, and sentenced him to death; "our reverend prior will draw out the sentence ready for your signing; but while he does so, pleasure me in one thing. Here is a paper, found, as you saw, in the breast-piece of yon wretched man."

"We did," they responded, one and all.

"The time for declaring its contents hath not yet arrived," continued the bishop; "please to affix your seal upon the back, that, when produced, none may question its authenticity."

Odo, and even Robert of Artois, hastened to comply with his request, so great was the ascendency the prelate had obtained by the discovery of their common danger.

"And now, my lord," said Odo, when the last signature was affixed to the deed which proclaimed Herman a traitor, and condemned him to the block, "what steps must be taken for the arrest of this most dangerous man."

"They are already taken," solemnly answered the bishop.

"And when the trial?"

"It is past," continued the prelate, in the same cold, unimpassioned tone.

"And the execution?"

"Behold!" exclaimed Herbert de Lozenga, striking with his crosier, as he spoke. The doors of the chapter-house flew open, and a guard, commanded by George of Erpingham, formed a semicircle in the space before them. In the centre was a kneeling man; Father Oswald, holding a crucifix; and the executioner with an uplifted axe. Ere a word, even of astonishment, could escape their lips, it fell; and the head of Herman of the Burg rolled on the blood-stained pavement.

CHAPTER VI.

THE recognition between Father Oswald and his wretched son was complete : the living and the long-thought dead met in the fearful judgment hall, where the monk, despite the sternness of his heart, his high resolve, and strong sense of justice, yielded to the throes of nature, and declared himself as the only means of inducing the wretched culprit to confess, and thereby save himself from the last fearful ordeal of the question. It was not without a severe struggle that he brought himself to make the revelation ; for, although now a Christian priest, he still retained much of the pride which had distinguished Haga the Arch-Druid. His very errors had been those of honour, love to his nation, and devotion to the proscribed order of which he was the chief. The mere thought that a son of his should have descended to aught like servitude was a bitter humiliation to his haughty soul ; but that he should have proved mean, base, and stained with crime, stung it into madness.

Immediately after the execution of Herman the priest retired to the solitude of his cell, and fortified his soul with prayer ; invoking many a saint and many a holy name, to touch with penitence the hard, bad heart of him he blushed to call his son. Gradually the suppliant's cheek resumed its paleness, and the unnatural excitement of his eye became subdued and calm ; Religion poured her soothing waters in his heart ; and the fierce volcano, if not extinct, at least for awhile slumbered in repose.

Rising from his knees, the aged man slowly crossed the cloisters, and directed his steps towards the prison of Ernulf—a low stone building which formerly existed on the site of the modern deanery.

The prison in which the captive was confined was a large square chamber, the only entrance to which was by a narrow door, thickly studded with nails and plates of iron, situated under a quaintly ornamented Saxon archway ; his couch was nothing more than a stone bench, projecting from the wall ; over it hung a crucifix, rudely sculptured by some former inmate, to beguile the weary hours of his captivity. So strong was the dungeon, that air and light were admitted only by a massive grating, cemented in the ceiling, too high for the prisoner to reach, too deeply imbedded in the solid masonry for any external force to remove. The bruised and maimed criminal still lay groaning on his pallet, where he had been cast by his executioners, after the torture, when Father Oswald entered the cell. Despite his resolution, he felt the kindlier sentiments of his nature struggling with his justice, as he gazed upon the being who, half-stripped of his armour, the dew of agony upon his brow, his eyes blood-shot and wandering, lay stretched on

the hard couch before him. Nature whispered to him that it was
his son—the being whose existence had been moulded from his own,
and towards whom, despite his crimes and degenerate baseness, a
secret yearning inclined his soul to pity. Perhaps conscience whispered him with some neglect of duty to his offspring, or demanded
whether, by precept or example, he had inculcated that high sense
of honour and love of virtue whose absence he so harshly blamed.
It was no longer, therefore, in the tone of an accusing spirit that he
addressed him, but almost in the accents of forgiveness.

"Ernulf," he demanded, "dost thou recognise me?"

The wounded man slowly turned upon his couch of pain, and
gazed upon the speaker; all excitement had passed from his pale
features. In recognising in Father Oswald his living parent, the
spell of his authority over him was broken; he knew that he was no
parricide; and even his obdurate heart felt lighter from the load
removed.

"I do," he coldly answered.

His interrogator started at the cool determination, the almost
indifference, evinced by the reply, and for a few moments they
regarded each other in silence, severally preparing for the mental
combat about to ensue; a silence as sullen as the pause which
precedes the burst of the tempest, or intervenes between the thunder
and the lightning's flash. The monk was the first to break it—the
pity excited by the sufferings of the prisoner gradually yielding to
indignation at his obduracy.

"Hast thou no word," he demanded, "for repentance?—to implore
forgiveness for the crime at which the angels shudder and e'en
demons tremble?—no prayer to appease offended Heaven and thy
father's wrath?"

"None."

"None!" iterated the priest; "none! Is then thy heart so seared
by crime that nothing less than the avenging bolt can penetrate it?
Knowest thou the punishment announced for parricides—the eternal
fires, the endless gnawing of the serpent tooth of an undying conscience, the sting of memory, and the hell of fear?"

"I am no parricide!" doggedly retorted Ernulf, his voice
slightly showing that the denunciation of the priest had moved
him.

"In thought and purpose," continued the speaker, "if not in
act. Thinkest thou thy crime is less because the blow inflicted on
thy father as he slept reached short of life? But it is just," he added,
mournfully; "thy childhood was impetuous, wayward, cruel; thy
manhood stained by violence and crime; 'tis just thy age should
proved a fitting sequal to thy youth."

"And whose the fault?" demanded Ernulf, starting from the
couch, regardless in his excitement of his bruised limbs and aching
brow; "demand it of the man who called himself my father, whose

pride revolted at a child's caress, whose want of confidence repressed each rising impulse of my heart towards him ; whose harsh, cold, stony, selfish nature withered my childhood, turned it on itself, to feed on its own diseased, corrupted heart. Wonder at my crimes ? —wonder they are not a thousand times more strange than those which madness, in her fever, paints ! Taught by no faith, accustomed from thy lips to hear blasphemed the truths which now it seems the Christian priest believes, but which the Druid Haga once abhorred, where was mystay, when passion's breath assailed me ?—where the arms to fight temptation in her Protean forms, resist her luring spells ? No ! " he added. " If I have fallen, thou art not my reprover ; if I have sinned, thou canst not be my judge. Man reads the crime, but Heaven the temptation."

Each word of Ernulf fell like a drop of molten lead upon the heart of Father Oswald. As he spoke, scale after scale fell from his eyes ; he saw and felt that the monster before him was of his own creation ; that the plastic clay of humanity had been trusted to his hand, and that, in his presumption, ignorance, or selfishness, he had moulded it into a demon's form. He found himself weak where he had thought himself most strong ; and the conviction brought bitterness and sorrow to his soul, silenced the fiery eloquence of his tongue, and humiliated his vaunted reason.

" 'Tis true," resumed the prisoner, " my hand has been raised against thy life ; but thou hadst first destroyed my soul. Pure it was committed to thy hands. Ask of thy conscience how thou didst execute the sacred trust. Unnatural father, I do reject thee for my judge. Priest of a faith thou never taughtest thy child, thus I breathe back the curse." The gaunt form of the speaker was raised to its full height ; and despite his haggard appearance, there was something even majestic in his look, as, with his arm raised, he was about to hurl back the paternal malediction with tenfold force upon the head that uttered it.

" Hold, wretched man ! " exclaimed Oswald, throwing himself at his feet, his heart crushed by the convictions his words awoke within it ; " I have sinned. and my sin hath become my punishment. I here retract my curse. Spare my grey hairs ; let me not hear the voice of my own son condemn me."

It was a strange sight to see the gifted Oswald prostrate at the feet of his rude offspring. Humiliated by the voice of conscience, subjected by the power of truth, he was no longer the same being. His spiritual pride, the defect of his character, was completely subdued ; for his heart had been exposed to his own view, and he felt sick within him. Even Ernulf was affected at the sight, for he knew well the nature he had humbled ; had trembled at it in its strength, and he respected it in its weakness.

" Not to me, father, not to me should the knee be bent," he answered, raising the old man as he spoke ; " at least let us part

friends, exchanging mutual forgiveness. I suppose," he added, " I
have not long to live, for Holy Church seldom relinquishes her grasp
except with life, and mine is a deed admits no chance of mercy.
What is the usual punishment of sacrilege ?—But I know—death—
death, at the least."

" The stake," faintly uttered the old man, scarcely conscious that
the words had passed his lips.

" The stake ! " almost shrieked the prisoner ; " and you tell me
so ? The stake ! Is there no sentiment of nature, no tie of blood, to
freeze the fearful word upon your lips ? The cord, the axe—any
fate, rather than to perish at the burning stake ! "

" Think rather of thy soul," interrupted his father ; " respect the
Church's judgments, as thou art a Christian."

" Well thou knowest I am no Christian," replied Ernulf ; " the
waters of baptism have never been poured on my obdurate head.
'Tis true that since I left my home and mingled in the world I
passed as such—perhaps, in creed, am one—but never yet hath
priestly hand sprinkled the regenerating drops upon my brow."

" Now Heaven be praised ! " exclaimed his father, a beam of
satisfaction illuminating his aged countenance ; " and thanks to every
saint !—the sin of my neglect may be atoned—the soul I trifled with
may be redeemed."

" What meanest thou ? "

" That were thy sins as scarlet as the crimes of all the earth, that
baptism would wash their stain away. Let us kneel," continued
the priest, " and let us both return thanks to Heaven for mercy—
thou for a soul redeemed, e'en at destruction's brink, and I for
undying anguish and remorse removed. Prepare thy soul by
penitence and prayer," he added, " to receive the wondrous boon
which Heaven in its wisdom hath reserved. Mine shall be the hand
to perform the sacred rite which numbers thee with the redeemed
on earth. May thy after-life inscribe thy name with the redeemed
in heaven."

" But the stake ? " interrupted Ernulf, listening only to his fears.
" Will it secure my body from the flames—must I quit the world
amid the execration of the yelling crowd—feel the fierce fire
melting the very marrow of my bones—my brain to boil amid the
raging heat ? Is there no hope—no mercy ? Speak, father, speak."

" None ! " said the old man, visibly affected by his son's despair,
whose countenance, distorted by the fearful terrors his imagination
conjured up, was but a feeble index of his mind. " Thou hast no
hope on earth."

" Perchance nor Heaven ! " added Ernulf, rolling again upon his
couch in an agony of fear and horror. " 'Tis but a dream, perhaps
—'tis but a dream—there is no Heaven, no mercy, or I should find
it. Fool ! to think that priests should e'er know mercy ! "

The priest began to pace the cell as if meditating some important

purpose, while Ernulf continued to exhaust himself by his ravings.
At times Oswald's eye would fall upon his son with a mingled
expression of scorn and interest—scorn at his unmanly terrors, pity
for the danger which excited them. At last, it seemed as if his
mind was resolved upon some important step, for he approached the
couch, and arrested the prisoner's wanderings with a look such as
that at which 'tis said the maniac trembles.

"And could thy life be spared, how wouldst thou use it, boy ? "
solemnly demanded his father; "speak, and let thy words be truthful
as thy danger's pressing ; for let me trace even the shade of falsehood
in thy mind, the hope but to equivocate with truth, and the chance.
the little chance that's left thee, is destroyed."

"Chance ! " eagerly repeated Ernulf, catching like a drowning
wretch at the word—"there is, then, a chance ? "

"Answer my question," coldly replied his father, who had little
sympathy with earthly fears, and who could, in his own person, have
regarded the stake with indifference, and even with triumph, had he
been condemned to suffer in a cause his conscience told him to be
holy—"how wouldst thou pass thy life ? "

"In prayer—in fasting in some hermit's cell," he answered ; "or,
pilgrim, staff in hand, I'd seek the burning plains of Palestine, and
wet with my tears the blessed Redeemer's tomb. Let me but live,"
he added, "and the mortal terrors of the present hour will keep my
soul from every future sin. Or do you prescribe a life of penance,
well will I keep it, father."

The priest gazed upon him as if he would read his inmost soul—
sift every working of his subtle mind. Perhaps the impression was
satisfactory ; for there was again something almost of kindliness in
his parting tones.

"'Tis well, my son ; dispose thyself for that which Heaven thinks
best ; for the rest, we are but potsherds in its hands. If, in the
solitude of thy dark cell, thy many crimes should preach unto thy
soul despair, let the remembrance of Heaven's unnumbered mercies
whisper hope."

The speaker quitted the cell as the last words fell from his lips.
and Ernulf sank once more upon his couch of pain, a saddened if
not a better man.

"My sin at last has found me," exclaimed the monk, as he paced
the cloister on his way to the chapter-room, where he expected to
learn the sentence pronounced upon his son. "Yon wretched being
answered truly. 'Tis I, unnatural father, who have destroyed
him—reared him in scorn of Christian faith—sought to impress
him with my own dark creed, or worse—left him in ignorance to
choose one. Shall Heaven, in its mercy, have left wide the path to
save his soul, and I do nothing for his mortal state ? No, Ernulf ! "
he added, sternly, "fallen as thou art, thou art still my son ; stained
though thou art, thy father is not pure ; degraded as thy nature

hath become, one trace of Eden lingers round it yet. Thou shalt not perish, if my life can save thee."

Full of this high resolve, he entered the chapter-house, where many of the brotherhood were assembled. By all present, even by those who loved him not, for his cold, unsocial nature, he was received with respect and sympathy, for all knew his connection with the prisoner, and marvelled at his firmness under a trial beneath which even manly fortitude might well succumb, and the calm endurance of which was almost miraculous in one of his advanced age and weakness. The sentence which declared Ernulf guilty of sacrilege lay signed upon the table, together with the re-script which gave him over to the secular arm, to be dealt with as mercifully as the nature of his offence permitted,—a recommendation of idle form, which was never permitted to interfere with the strict execution of the law ; a law which pertained more to the spirit of the dark age in which it was framed, than to the character of either the Church or priesthood. With a firm hand Father Oswald read the parchment, amid the silence of the brotherhood. To his ardent piety it seemed both natural and just that the crime of sacrilege should be expiated by blood : and he affixed his signature to the document without the least apparent emotion, thereby rendering the decision of the chapter both unanimous and valid. How he reconciled the conviction that the life of the guilty party was necessary to atone for his offence, with the desire to save that life, time will show.

" When is the execution appointed to take place ?" he demanded of the assembled monks, who stood gazing on him with admiration at his firmness and his self-control—a species of virtue as highly appreciated in the cloister as in the world.

" This very day," was the reply, given with an expression of surprise. " Surely," they thought, " he never will be there ! "

" And the hour ? "

" Sunset."

" So soon," thought their interrogator. " Then I must be brief ; for I have still much to perform."

In his own sorrow, he resolved not to be unmindful of Ulrick's safety. He had heard of the intention expressed by Mirvan in the church to be himself the champion in the lists ; and well he knew that the generous nature of the accused would submit to any alternative—even to death itself—rather than draw his sword against Matilda's brother and his bosom friend. He proposed, therefore, to withdraw him from his prison through the same passage by which he himself gained entrance to it.

On the same night on which the execution of Herman of the Burg took place, a female figure, closely veiled, attended by four men-at-arms, left the episcopal palace on foot, and directed her steps towards the ferry. Her disguised person and hurried step gave her more the air of a fugitive escaped from justice, than the widow of the powerful earl whose last obsequies were then being celebrated in the cathedral. Edith, for it was no other, was bound upon an expedition of no little moment, as well as danger, and her courage rose with the occasion ; the long-suppressed emotions of maternal love, now throbbing at her heart with hopeful energy, gave to her mind a strength and elasticity to which it had been long a stranger, and her decision had been prompt and clear. The men-at-arms who attended her were four of the Norman followers of Herbert de Lozenga, men who had not long arrived from his ancestral land, men who spoke not a single word of Saxon tongue, and who had never seen the countess. Their orders were to obey her will in everything, and to protect her person with their lives. Fearful of detection—for it was necessary that the world should still believe her dead—she hurried her steps towards the tower, where resided the ferryman, and where the faithful Judith was expecting her. As she hastened on, the broken chant of the monks fell occasionally on her ear ; still she paused not—her energies were but to save the living ; she had no time to mourn the dead. The ferryman, to whom on her arrival she presented a ring, bowed reverentially, for he recognised the signet of the bishop, and handed her into the boat, which already was in waiting, and took his place at the helm. The four Normans seized the oars—which, to their surprise, they found muffled—and directed their course towards Whitlingham.

"And whither go you, my dear lady ?" demanded Judith, in a whisper, as soon as her mistress was seated by her side.

"To Whitlingham—to the Druid caves," calmly answered Edith.

The reply struck terror to the faithful heart of her attendant. The caves of Whitlingham bore an evil name ; for superstition had clothed them in her shadowy terrors. Even in the day they were avoided ; but after nightfall few men would venture to approach them. Strange lights had oft been seen streaming through their rugged openings ; unholy songs and yells of triumph heard. And the idea of approaching, much more of entering, them seemed to Judith little short of madness and presumption. Nothing but this conviction could have induced her to offer even the approach to a remonstrance.

"To Whitlingham ! Gracious lady, did I hear you aright ? Unholy sounds have oft been heard there, and strange visions seen ; 'tis said the spirits of our pagan fathers nightly assemble there, to celebrate the accursed rites of Odin and of Thor. No Christian should approach them ; the Church rejects them ; let us not tempt their wrath."

"I fear them not," replied the countess. "Good spirits cannot harm us ; and Heaven will protect us against bad. But if thy courage fails thee, Judith, tell the men to pull to land ; thou canst regain the palace. I have no right to tax thee, girl, beyond thy strength ; it has been tried enough already."

The idea of leaving her mistress in danger was, to the faithful creature, more terrible than even her fears of Whitlingham.

"No, no," she said ; 'I have not lived so long to eat your bread, that I should desert you now. Be they pagans or fiends, where you go, mistress, my steps shall follow. The unholy sight may, perchance, appal, but it shall not drive me from you."

"The sight of human passions is indeed unholy ; but beyond that," said Edith, "thou hast naught to fear. The beings who assemble in the caves are men—some of them noble, though misguided ones. There may be danger to the body, but none unto the soul."

This explanation, imperfect as it was, afforded great consolation to Judith, who, however fearful where spiritual terrors were concerned, possessed more perhaps than a man's contempt for earthly danger. Born a vassal on the lands of Stanfield, in early life she had been accustomed to traverse the woods, and more than once had battled with the wolf. Drawing the long Saxon knife, which since the escape from the holm, she carried concealed upon her person, she whispered :

"They must be many that would harm you, lady, while I am by. If danger press I am prepared to strike."

"Thanks ; but be cautious," replied her mistress ; "if discovered, resistance would be worse than useless ; but I will hope the best," she added, "for Providence favours my design. The moon is now completely veiled, and not one single star, the gems upon night's mantle, is twinkling in the heavens. If once, aided by Father Oswald's instructions, we reach the cave, we are safe ; but whatever you may see, speak not, breathe not, even though it be a prayer for safety."

There was a solemn earnestness in Edith's manner which precluded further conversation, and Judith sat for the rest of the journey brooding over the mystery. A thousand times she was tempted to demand an explanation, but as often repressed her curiosity through affection and respect.

An hour's rowing brought them to Thorp, not as now, a lovely village, adorned by all that wealth and culture can bestow, but a low marshy swamp, dotted here and there with the rude wattle cabins of the Saxon herds, who tended the cattle of their Norman masters. From this point of their journey increased caution seemed necessary, and they crept slowly along the left side of the river, their noiseless course shadowed by the thick foliage of the trees and shrubs which overhung its banks. Twice in their progress they were alarmed by the sound of a distant oar, and compelled to lie flat within their boat, until the danger passed them. At last they contrived, unobserved, to reach the low shelving bank which conducted to the hills. Silently the rowers, who had evidently received their instructions, drew their boat from out the stream, and concealed it in the sedges, which grew in rank abundance on the banks. As soon as this was done the old ferryman struck into a narrow pathway, half hid by underwood and long dank grass. The countess and Judith followed him, the rear being protected by the men-at-arms ; and thus, without a word being spoken, the little party, in silence and in darkness, pursued their way till they came to a rude pile of unhewn stones, evidently the remains of some Druid temple. Here a light was struck, the men-at-arms searching the bushes round, to see if any curious eye had dogged their steps, their hands upon their long straight swords ready for immediate action.

The countess took an illuminated parchment from her bosom—it was a plan with which Father Oswald had supplied her for her enterprise—and compared the characters traced upon it with those graven upon a large upright stone, which, from its enormous weight, had resisted the zeal of the converted Saxons to overturn it. Apparently they were the same ; a sigh escaped her breast, as if the discovery had relieved it from some oppressive weight ; and for the first time she spoke, but in a voice so low it scarcely scared the genius of silence from the place :

"Thank Heaven ! they are the same. Quick—apply the instrument ! "

Judith, whom the transactions of the last two hours had completely bewildered, beheld with increased astonishment the old ferryman draw from his breast a kind of key, of curious form and antique workmanship, and apply it to one of the interstices of the stone, which, slowly turning on a concealed axle, disclosed a narrow passage descending into the very bowels of the earth. Two of the men-at-arms advanced, lit their torches, and disappeared through the aperture. The countess, without the least hesitation, was about to follow, when, unable longer to contain her apprehensions, Judith caught her by the robe.

"What wouldst thou ? " demanded the courageous Edith.

"Kill me, dear lady," replied her attendant ; "but do not ask me to descend with you through yon dark fearful passage—it leads to death, or to some charnel-house."

"To neither," interrupted her mistress ; "it leads to a recess within the Druid's cave, where unseen we may observe what passes. Patience, girl ; do not lose courage now ! That stone once closed, and we are safe."

"But should our enemies pursue us thither ? "

"Impossible ! " continued the countess ; " one being only knows of its existence, Haga the Arch-Druid, who revealed it to me. Come," she added, " one moment's hesitation may defeat my plans, peril my Ulrick's safety, and destroy my hopes. What ! " she exclaimed, with increased vehemence, seeing that Judith still hesitated, "wouldst thou belie a life of proved fidelity, and desert thy mistress in an hour like this ? "

The implied reproach, the mere suspicion of treason to Edith, stung the breast of her hearer with a far keener pang than her not unnatural terrors, or even her fear of death, and restored both her courage and self-possession—qualities which, under ordinary circumstances, she eminently possessed.

"Lead on, gracious lady," she replied ; "you are right, quite right ; why should I hesitate to follow where you lead !—e'en to the grave ? Should I expire at your feet, I should but end my days where I have passed the service of my life."

A quiet grasp of the hand was Edith's sole reply. She immediately descended the steps, Judith resolutely following. The concealed mechanism was again set in motion, and the Druid's stone resumed its accustomed place. For a long time they followed their guide in darkness through the many windings of the secret passage, for unfortunately the air was confined and too impure to admit of their burning torches. Their progress was rendered still more disagreeable by the unevenness of the road, and the flight of numerous owls and bats, whom their visit had disturbed. Their rugged pathway at last terminated in a species of hall or cave, where they could breath more freely. The chalky and flinty walls and roof had been shaped into something like form ; nay, even architectural ornament, such as it was, had been added. Here they again were enabled to light their torches ; for the air, from either natural or artificial fissures, entered with reviving freshness. A flight of rude steps, at the extreme end of the hall—if we may so call the cave in which the party were assembled—seemed the only means of further progress. Edith and her now courageous attendant mounted them, and discovered that they led to a sort of parapet, too high for them to pass, but which they were sufficiently tall to look over ; in fact, it was a species of wall separating the secret passage from Whitlingham cave, and contrived by the Druids for some now long-forgotten purpose.

The scene which presented itself to their astonished sight was one which Salvator Rosa's magic pencil might have well described. A huge fire blazed in the centre of the cave, which was far more lofty than at the present day, the gradual accumulation of sand and earth having considerably lessened its elevation. Torches of blazing pine were fixed at regular intervals in iron niches in the wall, their red glare falling on piles of arms, so arranged as to be ready for immediate use. Polished shields and shining helms reflected back the blaze, and rendered all that passed distinctly visible. A considerable body of men were assembled within the cave ; some were dozing off to sleep, others preparing food, or listening with excited attention to the tales of old which one or two bards, in under-tones. recited. But the chief personages of the scene were

standing together near the spot were Edith and her companion were
concealed. The principal personage was a tall old man, whose
muscular form and stately limbs, well squared shoulders, and firm
step, told he was still possessed of giant strength. A chain of
massive gold was twisted round his neck, and bracelets of the same
precious metal adorned his arms and wrists : his tunic of green
cloth fell to the middle of his legs, and was richly trimmed with
sables : his countenance was strongly marked, but more perhaps by
grief than age ; a lofty brow which so overhung the eye, that it
would have given a heaviness of expression to the face, had not
the eyes redeemed it ; they were of that piercing blue so peculiar to
the Saxon race, and so expressive of love or hatred, scorn, passion,
or revenge.

The heart of the concealed countess beat wildly, as she gazed upon
him ; for Edda, the friend of her father, the father of her murdered
Edward, stood before her,—not, indeed, as when last she saw him
in the brown pride of autumn's age, but changed by winter's snows ;
still they sat gracefully upon him. His voice was round and rich of
tone as ever. Involuntarily the tears coursed each other down her
cheek as its first accents fell upon her ear ; for the sweet memory of
olden times came over her.

" 'Tis well we are resolved at last," said Edda, addressing his
brother franklins, who were standing round him. "The Saxon
sword hath remained so long inactive, I thought 'twas glued for ever
in its scabbard. Thank Heaven ! 'tis drawn again. We have too
long been dreamers ; my blood has grown thick, dull, and heavy ;
a stirring bout," he added, " will once more send it, with youthful
vigour, dancing through my veins, or end my dreams at once."

Long and patiently did Edith listen to their various arrangements ;
each Saxon leader was assigned his post ; whilst Edda, the head of
the far most numerous sept, taking advantage of the weakness of the
garrison, who were nearly all expected to assist at the trial by battle,
was to storm the castle. Coolly she heard discussed before her
whether the signal should be given for the attack before or after the
death of Ulrick, the end of whose contest with so renowned a knight
as Herman seemed anything but doubtful. The last points in their
proceedings being settled, one by one the numerous franklins took
their leave, and Edda, with his followers, remained alone within the
cave. For a while he occupied himself in giving orders to his men,
who received them with that respectful alacrity which showed their
veneration for their chief, whose countenance, since the departure
of his brother nobles, had gradually lost its energetic expression, and
resumed its habitual melancholy. Drawing his ample cloak around
him, he began soliloquising, as he paced to and fro by the watch-fire's
light within the cave.

" So," he murmured, " the Saxon wolf-dog is again unslipt to hunt
its Norman master. 'Tis a desperate chance to rouse the slumbering

courage of a vanquished people—raise them from slavery to freedom. Should we fail, how many widowed dames and sireless sons will curse the day we drew the powerless sword ! "

" Many," exclaimed Edith, who had left the place of her concealment, and stood before him.

He started, and gazed on her with an expression of awe and fear. He was ignorant of the secret means by which she entered. He knew that the approaches to the cave were guarded by those upon whose fidelity he could depend. It seemed as if a warning spirit had risen from the earth to turn him from his purpose.

" Who and what art thou ? " he demanded.

Edith slowly raised her veil, and exposed her pale but still lovely features to his view. Though many a year had passed since they had met, he knew her at a glance.

" And what," he courteously asked, " brings Hugh de Bigod's widowed countess to this lonely cave the very night of her lord's obsequies ? Has the Norman heir driven his Saxon widow from her home ? If so, lady, thou art welcome—welcome for the memory of one most dear—of one whose love was the first spring-flower of thy virgin heart, though forgotten now."

" Never forgotten, father," answered Edith, " for there are lines so deeply traced upon the heart, death's icy fingers only can efface them. 'Tis true, to save my wretched race from death, my father's honoured age from beggary and shame, I gave my hand to Hugh de Bigod, whose generous nature ne'er wronged the sacrifice ; but my love was buried deep in Edward's lonely grave."

The name of his son, pronounced by the lips of the woman he had so fondly loved, agitated the old man ; the tone of her voice awakened many a long-forgotten thought, jarred many a broken chord ; a tear dimmed his deep blue eye, but with a hasty movement of his hand he dashed it aside.

" Speak not of Edward ! " he exclaimed ; " I am old, and age is weak. Make not a woman of me."

" I must speak of him, and you must listen to me."

" How ? "

" His widow asks," said Edith, throwing herself upon her knees, and clasping the old man's hand, " the mother of his son."

" Woman ! " cried, or rather shrieked, the aged franklin, " what have I heard ? My Edward's widow—the mother of his son ! I am a lonely man, crushed by my sorrows. Do not trifle with me. The storm," he added, " which once raged here, is now at peace ; but words like these break the icy barriers of my heart, to spread, like Etna's lava, desolation round."

The fearful energy of the old man's words alarmed the countess, but failed to check her resolution. In his passion he had grasped her wrist so intently, that the flesh quivered beneath his pressure ; still she felt it not. With her disengaged hand she took a paper

from her bosom, stained by time, but still more by her tears ; it was
the proof of her secret marriage with his son. Eagerly the old man
perused its contents. Twice he tried to speak, but his emotions
choked him. " True, true," he sobbed ; " none but a heart so seared
by treachery could doubt a voice like thine. Child of my friend,
bride of my murdered boy, come to his father's heart, which throbs
to pillow thee amid life's storms." In an instant Edith's arms were
twined round the old man's neck, her head reposing on his manly
breast ; the warm tears trickling down his venerable cheeks mingled
with hers. " But your son," he added—Edward's boy—my boy—is
he living yet ? A look—a sign—and I am happy." The anxious
tone of the speaker showed how deeply every feeling was interested
in the reply. He watched his helpless burthen ; fate seemed to hang
upon her lips.

" He lives," murmured Edith.

" Thank Heaven ! Oh, many a goodly rood of land, for this, shall
grace our Lady's shrine. Where is my boy ? "

" A prisoner in the castle."

" A prisoner ! " echoed Edda ; " I'll tear him thence, though a
Norman's blood cemented every stone. A prisoner ! Tyrants ! are
they not drunk with blood enough already ? A prisoner ! But enough
—he lives, and Edward's boy shall not long linger in the Norman's
hold. Life's purple tide rekindles at my heart ; my nerves thrill
with the energies of former years ; revenge and rage are struggling
in my breast for dreadful mastery. Spirits of my fathers," he
continued, casting himself upon his knees, " in whose veins the
mingled blood of kings and heroes ran—Odin and Hengist, from
your thrones look down, and let your power protect your wretched
race—rally, immortal spirits, round my sword, and guide it to each
Norman tyrant's heart ! "

" Not to the Norman's, but the Saxon's, father. From our own
race the serpent sprang whose venom hath undone us—Saxon the
sword which made thee childless and me a widow—Saxon the tongue
which would complete our ruin, and dares accuse our murdered
Edward's boy ! "

At the words of the countess a ray of light penetrated the mind of
Edda ; and he exclaimed, as the truth flashed upon him :

" Ulrick is thy son ! "

" He is ! " continued Edith—" the noble, generous, the heroic boy !
Father, thou needst not blush to own him ; not in the history of thy
honoured line, princes, or fabled heroes of thy race, will a nobler
heart or mind be found than Ulrick's."

Rapidly did the excited mother relate to the powerful franklin
the history of her early marriage—Ulrick's birth, supposed death,
and miraculous preservation by Herbert de Lozenga, by whose
direction she had been sent to warn him that the plans of the Saxon
insurrection were betrayed, and measures taken to defeat them. As

[ULRICK AND THE PRIEST CROSSING THE CHAPEL.]

H

she proceeded in her tale to support the truth of her assertions, she showed the signet ring, upon the production of which by Father Oswald, Herman had so unexpectedly declared the nobility of Ulrick's birth ; and in conclusion she placed in his hands a packet, bearing the seal of the prelate, the contents of which she was herself unacquainted with. Hastily Edda broke the seal, and found it to contain an agreement, signed by most of the Saxon chiefs engaged in the conspiracy, in the event of their success, to deprive him of the government of his vast possessions, and allow him during his life the enjoyment merely of a portion of his revenues, unless, to avoid the humiliation, he chose to adopt Herman as his heir. The parchment had fallen into the hands of the bishop, through the agency of Father Oswald.

"What," exclaimed Edda, as he recognised each well known signature and seal, "would they divide the lion's spoil ere he had fallen into the snare ? Fools, they have sealed their own most righteous doom ! The pitfall they have dug shall prove their ruin ! "

Long and anxiously did the countess remain in consultation with the chief, and morning had already dawned ere the lonely bark, with its silent rowers, was again launched upon the stream.

CHAPTER VII.

IT was late on the morning after the obsequies of Hugh de Bigod, when the seneschal entered the prison of Ulrick, to announce to him the decision of the Normans : that Mirvan should be permitted to appear in the lists as the champion of the deceased earl—a ceremony which he fulfilled with all the chivalrous courtesy of the age. The impression which the announcement made upon the generous heart of the prisoner may more easily be imagined than described ; love, honour, all opposed it. The haughty Saxon who had taunted him with the mystery of his birth, who had outraged his pride, infamously and falsely accused him of a crime at which his soul revolted, he could have met in the deadly strife of arms ; nay, thirsted for the encounter, which, in the opinions of the age, would have decided the question of innocence or guilt between them ; but Mirvan was a different enemy—he was the first friend of his youth—the brother of Matilda—the son called on, as he believed, to avenge his parent's blood. Friendship as well as principle forbade him to draw the sword in such a contest. The struggle was short but bitter ; and he determined, whatever might be the consequence, to refuse the combat, where victory would be worse than defeat—where every blow he struck would wound a

H 2

heart dearer than his own. Firmly, therefore, he declared his
refusal to meet any but Herman in the lists : nor could the friendly
remonstrance to the seneschal induce him even for a moment to
reconsider his determination.

" You are aware," urged his visitor, " that the trial by battle once
appealed to, and then declined, leaves you no other judgment ; by
the law of arms, you will be deemed guilty, and suffer not only death,
but dishonour."

" Be it so," replied Ulrick : " better to die with an unmerited
stain upon my name than to live to bear within my heart the fires
of remorse. I will not lift my arm against my earliest, though
misguided, friend."

" Not even to prove your innocence ? " demanded the officer.

" No," answered the youth, after a moment's pause ; " enough
that my own heart knows it."

" Who else will know it when thou art dead, branded with a
felon's name ? "

" Heaven ! " exclaimed Ulrick, with a look of resignation, " and
the good angels who watch the grave of peace."

The seneschal, whom the prisoner's firmness touched, bowed
respectfully, and withdrew.

Although unable to appreciate his motives, he respected them :
his rough soldier nature admired the martyr courage which could
so calmly contemplate the approach of death, rejecting the last
chance of safety.

" So ends my dream of life," exclaimed Ulrick, as he heard the
heavy iron bar drawn on the exterior of his prison-door. " Honour
has been its dream of youth—my manhood shall not shame it at its
close. Erect in my integrity, I can meet my doom, and march to
the scaffold as to the victor's car."

" Such," said a deep voice behind him, " is the Christian's courage
and the martyr's faith."

The prisoner started at the sound, and, turning, beheld Father
Oswald, who had entered his dungeon by the secret passage. His
astonishment was extreme ; for, from the state of insensibility in
which the poisoned wine had plunged him, he was ignorant of the
monk's previous visit.

" Father Oswald ! How, in the name, of every saint, gained you
admittance here ? "

" By natural means," replied the old man, pointing to the secret
passage, which he had left open ; " by the same means thou mayest
avoid thy fate. Follow me."

" Whither ? "

" To liberty."

An expression of scorn curled the prisoner's lip ; for, in his mind,
flight was connected with dishonour.

" What ! " he exclaimed, " fly ! and live to bear a branded name !

give truth the lie! and turn approver to my proper shame? Oh, never, never!"

"Then meet the Norman champion in the fight," replied the monk.

"Impossible!" said the youth, mournfully; "he is my friend—unkind, I grant you, still he is my friend!"

"Friend!" repeated Oswald, in a tone of pity. "Do such dreams linger in thee yet? Natures like thine are born to be deceived. Cold as this heart is, it can feel for thee."

"Hast thou no faith in friendship?"

"As much as in the sea's delusive calm before the tempest breaks," bitterly answered the old man; "as much as in the serpent's innocence because it sleeps. Friendship! I tell thee, boy, it is the coin with which man cheats his fellows—a wretch plotting against his neighbour's peace and life can find no mask so sure to hide his purpose as friendship's sullied name. The bird whose wings fan its own funeral pyre is not more purely fable than a friend. Wouldst thou be happy," he added, "dream not of friendship more."

"Mirvan is my friend," interrupted Ulrick.

"Yet he, unheard, condemned thee," coolly observed the priest.

The reply shot a pang to Ulrick's breast; for in the confidence of his nature, the generosity of his heart, he felt that he could not have judged unheard as Mirvan judged; still he endeavoured to defend him.

"His father's death," he faltered, "and the false words of an artful fiend, have blinded his better reason; so confidence has given place to doubt."

"And what is friendship, fi a doubt can shake it? But come," added the priest, "for I have still a solemn ministry to be performed, and I could wish that mercy should precede justice. The path to freedom lies before thee. Fly from the enemies who seek thy blood, to those who long to welcome thee."

"Never," resolutely answered the young man, "will I consent to stain my name by ignominious flight."

"Not though it lead thee to thy mother's arms?" demanded the priest, "to her maternal blessing, to a name proud as the proudest of thy Norman foes—a name which renders thee the mate of any line their pirate race e'er boasted?"

"What meanest thou, father, by these words?" demanded the youth, deeply excited. "Thou art a holy man; thy words should be of truth. Are these things so?"

The priest silently bowed his head in confirmation of his words—words which the prisoner had drunk into his very soul—words which assured him that his boyhood's hopes were no longer dreams.

"And yet," said Ulrick, despairingly, after a pause, "I cannot fly."

"Not," interrupted the monk, "if, the moment thou wert free, the evidence of thine innocence, attested by the hand of thine accuser, witnessed by those who now would judge thee, were produced, to clear thy fame beyond suspicion's breath ? "

"Is it possible ? "

"Canst thou doubt me ? " he added, seeing that Ulrick's last objection was shaken. "Men so near the grave as I am seldom lie. Here is a dress in which thou mayst pass unsuspected by the soldiery, should we encounter such when beyond the castle wall. Array thyself, for time is precious with me."

Ulrick hesitated no longer ; the assurance that the proofs of his innocence should be placed within his hands, when once beyond the castle, decided him, and he hastened to assume the disguise of a lay brother, which his kind protector had brought him. Just as he had drawn the cowl over his face, the door of his prison opened, and the seneschal, who had been directed to conduct the prisoner before the nobles, to explain his extraordinary resolution of not appearing in the lists against Mirvan, entered the cell. His astonishment at the sight of the two monks was extreme.

"Where is the prisoner ? " he exclaimed, after having cast a hasty glance round the cell.

"Beyond your reach," coolly replied Father Oswald.

"Treachery is here ! " exclaimed the seneschal, raising his voice. "What ho ! guard ! the prisoner hath escaped ! Warders, to your posts ! Treason, ho ! "

The effect of the alarm was to set every man within the walls on the alert. The word was passed from post to post, and the heavy tramp of the armed soldiery was heard upon the stairs ascending to the tower.

"Too late, too late ! " whispered the prisoner to Father Oswald ; "the guard are here."

A dozen men-at-arms rushed into the prison as he spoke. Firmly the monk grasped Ulrick's arm as he replied—

"Were their chains upon thy limbs, boy, they should melt like wax ; were the sword above thy head, I would shiver it ere it fell. Brute force is theirs—science and wisdom mine."

"Seize them ! " exclaimed the seneschal. "Cut them down if they attempt to pass ! "

The men were about to obey their chief, when Father Oswald scattered a powder upon the floor, which instantly ignited on coming in contact with the air, and filled the prison with a thick vapour, from which lurid flames occasionally flashed, and peals of thunder rolled. The affrighted Normans fell prostrate through fear and superstition, the belief in magic being universal at the time, though condemned by law, both civil and ecclesiastic.

"The fiend ! the fiend !" they shouted, and in their terror called upon every saint to save them. Gradually the flames subsided, and the dense vapour became dispersed ; when they recovered sufficient courage to look around them. The two monks had disappeared ; they found themselves within the prison, trembling and alone. A long, winding staircase, concealed in the thickness of the wall, brought the fugitives to the very foundations of the castle, where the air felt cold and damp. Here they paused for breath, and Father Oswald lit a torch which he had brought beneath his vest. Ulrick found himself, on looking round, in a cell something similar to the one he had just quitted ; the same rough-sculptured Crucifixion adorned the wall, representing St. William in the Wood. From another concealed passage opening from its back, they proceeded in the direction of the chapel, to which they mounted by similar winding stairs to those they had descended.

"Caution !" exclaimed the priest, as they reached the last step, which brought them to a panel of carved oak, which evidently answered the purpose of a concealed door, the complicated mechanism by which it was opened being on their side of it. His companion arrested his step at the word, for he heard voices in the chapel. By removing a small slide, Ulrick was enabled to peep through a portion of the fretwork and see what was passing in the sacred edifice, without himself being seen by those he watched.

Isabel and Matilda were standing near the altar in earnest conversation with Odo of Caen, who seemed to defend himself but weakly against some joint request. It was the voice of the former that first met his ear.

"Impossible !" she exclaimed, pettishly, as if repeating the words of the knight ; "there is nothing impossible to a willing mind or to a lady's prayer. What harm can possibly arise from my cousin and myself visiting the prisoner in his dungeon ? Think you that we shall smuggle him away beneath our wimples ? or all three escape on a fiery dragon ? "

"Not that," replied Odo, smiling at her earnestness ; "but he is under ward, and I am pledged in honour to admit neither friend nor enemy to converse with him. Be reasonable, pretty coz, and press me therefore no more upon this theme."

"Indeed, but I will press thee, and earnestly, too," answered Isabel ; "for thy objections, despite thy protestations, are as slight as thy wish to favour us. By thy vow of knighthood, thou art bound to succour innocence ; and Ulrick, I tell thee, again and again, is innocent. Had Herman been the champion, tongue of mine had never wagged to prevent the fight. Heaven, I doubt not, would have protected the righteous cause, and decided well between them, for I feel assured that Herman is——"

"Herman will never more appear as champion in any cause," gravely interrupted the knight, who shuddered as he remembered his midnight execution in the cloisters of the cathedral, and his own share in it.

" The better for the cause, if it be a good one. But come," she added, " brother Odo—for I suppose I must some day call thee so—pleasure us in this. Why, thou makest more mouths to perform an act of justice than others would to strain a point of honour. Matilda and myself both vouch for Ulrick's innocence ; and surely the word of two noble Norman maidens may outweigh a Saxon's slander. Would that my sister Jane were here !—thou wouldst not dare say nay to her."

Though not convinced, the knight was shaken in his resolution ; the appeal to her sister's name had touched a secret chord in his stern nature ; yet he yielded not at once. but continued to resist, more for honour than the hope of victory.

" Could I but see the use of such an interview—what chance ! " he muttered.

" Every hope," interrupted Matilda. speaking for the first time. " There is some fearful mystery concealed in Ulrick's accusation. Woman's wit will often find the key where man's boasted wisdom fails. We judge from sympathies ; cold man from reason. Did he not risk his own to save my brother's life ? Was not the sword with which 'tis said the felon blow was struck my parting gift ? A gift," she added, slightly blushing as the eye of the knight encountered hers, " sanctioned by my brother's presence and my cousin's smile ! Odo, should either Ulrick or my brother fall in this unholy fight, eternal must be their remorse who might have stayed the contest."

" 'Tis stayed already," answered Odo. " Know you not the prisoner hath refused to measure swords with Mirvan ? "

" Noble Ulrick ! " exclaimed Matilda ; " yet not more noble than my judgment painted him ; and what is the result ? "

" By the law of arms," he reluctantly answered, " he is condemned to die."

" To die !" exclaimed Matilda, violently excited. " Oh, no ! you cannot be so lost to every precept of humanity—to every voice of justice. Unheard to die ! to quit the gorgeous scenes of this fair earth—exchange life's hopes and gushing sympathies for the vile headsman's steel, with honour's impulses throbbing at the heart—to sink to a dishonoured grave, is e'en too horrible for thought. If it be so," she added, firmly, " e'en at the place of execution one voice shall still proclaim his innocence, and vindicate his name."

Our readers may well imagine with what transport the eloquent words of the speaker fell upon the listener's ear. The sinner who heard the angel of mercy pleading for him at the judgment seat could not have felt a deeper transport. In the excitement of the moment he would have quitted his concealment, and. regardless of the danger, have cast himself at Matilda's feet, to pour out his heart in grateful prayer, had not the hand of Father Oswald wisely restrained him.

" Patience," whispered the old man ; " that which is deferred is far from lost ; thou yet shall thank her like thyself, my son."

Even Odo was struck by the fair speaker's confidence and despair ; they naturally turned his thoughts to a fresh channel.

" Lady," he said, " thou lovest this unknown youth ; and love, too often, blinds our better reason."

" Odo of Caen," replied the maiden, with dignity, " this is ungenerously urged ; but since it hath been so, be this my answer, that never word of love from Ulrick's lips have fallen on my ear ; and I spring not from a race that could, unsought, be won. Ulrick, the unknown youth, can never be to me more than the preserver of my brother's life. De Bigod's daughter weds but with a line as pure and as illustrious as her own."

The deep blush which had suffused the speaker's countenance gave way to the mortal paleness which, since her father's death, o'ershadowed it. The rough soldier was awed by the dignity of her manner, and the hopeless tone in which her words were uttered. If not convinced, he seemed to be convinced ; though skilled to read the human heart, he generously closed the page, and strove to read no further. For a few moments there was a pause, which Odo was the first to break.

" Lady," he said, bending the knee with courtly gallantry, " that I believe my thoughts have wronged thee, be this the proof. I yield to thy demand ; I will myself conduct thee and the Lady Isabel to the prison door, and leave you to converse with the accused, of whom I'll think the better that his innocence is vouched by thee. Speak," he added, with a smile, " am I forgiven ? "

" Forgiven ? " said Isabel, who saw that Matilda was unable to reply ; " ay, and shalt be rewarded, too. I'll plead thy cause with Jane, and on her wedding-day my cousin and myself will braid her hair, and every pearl we have shall go to deck it. But when," she added, " shall we to the prison ?—to-morrow is the day appointed for the fight."

Odo was about to reply, when the alarm-bell of the castle caught his ear, as it sent forth its iron summons. He started at the sound : his first thought was of the intended Saxon insurrection. The possibility of the prisoner's escape never struck him. Before he had even time to draw his sword, Robert of Artois rushed into the chapel.

" Speak ! " cried Odo ; " what means the alarm ?—are the Saxon hounds upon us ? "

" The prisoner hath escaped ! "

Matilda and Isabel were in an instant upon their knees before the shrine in mute thanksgiving ; a weight seemed to have been removed from both their hearts—Matilda for Ulrick's, and Isabel for Mirvan's safety.

" Escaped ! " repeated Odo ; " impossible ! the tower was guarded

by my own and Bigod's followers. I'll stake my life on their
fidelity. There must be some witchcraft or devilry in this. But
follow me," he added. " Whate'er the mystery may be, we'll see the
bottom of it."

Odo, followed by Robert of Artois, left the building as he spoke.
" Now, then, follow !" whispered Father Oswald ; " we must
cross the chapel. On the opposite side is the entrance to another
passage, which leads us beneath the castle moat, e'en to the cloisters.
It were dangerous now to traverse the guarded plain between them ;
follow me, then, in silence."

He opened the concealed spring as he spoke, and in an instant he
found himself with his companion in the chapel. So absorbed were
both Isabel and Matilda in their prayers, that they heeded not the
echo of the priest's sandalled foot, or the yet heavier tread of Ulrick.
The latter could not, however, in his love and gratitude, forget the
generous defence of his honour made by the lips most dear to him.
Led by the passionate impulse of his heart, he cast himself at the
maiden's feet, and printed a burning kiss upon her hand.

Matilda started with surprise at such an action from a monk, and
was about to rebuke his insolence, when the voice whose tones had
so often awakened an echo in her heart reassured her.

" Angel of mercy," he exclaimed, " farewell ! thy judgment hath
not wronged thy goodness ; the spotless virgin in her cloistered cell
—the infant smiling at its mother's breast—are not more free from
blood than I am. At the hour of battle, fear not but that I shall be
there, to prove my innocence or brave my doom."

Before Matilda or Isabel could reply, Ulrick had again drawn
the cowl over his face, and disappeared after his mysterious
conductor.

Herbert de Lozenga, Edda, and the countess were seated in an
apartment of the episcopal palace, when Father Oswald, after
conducting Ulrick through the subterranean passages which
connected the castle with the cathedral, emerged with him into the
cloisters.

" Thank Heaven !" exclaimed the priest, " we are secure at last,
boy ; the danger is over, and I have kept my promise to thee."

He was about to leave him as he spoke.

" Stay, father," cried the youth ; " safety, indeed, thou hast
secured me ; but, remember, it must not be safety without honour ;
either the proofs you promised of my innocence, or I surrender
myself once more a prisoner."

" What !" exclaimed Oswald, with a melancholy smile, " doubtful
still ? " He advanced and took his companion by the hand, and
continued in a kinder voice : " Ulrick, I have been a man of sin
and sorrow ; my pride has been humbled into the dust, my wisdom
confounded by a child. Yet not to redeem the past—to avoid the
last fearful ordeal which awaits me—would I pollute these lips

with falsehood. The proofs I promised you exist ; another hand than mine will yield them to thee. Give thy present hour to nature's claims—another will be found for honour's. Remember that thou hast a mother, whose heart throbs as it would burst its bosom to enfold thee. Follow me—I will conduct thee to her."

There was a tone in the monk's voice which at once convinced Ulrick, and forbade reply. Its sadness touched him—its truthfulness confirmed him in his confidence. With the obedience, if not the simplicity, of a child, he followed his conductor to the room where his earliest benefactor and new-found parent awaited him. Eagerly did the prelate, on his appearance, advance to meet him, for he loved him like a son. Ulrick's heart was the first which in his sorrows taught him his own was human—recalled him to himself—restored him to the world ; and he was now returned to him, like the shipwrecked mariner whom all thought lost, through danger and through storm, doubly welcome to his lonely heart. Fervently, therefore, was the good man's benediction given, and grateful tears accompanied it.

"Ulrick," he said, as the youth rose from his knees, "there is a blessing as sacred even as the priest's—as grateful to the heart as the anointed prelate's holy words. Does not nature whisper thee it is thy mother's ? Go, ask it," he added, "of the heart which yearns to give it thee ; tell her she need not blush to call thee by the endearing name of son."

"I do believe thee," exclaimed the happy Edith, as she threw her arms around the neck of Ulrick, and imprinted a motherly, holy kiss upon his cheek ; "come to the widowed heart which through long years hath mourned thee as the dead, yet feels its sorrows overpaid in finding thee at last. Ulrick, my boy, my good and brave ! my Edward's image ! my life's only flower ! the thrill which struck me when I first beheld thee was Nature struggling to proclaim thee mine ; and, dullard as I am, my heart was deaf to her mute eloquence, or I had known my son."

A flood of tears relieved the o'erfraught heart, which else had burst with too much happiness. The prelate felt that there were scenes too sacred even for his ministry to witness. Silently he withdrew from the apartment, followed by Father Oswald, into the cloisters, which for a while he paced in silence, the aged monk watching his steps.

"Brother," he at last exclaimed, turning to Oswald, "thy penance upon earth hath indeed been sore, and this last blow surpasses human justice. Fearful as have been the crimes of thy son, I feel both for him and thee."

"I can bear it," replied the old man, with a firm voice. "His will who ruleth all things be accomplished ! "

"If Heaven can pardon," resumed the bishop, "should man

prove relentless ? May not the life of thy unhappy and misguided boy be spared—spared for repentance and for future hope ?"

"My lord, he is repentant. But the crime of sacrilege must be atoned ; the insulted altar calls for expiation. Our duties both are painful : yours to yield him to the arm which condemns him to the flames ; mine to reconcile the victim for the sacrifice. Shrink not from yours, I am prepared for mine."

The speaker hesitated for a moment, as if struggling with some internal weakness, and then threw himself upon his knees before the bishop, who instantly endeavoured to raise him, which the old man resisted.

"No !" he exclaimed, "this posture suits me best ; it is a suppliant's. Grant me the only favour I ever asked of man."

"Name it, my son," replied his superior, anxious to please him.

"Let not my son, the last of a line whose royal priesthood is lost in the mist of ages, be dragged like a peasant to the stake. Clad in his knightly armour, unshamed by degradation, let him die."

"Willingly, my son."

"The heart is willing, but the flesh is weak," continued Oswald "I cannot see him die ; but I will so prepare him for his fate, that you shall find an unresisting sacrifice. Till the last hour arrives, leave him with me and Heaven."

"Be it as you wish. Orders shall be given even in justice to remember mercy. His sufferings shall be brief."

"Not so," interrupted the monk ; "I would not abridge one mortal pang ; for, oh ! " he added, "they are too little to atone for sacrilege, neglected duty, and a soul perverted. Your blessing, holy father ! " be continued—"your blessing ! Pray for me at the hour of daily sacrifice, when from thy sacred lips the supplication for offending man rises to Heaven !—remember him whose youth was darkness, and whose age was sorrow ! "

The clanging of an iron heel upon the pavement caused them both to start. Meekly bowing, Father Oswald rose from his knee, after receiving the episcopal benediction, and directed his steps towards the prison, for his last interview with his unhappy son.

Even the approach of an armed knight—for such the stranger proved to be—would not have diverted the prelate's mind from the chain of thought in which his interview with the monk had thrown it, had he not recognised in the red-haired and coarse-visaged stranger the son of his Sovereign—the same, who, shortly after, under the title of William Rufus, succeeded to the Crown, and lost both his crown and his life by his vexatious tyranny. On recognising him, Herbert de Lozenga immediately recovered his courtly self-possession, and advanced to meet him.

"Thanks, my lord bishop, thanks," he exclaimed, with the bluntness which characterised his manners ; " we doubt not of your sincerity, but something to restore the inner man were more welcome now than compliments. We have ridden hard, my lord."

No expression on the features of his hearer showed the prelate's high-bred scorn of his unpolished guest. By a silver call, which, after the manner of the age, he wore suspended by his side, he summoned a lay brother to his presence, to whom he communicated the necessary orders for an ample refection to be instantly served in his own private apartment.

"And so the Saxon clods would rise against us!" continued William. "By the hand of Rollo, but I will break their stubborn necks, or bend them to the yoke! I will not leave a Saxon franklin in his hall; fire and sword shall purge the land of all who bear the hated name. I will make England one vast hunting-ground, and chase them at my pleasure. Our father's health, my lord, we are told, breaks fast; let me but once be king!"

"Never, with such views," said Herbert, "canst thou maintain thy seat; thy very nobles, William, would forsake thee. Think by how many ties the Saxon and the Norman bloods are linked, how many holy sympathies unite the conquerors and the conquered. By conciliation only canst thou hope to reign, or hold in peace thy crown."

"I'd rather hold it by my sword!" impetuously answered the fiery prince.

"Crowns have often by the sword been won, but seldom held by it. Thou saidst but now thy father's days were numbered. Ask thyself, hast thou no rival near the throne whose claims may clash with thine, despite thy father's favour?"

William started, and remembered his elder brother, the unfortunate Robert, whom he eventually supplanted both in England and Normandy, and whose eyes were barbarously put out, to render him incapable of reigning, while he was a prisoner in Cardiff Castle—put out by order of his cruel brother.

"My father by his sword won this fair isle, and may will it as he pleases," proudly answered the prince. "I am not to be checked by fears like these. By Heaven, prelate, did I deem thee false, I'd place thee where thy treason should be hurtless."

A transient flush for a moment clouded the unusually pale features of the bishop, and his eye was lit by a fire which showed he had once been dangerous. Still, ever master of himself, he paused till the sentiment of anger had passed away, and then answered, in his usual cold and unimpassioned tone—

"I am not of those whom princes judge. Reserve, young man, your threat for those who fear them. Were it my will, prince as thou art, to send thee bound in chains unto thy elder brother, or place thy head upon the Tower of London, I'd find the means to do it. Treason, to me! Forget not, prince, I am of a line as noble as thine own."

The young prince, who well knew the influence which Herbert de Lozenga possessed amongst his countrymen, felt that he had gone too far. The right of his father to leave him the crown he had acquired, to the prejudice of his elder brother Robert, might be disputed ; in such a case the bishop's voice would be most important. He smothered, therefore, his secret wrath, and had recourse to that hypocrisy for which he was distinguished.

"Forgive me, my good lord," he exclaimed, with an expression of frankness too transparent not to be seen through ; " but children will sometimes quarrel with their ;tutors—you know your pleasure ever is our will."

At this moment the lay brother returned to inform his superior that the refection waited them.

" 'Tis well," said the bishop. " Prince, I attend you."

His guest for a few moments hesitated ; in his own treacherous, cruel nature he doubted the sincerity of all men. He was alone, in the power of a man whom he had indiscreetly threatened, and he judged his conduct from what his own would have been on such an occasion.

" We are friends, my lord, I trust," he said. " Remember that I came hither on your summons, slightly attended, with full confidence in your well-known loyalty and faith. You will not wrong it ? "

"The man who came on Herbert de Lozenga's summons," replied his host, " were safe, even though my brother's blood crimsoned his hand. Eat of my bread, drink of my cup, and sleep beneath my roof in peace as well as safety."

But half-satisfied, the young prince followed the prelate from the cloisters. The collation once despatched, they remained for several hours in council, where the strong mind of the ecclesiastic completely subjugated the weak one of his guest, who determined, at least on the present occasion, to be guided by his experience, and conform himself to his wishes.

* * * * *

Long after the preceding interview, Father Oswald was still occupied in prayer with his son, whose repentance, at least, appeared sincere ; humbly and devoutly he had received from his parent's hand the baptismal rite, whose regenerating waters wash all guilt away ; a holy calm had succeeded the frantic ravings of despair, and Ernulf felt almost resigned to die. His armour, which he had taken off for the ceremony, was piled in one corner of the room ; the font and tapers occupied the centre. As the penitent rose from his knees, his father removed the stole from his neck and placed it on the couch ; as he did so the great bell of the church began its solemn peal,—a signal to the citizens and inmates of the abbey that the execution was about to take place. Ernulf started at the sound ; despite his resignation, he turned pale.

"Fear not, boy," said the old man ; "in reconciling thee to Heaven, I have saved thee from the penalties of earth. It were not just that thou shouldst suffer for thy crimes, while he whose neglect perilled thy soul escaped."

"What meanest thou, father ? " demanded the prisoner, a faint ray of hope once more returning to his heart.

"That I have provided for thee the means of safety," answered the old man. "Thinkest thou," he added, "I would see thee perish in the flames, and feel my sins had lit thy funeral pyre ? Take this packet—it contains that which in a far distant land will guard thee against want ; take it, together with my robe, and fly."

"And leave you here a prisoner in my place ? Never, father— never ; I am not so base as that."

"Even so," impassibly answered the monk ; "what should I fear ? "

"The vengeance of the Church," replied his son.

"Ernulf, dismiss the thought ; I swear to thee no human judgment shall ever reach me for the act. Besides, if my own heart approves, I value not the censure of other men's tongues. My robes will pass thee safe and unquestioned through the city. Once beyond the walls, thou knowest too well the country to be retaken. Hark," he continued as the bell again struck upon his ear, "time grows short. By the obedience which a son should pay his father, I command thee assume my robe and fly ! "

The love of life is perhaps that sentiment which abandons us, and Ernulf felt it with renewed force at every sound of the signal bell. The natural horror of death—and of such a death—decided him, and he hastily assumed the robe and cowl which Father Oswald had already laid aside. Calmly, and with an untrembling hand, the old man assisted him to arrange the disguise, and placed the packet in his hand.

"Farewell, my son," he exclaimed in a firm voice ; "on earth we meet no more. Thy safety for ever banishes thee from England, and my career on earth is short; pray that its end be happy. Forgive the harshness that oppressed thy youth, the cold neglect which closed thy opening heart, as I forgive thy disobedience and thy crime. Farewell ! A priest's and a father's blessing rest upon thee ! "

The speaker extended his arm over the disguised criminal as he spoke, and remained for a few moments absorbed in mental prayer. Gradually recovering himself, he led him to the door of the dungeon, opened it, pressed his hand for the last time as he passed through, then closed it between them for ever.

For some moments he listened to the receding footsteps of his son, and breathed more freely as they fell fainter and fainter upon his ear.

"He is safe ! " exclaimed Oswald, with a smile of triumph. " I

thank Thee Father that the soul Thou gavest has not through my
most grievous sin been lost. Father and son may meet again with
Thee."

The old man advanced to the corner of the room, where the
armour of Ernulf was carefully piled together, and began to pray.
Louder and louder the bell of the cathedral tolled, as the crowds of
citizens, soldiers, and knights entered the precincts of the cathedral
to witness the execution. The fat, greasy burghers of Norwich
hustled each other for the best places, with as much brutality as
ever attended a public execution in later times. A compact crowd
filled the space between the west front and the old tower, since
replaced by the old Erpingham gate, leaving little more than sufficient space for the procession and the execution of the criminal. A
large body of the bishop's retainers kept the ground, headed by
their commander ; and the abbatial and episcopal banner floated
from the turret of the church. The bishop's throne was erected on
the right of the square formed by the soldiers, and the seats for the
secular judges faced it. The latter had long been seated before the
procession issued from the gates of the cathedral. The chant of the
priesthood fell upon the ear, raising the solemn hymn of the Church,
the *Dies Iræ*—

> " The day of wrath. the dreadful day,
> When all that lives must pass away ;
> When time shall feel that he is old,
> The sun his glorious race is told ;
> When every blazing star shall fall,
> And nature wear one funeral pall ;
> When death and sin shall cease to reign,
> Thy justice shall unchanged remain.
> Dies iræ, dies illa,
> Solvet seclum in favilla.

> " The day of wrath—the trumpet's sound,
> Shall call earth's varied nations round
> As, to meet eternal doom,
> They rise in myriads from the tomb.
> 'To judgment come ! ' the angel cries,
> The groaning earth, the bursting skies,
> Piercing creation's utmost bounds,
> Shall echo back the appalling sounds.
> Dies iræ, dies illa,
> Solvet seclum in favilla."

" They come at last," exclaimed one of the Saxon franklins, at the
end of the hymn ; " and see, the proud prelate heads them. His
own turn," he muttered, " may not be long."

" What's that, friend, you murmured ? " demanded George of
Erpingham, who had overheard the words.

The indiscreet Saxon quailed beneath the glance of the fierce
knight, like a whipped hound. Much as he feared the Normans,
he feared the Church still more—a sentiment which the scene he
had come to witness was not likely to decrease.

[HERBERT DE LOZENGA POINTING TO THE HEAD OF HERMAN.]

"Nothing, sir knight," he stammered, confusedly; mere idle thoughts—no more."

"Such thoughts are dangerous here. Keep them to thyself, Sir Franklin, and it shall go well with thee."

The arrival of the procession cut short all further reply.

First came a noble, bareheaded, bearing the banner of the clergy, followed by the monks, two and two, chanting the Litany of the Saints : after them marched the dignitaries of the cathedral, followed by the bishop clothed in the pomp of purple, but in black cope and stole, in sign of penitence. On the appearance of the prelate a suppressed murmur arose among the people—on any other occasion they would have shouted—for they loved him for his charities, had mourned him dead, and rejoiced to find him living. The prisoner followed in complete armour, surrounded by his guards.

The bishop and the clergy were no sooner seated, than the criminal walked deliberately up to the stake, to which the executioners immediately attached him, while the civil judges pronounced his sentence. "How dost thou die ?" demanded the marshal of the city, whose duty it was to record the answers of the prisoner.

"A penitent," replied a deep voice, which issued from the helmet of the victim, like an echo from the grave ; "a Catholic and a Christian."

A shriek of mortal agony was heard at a distance in the crowd ; and a monk, whom all took for Father Oswald, was seen trying to force his way through the dense mass of people.

"Apply the flames," firmly exclaimed the prisoner, upon whose ears the scream had fallen. "At once perform your office—my soul to God, my ashes to the winds."

The fire was applied, and in an instant the flames blazed with fury ; for Herbert de Lozenga had humanely ordered the wood which composed the pile to be saturated with spirits and resinous gums. Again the monks raised the *Requiem* which implored mercy for the departing sinner's soul. But a voice was heard, louder than all their music, crying "Forbear !" and the form of a frantic monk was seen, with superhuman strength, fending the yielding crowd, which gave way like a cleft stream before him. With a last effort he broke through the inner circle, sprang into the blazing pile, and endeavoured to release the victim from the stake ; his cowl fell back, as he did so, and all recognised Ernulf, the squire, at whose execution they imagined themselves assisting.

"Save them !" exclaimed the bishop, starting from his seat, as a fearful suspicion crossed his mind—a suspicion, alas, but too true ; for at the same moment, the straps which fastened the helmet of the supposed criminal gave way, and fell into the flames, exposing to the horror-stricken gaze of all the well-known features of Father Oswald, who, to save his son, had thus contrived to take his place.

The very precautions taken to shorten the sufferings of the criminal rendered it impossible to save him; but he did not die alone; for his repentant son shared his death, and mingled his ashes with his. Sadly and silently the crowd dispersed, like men stricken with a mental palsy; the scene they had witnessed having displayed another page in that mysterious book, the human heart.

CHAPTER VIII.

IN the plain extending from the moat which surrounded the hill upon which Norwich Castle stands the lists were erected. The simplicity of the preparations showed that they were intended for no courtly tournament, but for an encounter where life and death were set upon the issue. Close to the exterior palisades a large lodge was built, adorned with purple hangings; over it floated the banners of Odo of Caen and his brother nobles, who were to act as judges of the fight. But the rest of the buildings were plain in the extreme. In the midst of the inclosed arena were a block and a post, on the former of which the accused, if defeated, was to suffer death; while to the latter his name was to be affixed by the hands of the executioner in the event of his non-appearance, a mark of infamy more degrading than even the pillory or modern outlawry.

The sun shone brightly on the scene; and, at an early hour, the troops of the confederated franklins marched to the spot, most of them wearing the long white frock peculiar to their nation, and which the carter's smock of the present day nearly resembles. Beneath it they could conveniently hide their arms, and appear to a casual observer a peaceful body of serfs and peasants, drawn together by curiosity to witness the approaching fight. Soon after the parties began to arrange themselves, the leaders of the enterprise observed, with secret dissatisfaction, that immediately a party of Saxons arrived, and took up their position on the ground, an equal number of Normans, all of whom were well armed, placed themselves beside them, and, without seeming to do so intentionally, so intersected them that all possibility of the conspirators acting in concert was destroyed. Several times they manœuvred to change positions, but were as often outmanœuvred by the Normans, who, whether by accident or design, thwarted by their evolutions every attempt which the Saxons made to unite themselves in one or more compact bodies.

The only party which presented anything at all like an appearance of having unity were the followers of Edda, a numerous body of men, well armed, and commanded by a youthful knight, whose face was hid by his visor, but whose firm step and active movements showed him to be in the full pride of strength and manhood. The Norman nobles were the last who made their appearance upon the ground ; most of them, as they did so, resigned the command of their vassals to their esquires, and proceeded to the castle, where a council had been summoned by the bishop, to be held previous to the proceedings in the lists. One by one the Saxon franklins were sent for on different pretexts ; so that, by the time Herbert de Lozenga arrived, escorted by a large body of his followers, under the conduct of George of Erpingham, most of the leaders, whether Norman or Saxon, were assembled in the great hall.

Edda, the most powerful chief of the conquered race, walked by the side of the prelate, who divided his conversation with him and the red-haired stranger, whose real rank was known only to himself. Many a knight and vavasour followed in his train, bound by the tenure of their lands to do him feudal homage. As a Norman baron, he ranked with the most powerful ; and in his double capacity of Bishop of Norwich and Abbot of Hulm, with the richest ecclesiastics in the kingdom ; added to which, his known favour with the Conqueror, and office of Chancellor, made him one of the most important personages in the realm, and his influence was courted and respected by all.

A tall, gaunt man appeared amongst the stragglers in the bishop's train, the mere sight of whom seemed to excite the indignation of the crowd ; even the men-at-arms, who escorted him, to protect him from the insults of the mob, kept at a respectful distance from him, and laughed whenever a gibe more bitter, or a curse more fierce, saluted his appearance. It was the city executioner. Whether indifference or philosophy rendered him insensible to the degradation of his position, it might have been difficult to decide ; but he walked on, amidst the jests, curses, and hootings of the people, with an impassibility of feature which a Stoic might have envied. He was clothed in red—the colour of his office—and wore a large black barret, which rendered the ghastly hue of his features more apparent ; in his hand he carried a leathern bag, sufficiently capacious to contain either the head of a victim or the implements of his fearful and disgusting office.

" Is Saint Peter taking tithe of heads to-day ? " whispered Brenner, one of the few Saxon leaders who remained upon the ground, " that he walks with such a collector in his train ? The headsman is a bird of evil omen ; ill befalls the purpose or the man whose path he crosses. Would I had met his sight on any day than this."

" Amen ! " replied his companion. " The only consolation is, he is without his axe. Have you observed," he added, looking cautiously around to assure himself that no one could overhear him, " how the Normans flank our men ? I trow there is more of purpose than of chance in it. I fear we are betrayed, or, at least, suspected."

Brenner had previously, in his own mind, made the same observation, but remained silent, not wishing to alarm his companion by acknowledging his suspicions. At this moment they were joined by a third party—Armand of the Wold, one of the petty franklins, compelled by his position to follow blindly in the wake of his more powerful chief ; a shrewd, keen, calculating man, always ready to turn with the tide he was too weak to stem. The gloomy restlessness of his nature showed that he was ill at ease.

"Who has seen Herman of the Burg ? " he demanded ; " why is he absent at such a moment ? For two days he has not appeared amongst us. I like not this."

The first two speakers confessed that they had neither seen nor could explain his absence—an avowal followed by immediate silence, each calculating how far his neighbour might be a partner in the treason, if any such existed. Brenner was the first to break it.

" Most of our party, on one pretext or another, have been summoned to the castle," whispered the first speaker. " There are invitations a prudent man always should decline."

" Especially an enemy's," observed Armand.

" And above all a Norman's. Ill befall the day when they first set foot on England's happy soil. But look," continued Brenner. " how the bishop lures the noble Edda to the council. I thought his white hairs covered more wisdom."

" Or less treason," muttered Armand.

At this moment the seneschal, wearing his chain and carrying his wand of office, approached the speakers, and commanded them to attend the council about to sit in the castle. The summons was given in the name of the bishop chancellor. As the officer was attended by a party of men-at-arms, resistance would have been equally foolish as useless. After a mutual glance, which seemed to say, " We are fairly caught," they bowed in acquiescence, and followed their conductor to the council.

The great hall of Norwich Castle was lined with men-at-arms, and a strong body guarded the different doors. All whose rank entitled them to the *entrée* were freely admitted ; but once there, none but the Normans were allowed egress. Whenever a Saxon approached the entrance, he was respectfully informed that the council was about to commence, and invited to remain in his place—the tone of the invitation rendering it equivalent to a command. Thus suspicion and mistrust were at their height. The absence of Herman was the subject of many a comment ; nor did the appearance of Odo of Caen and his brother nobles, in complete armour, tend to tranquillise the doubts of the conspirators, which at last became so painful that the clash of arms which announced the arrival of the bishop sounded as a relief to them ; at least, they would learn the worst, for the doubt of ill is sometimes more difficult to bear than even ill confirmed.

As if with an instinctive feeling of hostility, or of an approaching contest, the two parties had formed into separate groups, engaged in hurried whispered conversation, when Herbert de Lozenga, with his train, entered the hall. There was an expression of care upon his brow, although both step and air were firm as ever. Mirvan raised his visor as he advanced to meet him.

" Welcome, my lord and father," he exclaimed ; " we attend your summons. Please you, we have business which the sword must judge, if the accused appears ; if not, the executioner. Let us to the council, and at once."

The cold, though respectful, tone of the speaker showed that he looked upon the prelate as his enemy. Indeed, he doubted not but that it was by his secret contrivance Ulrick, whom he still continued to regard as his father's murderer, had been so singularly removed from prison.

" Patience, young man ! " replied Herbert. " Is the thirst of blood so strong within thee, thou canst not wait an hour ? Fear not but the accused will appear ; my word shall be your gage that he will meet you."

The young earl bowed respectfully, and pointed to the chair at the end of the daïs for the bishop to take his seat.

" Not so," he said, in answer to the mute invitation ; " there is one amongst us to whom all claims must yield. " Prince," he added, turning to the stranger, " assume your seat, and let us to the affairs of moment which detain us."

The appearance of the Conqueror's favourite son produced a varied feeling in the minds of the assembly. By the Normans he was greeted with a shout of triumph ; by the Saxons he was received in sullen silence. They felt that they were betrayed—that the last hope of shaking off the Conqueror's yoke was lost.

" Venerable prelate, and you, noble peers," said the prince, as soon as he was seated, " our first duty is to inquire into the cause of the death of our faithful friend, Hugh de Bigod, to avenge his memory, to track the murderer's steps, if living ; if dead, to consign his name to infamy and execration. Who are the accusers ? "

" I am," exclaimed Mirvan, eagerly advancing.

" And I," calmly repeated the bishop.

" But whom do you accuse ? " demanded the prince, first addressing himself to Mirvan.

" The man whom I once called my dearest friend ; the man I would have trusted with more than my life—with honour ; the man whose soul I once held so pure—I almost blushed at my unworthiness to call him friend—Ulrick, of what race I know not, but proved by the word of a noble knight, now absent, to be of gentle blood— Ulrick, the ward of my lord bishop there," he added, pointing half-

scornfully to the prelate, " whose word e'en now, I pray you all
remember, was given for his appearance in the lists to meet the
charge against him."

" Fear not, sir earl," interrupted Edda, proudly, " but he will
keep his word."

" And you, my lord, whom do you accuse ? " demanded William,
addressing Herbert de Lozenga, whose countenance had never varied
during Mirvan's speech.

" Herman of the Burg," he calmly replied.

Several of the Saxons started, for they knew by whose hand the
deceased earl had fallen ; indeed, the murderer had avowed it to
more than one or two ; but on Mirvan the accusation fell like a
thunder-clap. 'Tis true that from his rough, unamiable manner, he
had never liked his kinsman, but he had ever looked upon him as a
man of unblemished honour, and as such would have defended his
reputation with his life. His indignation, therefore, at the accusation
was as unbounded as his astonishment, in which latter sentiment
the Norman nobles, great as was their dislike to Herman, shared.

" Prince," he exclaimed, " this is a mere mockery of justice ; the
accused retorts on his accuser. I dare not further trust myself to
speak, lest I forget the reverence due to age, to sacred function,
and this royal presence ; but ask him, pray ask him, upon what
grounds he dares accuse my absent kinsman."

" You hear," interrogatively observed the prince ; " on what proofs
do you accuse him ? "

" On his own confession," solemnly answered the bishop, "witnessed
by these noble peers."

" His own confession ! " mechanically repeated the young earl, as
if doubting the evidence of his senses.

" Thyself shalt be the judge," continued the prelate, drawing from
his breast the parchment which had been found in the breastplate
of the unhappy Ernulf, and which our readers will doubtless
remember had been attested by the signatures and seals of Odo of
Caen and the Norman nobles on the night of Herman's execution.
The document, which detailed every circumstance, had been written
by the murderer, and given to his esquire, to convey to the assembled
franklins in the caves of Whitlingham, as a still further proof of his
devotion to the cause of Saxon independence. Every word was in
his own handwriting, which Mirvan was well acquainted with, and
witnessed by his arms.

" What have I read ? " exclaimed the astonished and horror-stricken
youth, as he let fall the scroll. " If this be true, as I confess it is, I
am indeed doubly unhappy. I have lost my father, and have
wronged my friend."

" That word regains him," exclaimed Ulrick, who, on a signal
given by Herbert de Lozenga, entered the hall, and advanced
gracefully to his accuser. " Mirvan," he added, "my heart hath

never done thee wrong ; e'en in my dungeon I accused not thee ; e'en at the scaffold had not cursed thy name."

A tear dimmed the eyes of the two friends as they embraced. Let not the worldling sneer at the confession of their weakness. Such weakness is more beautiful than strength. Earth hath many a gem more prized, but none more pure than manly friendship's honest, priceless tear.

" But where," exclaimed Mirvan, " is the fiend who hath deceived me, whose hand is stained with my dead father's blood ? Prince and nobles," he added, turning towards the daïs, "I demand on Herman of the Burg the judgment of his peers. The felon hath confessed. The doom, the doom ! I claim the murderer's doom !"

" Herman," solemnly answered the bishop, at the same time taking the speaker by the hand, and leading him to the window, " can fear no human judgment more ; he hath already passed a tribunal more awful far than man's. Behold !" One of the men-at-arms threw open the window as the prelate spoke, and Mirvan beheld, with surprise, the executioner in the act of affixing the head of the assassin on the post in the centre of the lists. For a moment he gazed upon it with a feeling of fierce satisfaction, which gradually yielded to a nobler sentiment ; he felt that human justice was accomplished, and shudderingly withdrew from the hideous spectacle as the soldier closed the casement. The effect upon the assembled Saxons was to produce consternation and dismay. Ignorant of the real cause of the culprit's death, they felt convinced they were betrayed, and slowly began to disperse, too happy in being permitted to escape. The Normans suffered their departure unopposed—such were the instructions they had received ; but the leaders of the contemplated insurrection were not so fortunate ; they still remained virtually prisoners in the castle. Shortly afterwards, the countess, Matilda, and Isabel entered the hall ; and as the subject of Ulrick's birth was gone into, it is unnecessary to repeat the proofs by which his rank and claim to Stanfield and the vast inheritance of Edda were established ; even the Normans confessed themselves satisfied, and frankly admitted him as their peer amongst them. If the heart of the acknowledged youth beat high, it was when his eyes encountered the blushing cheek of Matilda ; if he felt the sentiment of pride, it was when he grasped the hand of his recovered friend, and felt that he could claim his friendship upon equal terms.

Herbert de Lozenga approached the seat of the young prince, and whispered to him—

" Your promise, prince ! your promise !"

William turned uneasily upon his chair, like a man who sought to escape from something distasteful to him, but in vain ; the calm, cold eye of the bishop followed his every glance ; he felt that there was no escape from his plighted word.

" Herald," he said, " perform your duty."

The officer advanced into the midst of the hall, and thrice proclaimed Ulrick Earl of Stanfield, and heir of the Saxon Edda ; calling upon all who felt disposed to dispute his claims to stand forth and speak, or remain for ever dumb ! No voice replied to him. At each pause in the ceremony the prince cast a scrutinising glance on the young earl, whom the decision stripped of a fair portion of his large inheritance ; but the heart of Mirvan was too generous to entertain any selfish feeling. William, therefore, had no choice left but to proceed.

The prelate and Edda led the newly-acknowledged noble to the prince's chair ; who, taking his hands between his own, received his oath of allegiance ; and solemnly confirmed, as regent of the kingdom, and his father's representative, the act of investiture ; the prelate, as he did so, pronouncing aloud "Amen ! "

"And now, Saxons and Normans," exclaimed William, "a few words with each. To you," he said, turning to the discouraged franklins, "your plots are known ; your treasons all unveiled ; you are here within our judgment-hall, surrounded by our faithful barons and our loyal troops ; the block within the lists ; the headsman ready at our call. What ransom can ye offer for your lives ? "

There was a silence ; the Normans gazed sternly upon their rivals, who felt that they were powerless within their hands ; and each internally cursed bitterly the memory of him by whom they had been deluded to their ruin.

The prince enjoyed their confusion, for he was no generous enemy, and again demanded, in a tone of taunting mockery, which displayed the natural cruelty of his disposition, and augured ill for the future—

"What ransom, Saxons, for your lives ? "

"Thy princely word," exclaimed the bishop, anxious to end the scene.

"And your intercession, my good lord," continued William, recalled by the grave tone of the speaker's voice to the prudence of conciliating the conquered race, as a means to his own accession to the Throne. "Franklins," he added, "you are pardoned ; your forfeit lands and lives are spared upon the payment of such fines as we hereafter shall impose. But remember, 'tis the last time that Mercy speaks ; be wiser for the future, and tempt the lion's wrath no more, lest he should turn and rend ye."

"And for the future," said Herbert de Lozenga, advancing to the centre of the hall, "let discord end between the Norman and Saxon race ; let hostile blood unite to heal the wounds which long have drained this war-divided land. Lady," he added, advancing and taking Matilda by the hand, "this is a bond would prove a pledge of unity more strong than Saxon force or Norman steel could break —a bond of peace and love. Read I aright that blush ? "

Matilda turned from the impassioned gaze of her lover, who looked as if life and death hung upon her reply, to read her brother's will, whose consent alone could ratify her union.

The generous Mirvan knew too well his sister's heart not to interpret its unspoken wishes. First embracing Ulrick, he led him to the prelate, saying as he did so—

"Father, thy wisdom interprets our unspoken wishes ; complete thy holy purpose."

"Thus, then," resumed the prelate ; "I do betroth ye. May Heaven bless the union of two hearts formed by their virtues for each other."

Devoutly did the countess and the venerable Edda join in the benediction upon the last descendant of their ancient race ; and every voice within the hall, *save one*, joined in the shout, "Hail to the Lord of Stanfield ! Hail to his promised bride !"

   *   *   *   *   *

On the evening of the important day on which the scenes we have endeavoured to describe took place, William had retired to his chamber in the castle, for he had become the guest of the unsuspicious earl, and was arraying himself for the approaching banquet.

Robert of Artois, who had long been in his confidence, was standing near a table, covered with open caskets full of jewel-work, and which supported the rude mirror in which the prince was complacently contemplating his person—for, like most plain men, he was excessively vain. His hasty, snatchy manner showed that he was either discontented or ill at ease—his companion could not tell which, but waited patiently for the enigma he had undoubtedly been summoned to hear.

"Normans !" muttered the prince, "Normans ! We are no longer worthy of the name. The hound hath changed places with the deer ! We raise the head we ought to tread on ! Ah, Robert," he added, pretending to see his companion for the first time, "what thinkest thou of this goodly marriage, this coupling of the carrion raven with the generous falcon's blood ? We had better all turn Capuchin, and preach on Christian charity. Our swords are useless now, unless we turn them into hooks to reap with. We shall soon, good Robert, be no longer masters in the land we won."

"Not if your highness wishes to prevent the knot the holy bishop fancies he has tied. Norman hearts and hands may still be found asking no better warrant for the deed than the expression of your royal will. Speak but the word, and it is done."

"Sayest thou ?" said William, turning suddenly round, and fixing a scrutinising glance upon him, as if to read his very soul ; for long habit of dissimulation in himself had taught him to suspect the sincerity of others. The ambitious noble met his gaze, and in an instant they understood each other, so prompt is the intelligence of guilt. "But how to be accomplished?" demanded the prince, leading him to propose the crime he feared to ask him.

"Remove the bridegroom," coolly answered his companion; "that were the easiest way to solve the riddle."

"No; that were dangerous. Let the clown mate him with some Saxon wench, and hold his lands in peace—at least," he added, "for the present. Lozenga loves him like a son, and I have no wish to play my future sceptre against his pastoral staff. His is a temper not to be trifled with. Wouldst thou believe it, Robert? The proud priest threatened that he would send me to my half-witted brother if I presumed to cross his path again; nay, dared to vaunt his vassal line as equal to my own."

"The ambitious traitor!" exclaimed Robert of Artois; "he must be silenced. Such men are dangerous."

"Let him rest; he is as much beyond our reach as Ulrick is beneath it. The prelate and myself, we understand each other. Whilst I act with what he is pleased to call justice and conciliation, he will not oppose our father's disposition in our favour. Let me but once securely feel the crown upon my brow, fear not but I will reckon with him fully for this day. The dotard dreamt not that, with every threat, he aimed an arrow at my brother's life—curse on the chance which made him born before me!"

"Why not, then, secure the bride?" demanded the ready panderer, who more than suspected the cause of the speaker's humour, well knowing how susceptible he was to the thrall of beauty, and how reckless by what means he gratified his licentious passions.

"Thou hast hit my very thought," said the prince, with a smile of approbation; "but how may this be done?"

"Nothing more easy."

"Explain thyself."

"This very night the noble maidens propose to attend our Lady's shrine, where prayers are nightly offered up for the repose of Earl de Bigod's soul. They are too coy to grace your highness's banquet with their presence. What if some able fowler spread the net, and cage the birds on their return?"

"Where to find such a friend?"

"I'll be that friend," replied Robert. "Your highness knows that I would peril body as well as soul to serve your pleasures. My castle at Filby is but three hours' ride; it hath ere now contained as fair a prize as these sweet piping dames. Besides," he added, "the distance is so short you might yourself visit my stronghold, whenever charity inclined your heart to solace the lone captive."

A smile of mutual understanding followed, and the prince and his unworthy favourite separated; the former to lavish hollow courtesies where he meditated the foulest wrong; the latter to arrange the treacherous snare in which he hoped to entangle the unguarded steps of trusting innocence.

The banquet, after the fashion of the times, waxed rough and boisterous in the hall of the old castle. Never had the fickle William seemed in a more gracious mood ; twice had he pledged to the union of Ulrick and Matilda in the circling cup, calling on Saxon and Norman hearts to join him in the toast. All were fascinated with his open manner and seeming sincerity ; and all, save one, deceived by them. Herbert de Lozenga had watched his impassioned glances when he beheld Matilda in the hall—the look which followed her retiring footsteps ; and, although he anticipated no attempt at outrage, he determined to have an eye upon him. As the banquet proceeded, his suspicions were still further strengthened by the look of triumph which flashed from his fierce eye whenever the maiden's name became the theme of conversation.

Amongst the minstrels who occupied the gallery opposite the daïs, was Hella, the Saxon—admitted by all who loved the joyous science to be the chief of the all but extinct bardic tribe. Many doubted, indeed, if he were even Christian, so devoted did he appear to the old superstitions and traditions of his race, so intense was his hatred of the conquerors. It had needed all the eloquence of Edda, whom he venerated as one of the last who shared in the blood of Hengist, to induce him to be present at the banquet ; nor was it till after he had been repeatedly called for that he descended into the hall with his magic harp to sing before the assembly. So great was his renown, so intense the expectation of the Normans, few of whom had ever heard his song, that even the voices of the noisiest were hushed ere the gifted strain broke forth—

> "What spell can consecrate the sword ?
> Not priestly prayer, or kingly word ;
> Nor e'en the deeper spell which lies
> In woman's wondrous, sunlit eyes ;
> No ! nor the minstrel's verse of flame,
> A nation's shout, the breath of fame,
> Can yet the holy spell afford
> To consecrate the warrior's sword.
>
> "But when drawn for broken laws,
> In nature's right he sternly draws,
> When liberty expiring cries,
> And wrongs from hill and valley rise,
> The blood by tyrants rudely shed,
> A nation's tears for freedom fled,
> These, these the holy spell afford
> To consecrate the warrior's sword."

The few Saxons who were present hung their heads in shame ; to them it was like the song of their captivity. The Normans heard the strain in gloomy silence ; it sounded like a reproach upon their tyranny and misrule.

"Thou hast chosen a strange theme for our banquet, friend!" exclaimed the prince ; "but though our ears are nice, thy skill must not go unrewarded."

He took from his neck a chain of gold, of no great value, and sent it by his page to the aged bard, who received it with a courtly reverence, although he answered with a mocking tongue—

"The praise of princes is our noblest guerdon. Gentle page, it must not be said that Hella was ungrateful to the bearer of so precious a gift ; wear this," he added, taking from his own neck a chain whose value more than doubled the Norman's, and which he hung carelessly round the neck of the youth ; "and sometimes think upon the poor bard's gift." So saying, he directed his harp-bearer to take up the instrument, and with a stately step left the hall.

At a signal from the bishop, the Norman minstrels sang the praise of Rolla, and the glories of his race ; the nobles listening to the exciting strain, and in their enthusiasm forgot the aged Saxon and his song.

For the third time, with a flushed brow, William arose from his seat to give forth the hollow pledge of amity and peace ; when an alarm was heard without, and the seneschal, bleeding and unhelmed, rushed into the midst of the assembly. All started at the sight, and the hand of many a knight was laid upon his sword.

"Speak," demanded the bishop ; "what has befallen ? "

"To arms, nobles and knights!" exclaimed the faithful officer. "Returning from the cathedral, the noble ladies, Isabel and Matilda, have been carried off ; their escort was too feeble to protect them."

The eyes of Mirvan and Ulrick remained riveted upon the speaker, as if they scarcely comprehended the intelligence, so completely were they stunned by the blow. The prelate's searching glance was fixed upon the prince, who quailed beneath it.

"Doubtless by Saxons," he stammered.

"By Normans, noble prince—by Normans ! I knew too well the taste of Norman steel to be deceived, despite their Saxon dress. I'll swear their brands were Norman."

William scowled upon the officer with a look of hate. The sturdy soldier, conscious of his integrity, met his gaze unmoved. While the nobles were busy in consultation, Herbert de Lozenga drew the commander of his troops, George of Erpingham, aside, and whispered something in his ear. Whatever was the nature of the communication, it evidently surprised the stalwart knight, for, for the first time in his life, he hesitated to obey. The rapid conversation which followed removed, however, his objections ; for, touching his sword, in sign of fidelity, he withdrew. The bishop, instead of following his example, concealed himself behind the floating arras, with which the walls of the banquet-hall were hung. At the same moment Hella, the bard, entered the assembly, and approaching Ulrick with a stately step, exclaimed—

" Thy sword ! thy sword ! The wolf is in thy fold ! The vulture
bears the trembling dove to its dark nest ! Last of a race I love !
why standest thou idly here ?—to horse ! Let manly deeds answer
unmanly outrage ! Strike for thy country's wrongs, thy outraged
love, or see thy bride become the Norman's scorn ! "

All the nobles present, Saxons as well as Normans, deeply felt
the outrage, and rushed into the chamber, calling to arms as they
did so ; the alarm bell sent forth its deep, loud note, and added to
the horror of the scene. The treacherous prince, the contriver of
the cruel scheme, paced the rush-strewn floor, triumphant in his
villainy, and, as he thought, alone. His meditations were soon
interrupted by Robert of Artois, who, having succeeded in his
expedition, had thrown off his disguise, and returned to the castle,
lest his absence should be remarked ; leaving his followers, long
accustomed to such deeds of violence, to conduct the prisoners to
his stronghold of Filby.

" Thou art a bold falconer," whispered the prince ; " thou hast
struck quarry fairly. Hadst thou silenced yon prating seneschal, all
had been unsuspected. Despite your followers' disguise, he swears
they are Normans."

" Let him swear ; oaths cannot harm us, prince. I must away to
join in the pursuit, lest I should be suspected. In the morning
take your departure as if for London. Once beyond the city,
dismiss your train, and turn your horse's head to Filby, where thou
wilt find the sweetest bird that ever pined within its iron cage.
Thou knowest the way to tame her."

With these words the ready panderer bowed and withdrew.
William was about to follow his example when the prelate, quitting
his concealment, boldly confronted him. The tyrant saw in an
instant that he was discovered. For a few moments they stood
gazing on each other—the countenance of the prince pale with fear
and confusion, that of the bishop full of contempt.

" So," exclaimed the latter, " this is the way thy royal word is
kept ! Thou hast broken thine oath, outraged the roof which
shelters thee, risked plunging the land in civil war, to gratify thy
passions. What prevents that I proclaim thy treason, and yield
thee to the Saxons ? "

" Thine own ambition, priest," doggedly answered William.

" My ambition ! "

" Once a king, thou knowest this hand can raise thee to a height
but second to my own—the primate's envied throne."

" Vain man !" replied Herbert, " the hermit's cell would please
me better than the mitred stall. Power is worthless when the heart
is ashes. I came not to implore, but to command thee. Resign
thy victims, and I may consent once more to spare thee the brand
of public scorn—to shield thee from the avenging swords of those
whose honour thou wouldst stain. Decide ! "

"Never!" exclaimed the prince, foaming with rage. "I love the fair Matilda, and rather would forego the Crown itself than yield her beauties to thy favoured minion. Thou hast heard my answer."

"But mine is yet unspoken," as proudly replied the bishop. "For thy brave father's sake I would have spared thee; but now the will of Heaven and justice must be done."

He advanced towards the doors which opened from the banquet hall, as if to quit the apartment or to summon aid.

The baffled tyrant, perceiving his design, threw himself between, and drawing his sword, held it levelled at the prelate's breast, to impede his departure. For a moment they stood like the stag and hound at bay, gazing on each other in silence—the churchman calm and stern, the prince trembling with passion and excitement. "You pass not on your life!" he cried.

"Advance one step," said Herbert, drawing up his person to its stately height, "lay but a finger on my sacred robe, and I will bind thee in a spell shall paralyse thy soul! Not to thy honour or thy sense of justice do I now appeal. Thou lost to every tie of honour and humanity, thy terrors are my safety. The brand of Europe and the Church's curse thou darest not meet. Fool!—coward—villain!" he added, as the sword of William gradually inclined towards the ground. "I scorn, deride thy vain attempt. Back, ruffian, back—I pass thee or I perish!"

With his eye sternly fixed upon the prince, the prelate moved towards the door. Thrice the weapon was raised, but its point was as often turned aside when the glance of Herbert de Lozenga encountered his. With frantic rage, he dashed it to the ground, muttering as he did so—

"'Tis true; I dare not take thy life."

William had already determined in his own mind the line of conduct to pursue. Once freed from his accuser's presence, he would mount his horse and ride to Filby. There he doubted not but he might defy the outraged lovers and their friends; for what Norman chief would march against him when once the royal banner was displayed? Herbert knew too well the risk to Matilda's honour to leave him even for a moment alone. Advancing to the door, he merely waved his hand, when George of Erpingham and a body of about sixty men, all completely armed, and wearing their visors down, entered the banquet hall. William trembled at the sight, and involuntarily looked around to find his sword.

"Wouldst murder me?" he cried, glaring on the prelate.

The bishop deigned not to reply, but addressing himself to George of Erpingham, who awaited his orders, said—

"Danger and treason are abroad. His highness goes to my poor palace; escort him thither with all due honour; let none approach him, or exchange a single word. I rely on thy fidelity and knightly faith in this."

[MATILDA PROTECTING ISABEL FROM ROBERT OF ARTOIS.]

K

"Traitors!" exclaimed William, "know ye not who I am? Dearly shall ye rue this outrage on your prince! Rather arrest yon plotting priest! Obey my orders, and I swear, e'en by my honour, that riches, favours beyond ambition's dreams, shall recompense the deed!"

"Honour!" interrupted Herbert, contemptuously; "does not the word blister thy tongue, palsy thy craven heart? The violator of innocence, the perjurer, and the robber dares talk of honour! Prince, spare thy eloquence; thou canst not corrupt thy guard; they speak no Norman tongue. Away with him!"

"Should he resist?" demanded Erpingham, through his visor.

"Force must be employed."

"Should he escape?"

The bishop fixed his glance upon the prisoner, and paused ere he replied, wishing the import of his speech to be truly understood.

"Level thine arquebus, and strike him dead."

With these last words he quitted the apartment; and William, seeing that resistance was in vain, resigned himself to his fate. His guards closed around him, and conducted him to the bottom of the staircase, where a close litter was in waiting. For an instant he hesitated, and looked around, as if to summon assistance. None appeared; and the few torches held by the soldiers showed him the arquebus in the hands of the mysterious knight.

Inwardly cursing his fate, and the being who had crossed it, he entered the litter, and in less than an hour found himself a close prisoner in the loftiest tower of the bishop's palace.

CHAPTER IX.

ON their arrival at Filby the fair captives were conducted to a strongly-barred chamber, in the centre of the keep, and left by their ruffian captors to themselves. For a while they sat on the rude couch—the only attempt at comfort in their prison—in speechless dismay. So sudden was the transition from happiness to despair, that both were equally stunned by the blow. To all their entreaties for an explanation, and tempting offers for freedom, their conductors had maintained a sullen silence, and imagination conjured up a thousand terrors more fearful than even the dark reality of their fate.

Isabel, from the natural buoyancy of her disposition, was the first to recover something like composure. "Do not weep, coz—do not weep," she exclaimed, endeavouring to soothe the wretched Matilda,

K 2

who sat beside her, clasping her hand in hers. "Perhaps we are only captured for the sake of extorting ransom ; we are no village maidens, to be spirited from our homes without an effort being made to succour us. Many a lance ere this is laid in rest, and many a pennon given to the winds. Ulrick and Mirvan will search the world but they will find us ; nor will Odo of Caen tenderly bear this insult to the sister of his affianced bride. Trust me, that many an hour of future joy will well repay us for the present hour. Dearly the Saxon ruffians shall repent this insult ! "

" These are no Saxon outlaws," replied Matilda, struggling for firmness as she spoke ; " but Normans, girl. This blow is struck by those of our own race. Didst thou not mark the armour of the knight who headed the foul enterprise ? "

" Normans ! sayst thou, coz ? Impossible ! they must be Saxons ; who else would dare assail De Bigod's daughter ? "

Matilda mournfully shook her head in token of denial. Accustomed from infancy to the military peculiarities which distinguished the two races, her practised eye was not to be deceived ; she had recognised the Norman chief in Robert of Artois, despite his simple visor and disguise, and could not root the strong conviction from her soul.

" Normans ! " again iterated Isabel ; " what can be their motive—plunder or revenge ? "

" Whom have we ever wronged, to provoke the latter ? " said Matilda. " And who would dare avow the lass'ness of an act like this, by demanding of Ulrick or my brother ransom for their brides ? No," she added bitterly ; " I fear worse outrage yet."

Isabel bounded from her seat like the fawn startled by the hunter's step. Her cousin's words revealed a danger more fearful than her terrors had yet painted ; but her courage rose with the peril : indignation filled her heart ; and although her cheek was pale, insulted virtue flashed from her speaking eyes.

" Let not the ruffian leader of this enterprise hope to find in a daughter of my race," she cried, " a reed, whom the storm of violence can bend, or captivity appal ; there is a refuge which even insult must respect, and vice cannot approach."

" True," replied Matilda ; " death—honour's last shield, and virtue's sure defence."

The word sounded dismally in the vast and dimly lighted chamber where they sat. It was evident, from the preparations made to receive them, that they were expected, for a coarse repast had been prepared, mingled, however, with some degree of luxury ; for although the viands were of the plainest description, the flagons and drinking cups were of silver, then only used in the monasteries and castles of the nobles.

" Stay," said Isabel, whose eye had been mechanically resting on the ill-assorted banquet, and who, struck by a sudden idea, advanced towards the table, "this may, perchance, afford some clue to our vile gaoler's name." She caught up the massive flagon as she spoke, and advanced with it to one of the torches stuck in an iron sconce upon the wall. The light fell upon a shield rudely graved upon the precious metal ; its blazon was a bend ingrailed, surmounted by a lion's head. Both started as they gazed upon it, for they recognised at once the well-known arms of Robert of Artois. To Isabel of Bayeux this was an additional cause of fear, for she well knew the desperate character of the bad man who bore it. Twice had she rejected his unwelcome suit ; the last time with a contempt she well knew had deeply stung his pride. Rather would she have found herself the captive of the vilest chief who lived by petty plunder than in the power of that bold, revengeful man.

"Matilda," she cried, clinging to her cousin, and giving way to her not unnatural terrors ; "thou hast read the fearful mystery aright ; these are no Saxon plunderers ; ransom is not their object, for twice hath Robert of Artois dared to pollute my ear with his false tale of love. But I am rightly served," she added bitterly. "Why did I not unfold his insolence to those who would have crushed the hateful serpent ere it had twined its venomed folds around me ?"

It was now Matilda's turn to soothe her affrighted cousin, whom the discovery of her captor's name had quite unnerved ; like most persons of a quiet and retiring nature, she possessed that latent courage which rises with the danger of occasion, and in the deep recesses of her innocent heart she found a strength where late was nought but timidity and weakness.

"Courage, courage," she cried, repressing her own tears, to assuage her companion's, "all hope hath not yet abandoned us ; though, human eyes may fail to penetrate our prison, the eye of Heaven is on us, and doubt not, coz, but our guardian angels watch us even here. Soon may my brother's banner circle round these walls, and lay their towers in the dust. Mirvan will come and find thee."

"Dead !" said Isabel, interrupting her ; "for if he come not soon, terror too sure will kill me. Matilda," she added, throwing her arms suddenly round her cousin's neck, "by our girlish friendship, our sister love, the tie of blood between us, promise me one thing, or my brain will turn, and reason totter on her seated throne."

"Name it, dearest girl."

"Let not the ruffian tear us from each other ; while with thee, I can endure his threats ; alone, I should go mad. Thou," she added, passionately, "canst have nought to fear ; I am alone the victim. Had not thy ill-starred fortune held thee to my side, thou hadst escaped this last extreme of fate. 'Tis I who have undone thee. Wilt thou not promise me ?"

"I will," replied Matilda, willing to soothe her ; "nothing but violence shall tear thee from me. Should force be used ?"

" Kill me," exclaimed Isabel ; "arm thine hand with Roman courage, and strike me dead before thee. By thy brother's love, thine own unsullied purity of soul, thy house's honour, and thy virgin truth, pledge me to this."

There was a mutual pause ; Matilda eyed the no longer trembling girl, who stood erect before her, and read the sincerity of her request in her firm glance and look of almost prayer. The request was terrible to one of her gentle nature—terrible from the love she bore the tender victim—terrible from the danger which surrounded them.

Calmly she advanced from the couch on which they both had been seated towards the table, and taking up a small, sharp knife, concealed it in her bosom. Isabel saw the action and understood it. A slight flush suffused her pallid cheek, but passed as quickly as it came ; her only comment was a kiss upon the brow of the heroic girl. Matilda understood it.

" It is, indeed, a terrible and last resort," she said ; " but should all else fail, I will be near thee ; fear not, Isabel, by our mutual love, living, the villain's arms shall never clasp thee."

The exhausted girl, overpowered by the violence of her emotions, sank into the arms of her courageous cousin, in whose promise she beheld her last resource against dishonour or a life of misery.

* * * * *

The same night Herbert de Lozenga was seated in his oratory. He had much to reflect upon, for his own position was not without considerable danger. In arresting the person of his monarch's favourite son, and probably future sovereign, he had irretrievably committed himself with that bold, bad man, whose cruel nature never forgave an injury or a slight. But still he quailed not ; personal consideration had never yet influenced him in the path of duty, and he was determined to pursue it, regardless of all consequence to himself. Ulrick's happiness was dearer to him than his life, and he resolved at all hazards to secure it.

It was necessary, therefore, that his dangerous prisoner should be securely watched ; and he determined to trust his guardianship to Walter Tyrrel, a young knight who had long been attached to his service, and over whose birth, like Ulrick's, a cloud of mystery hung.

In the age at which we write, it was by no means uncommon for the great nobles and prelates to attach to their households esquires and knights of gentle birth, who were trained to arms or letters, as their respective tastes or inclinations might incline them. Raising his silver call, he summoned a lay brother to his presence, and directed him to find the youthful knight in question.

" Yes ! " he exclaimed, " Tyrrel will be his surest guard. The youth whom he would deprive of his inheritance, whose life long ere this he would have taken had he but dreamt of his existence.

Poor boy ! " he added ; "cruelly he crossed thy sainted mother's path. May he prove less dangerous to her son."

The young knight entered the oratory as he concluded, flattered by the unusual confidence, for he was not only ambitious in his nature, but reckless in the means by which he advanced his fortunes. From his cold and selfish nature, the prelate had never loved him ; still he was far from suspecting the deep treachery and heartless vices which his calculation hid from even his observance. Perhaps the kind man's heart was too full of love for his first *protégé* to interest him deeply in the second ; for Ulrick was to him even as a son.

" Tyrrel," said the bishop, " I am about to bestow on thee a mark of confidence—the precursor, chance, of future favour. Thou art not ignorant that I have an inmate here—something between a guest and a prisoner."

" I am aware," answered Sir Walter ; " my leader, Sir George of Erpingham, told me as much when he arrived."

" Know you his rank ? "

" I guess it, my good lord."

" Then you must know how necessary 'tis that unusual ward be kept. To you I confide the custody of his person ; guard him with all honour, but as strictly as you would watch your mother's fame and own inheritance. Perhaps," he added, with a smile, " you may one day thank me for his capture, and the trust I now repose in you. You know where he is lodged ? "

" In the eastern tower, beyond the cloisters. He must be skilled indeed who could break prison there."

" Go," continued the prelate, at the same time giving him a ring. " George of Erpingham, on the sight of this, will resign his post ; send him to me, for I have further employment for his zeal. Remember, young man, those who would gain my confidence must win it by fidelity and honour. Farewell."

Walter Tyrrel quitted the oratory with a gratified air, which resulted less from pride in the confidence reposed in him, than the conviction that it was something which might be turned to his own advantage and aggrandisement, before which honour and breach of trust were idle names. Besides, he never loved the prelate. He had long been jealous of his partiality for Ulrick, whose elevation galled him, and whose agony, on the abduction of his bride, he had seen with secret pleasure. The opportunity of thwarting them was too tempting to be thrown away.

" My lord bishop plays a daring game," he muttered, as he directed his steps towards the tower where Prince William was confined ; " others, perchance, may play as bold a one. 'Tis not the first time both gaoler and captive have been missing. If the Red Norman bid but high enough, the path to liberty lays straight before him. I will not baulk my fortune."

So saying, the newly-appointed guard entered the chamber in the lower basement of the tower, where George of Erpingham and a company of his men were keeping watch. At the sight of the prelate's signet the brave old soldier resigned the command to the treacherous knight, and withdrew to his own quarters, to remove his armour, ere he sought the bishop. Herbert de Lozenga had not been long alone when the lay brother whom he had despatched in search of Tyrrel returned to inform him that a pilgrim from Normandy was at the gate, and demanded to speak with him.

"Not now," replied the superior; "not now. My mind is occupied by thoughts of too much moment. Give him hospitality for the night ; in the morning I will see him. Tell him this, and speak him welcome in my name."

"I told him so," replied the old monk. "I told him so ; but he was obstinate, called me a prating dotard, and swore by Rollo that he would see you, holy father, ere he slept ; then called for wine, and ordered Father Felix to bring him a manchet, as if he were in an hotel, instead of a community of Christian priests."

"Quick," exclaimed Herbert, starting from his seat, "conduct him to our presence instantly. If it be as I suspect," he murmured, after the old man quitted the oratory, astonished at the vehemence of his superior's manner, "the game is in my hands, and Ulrick, wronged boy, the tyrant shall himself restore to thee thy bride, or pay his crimes with forfeit of his crown."

The moment the lay brother ushered in the stranger, Herbert de Lozenga recognised, despite his disguise, the eldest son of the Conqueror, whose fate has been the theme of many a minstrel's song ; who, born to inherit a crown, passed the greater portion of his life within a prison ; whose courage was always rendered useless by his recklessness, and who consoled himself for the loss of liberty and power by the wine-cup and the song.

"Prince, in the name of every saint. what brings you to this land," said the ecclesiastic, "where your path is beset with perils ? Know you not that your father hath decided to bestow England on your brother William, leave you, as eldest born, the ancient fief of Normandy, and that many of the nobles approve this disposition of the crown ?"

"Hang the crown," replied the impetuous Robert; "if England boasts no better wine than the lean draught your cellarer set before me, William may govern it for me ; but, perhaps," he added, bursting into a jocose laugh, "where the charity is large the wine is weak. I'll wager a hundred pieces, my good lord, none of the same vintage ever graced your table : were the fat and pious brother who served me to drink no other until Easter, he would require a few yards less of broad-cloth in his frock."

"The draught shall be amended, prince," said Herbert; "but answer me my question : what brings you here ? "

"Caprice! Caprice! the whim of an heir who rides over his estate *incog.*, while its possessor recites his last *Confiteor.* Our father keeps his Court at Rouen ; but we know, from a sure hand, his health breaks fast. Like the dying bear, 'tis dangerous to approach him ; he hath already hanged two physicians, and engaged a third, an unbelieving Jew."

"What is his malady?" demanded Herbert de Lozenga, anxiously, for he foresaw the conflict which would probably follow the Conqueror's death.

"The same which ails your wine," replied the prince, with a heartless laugh ; "he hath too much water in his barrel. The French king asked when his vassal brother would be brought to bed : 'twas a good jest, but must be dearly paid."

"How so?"

"Our choleric father swore to be churched in Nôtre Dame, with twenty thousand lances in his train. He is the man at least to keep his word ; he hath already wasted the Seine with fire and sword, as first-fruits of his oath."

"And for a jest," exclaimed the bishop, "an idle jest, spoken in an hour of mirth, when wine had tempted reason, and the unguarded lips utter the wayward fancies of the brain, blood must be shed, houses desolated, cities destroyed, and kind hearts broken! Earth! earth!" he added mournfully, "such are thy rulers!"

"Earth soon will count one more and less," interrupted Robert, who contemplated his father's approaching death with anything but dissatisfaction ; indeed, the conduct of the former had been sufficiently harsh towards him to break all tie of blood between them. He had thwarted him in his dearest wish ; and, urged by his partiality for the unworthy William, would have stripped his elder son even of his inheritance of Normandy, had not the consent of the King of France, as suzerain, been necessary—a consent, he well knew, it would be hopeless to solicit, the policy of the French Court being to disunite the Crowns of England and Normandy : their descending on one head rendered the ducal vassal more powerful than his master.

"Prince," said Herbert, gravely, "Heaven only knows whether thou art come for good or evil ; but thou art come in an eventful hour—thy brother is an inmate of my palace."

Robert heard the information with evident surprise, and for a moment eyed the speaker keenly, as if to read his very heart. The examination was apparently satisfactory ; for he almost instantly resumed his former expression of careless confidence, and demanded, as if it were the most important circumstance in the world to him—

"A guest?"

"No," gravely answered his host..

"A prisoner?"

"Yes."

The prince's reply was a loud, careless laugh ; the jest seemed to strike him more than the advantage to be drawn from it, so contradictory was his character : at one moment all energy, at the next indifference to everything ; capable of conceiving a bold design, but wanting the perseverance to insure success. Well had his mother, the Queen Matilda, designated him as the weathercock of impulse and of—folly she might have added, and of fortune also.

"And so you have caged the wolf," he cried—"or rather the fox, I should say, designating our royal brother from the colour of his hair. Leave a priest alone to bait a snare ! How fell he into it?"

"Prince," answered Herbert, with offended dignity, "I am not one of those who traffic in pitfalls or in snares. Your brother is my prisoner, to answer for a cruel outrage on a maiden's liberty ; openly I arrested him, openly I'll guard him, till the outrage is atoned and the lady free. But come," he added, "the time is dark with import, and I have matter which concerns you deeply. Lay for a while that reckless levity of heart aside, and let us speak like men who watch the game of life."

"Willingly, my lord," replied the prince, brought to something like seriousness by the prelate's tone ; "but answer me first one question—the boy whom I confided to your care—speak—lives he yet?—and may I not behold him ?"

"He does. His training hath not shamed his birth. Fifteen months are passed since the sword of my good lord of Kent hath dubbed him knight ; he hath remained ever since attached to our Court ; e'en now he guards my prisoner in his tower."

A singular smile, half of mischief and half fun, passed over the still handsome features of the Norman prince at the intelligence, but it soon passed away ; and motioning to the prelate to precede him, he followed to a small recess at the back of the oratory, where we will leave them to converse on business of deep import, the result of which may soon become apparent to our readers.

     *   *   *   *   *

The first beams of the rising sun had already tinged the east with gold, and gilded the graceful spire and turrets of the cathedral, as Ulrick and Mirvan, attended by most of the nobles who had been present at the banquet, returned from their unsuccessful pursuit. The men looked jaded, and their horses worn ; still not a single complaint was heard ; for rough and careless as the soldiers were, they sympathised with the despair of their two leaders, who, pale as marble, and with bloodshot eyes, gazed hopelessly upon each other. Robert of Artois, the unsuspected author of the deed, had been one of the foremost in the pursuit, carefully directing the pursuers, by his well-feigned zeal, far from the path they should have taken. As the various stragglers came slowly up before the castle, he reined his tired steed, and said, "Farewell, my friends. Should chance discover the author of this outrage, which fills each heart with rage and every honest tongue with scorn, send but a glove to Filby in token of your need, and in an hour my banner shall be spread to meet you. This present hour business of import calls me home. That once despatched, I am again your servant."

" Thanks ! " exclaimed the broken-hearted Ulrick ; "he is a friend indeed who shares a sorrow as if it were his own. On your return send out your men to scour the country round. I'll fill his gauntlet with gold who brings intelligence of my lost bride, or names the villain who has wrought this mischief ; dearly the heartless ruffian should abide it."

Courageous as Robert of Artois naturally was, he quailed beneath the expression of Ulrick's eye as he pronounced the threat. A desire to find himself within his stronghold of Filby seized upon him. Raising his helmet, therefore, in sign of adieu, he cried—

" Doubt not, noble youths, all that friendship can achieve shall be attempted ; my men shall spare nor spur nor rein till your lost treasure's found."

Hella, the bard, who had, despite his vast age, been one of the first to mingle in the pursuit, cast a suspicious glance on Robert of Artois as he rode off. Odo of Caen observed it ; he had not forgiven the bard his song, which seemed indirectly to call upon the Saxons to throw off the Conqueror's yoke, and to censure the misrule of the Norman race. He gladly seized, therefore, the opportunity of venting his spleen, which the unsuccessful result of the pursuit had still further tended to increase.

" Sir Saxon," he cried, "thou lovest not our brother of Artois. Heaven defend me from as dark a greeting as thy look conveys. In what hath he displeased thee ? "

" His deeds," coolly answered the aged Saxon.

" Humph ! " replied the questioner ; "'tis difficult for Norman deeds to please a Saxon's judgment ; but what particular deed of Robert of Artois hath merited the harshness of such judgment ? Sir bard, explain me that."

" His share in this night's outrage."

All started, and even Odo of Caen was staggered by the coolness and firmness of the reply. Ulrick and Mirvan gathered with the rest of the nobles round the old man, and eagerly demanded upon what proofs he grounded his assertion. Some, who saw in it only a splenetic attempt to sow dissension between the Saxon and Norman chiefs, cried shame ; and had not the bereaved lovers and several of their friends drawn their swords, the old bard would have rued his temerity in daring to accuse one of the most powerful of the Norman chiefs. After much quarrelling and confusion, Mirvan, whose office of Marshal of the Angles gave him most authority amongst them, at last obtained something like silence.

" The wisdom of age," he cried, " is not slightly to be contemned ;

let Hella be heard! First I demand upon what proof he founds his accusation—an accusation monstrous if false, and terrible if true."

"Upon no proof," replied Hella; "but upon——"

The rest of his speech was lost in the clamour which the friends of Robert of Artois contrived to raise. Crowding, they thronged around the old man, who gazed unmoved upon them; their looks and words were menacing, when Ulrick thrust himself between; like the young lion who first sees his prey, his blood was roused—despair had made him reckless.

"Back!" he exclaimed, tracing a circle with his sword; "let him who is most tired of life first cross it. Were ye the friends of the Norman devil whose name Robert of Artois bears, I'd brave ye all in such a cause as this. Is this the amity ye lately swore?—is this the justice Saxons must expect at Norman hands?—against an old man, too! Shame on your courage, sirs."

The vast body of Edda's troops, hearing the voice of their lord, thronged instantly around him. Odo and the more reasonable of the Normans felt that he was right; and the assailants, seeing that they were outnumbered, sheathed their weapons.

"Let him explain his words, and justify them, if he can," they cried. "Public has been the accusation; as public be the proofs."

"Who saw Robert of Artois at the banquet?" demanded the old bard. There was a pause—none remembered to have seen him. "Who can tell when and where he first joined in the pursuit?" he added.

"I—I," exclaimed several of the younger nobles; "he joined us in the market-place, and all have seen how eagerly he conducted the pursuit."

"Ay," exclaimed a third, "and well he hath been recompensed."

"Conducted the pursuit!" echoed Hella. "True, he did conduct it everywhere but to the road which led to his own felon den. Who twice misled us by false intelligence?—Robert of Artois. Who of all the nobles was absent at the banquet when the outrage was committed?—Robert of Artois. Who alone, of all those who swore to avenge the crime, hath withdrawn from the pursuit?—Robert of Artois. And who," he added, with increased energy, "is the vile ravisher of innocence?—Robert of Artois."

Conviction flashed in an instant upon both Mirvan and his friend, the former of whom had frequently remarked his passionate glances directed towards Isabel. So profound was the impression Hella's words produced, that even the culprit's nearest friends were dumb. Odo of Caen was the first to break the silence.

"It must be seen to," he exclaimed. "Let the esquires give orders to refresh our men; and then towards Filby."

The words had scarcely passed the speaker's lips, when a servitor, bearing the badge of Herbert de Lozenga on his vest, galloped to

the ground, and, without waiting to dismount, placed in the hands
of Ulrick, who hastily tore the seal, a missive from the prelate, which
detailed the treachery of Robert of Artois, but without alluding to
his prisoner's share in it—a circumstance which, for many prudential
reasons, he wished for awhile to remain concealed.

" It is confirmed," he cried, glancing over the letter. " Robert of
Artois is the vile ravisher—the traitor who hath broken the bond of
peace—stolen like some midnight thief upon my path, and robbed
me of my happiness. Who will dispute his guilt when it is known
that the venerable bishop is his accuser ? But I will have revenge ! "
he added, drawing his sword—an example which was followed by
the aged Edda and his Saxon followers.

" By Him whose name yon stars pronounce," continued Ulrick,
" whose might the roaring sea and tempest's breath alike make
manifest, I here devote my soul to its fulfilment—a wild, exter-
minating, deep revenge ! "

A shout of execration from the Normans and Saxons followed the
words of Ulrick, for the insult to both was equal in the outrage
offered to the brides of their leaders ; eagerly they demanded to be
led against the stronghold of the knightly robber, vowing not to
leave one stone upon another till they had rescued his prisoners.
The preparations were quickly made, and ere the sun was an hour
higher in the heavens, the united hosts, under the conduct of Mirvan
and Ulrick, were on their way to Filby.

    *   *   *   *

Matilda had beheld with joy the excitement of her cousin at last
relieved by tears, as she sank exhausted with her griefs upon the
couch beside her. By a benevolent provision of nature, sorrow or
pain, beyond a certain limit, stupefy the brain, or life would succumb
beneath them. Isabel had gradually sobbed herself into a feverish
slumber, disturbed by fearful dreams and visionary terrors, from
which she would occasionally start, but recompose herself on hearing
the low, sweet voice of Matilda, or feeling the affectionate pressure
of her hand. The latter slept not, but had passed the night in prayer,
tempering her soul with courage. On considering her position, she
felt convinced that her imprisonment was but the consequence of
her companionship with Isabel. The purity of her nature did not
allow her to suppose that her beauty had excited the lawless desire
of anyone ; for, like the flowers of the field, she was unconscious
of her loveliness. Partially reassured, therefore, on her own account,
she resolved to devote herself to the protection of her cousin, whom
she loved as a sister, and the affianced bride of her brother. The
rays of morning began to penetrate through the strongly-barred
windows, when the watcher, seeing that her charge still slept,
advanced to the casement, to see if she could recognise from the
surrounding country the place of their imprisonment. The view
fully confirmed her suspicions that they were the captives of Robert

of Artois ; for Filby Broad, with its sedgy islands and woody banks,
lay stretched like a clouded mirror in the morning mists before her.
As the sun advanced in power, the lake became more and more
distinct, till she could trace the wild duck leading her brood in
matronly pride on its placid bosom, or the stately heron, patiently
watching for its finny prey from some projecting stone close by the
shore, where the waters were not too deep for its long legs to wade,
or neck to plunge. Sometimes she would watch the solitary drake,
as, with its sharp cry, it rose from the water, and directed its arrowy
flight over the distant woods of Ormsby, or the low, marshy grounds
which lie between them—envy its rapid flight, and sigh for
freedom.

Her reveries were broken by the gentle closing of a door. In an
instant the terrible reality of her position pressed upon her ; and,
turning to confront the intruder, she beheld, to her great relief, that
it was a woman. So completely was she shielded from observation
by the recess in which she stood, and so quiet had been the movement,
that the stranger failed to perceive her ; and there was something so
peculiar in her manner, that Matilda determined to observe her.
Her apparel, which was extremely rich, partook more of the Eastern
than European character ; a saffron-coloured short vest fell over a
white cymar, which descended to the wearer's ankles ; both were
embroidered at the hems with gold. Her figure was tall and
commanding, and her features, which were still beautiful, although
marked by the strife of passions, bore the peculiar characteristics of
the Jewish race. It was evident, from her costume, that she could
not be a menial ; for, independent of the richness of her dress, gems
of considerable value glittered upon her arms and neck, or were
braided in her long, dark hair. Cautiously she approached the couch,
and gazed upon the sleeper ; her features became dreadfully agitated
as she did so.

" She is beautiful," she murmured, or rather hissed through her
clenched teeth ; " young, too ; perhaps nobly born—innocent and
fair ;—what chance have I, withered as I am in form and
mind, to retain his heart against such a rival ? He will
soon arrive to clasp her in his eager arms, to breathe his serpent
vows into her ear, to press his poisonous kisses on her lips, and
laugh to scorn the lost, degraded Rachel. Let him come," she
added, firmly ; " he shall find the kiss of death upon her lips before
him ; the worm shall first supplant him in her love ! " As the last
words fell upon the astonished listener's ear, the Jewess drew a sharp,
glittering blade from beneath her vest, and advanced yet nearer, with
the stealthy pace of a tigress, towards the couch. Matilda had
gradually become spell-bound with terror at the evident purpose of
the stranger. Her limbs were rooted to the spot, and the powers of
speech and motion seemed alike denied her ; her agony became
intense ; vainly she struggled with the torpor which oppressed her.

Nor was it till the arm of the woman was actually raised over the unconscious Isabel, that, with a piercing shriek, she burst the horrible species of fascination which bound her, exclaiming as she did so—
"Think on thy soul! Shed not the blood of innocence."
So thrilling was the cry, that the affrighted Isabel started from her slumbers, waking from fearful visions to a more fearful reality before her. The murderess was equally startled; it seemed as if the appealing voice of conscience had thundered in her ear, "Thou shalt do no murder!" She gazed in surprise upon the fair girl who had so suddenly interposed between her and her intended victim, and who, with arm encircling the agitated Isabel, boldly confronted her.
"Who art thou?" she falteringly demanded.
"Victims, like yourself, to the foulest treachery," replied Matilda; "though, perhaps, unlike you, unwilling ones. How can this poor girl excite your hatred, that you should seek to stain your hands in blood? Rather assist us to escape our tyrant's power, for the honour of your sex and the memory of your mother's love."
The word mother seemed to touch a chord whose every tone vibrated in agony. Dropping the still upraised weapon, she clasped her hands upon her brow, as if stricken by a sudden pain. The flush of passion on her features was replaced by the purer blush of shame, and in an instant the tears gushed from her burning eyes, and relieved her overfraught heart; for, fallen as Rachel was, one trace of Eden lingered in her yet. In a voice broken by sighs, she murmured—
"Speak not of my mother, lest from the grave she rise to curse her child."
"She is mad," whispered Isabel—"mad. If friends come not soon to rescue us, reason will leave me too."
"No!" said Rachel, dashing the tears from her dark eyes, as if ashamed of her momentary weakness, "I am not mad! Would to our Father Abraham I were! For madness cannot equal the pangs of a despised and unrequited love."
"You love our captor, Robert of Artois, then?" exclaimed Matilda, a ray of hope dawning on her soul.
"Ay, maiden, love him as the lost daughters of our race alone can love—beyond home, parents, honour, life—more," she added, with still increasing excitement—"more e'en than Heaven itself: all but life I have already sacrificed for him, and would again, though but for one kind smile; alas! 'tis long since I received one."
"And he requites your sacrifice——?"
"With scorn!" interrupted Rachel; "with scorn! whose serpent tooth gnaws deeper into a woman's heart than aught on earth beside. I once was good," she added, "gentle as yourselves, not meanly nurtured or ignobly bred. What hath it made me? A raging tigress;

changed my woman's heart into a fiend's ; destroyed the kindlier impulse of my nature ; made me in heart, if not in deed, a murderess ! "

"Alas ! " said Isabel ; " what have I done to cause such fearful hate ? "

" Loved him I love," replied Rachel, whose jealousy returned as she gazed on the lovely girl before her, and mentally compared her opening loveliness with her own fading beauty ; " is it not enough to give me cause to hate thee ? "

" Woman," exclaimed Isabel, with dignity, " be the words thy happiness or bane, be they for good or ill, know that, if Robert of Artois were king, Isabel of Bayeux would never share his throne ; but would prefer the convent's gloom, the meanest hut, the shelter of the grave itself, to his polluted couch.   I loathe and scorn him."

There was a tone of sincerity in the speaker's words which carried conviction to the heart.   The Jewess gazed attentively upon her for a few moments—at first suspiciously, but at last with confidence, for the candid brow of the fair girl was not one where falsehood had ever traced its crooked characters.   Despite herself, she could not but believe her.

" Deceived ! " she muttered to herself, " again deceived !   Thank Heaven, this crime, at least, is spared me !   Forgive me, maiden," she added, " my evil purpose ; but I was stung—deceived—wrought on by jealous pangs ; they told me thou wert come to be his bride —his willing bride—and I, who loved, too easily believed them. But if thou lovest him not," she added, " why art thou here ? "

" Ask of the vulture," said Matilda, " why the wounded dove was found within his nest ; ask of the tiger why the bleeding fawn is trembling in his den.   Art thou answered ? "

" I see—I see," exclaimed the Jewess, struggling with her evil passions, which were again excited by the idea of Robert's love for another ; " but I will save thee.   The fool who poured this tale of poison in my ear did it to gain my love—fool !   not to know that hearts like mine can feel but once its spell, and break when it is broken.   Wouldst thou be free ? "

" Gladly," exclaimed both Matilda and Isabel.

" But you must swear," she added, " that if by my means the path lies open to you, no injury shall fall upon your captor.   False as he is, I would not, e'en to save my perilled soul, harm one hair of his ungrateful head.   Promise me this."

" Easily answered :   Matilda, my cousin, and myself solemnly swear never to breathe, save in confession, our captor's fearful name."

" Away, then," said Rachel, hurriedly ; " morning advances, and he may soon be here—here to mar our plans, and to prevent your flight."

" It is prevented," exclaimed a stern voice behind them.   They

[RACHEL'S REVENGE ON ROBERT OF ARTOIS.]

L

started, and Isabel beheld the object of her hate and terror, Robert of Artois, who, after leaving Ulrick and Mirvan, had returned to Filby, to await the arrival of his royal accomplice in the act of villainy. The effect of the appearance upon the Jewess was even greater than upon his trembling victim ; in an instant her fit of jealousy returned, and springing towards Isabel, she would have completed her original purpose, had not the swift arm of her seducer arrested her.

"Release my hand !" she cried, or rather shrieked. "I'll not be held ! Her life or thine, Norman ; ravisher ! villain ! coward ! Christian, I spit upon and curse thee ! "

It is difficult to say how the contest with the frantic woman might have terminated, had not several men-at-arms rushed into the room, on hearing the voice of their master. They were accompanied by a young esquire, whose agitated countenance, when he beheld Rachel struggling with his lord, told a deeper interest than mere pity ; his hand involuntarily grasped the hilt of his poniard, but reflection held it.

"Convey this wanton to a secure cell within the keep," cried Robert, spurning the unhappy woman brutally from him. "Guard her well, Aymer, and see that I am pestered with these frantic scenes no more."

"Dog," said the Jewess, still resisting the men-at-arms, who were dragging her from the apartment, "thou hast spurned me like a hound ; beware my fangs ! Thou hast broken the last tie between us ; beware when next we meet ! "

"Believe me, I regret, fair ladies, you should have been exposed to a scene like this," said Robert of Artois, as soon as the unhappy woman was removed ; "but jealousy of your superior charms has driven her mad. I will give orders she shall not mar our happiness again."

This was said with an affectation of courtesy which rendered its insolent familiarity more bitter. Isabel, on whom his eyes were licentiously fixed, shrank trembling to the side of her cousin, whose hand alone prevented her from falling, so excessive was her terror at his presence.

"Robert of Artois," said Matilda, with dignity, "I appeal not to thy honour—for this deed of thine proves that my words would wake no echo there—but to thy fears. Canst hope our presence can be long concealed within these walls ? Normans and Saxons will alike unite to punish thy aggression. Release us, then ; and here-I solemnly renew the oath never to yield thy name to those whose swords would punish thy unmanly crime."

"Filby," replied the knight, carelessly, "hath held birds of a nest as lofty, maiden, as thine own ; and I have kept the fledgelings. But a few hours since I left thy brother and his new-found friend ; we parted in honest fellowship. Suspicion's self can never glance

L 2

at me ; and if it does," he added, "Isabel will by that time be my
bride, and thou be caged by one who knows how to put a gag upon
that scornful tongue, and tame thy haughty nature."

"Thy bride !" exclaimed Isabel, gazing on him with loathing.
"Never !"

"These walls have echoed often to that word," sneeringly
observed the knight ; "spoken as oft in vain. I know a trick to
make thee sue to be the bride of him you so long have scorned. I
have humbled hearts, ere now, as proud, and firmer far than thine.
But why are you in this chamber ? My orders were you should be
separated. Solitude may tend to tame your spirits. Come," he
added, approaching Isabel as he spoke, "I have a dove-cot prettier
far than this ; let me conduct thee thither. There I will woo thee
as thou shouldst be wooed, and teach thee, maid, how Robert of
Artois loves."

The flashing eyes of the speaker declared but too plainly his
guilty purpose. So completely did he deem the unprotected girls
within his power, that he would not even give himself the trouble
to dissemble, but felt a savage joy in humbling, by brutal outrage,
the high-spirited being who had scorned his proffered love. Isabel
read his purpose, and exclaimed, as she sank fainting in the arms
of her cousin—

"Thy promise, coz, thy promise !"

The appeal was not made in vain. In the purity of her nature
Matilda would rather have seen her cousin dead—nay, with her own
hand have offered up the spotless victim on the shrine of honour—
than polluted by the touch of the base ravisher. Drawing the knife
which from the hour of her arrival at Filby she carried concealed
in her bosom, she held it over the insensible form of Isabel.

"Advance one step nearer !" she cried, "and I consign her soul
to God and His good angels. Robert of Artois, doubt not my
purpose. Mark if my hand trembles or an eyelid quivers. I have
sworn, living, thy arms should never clasp her. Lessen the
distance between us but one step—a line's breadth, a hair—and her
pure blood shall rise to heaven against thee."

So firm was the voice of the speaker, so resolute her eye, that
even Robert of Artois, accustomed though he was to scenes like
this, could not for one moment doubt her purpose. The sharp,
glittering blade was within an inch of her fair cousin's breast, her
eye unflinchingly fixed upon his. Involuntarily he started back,
saying, as he did so—

"What wouldst do ? "

" Preserve her honour at the expense of life."

" Murderess ! "

" Thou art the murderer," replied Matilda, "I, the priestess.
Thine is the victim—mine the sacrifice ; approach, and it is offered.
If Heaven will not prevent, its mercy will accept it."

"Foolish girl!" exclaimed Robert; "it can neither prevent nor interfere to save thee."

Scarcely had the words passed his lips than the blast of a trumpet rang loud and deep before the drawbridge. Matilda started, for she knew the challenge of her house. 'Twas Mirvan's trumpet.

"It has interposed!" she cried. "Robber, thy ruffian hold is close beset ; our friends are round thy walls! Well may thy cheek turn pale. In Heaven has been our trust, and Heaven hath answered us. Living, thou canst not guard us ; dead, our friends will pile these towers in ashes o'er our grave."

"Confusion!" muttered Robert, and rushed from the apartment.

Matilda laid her insensible burthen on the couch, and sank in grateful prayer upon her knees beside her.

CHAPTER X.

ROBERT OF ARTOIS rushed from the chamber of the two captives, and with hasty strides gained the battlements of his stronghold, from whence the sight which met his gaze might have quailed a stronger heart than his, for the united Saxon and Norman hosts were marshalled on the plain before him. So universal was the indignation at the unmanly outrage he had committed, that even amongst those whom he called his friends not a single banner was absent. Men who would have supported him in almost any other cause, who had shared with him in the plunder of the oppressed Saxons, were now in arms against him. Had his victims been of the vanquished race, it would have been long ere a single pennon had been given to the wind ; but the insult to the daughter and niece of so popular a man as the late Hugh de Bigod could not be passed over : it was a crime which might come home to every noble's hearth ; and they determined, however they might violate the rights of others, that none should tamper with their own.

About twenty paces behind the herald, whose trumpet had called the lord of Filby to the walls, stood the chief leaders of the expedition —Ulrick and Mirvan, to whose anxious hearts it seemed an age until their enemy appeared. Edda and Odo of Caen left the parley to the two lovers, and were busily occupied in directing the franklins and nobles where to place their men. Under the direction of such experienced commanders, every point of vantage was taken possession of, and the castle was completely invested before the inmates knew of their approach.

"Unless the fox's den be well supplied," said Odo, casting a satisfied glance on the military dispositions, "we shall starve him to

a surrender ; for I defy horse or man to pass by lake or plain
without being exposed to the arrows of our soldiers. But see," he
added, " the ravisher appears upon the walls. May the caitiff's
shrift be short and speedy, for it will be his last ! "

" 'Tis a strange greeting you have called me to ! " exclaimed
Robert, after casting a hurried survey over the scene. " Is Filby
hold a robber's den, nobles and knights, that you appear before it,
banner displayed and lance in rest ? 'Tis well our walls are strong
enough to bid defiance unto all who come. Come ye in hostile
guise, or is't some riddle beyond a plain man's guessing ? "

" Robert of Artois," said Ulrick, with a strong effort to master his
indignation, " though this deed of thine is of so black a treachery,
it merits more the hangman's office than knightly chastisement.
Descend, and let the sword decide between us. If vanquished, thou
shalt release thy captives ; if conqueror, Heaven will raise them up
another champion."

" Captives ! what captives ? " demanded the villain in well-
dissembled surprise ; " my castle is not a prison."

" Lying will not serve thee now," cried Mirvan : " despite thy
arts, thy treachery is known. Where is my sister—where my cousin
Isabel ? Release them, or I swear not to leave one stone upon
another of this den of treachery and blood—one living soul within
its ruined walls ; thy knightly spurs shall be hacked off—thy
escutcheon reversed, in sign of infamy, upon thy grave."

" Boys ! " replied Robert, " I hear and scorn you both. First, for
the base-born Ulrick,—for such, despite the bishop's juggling tale, I
do believe he is—I cross no sword with men of doubtful birth. As
for my captives, if I have such, I have good warrant for detaining
them. For the rest, exert your strength on Filby—bend bow and
mangonel ; our walls can boast of hearts and hands who know how
to defend them."

" Coward ! " exclaimed Ulrick, maddened by the sneering tone of
the speaker ; " cool, calculating, spiritless coward, bold only when
women are to be assailed, hath thy cheek no blush of shame ?—thy
heart no drop of knightly blood ? "

" If not with Ulrick, measure swords with me ; my birth, at least,
is equal to thine own," said Mirvan ; " felon as thou art, I offer thee
the chance of equal combat, a noble's sword for the vile headsman's
axe. Descend, and Heaven decide between us."

Mirvan's challenge, and the epithet of a coward which Ulrick had
previously applied to him, stung their enemy to the quick ; for, like
most cruel and licentious men, he was excessively vain, and
consequently susceptible of shame. It was not, therefore, without
an effort that he determined to decline the contest ; for he well
knew how such an act must lower him in the estimation of his
chivalrous countrymen, with whom courage was held the highest
virtue. Perhaps he was influenced in his decision by the belief

that the arrival of the royal partner of his crime would relieve him from his embarrassing position by causing the Normans to desert their new allies, or turn their swords against them. Perhaps, too, he lacked the moral courage to face the glance and swords of those whom he had so cruelly injured. Whichever was the motive, his face was livid with contending passions, as he replied—

"If, for the present, I decline the contest, think not it is I fear it; the bridegroom never longed more for his bride's first kiss, than I to vindicate my honour and chastise thy boyish insolence; that which I have done I dare defend. Normans and Saxons, I defy ye both. What ho!" he added, calling to the warder, "fling out our banner; man the walls; let your keen arrows count every rivet of their armour. A hide of land and twenty silver marks to him whose arm strikes down a leader of yon vaunting host."

Scarcely had the words passed his lips, than a body of his men, who had been crouching behind the battlements, suddenly started up, and discharged a flight of arrows at the group of nobles near the herald. Thanks to the goodness of their armour, Ulrick and Mirvan both escaped. Odo of Caen was slightly wounded in the head, but the unfortunate herald was slain. The assailants raised a shout of execration as they beheld him fall; and even the cheek of Robert of Artois blanched—for his office, like his person, was sacred, and the wounding or injuring one of them was ever considered a most unknightly deed.

"Villain!" exclaimed Odo of Caen, shaking his sword, "the blood thou hast shed must be atoned. I swear never to quit this spot alive, till I have levelled thy castle with the dust, and fixed thy head upon the ruined pile. So help me Heaven, our Lady, and St. George!"

The speaker, his face streaming with blood from the treacherous arrow, drew his sword and kissed the golden cross upon its hilt. It was no unusual circumstance at the period of the Conquest, and the ages of chivalry which succeeded it, for one or more nobles to bind themselves, like Odo of Caen, to some particular undertaking; such oaths were always most scrupulously kept by all who valued their knightly reputation; to break them was considered such dishonour that it released the affianced bride from her contract, should her lover be proved guilty of it.

"A vow! a vow!" cried Mirvan, as Odo ceased speaking, "to which I join myself heart and soul."

"And I!" exclaimed Ulrick and most of the younger nobles; at the same time touching the sword of Odo, in token of their companionship in his oath, and pronouncing the formula, "So help us Heaven, our Lady, and St. George."

The followers of Robert were preparing to send a second flight of arrows, when Edda, who marked the action, gave the signal to his men, and in an instant a cloud of missiles swept the wall; several of the besieged fell, struck by the heavy stones which the Saxons sent from their slings with remarkable precision. Their leader received one upon his breast, which reminded him that he was without his armour by the pain it occasioned ; he retired, therefore, behind a bastion, calling to his esquires to bring him his coat of mail and casquet as he did so.

Filby Castle was a regularly fortified hold, built with more regard to strength than either beauty or convenience. Like most of the fortresses of the age, it consisted of a lofty keep or donjon, surrounded by offices, forming a kind of courtyard, the only entrance to which was by a strong tower ; the latter generally served as storehouses for the corn and provisions of the inmates, as well as the dormitories of the guards, its flat roofs serving, in case of attack, as a battery, from whence the besieged could pour down molten lead and hurl masses of stone upon their enemies. The keep and tower were the only buildings of stone ; the rest were mere constructions of sun-burnt brick and timber, easily destroyed by fire, and whose loss would but slightly affect the carrying of the rest of the stronghold.

From the determined manner of Robert of Artois, it was evident that all hope of capitulation was in vain ; he was prepared to defend himself to the last, and, after a brief consultation between the Sxon and Norman leaders, it was resolved to continue the seige in due form.

"Nobles," said Edda, as soon as the resolution was concluded, "if the peace between our races is to be a lasting one, it must be cemented by an act of stern but necessary justice. The wrong which brings us here hath been offered by Robert of Artois alike to both, and both are joined to punish him. Let the gallows be erected in sight of his vile den, his name attached to it, like that of the meanest criminal, together with a parchment, signed by us all, declaring him degraded from the dignity of knighthood, and doomed, for the murder of our unoffending herald, to die a felon's death. Are we agreed ? "

"We are ! " exclaimed Ulrick and Mirvan in the same breath.

Odo of Caen and his brother nobles approved the proposition ; the gibbet was accordingly erected, and the act of degradation solemnly affixed by sound of trumpet. Robert, pale with rage, witnessed the ceremony from the walls of his stronghold, and his cheek changed with rage and fear, as he marked the effect it produced upon his followers, men who, under ordinary circumstances, would have abetted him in any act of villainy. Quickly, however, recovering himself from his confusion, he observed, with a loud, forced laugh—

"A slip of parchment will not win Filby hold. Courage, friends ! we shall soon behold a royal banner in the boaster's rear. William of Normandy, our future monarch, by whose orders I am acting, will soon be here to punish these presuming traitors, who would usurp the prerogative of justice, and dispute his will."

The words had scarcely passed his lips when the sentinel who was placed upon the highest tower called out that he beheld an approaching force, headed by several knights in armour, who were directing their march towards Filby ; and that, from the movement amongst the besiegers, he doubted not but that they perceived it too. The intelligence gave fresh courage to their audacious leader, who doubted not but that it was his patron marching to his succour.

"See you no banner ?" he demanded.

The soldier paused a moment ere he replied, for the new actors were still at a considerable distance from the scene.

"I do," at last he answered. "There are three ; one borne in advance of the others—a herald precedes it."

"By whom is it borne ?"

"A knight in full armour," shouted the man. "Three leaders follow it—one is a priest."

"Can you discern the blazon ?" replied Robert of Artois, at the same time straining his sight to catch it, his fears reverting to Herbert de Lozenga at the intelligence that one of the leaders was a priest.

"A lion rampant in an azure field, surmounted by a ducal crown. It is a royal banner," added the man.

"Thanks to our Lady," shouted the degraded man ; "it is the prince. Now then we shall see you scum dispersed like chaff before the wind. Shout, men, and wave our banners from the walls to welcome them ! Shout, in sign of recognition for their aid ! See, the enemy marshal their ranks to meet them. Would they resist their prince ? Aymer," he added, turning to the young esquire who attended him, "lead a party of our men into the courtyard below. Be ready for a sally. This is the day to win thy spurs ; and tell the warder at the first signal to be ready at the drawbridge ; we must attack them in the rear."

Robert of Artois watched with eager eyes the expected encounter of the two hosts. What was his consternation when he beheld their leaders mutually advance in sign of amity, and their troops mingle together till they formed but one body, which, after a few moments' evolution, directed its march towards Filby ! From that instant he felt the first misgiving for the success of his villainous scheme, and half-repented that he had undertaken it.

"Can the fickle-minded tyrant," he muttered "have betrayed me ?—or have both Normans and Saxons yielded to the *prestige* of his birth ? No, no," he added, bitterly, as the banner of the leader distinctly met his view—"by my evil star, it is the blazon of my namesake, Robert Curthose, the Conqueror's eldest son. What devil brings him to this country to mar our plans ! Where can his brother be ? The wily bishop, too !" he added, as George of

Erpingham advanced with the pennon of his master; "the game hath fearful odds against me. No matter, I will fight it to the last. Victory or revenge shall at least be mine. I will not fall alone."

Lowering their visors, to guard against any fresh act of treachery on the part of the besieged, the leaders of the now united army, preceded by a herald in the royal tabard, and a knight bearing the prince's banner, advanced close to the walls of the castle; its commander was waiting to receive them. Thrice did the herald summon him to open the gate to his highness Robert of Normandy, on pain of treason and forfeiture in case of a refusal. There was a pause, during which the traitor whispered something to one of his arquebussiers, a man equally noted for skill and determination ; a nod of intelligence was the fellow's only reply, and immediately he concealed himself behind one of the projecting bastions, taking his weapon with him.

"And how am I to know," answered Robert of Artois, " that the prince is really with you ? Report speaks him in Normandy. Men ere now have fallen into a snare as plain as this ; the royal banner may be assumed——"

" But not the royal person," interrupted the unsuspicious prince, spurring his horse, and advancing from the group of nobles by whom he was surrounded still nearer to the walls. " Behold ! "

He raised his visor as he spoke, exposing to the full gaze of the besieged his frank, manly countenance. Scarcely had he done so, than the concealed ruffian, obedient to the orders he had received, discharged his arquebus ; but, fortunately, from the crouching position he had been compelled to assume, in order to conceal himself, he had not taken aim with his usual precision. The arrow missed the prince's face, but struck the golden crown upon his helmet—an emblem of the prince's future destiny—and the royal insignia fell to the ground, shivered by the shock. Its incautious wearer instantly closed his visor, and, raising his hand in defiance, exclaimed—

" Robert of Artois, thou art a doomed man ! By the oath of my race, I swear to show no mercy to thee or any of thy fellows. The axe and cord shall be the doom of all. No further parley now. The lion's on thy track. His thirst of blood is roused ; fear not but he will quench it to the full."

At the end of this imprudent speech, the prince returned to his followers and friends, who, however they regretted his incaution, were silent through respect ; for the resolution he had sworn to left no room for hope of an accommodation with the besieged ; many of whom would perhaps have hesitated to defend their master against their monarch's son, but that he had sworn their death by an oath which none of his family were ever known to break. No other resource, therefore, was left to them but a desperate resistance ; they knew that the attack would be fearful, and they prepared with alacrity for their defence, their wily leader rejoicing in the indiscretion of his reckless enemy.

"We have had words enough," exclaimed Ulrick ; "and nothing now remains but to draw the sword and throw away the scabbard. Beloved Matilda !" he added, "if too late to save, at least I'll honour thy loss with Filby for thy funeral pile."

Under the direction of their leaders some of the men commenced cutting down the reeds and sedges which grew upon the banks of the lake ; others were sent into the wood to fell trees and brushwood ; the whole of which, despite the efforts of the beseiged, they succeeded in piling against the offices which, as before stated, formed the courtyard of the castle, by connecting the keep with the tower. During this operation the Saxons, under Edda, rendered good service ; for no sooner did the Normans appear upon the walls than they were swept down by their arrows and the heavy stones flung with astonishing dexterity from their slings. Many a cauldron of seething pitch fell from the hand prepared to turn it on the besiegers' heads ; on more than one occasion, however, it fell on the unprotected limbs of the Saxons, burning them to the very bone. The Normans saw this, and knowing they were better protected by their armour, called upon them to retire whilst they took their place—an offer which the former accepted in the same generous spirit in which it was meant. Nothing, however, could induce either Ulrick or Mirvan to withdraw ; reckless of the danger they ran of the missiles which were showered upon them, they continued to share in the labours of their men. In the course of a few hours the pile had reached a formidable height ; the boiling matter which the enemy had poured from the walls only rendered it the more inflammable ; and as soon as the torches were applied, the flames rose quickly and strong. Robert of Artois, seeing that all attempts to stop the conflagration would be vain, retired with his men to the shelter of the keep, which, from its strength, seemed to bid defiance to the besiegers' efforts.

    *   *   *   *   *

Whilst these proceedings are being carried on, it is a fit opportunity for us to return to the Jewess, and the young squire to whose charge her seducer had consigned her. On entering her dungeon, Rachel paced its cold, damp floor with the angry mien of an excited lioness ; her feelings had been hurt where they were most susceptible—in her love. Pride, womanhood, and affection had alike been outraged ; the man for whom she had sacrificed her own esteem, the respect of her people, the prejudice of her faith, and her mother's love, had spurned her from him like the vilest thing. The blow had so crushed her heart that even its passion for the idol once enshrined there became extinct; it throbbed with but one sentiment—revenge.

"'Tis just !" she cried, "'tis just I should be used so ; gathered like a toy in a moment of caprice—cast aside like a faded flower the moment satiety had palled. What will be my fate? I have now no refuge but the grave."

"Yes, one other!" exclaimed Aymer, throwing himself at her feet. "I have long loved you—lived but in your presence—have borne the burning pang of seeing you another's but in the hope that you would one day smile upon my persevering suit. Speak but the word—I will contrive the means to bear you from these hated walls to a home of happiness and peace."

"Happiness!" iterated the Jewess, scornfully—"happiness with one of thy cruel race? No—I have had enough of Christian faith, of Christian love—I'll trust to them no more."

"Hear me swear—by every saint, by every knightly oath," said the esquire, casting an impassioned glance upon her.

"He, too, hath sworn," interrupted the captive, "and every vow is broken. It needs but a Christian oath to make me doubt thee more than I do already. False as he is, this withered heart will never know another love, or dream again the dream its girlhood dreamt. Stir not its slumbering ashes, Aymer, lest thou wake a flame which may consume, but never burn for thee."

"Be calm, this storm of passion else must soon destroy thee."

"Yes, I will be calm," said Rachel, sternly, "as seas opposing winds, as the torn earth convulsed by fires. God of my fathers!" she added, with an increased burst of passion, "was it for this I left my peaceful home—lived the companion of his guilt and shame? Yet let the desperate libertine beware! Not the fierce tigress raging for her young—not the red lightning from Jehovah's hand, strike with more fury than a woman scorned."

The still beautiful creature stood, as she uttered her fearful denunciation, more with the aspect of an enraged pythoness than a human being; her dark black eyes flashed with intensity of hate. Aymer regarded her with pity as well as love, for he guessed but too well the fate to which Robert of Artois, to secure his own safety, would find it necessary to doom her, and from that he resolved at any rate to save her, wished her to live, though not for him.

"Rachel," he cried, at the same time taking her by the hand, "listen to me. It is not now the voice of passion, but of pity, speaks; thou hast said truly that all ties between thee and thy seducer are for ever broken; thou canst no longer hope to retain his heart; hast thou no danger to encounter from his hate?"

"His hate!" answered the wretched woman, scornfully; "can it do more than his destroying love?"

"It can," replied the young man, "it can kill."

"And callest thou mercy hate?—the best boon Robert of Artois can bestow is death; for in the grave is peace."

The deep tone of sadness in the wretched woman's voice, as she answered the esquire, told him how vain were all his hopes of love; still he resolved, if possible, to save her, for, like most ardent natures, there was a sentiment of generosity mingled with his wildest passions ; every manly feeling was interested in a creature so outraged and so helpless ; his emotion increased, therefore, as he resumed—

"There are outrages worse to a noble mind than death. Should he first resign thee to his brutal followers, to be their prey—their scoff—their victim——"

"Hold !" shrieked the Jewess ; "naught which wears a human form could consign the being it had loved to such a fate ! Fiend, devil as he is, Robert of Artois would never contemplate so foul a deed ; thou sayest this but to terrify me—to win me to thy purpose."

"No !" exclaimed Aymer ; "deeply as I prize thy love, wondrous as is the enchantment of thy beauty, on my soul I would not win thee by an act of baseness. Hear me : I will provide thee with the means of flight. The lower postern by the water's edge is under my especial care, the key in my possession ; soon as night draws on, I will unbar thy prison door, and thou mayst fly far from this den of infamy for ever."

"Alone ?" demanded the Jewess, fixing a searching glance upon him.

"Alone," firmly replied Aymer. "If I live not for thy love, I may as well die here. Men may call me traitor ; but none shall ever live to brand me with a coward's name. I could have borne that men should say, ' He fled his post in danger's hour for love ' ; but none shall have the right to think I quitted it through fear."

"The God of Abraham bless thee, Aymer, for thy generous heart !" exclaimed the Jewess, kissing his hand with deep emotion ; "and He will bless thee, boy, with a far purer, better love than mine—a love whose innocence shall cast its flowers around thy path, reminding thee of Eden's lost'inheritance. I do accept thy offer ; and for the remnant of my wretched days, deeply as I have suffered from Christian treachery, I will think better of its faith for thee. But why remain behind ?"

"I have told thee," said the young man, calmly ; "love only could, even to myself, excuse my flight in danger's hour."

Rachel gazed upon him long and sadly, and seemed, while doing so, to commune with herself. Once or twice she murmured, " So young !—so brave !" Her resolution, whatever it was, at last was taken. Her voice was calm as an infant's while she uttered it—

"Aymer," she said, "thou hast prevailed. To save thy life, I give thee the little that remains of heart within this blighted bosom. If the wreck be worth thy acceptance, take it ; for it is thine. Would it were better worth thy noble nature."

"I understand thee, Rachel," answered the esquire ; "I read thy generous purpose. Thou wouldst save me, despite myself, from the dangers which now threaten Filby, and then leave me to my fate, alone."

"Not so," she answered. "Thou hast no right to doubt my
words, for they have ever been to thee a voice of truth. I do repeat
it," she added, with a slight blush—" once beyond these walls, all
thou canst ask is thine."

Aymer could no longer doubt ; he was like a man who, in the
moment of despair found the path of happiness suddenly opened to
his view. Taking her hand, he covered it with passionate kisses,
thanking her a thousand times, as he did so, for the generous
sacrifice, and vowing that his life should be devoted to the task of
effacing from her mind the recollection of past sorrows, and
guarding her future happiness. There was a smile of incredulity
upon the face of the Jewess as she listened to him with something
like pity at the extravagant joy he manifested—a joy which she well
knew was doomed to be changed to bitter disappointment.

"Leave me," she cried, gently releasing her hand. " I require to
be alone. I must commune with my heart, and draw courage and
resignation from myself. At the hour of escape you will find me
ready. Hark ! " she added, as the trumpet of the besiegers a second
time echoed through the castle, "the enemy are already at the
gates ; hasten to thy post to avoid suspicion ; but first leave me thy
cloak, for my blood runs coldly, and my heart is chilled in these
damp walls."

Aymer carefully enveloped the speaker's form in his ample
mantle, whispered the word "Adieu," and would have pressed a
kiss upon her lips had not the sudden paleness which came over
her warned him to desist.

"Not now—not now," she murmured ; "wait but a little, and I
am wholly thine. At the appointed hour of flight thou wilt find
me in my dungeon, and must lead me from these cursed walls in
silence. Mark me, in silence ; for my heart will be too full of the
bitter memories of the past to bear the sound of human voice, even
in sympathy."

"All, dearest Rachel," whispered Aymer, soothingly, "shalt be
as thou hast willed it. Till the hour arrives, farewell."

The young squire contented himself with once more pressing his
lips upon her hand, and hurried from the cell.

"Poor boy ! " sighed the Jewess, as the echo of his footsteps fell
fainter upon her ear, " had I met a heart like thine, how different
might have been my fate ! Mayst thou live to find a destiny more
pure and happy than I could make thee. 'Tis past," she added,
brushing the tears from her dark lashes ; "one sigh to recollection
of my abandoned home, my blighted youth, my broken heart ; and
then, like the daughter of my race of old, who smote Holofernes on
his silken couch, to right my injuries in the vile Norman's blood."

For awhile Rachel continued to brood over her resolve, and
arrange the means of its success. A proud smile lit her beautiful
features as she contemplated, in the mirror of her mind, its

concluding triumph. There was nothing of fear or doubt in its expression. For herself, she was equally insensible to danger as her heart was dead to hope. Drawing her tablets from beneath her vest, she seated herself upon a stone, and hastily traced a few lines, read them twice over, seemed satisfied with their contents, and drawing Aymer's cloak around her, left the dungeon, which he had unfastened. It was evident, from the ease with which the Jewess threaded her way through the winding passages, that she was well acquainted with the locality of her prison. As she approached the battlements, however, her step became more cautious, and she drew the capuchin of the esquire's mantle over her head, so as completely to disguise her features. Of those whom she encountered, some took her for a young knight who was but just recovering from his wounds, and who for some time had inhabited the castle ; others passed her without troubling themselves with a conjecture, so occupied were they with their individual danger, and calculating on their respective chances of safety in the coming contest.

Like a spectre, the unhappy woman glided along the ramparts, still carefully veiling her face, and reached a solitary tower, where an old soldier kept watch ; he was leaning on his bow as she approached, and seemed to contemplate the approach of the enemy with an air of sullen indifference. So absorbed was he in his thoughts, that the light step of. the intruder failed to disturb him ; nor was it till he felt the pressure of her hand upon his shoulder that he started from his reverie.

"Harro," she whispered, "hast thou forgotten me ?" She threw back the hood which concealed her features as she spoke.

"No, lady," replied the old man, bowing reverentially ; "this heart must indeed be cold when I forget the ministering angel who watched over the sick couch of my dear child ; my heart may be a hard and rough one, but it retains the characters graved by the hand of gratitude the more indelibly. What brings thee to a scene like this ?"

"Revenge," replied Rachel, calmly. "I have been spurned like a hound by him for whom I sacrificed all that woman can—honour, respect, and Heaven. Thy master, and my destroyer, has doomed the victim he has made to death."

"To death !" echoed the soldier, with a look of astonishment ; "surely you dream."

"Not so," she answered ; "my dream at last is ended. Wilt thou serve me in this my hour of peril ? or are thy professions like those of the world, hollow and unstable as the breath which made them ?"

"Speak," said the old man, "and prove them. Though it cost me my life, I will not belie my words. What am I to do ?"

"Give me an arrow from thy quiver," answered the Jewess.

"Harro did as he was requested, and Rachel, receiving the weapon, seated herself upon the ground, and endeavoured to affix

the tablets, on which she had written in her dungeon, to the point.
After searching her person for a ribbon or a cord to tie them with,
she quietly demanded of her companion if he had a knife. He took
one from his girdle and gave it to her. Without a moment's
hesitation she drew one of the long glossy tresses, which it had
once been her pride to ornament, through her fingers, and severed
it. In a few moments the tablets were securely fastened to the
steel head of the instrument. Rising, she cast her glances round
the scene before her till they rested on a distant banner, round
which several knights and a man in the dark flowing robes of an
ecclesiastic were assembled.

"Dost see those men?" she demanded, pointing to the group,
"those close by the prince's banner?"

The archer nodded his head in token of assent.

"Send me this shaft amongst them," she resumed, "and I will
deem my kindness to thy child o'erpaid—thy every promise kept.
Draw well thy bow," she added, as the man took the arrow and
fitted it to his weapon, "for life and death hang on thy strength.
Let thy arm be nerved by gratitude, as mine has been by vengeance
—shoot as thou wouldst for freedom or for hate."

Harro did as she requested. Using his still great strength, he
drew the missile to the very head; and so sure was his aim, that
despite the vast distance between him and his mark, he hit the very
flag.

Rachel watched with eager eyes its flight, and saw with
satisfaction that her design was answered; for an esquire raised the
arrow, and bore it with its burden to Herbert de Lozenga, the
ecclesiastic, who was conversing with the knights. The prelate read
the writing to those around him; and Ulrick and Mirvan waved
their scarfs, in token that, whatevever the request or information it
conveyed, it was joyfully accepted.

"Thanks, old man!" exclaimed the Jewess; "thou hast done me
the last service I shall ever ask of man; thy promise has been kept; a
wretch's blessing rest upon thee! Shouldst thou escape the siege,"
she added, taking a collar of jewels from her neck, "these will
provide thee comforts for thine age. Mayst thou live long and
happy."

She placed her gift in the archer's hand, and drawing the capuchin
once more over her features, retraced her way cautiously towards
the keep; her step was lighter as she did so, for she felt sure of
vengeance.

"Let me but triumph in life's parting hour," she murmured to
herself, "and I will deem my sufferings o'erpaid; let the fatal star
which didst preside over my mortal destiny shine but propitious
now, and I no more will curse its influence. Robert of Artois, I
have kept my oath; I feel that we shall meet again."

Instead of returning to her dungeon, she passed along the now

[THE DEATH-BED OF ROBERT OF ARTOIS.]

M

deserted armoury, nor paused till she reached the door of the apartment where Matilda and her cousin were confined ; a sentry had been placed there, who raised his partizan at her approach : his orders were that none should enter. Fortunately for Rachel's enterprise, she still retained the signet-ring of her betrayer, given to her charge in an hour of confidence, which her self-sacrifice had but too well merited. Extending her hand, she showed the glittering gem, exclaiming as she did so—

" This signal all within the walls obey. I am charged by thy master to hold converse with his prisoners. Give me way."

The man, not doubting the truth of her assertion, unhesitatingly lowered his weapon, and gave her ingress to the chamber, where we must leave her for awhile, and return to the operations of the besiegers.

The flames had destroyed the buildings which connected the keep of Filby Castle with the lofty tower which served as principal entrance to the edifice. The two latter, however, still held good ; the threat of Robert of Normandy binding the garrison and their chief by a sense of mutual safety. The principal efforts of the enemy were, however, directed against the keep, where they knew the captives were confined, and to which Robert of Artois and the greater number of his followers had retired. Herbert de Lozenga's men had brought several battering-rams with them, which, under the direction of George of Erpingham, they were suspending from their massive swings before the iron-plated gates of the stronghold. It was an object with the besieged to impede the progress of their labours, and it was the spot where the contest raged most fiercely. The northern side of the donjon, next the water, was unassailed, and comparatively unguarded.

It was from an angle of this position that Harro had winged the shaft at the request of Rachel.

" Listen ! " cried the prelate, as he perused the billet. " We have friends within the walls. Heaven will bless our cause ! Perhaps ere morning's dawn the lost brides may be restored to us."

" Read, father, read ! " impatiently exclaimed both Ulrick and Mirvan.

The bishop did so :—" When the first hour of twilight falls, the little postern 'neath the northern bastion will be opened. Place your men in ambush. An esquire and a female will issue from the keep. As you would avoid the sin of deep ingratitude, harm not a hair of that man's head. His companion will explain the means by which the keep may be secured. Keep up the assault upon the western side, draw the attention of the beseiged to that spot ; and that alone. Once within the walls, courage and your own good swords must do the rest."

" Perhaps some snare," said Odo of Caen ; " can you guess the writing ? "

M 2

"Evidently a woman's hand," replied the reader, handing it at the same time to the two bereaved lovers.

Ulrick and Mirvan each in turn eagerly took the scroll, and returned it to the prelate with a feeling of disappointment, for it was not the handwriting of either Isabel or Matilda.

"Be it from friend or foe its counsel shall be tried," exclaimed Ulrick ; "I will not lose one chance of vengeance."

"Right, boy !" cried his grandfather, the venerable Edda, who, despite his years, had been one of the foremost in the attack. "See ! George of Erpingham waves his sword in signal that the battering-rams are placed. Odo and I will conduct the assault, whilst you and your all but brother lead a party of your men by the wood, to avoid suspicion. Once within its friendly shade, let them steal one by one to the northern postern. If, as the writer promises, the door should open——"

"Leave us to answer for the rest," interrupted the two young men, as they hastened to follow his advice, and draw off their men ; "perhaps, when next we meet, we meet as victors. Farewell."

Ere the aged Saxon could reply, they were on their way.

"Allow me to join you," said Robert of Normandy, as Odo and the veteran marched to the scene of action. "My honour is engaged in this as deeply, knights, as yours. 'Tis long since I have joined in the noble game of war. My blood is warmed, and I feel eager for the sport."

The besieged, who well knew that the destruction of the portal must entail the surrender of the keep, used every means to defeat the efforts of their enemy. Huge benches were brought from the banquet hall, and hurled upon them, crushing numbers beneath their massive weight. Robert of Artois, with the courage which despair will often give, displayed a perseverance worthy of a better cause ; armed with a large iron bar, he laboured to loosen one of the enormous stones which formed the battlements of his strong-hold, the fall of any one of which must have been fatal to his enemies, and rendered their battering rams useless. He would doubtless have proved successful had his men seconded his efforts with equal ardour to his own ; but the slings of the Saxons, who were posted at a distance, so annoyed them that they shrank behind the buttresses, and their leader only owed his safety to the strength of his armour, which was, however, bruised by the heavy blows it had received. As the battering of the huge beams fell upon the portal, he redoubled his frantic efforts, till the vast mass of stone trembled beneath his repeated shocks. So desperate did the besieged at last become, that they used the bodies of the dead and dying of their own party as missiles, and hurled them on the persevering foe.

The attention of all within the walls was directed to the western side so entirely that, as Edda had suggested, the body of men under the conduct of his grandson and Mirvan reached the postern by the lake, as their unknown correspondent had directed. The last rays of the setting sun had already kissed the bosom of the lake in token of adieu as they arrived there. With breathless impatience they waited for the promised opening of the gate ; every moment seemed an age of suspense—an agony of expectation—whose endurance was torture to the mind. The massive doors at last turned slowly upon their rusty hinges, and the esquire Aymer appeared, leading a female closely veiled ; in an instant he was secured and disarmed, and the postern closely guarded.

"What treachery is this ?" cried Aymer, in astonishment at the unexpected attack ; "am I betrayed ?"

The youth was destined to a still greater surprise ; for his supposed mistress, who was clad in the garments of Rachel, threw herself into the equally astonished Mirvan's arms ; and raising her veil as she did so, discovered the features of Isabel of Bayeux, whom the Jewess, in atonement for her former attempt upon her life, had thus contrived to save.

"Where," demanded Ulrick, "is Matilda ?"

"Still in the tyrant's power," sobbed the excited girl ; "haste, if ye are men, to save her."

The words had scarcely passed her lips than Ulrick disappeared, followed by his men ; he needed no clue—instinct seemed to guide his steps to the rescue of his betrothed. And Mirvan, after consigning his rescued cousin and her companion to a party of his archers to conduct them from the scene of danger, followed his example ; for his heart was too generous to taste of happiness while his sister's safety or his friend's peace of mind was still in peril.

The shrieks of despair and the groans of the dying within the walls soon told to Robert of Artois that his den was in the hunter's power. Casting aside the bar which he had continued to wield, he rushed to the apartment where he had confined his captives, and seizing on a female whom, from her dress, he recognised as Isabel of Bayeux, he dragged her with him to an isolated turret which rose by the side of the keep, the only communication between them being a wooden platform, which, with a few blows of his sword, was easily destroyed.

In a few moments Mirvan and Ulrick were masters of the keep, the enemy being entirely subdued.

"Yield thee, traitor !" cried the latter, gazing with agony on the veiled woman whom Robert of Artois still held firmly by the hand, and whom he believed to be Matilda ; "yield, and I spare thy life. But as thou art a man, harm not that trembling dove beside thee."

"Hear me, vile Saxon," replied the baffled villain. "I have sworn that Isabel of Bayeux shall be mine ; and here, amid the ruins of my house, the destruction of my friends, I keep my oath, and triumph still."

"And I," exclaimed the Jewess, dashing aside her veil, and gazing sternly upon the destroyer of her peace, "keep mine. In life or death I swore to be beside thee. Where is now the blooming bride thou didst prefer to Rachel's fervent love ?—safe in her kindred's arms. Where is now thy hold of tyranny and blood ?— the despised Rachel gave it to the triumphant foe. In death—in death we are united ! This is a fitting scene for nuptials such as ours. Receive my bridal kiss."

Before the astonished Norman could recover from his disappointment and surprise, Rachel drew the knife which Harro had lent her on the bastion, and plunged it into her seducer's throat. Although her heart beat wildly as she did so, her hand was firm.

"My oath, my oath is kept !" shrieked the wretched woman, as she beheld her victim fall. " God of my fathers, have pity on Thy guilty child !"

Still holding the weapon with which she had struck the blow firmly in her hand, she sprang from the lofty battlements; one shriek, like some despairing angel's cry, and all was still.

"Such is the end of crime," exclaimed Herbert de Lozenga, who, with Edda and Odo of Caen had found the person of Matilda, and conducted her to her betrothed ; "let Filby Hold be levelled with the dust, that men may shun its wretched master's crimes."

CHAPTER XI.

FILBY HOLD having been completely destroyed, the victorious party returned to Norwich, where, in a few days, by the bishop's advice, the double marriages of Ulrick and Mirvan were celebrated, amidst the rejoicings of the assembled nobles, and the vassals both of Stanfield and the young earl's wide domains. Normans and Saxons equally rejoiced. The double tie, which cemented the union of the two most powerful leaders of the rival races within the Angles, promised to that portion of the distracted kingdom at least a temporary peace. Herbert de Lozenga had urged the immediate completion of the ceremony, despite the recent death of Matilda's father, for the experienced, wary statesman saw the contest likely to ensue on the death of William the Conqueror—an event of which he daily expected to hear ; and he determined to place the happiness of his favourite beyond the chance of war, by a tie which, even in that rude age of despotism and cruelty, was too powerful to be broken—the sanction of the Church.

"Bless you, my children !" he exclaimed, as the two noble youths and their trembling brides knelt to receive his benediction ; "may your lives flow on pure as the current of your thoughts, calm as the exercise of your virtues ; may children, who resemble you, spring like fragrant flowers around you, adorn your path of life, and cheer it at its close ; may the future crown you with its hopes, and past sorrows be repaid you in the present."·

Tears—but they were now tears of joy—bedewed the cheeks of Edith as her maternal heart echoed the prelate's benediction ; and she breathed a silent prayer that Ulrick's life might prove happier, far happier, than her own. Edda, too, the venerable Edda, beheld, in his grandson's marriage, the promise of his race renewed ; and adding a blessing equally sincere, but equally destined to be vain. The day was passed in rejoicing, usual at the period ; the poor were plentifully regaled, the vassals contended in trials of manly skill and strength, whilst their lords jousted in the lists, where Matilda and Isabel, as Queens of Beauty, sat to reward and encourage by their smiles the victors and the combatants. The day was a glorious one, and the shields of the nobles and knights, which were affixed to lances round the lists, showed their rich blazonry in the rays of the sun. The two bridegrooms had proved successful in almost every encounter, and thrice laid their trophies at the fair umpires' feet. Even Odo of Caen had been unhelmed by Ulrick, and laughingly observed that if marriage gave such strength of arm, he too must become a Benedict. Robert of Normandy, although passionately addicted to the knightly sport, gallantly declined to joust, declaring that the champions of two such dames must be invincible. It was the law of the tournament that any knight who wished to try the prowess of another should challenge him by touching the shield affixed for that purpose beneath his pennon with his lance—its owner, fully armed, generally remaining on horseback by its side, unless when engaged in the *melée*, or in some separate contest. The sports were nearly ended, when an arrow, sent by some unknown hand amongst the crowd, transfixed the shield of Ulrick. The method of conveying a challenge was so unusual, that most men thought it accident, till Edda, as marshal of the lists, drawing it out discovered a label of parchment affixed to it, with these ominous words : " Foiled, but not subdued ! " The old man mournfully shook his head as he read the inscription, which he crushed quickly in his hand, to conceal it from his grandson, unwilling that a cloud of doubt should mar the sunshine of his present hour.

" This is no common arrow," said Odo of Caen, regarding it attentively. " Its feather has been plucked from the ill-omened raven's wing ; the spirit of Robert of Artois hovers round us still. I fear more evil yet."

" I fear so too," observed Hella, the bard, who was standing near his patron, and to whose excitable imagination the circumstance seemed fraught with evil fortune. Had he seen the writing, the impression would have been even more gloomy and profound, for he was one of those who drew omens from birds, and mysteries from everything. " Who saw the traitor's body ? " he demanded.

Neither Edda, Odo of Caen, nor any of the nobles who were standing round, remembered to have seen it.

" Perhaps," resumed the speaker, " the wolf's only wounded, not destroyed. Ulrick may live to feel its fangs again."

" Pshaw ! " interrupted the bridegroom, who had seen the flight of the arrow, and who arrived on the spot in time enough to hear the last observation ; " the Jewess struck home ; and there is no blow as sure as that which is nerved by hate. Besides, tower and keep are both levelled with the dust, and our enemy's bones, doubtless, lie crushed beneath them. But be he living or dead, in body or in spirit, with my good sword, and friends like these around me, I can defy him."

Many a friendly glance answered the appeal ; and Ulrick, in the sincerity of his own heart, believed them.

At this instant the prince gave the signal to end the jousts by throwing down his truncheon, and the brides were conducted to the castle, amid the shouting of the multitude and the benedictions of the poor, to keep their marriage feasts. This time the gifted Saxon bard poured out no unwelcome song as his harp sent forth its strain in honour of the bridegrooms and their brides :—

> " Lady, although thy cheek be pale,
> Thy grief is but the bride's sweet sorrow ;
> Fling over her the silver veil,
> Her eyes will sparkle bright to-morrow.
>
> The jewels in her bridal wreath,
> Like rays of light and dewdrops clashing,
> Are rivalled by the gems beneath—
> The eyes through beauty's glad tears flashing
>
> Fill to the bride a ruby cup,
> And twine it with the choicest flowers ;
> With wine and nectar fill it up,
> As emblem of her future hours.
>
> Hail to the bridegroom and the bride !
> Warm hearts are now around them pressing,
> Hands that would aid whate'er betide,
> And kindred lips pronounce their blessing.
>
> Then, lady, though thy cheek be pale,
> Thy tears are but the bride's sweet sorrow ;
> Fling over her the silver veil,
> Her eyes will sparkle bright to-morrow."

The revel was continued to a late hour ; and long after the wine-cup had been pledged to the new-made brides, the song and merry laugh echoed through the old walls of Norwich Castle.

* * * * *

In a remote corner of the city, near the old church of St. Julian, stood a lone house, whose neglected and time-stricken exterior would have conveyed the idea that it was uninhabited, had not the well cultivated garden, which extended from the back even to the cemetery, proved that careful hands attended it. Plants of a foliage and blossom unknown to Europe were to be found within its low-walled inclosure. This garden was an object of considerable interest and curiosity to the thinly-scattered inhabitants who dwelt between it and the water's edge. No human eye had ever seen the mysterious gardener at his work ; still his labours were evident in the well-weeded walks, and careful training of its flowers and fruits. The house, unlike the ordinary buildings of the period, was entirely of stone. The only apertures for the admission of light were at the back, and those so narrow, and guarded by coarse wooden slides, that it more resembled a fortress than an ordinary dwelling. Its doors—for it had but two, one to the back and front—were studded with thick iron nails. Few persons, however, had ever seen them open ; and such casual passengers or watchers who had, shrank with terror from its inmates, for they were of the despised race of Israel— a people looked upon with abhorrence by the lower orders, and cruelly persecuted, on account of their wealth, by the nobles and petty vavasours of the lands on which they dwelt. Sometimes, however, they secured toleration from their skill in medicine ; and many a feudal lord, who would have wrung the last mark from the Hebrew, protected his physician. In their last character even the Church respected them ; and mitred abbots and dignified prelates, when suffering from the surfeit or the spleen, condescended to invoke their aid.

It was to the reputation which the master of the lone house in question had acquired in the capacity of leech that he owed the degree of safety which he enjoyed. Abram, for such was his name, was from the East—the land of gold and gems, of mystery and beauty—alike the cradle of the faith and superstitions of mankind. 'Tis strange when we reflect how little Europe has really given to the world ; it has perfected science more than created it ; it has accepted religion—split and divided it into sects, but founded none. The East seems to have been like the first-born child, endowed with the Creator's peculiar blessing.

On the night of Ulrick's nuptials, a boat, carefully rowed, glided down the river which half-encircles the city, past the Abbey of Carrow, and stopped only when it reached the shore facing the mansion of the Jew. The rowers carefully drew the boat from out the stream, and having formed a sort of litter with their oars, placed something like a human form upon it ; it was difficult to distinguish what, so carefully was it enveloped in the boatmen's cloaks. Gently they raised their burthen on their shoulders, and, preceded by a man in armour, who had conducted the operation, slowly directed their steps toward the house we have described. Whatever might be the purport of their visit, it was evident that they were expected ;

for, on the first signal, the door was opened to them, and closed the instant they had passed the threshold with their burden.

They were received by a tall, aged man, bearing a brazen lamp, whose strange costume and venerable appearance impressed even the leader of the little band with awe and respect. His beard, of silvery whiteness, worn long, after the fashion of the East, flowed loosely over his dark gaberdine, which, although made in the prescribed form, differed in richness of materials from those generally worn by his persecuted race; a girdle of silver confined it to his waist; the plates which composed it were graved with Hebrew characters, as was the case of writing materials, and the clasp of a pocket, curiously ornamented with needlework, which, by chains of the same metal, depended from it. The wearer's features were sharp and intellectual; the forehead was magnificently high; the eyes, despite his age, quick and penetrating, but characterised by that restlessness of expression which long habits of watchfulness in scenes of continued danger give; the aquiline nose and peculiar lip marked his descent from the despised nation of the Jews.

"Place your burden there," said the old man, pointing to a low couch, covered with deer-skins and soft matting. "Holy Abraham! but 'tis a fearful risk to run. The prince and nobles have doomed him to the gibbet, and should it be discovered that I have aided him, little would they reck in their fury of the poor leech's life. 'Tis a fearful risk; but it must be run—it must be run. Persecuted as we are ourselves, we owe something to humanity."

"And something to thine interest, Jew," replied the squire. "The day will come when he who sheltered Robert of Artois may lift his head with the proudest. My master has friends more powerful than thou wotst of. This unnatural league between the Norman and the Saxon race cannot last long. The Conqueror draws near to his last breath; his successor will dearly avenge his favourite's wrongs on those who have assailed him; and my master's blazon will once more shine with the proudest. His future sovereign's favour awaits him, should he live; if not, it will avenge him."

"I am no stranger to the value of a prince's gratitude," replied Abram, with a quiet smile; "but say, how didst thou save him from the ruins of his strong castle? The world reports him dead; and those who trembled at his name, whilst living, now fearlessly curse his memory."

"I alone," replied the esquire, "was with him in the tower, except the daughter of thy accursed race whose jealous hand struck the fatal wound. I saw him fall, and would have avenged him, had not the traitress done justice on herself by plunging from the dizzy height, ending her vile career by death. I drew him from the battlements to a secret vault beneath, where for days he hath remained concealed alike from friend or foe; the fools who

levelled both keep and tower in dust little thought that every
stone which fell but added to my master's safety, by hiding the
entrance to his concealment. Thou knowst the rest."

"A Jewess!" exclaimed the old man, endeavouring to suppress
his agitation ; "how came one of our nation to raise her rebellious
hand against a Christian's life ? But thou hast answered me ; thou
spokest of jealousy—knowest thou the maiden's name ? "

"Rachel," replied the Norman ; "she was the daughter of the
chief Rabbi of Rouen ; my lord took her at the sacking of the city,
when Duke Robert seized it from the French. For awhile she was
all in all, but at last became so jealous, that his love soon tired ; too
much fondness fatigues us in a woman : it is the chasing of the
deer gives pleasure to the hunter : few prize the game which is so
easily won."

A half-suppressed groan broke from the bosom of the old man
when he heard the name of the unfortunate being who had been
alike the victim of her own passions and Robert of Artois' cruelty.
With a violent effort of self-control he mastered his emotion, and
pointed to the men who had borne the wounded noble to his house,
to remove the cloaks in which he had been wrapped. Brantone—
for such was the name of the esquire—would have started had he
seen the fierce glance of hate which flashed from the eyes of the
leech when the pale features of the wounded man first met his
view—the basilisk's alone could have been more fearful. Drawing
a small silver probe from the case of instruments which he wore
suspended by his side, he proceeded to examine the wound,
which was situated in the lower part of the throat, just between
the juncture of the neck-piece and the coat of mail."

"Has thy master no friends or kinsmen near," demanded the
Jew, "in whom he can confide ? "

"I know but one," replied Brantone ; "the prior of the
Dominicans—his uncle by the mother's side ; all else have failed
him."

"Send for him quickly, then," resumed the old man ; "for in
twenty-four hours he must answer for his sins. All human aid is
vain. The blow hath been too deeply struck for human aid to save
him ; and I would not, for the world, a Christian noble should
expire beneath my roof."

"Dog ! " said the soldier, raising his hand to strike him, "were
it a palace, he would honour it."

Abram started back, and drew a long, sharp-pointed weapon from
his bosom, and calmly awaited the attack of the infuriated esquire,
who paused, half-ashamed of his own violence, and half-awed by
the calm attitude of the aged man before him, who seemed so
bowed by years that he felt he could crush him with a breath.

"Back ! " exclaimed the Jew ; "for did the blood of thousands
circle in thy veins, thy death were instant. Willingly I would not

take thy life ; for the fierce storm which once raged here is now at peace. A blow would thaw the frozen barriers of my blood, and spread, like Etna's lava, desolation around."

"Patience, old man !" cried the superstitious Norman ; "I did not mean to harm thee. Let there be peace between us."

"Fear not," resumed Abram ; "I am cool—quite cool. Reptiles only sting without discernment. Approach, young man," he added, willing to increase the impression he had already made upon the terrors of the strong soldier ; "nay, fear me not. Observe how wisdom may contend with strength—how palsied age may bid defiance to the force of youth. Look on this tiny instrument—observe it well ; 'tis formed of that precious steel which in the East men prize far more than gold. Tempered in fires lit first by nature's hand, then quenched in snows coeval with the world,.the slender point inflicts no gaping wound, but a slight puncture merely—a sempstress's needle would give as deep a scratch ; but the point is venomed—anointed with——Enough, this land breeds not the reptile from whose sting 'twas ta'en."

"It might serve thee against one," doggedly answered Brantone, struggling to conceal his terrors, "but would be useless against our numbers, were we inclined to outrage."

"Thou would'st not be that one," said the leech with an accent of cold contempt ; "but I am armed, were it against thousands. Fearing not death, I have surrounded my lone hearth with him. Norman, there's not a step within these walls but hides a grave ; one blow," he added, catching up an ebony staff, and pointing to a globe of coarse glass suspended from the ceiling, "and a storm more fearful than the simoom's breath would shatter these strong-built walls, and tear their inmates limb from quivering limb. Away !" he added ; "thou knowest my power—knowest how little the old leech fears thee. Away, and do my bidding to the prior. Tell him, when four-and-twenty hours shall pass, his nephew's sleep will be eternal. I have stanched many a wound—recalled the fleeting life to many a lance-pierced breast ; but here e'en Abram's skill must fail."

Whether the physician spoke from really conscious power, or from his knowledge of the human heart, so prone to superstition, it would perhaps be difficult to decide. Certain it is, that he possessed vast knowledge, with some charlatanism mixed with it. His words, however, produced the desired effect upon his hearers—ruffians who, under ordinary circumstances, would have desired no better sport than to ill-treat and persecute a Jew. Without a single word, they retired from the house, nor breathed freely till they found themselves beneath the shadow of the church, where alone, according to the superstition of the age, no evil power could approach them.

"Praise be to our Lady !" exclaimed one of the men, devoutly crossing himself, "we are safe from yon den of sin. I would rather have another such a siege at Filby than pass an hour in it. Think you, sir squire, it is a Christian's part to leave our master in his keeping? 'Tis true his body is past caring for, but then his soul?"

"Pooh!" answered Brantone; "his uncle, the worthy prior, will care for that; the old sinner will be too well paid to play him false; the Church would know how to deal with him, should the Jew attempt aught against his salvation."

"Ay, ay," interrupted a third; "leave the Church alone to deal with infidels and sorcerers; a sprinkling of holy water would take the devil from out of the best of them. I saw the Archbishop of Rouen lately burn three of them; they were fine robust fellows when they went into prison, and fought with their guards like troopers, but the Church soon tamed them; they walked on the morning of their execution as meekly to the stake as a lamb does to the slaughter-house, and sang their own funeral service as piously as any monk of them all."

"Our master, I tell you again, is safe," interrupted the esquire, who well knew his companion's tediousness when once mounted upon his favourite hobby—sorcerers and infidels. "'Tis time that we should separate; I must to the holy prior, who will doubtless repay our fidelity to his nephew with something more solid than benedictions, and you to your hiding-place in Filby woods. When all is over we can pass to Normandy, where a good lance never lacks employment, or a good sword need hang rusty in its scabbard." With these words the group separated; the men to regain their boat, and the esquire to the distant monastery of the Dominicans, where dwelt the uncle of the unworthy Robert of Artois.

As the party left the house of the Jew, the old man carefully closed the iron-bound door, and secured it by a massive chain and many a well-forged bolt; then, raising his lamp from the stone floor, where he had placed it, he slowly directed his steps to the chamber where he had left the wounded man. Going to a small cabinet, he carefully drew from it various balsams and dressings, and spread them on the table in the middle of the room. To have gazed upon him, few would have suspected the storm of passions raging in his breast, his manner was so calm, his actions so deliberate. A slight impatient quivering only in his fingers, something like the half-clutch of the impatient vulture's claw, might have indicated to a very close observer that his office was not one of love, but a ministry of hate. Cautiously he cleansed the wound, and poured in the healing styptic, bound the throat, and then prepared the draught for his exhausted patient.

"Precious elixir!" he murmured, "few in this island have ever tasted of thy healing virtues. I shall never more behold the flowers from which thy subtle essence was distilled. Little did I

dream, when first in Syria's land of wisdom I prepared it, that I
should ever waste it on my bitterest foe. But he must live," he
added, fiercely, between his teeth ; " live for a vengeance unheard of
until now ; for a vengeance which alone can expiate a wrong like
mine."

The sweet perfume of the balsam filled the chamber as it flowed
into the cup. Highly as the Jew prized it, he poured it with no
niggard hand ; so true is it that hate can sometimes be as liberal as
love. With almost a mother's care, he raised the head of the
wounded man, and poured the rich draught down his throat, then
gently replaced him on his pillow, and, with his finger fixed upon
his pulse, watched by him till he slept.

As soon as the deep breathing of Robert of Artois convinced the
old man that the medicine had taken effect, he rose from his seat
beside him, and walking to the foot of the couch, gazed upon him
for a few moments in fearful silence.

"Yes," he exclaimed, "the God of Israel, though slow, is just ;
the destroyer of my fair and innocent child, like a helpless infant,
is prostrate at my mercy. Rachel," he added passionately, "why
did not I sooner know thy destiny ? " For years so near thee, yet
ignorant of the casket which contained my treasure. I would have
ransomed all thy tears with pearls : as it is, they shall be repaid
thee by his groans. He scorned thee, too, poor girl ! He shall
have scorn for scorn, become his brother nobles' jest, be scourged
from the halls of his fathers, like some vile impostor, and die
despairing and accurst. If I could not save my offspring, I can at
least avenge her. But stay," he added, "something the Nazarene
spoke of thy heroic death. Thy bones must not bleach amidst the
ruins of thy tyrant's hold ! No Christian foot shall e'er profane
them. I will myself go forth while thy destroyer sleeps, and, as
the patriarch of old sought for the body of his son, so will I seek
Rachel, lost child, for thine."

The bereaved parent struck a gong suspended by the side of his
cabinet : its low musical sound was echoed through the house, and
answered by a being who seemed half-giant and half-dwarf, so
disproportionate was the contrast between his height and the vast
breadth of his shoulders, the length of his arms, and the shortness
of his legs, the muscles of both of which indicated agility and
strength. Although somewhat advanced in years, he was far less
aged than his master, whom he looked upon with a love and veneration amounting to idolatry, not only as a high priest of his nation,
but as one of the wisest and best of created beings. To him his
will was law ; and he would as soon have thought of questioning
the slightest expression of it, as of disputing the Law of Moses, or
the authenticity of the Pentateuch. Unlike most persons of his
peculiar formation, there was nothing repulsive in his features ; on
the contrary, they were indicative not only of benevolence and

intellect, but were distinguished by manly beauty. From his earliest childhood he had lived in the family of Abram, had partaken with him of persecution and sorrow, as well as shared the brief moments of sunshine in the old man's chequered, wandering life.

"Ezra," said his master, "hast thou heard of the destruction of Filby hold, the castle of the bold, bad man, who now lies sleeping here?"

"I have, father of the faithful race of Israel," answered the dwarf. "Eli, who purchased many vessels and much goodly plate of the spoilers, told me a strange tale concerning it. It seems the castle was betrayed into the hands of his enemies by some wanton daughter of our race, the discarded paramour of his fierce lusts."

"Speak not thus harshly of her," interrupted his master; "for, oh! she was my child—flesh of my flesh, blood of my blood; my long-lost, only child! When," he added, bitterly, "shall Israel efface the stains of her captivity among the heathen?"

The dwarf was struck to the heart by the tone of anguish in the old man's voice; he, too, had known and loved the erring Rachel, had watched her little footsteps when a child, heard her repeat her infant prayers, and when her ripening beauties opened to womanhood, guarded her with a parent's love, with almost a jealous lover's care. Her loss, which occurred during the siege of Rouen, was scarcely more felt by her father than himself. Madly he rushed from street to street, calling frantically upon the name of Rachel, and proffering sums so fabulous for her recovery that all who heard him deemed him mad. The sight of the being who had caused so much misery to himself and master excited his fury, and with a spring he bounded towards the couch, and doubtless would have strangled him, had not the voice of Abram restrained him from his purpose.

"Hold, Ezra!" he cried; "would that be vengeance?"

"No!" answered the dwarf, turning his eyes from the sleeper, as if fearful to trust them further.

"Leave him to me," resumed the old man; "at present we must go forth, whilst night favours our design. My Rachel's bones shall not be left to be trampled on by Christian feet. Bring our cloaks, and let the boat be ready."

Carefully securing the house, the disguised Israelites made their way to the water side, from whence a boat, rowed by the strong arms of Ezra, took them to Acle, where horses were easily procured to Filby. Abram found, by inquiries from one of his people, whom the thirst of gain led to remain all night about the ruins, that his daughter's remains had been interred, by order of Ulrick, under an oak, at a bowshot from the spot where she had fallen. By the aid of his companions, it was quickly removed; and the dwarf, taking it in his arms, mounted with it on horseback, the living and the dead both being covered by a cloak. Daylight had dawned when they reached the house.

* * * * *

The lordly prior of the Dominicans was seated at his morning repast, when a servitor announced the arrival of the esquire of his nephew, whose supposed loss he bore with wonderful equanimity, although the world had previously given him credit for entertaining a sincere affection for him. The order to admit him was immediately given, for he hoped to find him the bearer of certain letters which had passed between himself and his relative, the discovery of which would seriously compromise him with Herbert de Lozenga, his spiritual superior. Hastily draining the remainder of the spiced hippocras in the flagon before him, he wiped his full lips with his linen kerchief, and prepared to receive him. Brantone, as was usual when approaching churchmen of his rank, bent the knee as he entered the apartment, exclaiming as he did so—

"Your benediction, reverend father ! your benediction ! "

" *Pax Dei sit semper vobiscum !* " muttered the priest, at the same time swallowing the remaining morsel of the manchet bread. "Hast brought me any letters from my nephew ? "

" Alas ! reverend father, you must be aware that he is unable to write."

" I should think so," drily answered the prior, who imagined that the esquire was trying the depths of his feelings, and the soldier on his part supposing that the uncle had been informed of his nephew's almost miraculous escape.

"It will be some time before you will hear from him again."

" I should hope so," muttered the priest, not altogether pleased with what he considered Brantone's familiarity.

" Besides, even if he could find strength to write, it would be difficult to find a messenger in his present abode."

" I should think so, friend," replied the ecclesiastic, crossing himself ; " but answer me, Did your master, previous to his death, confide any papers to your charge ? If so, quickly let me have them. Poor fellow," he added, "his fate should be a warning to us all how we indulge in our sinful passions, or engage in dangerous enterprise."

" How, reverend father ? " exclaimed the soldier. " You are not yet aware that your nephew, Robert of Artois, still lives ! "

" Lives ! " echoed the uncle, with an expression of anything but agreeable surprise ; " and what does he want with me ? Doubtless gold—more gold. I had need hold the primacy, and my poor priory to boot, to supply half his extravagance ; it hath nearly ruined me already."

" My noble master will never need gold more : he is wounded unto death."

" And where is he concealed ? "

[ROBERT OF NORMANDY PROCLAIMED KING OF ENGLAND.]

N

"In the house of the Jew leech, Abram, whose skill none can question, however they may his honesty. He will not answer for his life more than for four-and-twenty hours. He must not die," added the man, "without the Church's aid."

"Doubtless! doubtless!" muttered the priest. "I will despatch Brother Felix—he is zealous and discreet; besides, I will order Masses to be said for his repose. The Church, though poor in worldly wealth, is rich in spiritual grace."

"Had you not better shrive him yourself?" demanded the esquire, bluntly. "Methinks it were but kind to do him that last good office, considering he is your sister's son."

"I enter the house of an unbelieving Jew? Anathema! Think on the scandal, my dear son. Should the prior of the Dominicans be seen to enter such a den of wickedness, it would be a blister on my name."

"Better that, than other ears should listen to the confession of your nephew," replied Brantone, who began to see through and despise the selfish nature of the churchman's fears. "You know best what has passed between your kinsman and yourself; besides, none but you can prevail on the curate of St. Julian to receive his body into consecrated ground. Sir Prior, you must come."

"Well, I suppose I must. Blessed St. Dominic! shield thy unworthy servant—lead him from this labyrinth; and if ever again—But how," he added, interrupting himself in his invocation, when he observed the soldier regarding him—"how, without scandal, am I to get there?"

"Of course, reverend father, you are free to leave the convent at your pleasure."

"Certes I am," answered the prior.

"Nothing more easy," continued Brantone. "As soon as nightfall, conceal your habit in my horseman's cloak; I will be your escort to the Jew's, where you may give my master a cast of your holy office, and none the wiser; long ere the matin bell, you can return in safety to your nest."

"Thou sayest he has not many hours to live?" said the priest, regarding him with a keen glance.

"Thou mayst take the Jew's word for it, father, if not mine."

"Then I will go," said the prior, firmly, "and trust my person to thy escort. Return at evening's close;—and here," he added, drawing a piece of gold from his pouch, "is something for thine entertainment; but first go to the curate of St. Julian's, and tell him in my name to meet me at the house of the accursed Jew. Fortunately his cure is a dependency upon our priory, and he may look for advancement at our hands. Heaven speed thee, my son; be fortunate, and, above all, discreet."

The esquire bowed reverentially to the dignitary, pocketed the coin, and quitted the apartment.

N 2

At the hour following the curfew, the reverend uncle was seated by the side of his wounded nephew in the lone house of Abram. Contrary to his expectation, he found the wounded man apparently recovering from his hurt ; his voice, though low, was clear, and his eye bright as ever, although his cheek was pale.

" Dog of an unbelieving race," said the ecclesiastic, who stood calmly beside the couch of his patient, " didst thou not send me word the days of my nephew were numbered, nay, his very hours ? —and yet I find him strong ? "

" My words are of truth," replied the leech ; " the strength thou seest is but the last rallying of life—a flash before the lamp expires. The sun which gilds the coming day will shine upon his corpse."

"Liar !" shouted Robert of Artois ; " I have been wounded nearer to death than this ! I shall live—I will live for vengeance ! I will be a brand to thy accursed race ! My enemies shall bite the dust before me ! Exert thy skill—thou hast not expended all thy nostrums. Stretch the utmost effort of thine art ; mine uncle here will glut thine avarice with gold, pour it like water on thy thirsty palm ; he hath my hoarded treasure in his keeping ; all shall be thine, save but my fleeting life ! "

The dignitary winced uneasily upon his seat, and muttered something about his nephew raving.

" It shall be tried," murmured the old man, " not so much for the gold as for the pleasing your reverend kinsman."

Abram left the room for a few minutes ; when he returned he bore a small silver cup in his hand, which contained a highly balsamic liquid, and offered it to the lips of the impatient knight.

" Drink !" he exclaimed ; " 'tis thy last chance of life—a frail one it is true. Should it fail, all human aid is hopeless ; a few, a very few, short moments will decide."

Robert of Artois eagerly drained the draught, and sank exhausted upon his pillow. The old man quietly took his seat beside him. Something like a smile of satisfaction was visible on his features, as his long, sharp, bony hand encircled the wrist of the drinker. For more than a quarter of an hour he watched his patient in silence, accustomed to veil every emotion of his heart under a mask of cold impassibility. He hid, even from the keen churchman, the fierce joy he felt as the pulse beat fainter and fainter beneath the pressure of his finger. Seeing that the draught had operated, he rose from his seat, and whispered to the prior—

" All that human skill can accomplish hath been done ; what now remains rests between the priest, his conscience, and his God. In an hour Robert of Artois will slumber with the dead."

" I'll have no priest !" shrieked Robert, as Abram left the chamber. " I call upon the fiends to save me ! Can I not make a compact but for one year of life ? I'll give my wealth, possessions —my soul," he added, " but to live ? Will not the tempter hear, or is it but a fable? Is there no heaven, hell, angel, or demon to assist me?"

The Jew smiled as he withdrew yet farther from the chamber. The despairing curses of the destroyer of his child fell like music on his ear. They were the promise of the completion of his deeply-meditated vengeance.

The hour, as the leech had predicted, had scarcely passed, when the prior summoned the curate of St. Julian's to his presence; he was followed both by Brantone and Abram. It was clear, from the livid cheek of the churchman, that his nephew's confession had been a fearful one, for the blood had entirely forsaken his florid face, and the perspiration hung in thick drops upon his clouded brow. The apparition of the corpse was yet more terrible; the teeth were firmly set, the eyes distended as if they would leap from the head, and its fingers entangled in the fragments of the coverlid, which had been torn in its last fearful agony. So terrible was the appearance of the body, that all but the Jew turned from it in disgust.

"Brother," said the dignitary, addressing his subordinate with that tone of.blandness with which a superior intimates a command which the conscience of the hearer should reject, "thou knowest of the misfortune which hath fallen on my house; my nephew is no more. Praise to our Lady! he died penitent. See the body secretly interred this very night within the vaults of the chapelry, and in the morning visit me at my priory. We have long watched thy zeal and diligence in the fold of which we are but an unworthy shepherd, and it is our intention to remove thee to a more extended field of usefulness. For thee, Jew," he added, "the worthy curate on his return will pay thee for thy skill and kindness shown towards the deceased; although the former was but valueless. I need not tell thee to be silent on the events of which thou hast been a witness. Remember this—I caution not twice. Brantone will escort me on my return. Farewell, and *benedicite!*"

Abram and the priest both bowed low, as the prior, without casting a glance upon the couch where lay the body of his nephew, quitted the apartment, and hurried from the house. That very night, Robert of Artois, the noble Norman, whose sword had been the terror of the country, whose exactions desolated the hearths of many a peasant and petty franklin, was consigned to what the world deemed his last resting-place, by the hands of two Jews; no knightly banner waved over his remains; no gilded escutcheon marked his resting-place.

"He will rest securely there," said the curate, as he turned the key in the massive lock of the vault; "his funeral rites must be celebrated at some fitting time. Farewell, friends! I will convey the prior's benefaction to you in the morning; that once done, forget that we have met."

And the pious man pursued his way towards his quiet cell, wondering as he went at his good fortune. The Israelites dogged his footsteps till they saw him housed, and retraced their pathway to the church.

CHAPTER XII.

THE two Israelites cautiously entered the church, and groped their way to the steps which conducted to the vaults where rested the body of Robert of Artois. It was not till they had descended that they ventured to light the torch which the dwarf had brought with him for that purpose ; for the expedition they were engaged in was one of danger, should any curious eye discover their proceedings. The superstitious as well as religious feeling of the age being opposed to the mere entrance of any of their hated nation within the consecrated precincts even in open day, much more so at the lone hour of night, when, according to popular belief, pale witchcraft celebrated its fearful rites—their mere presence under such circumstances was sufficient to condemn them to the stake. The body of the knight had been deposited in an old stone coffin, which had previously served some former inmate, but which in the revolution of time had been despoiled of its original tenant ; the rudely-sculptured cross upon its lid indicated that it had been intended as the final resting-place of an ecclesiastic :

> "Some lordly abbot or some mitred priest,
> Whose hand had grasped the crosier's holy staff,
> Or scattered benedictions on the crowd."

"Help me to raise the lid," whispered Abram ; "the carrion may be stifled else within its narrow cell. Holy Jacob ! how these Nazarene dogs guard their vile ashes from their heir, the worm ! Their pride revolts lest their polluted dust should mingle with its purer kindred earth. So much for Christian vanity in death ! "

By the aid of Ezra's powerful arm the lid of the sarcophagus was soon removed, and the features of the supposed corpse once more exposed to the sweet air of heaven. The elder Israelite gazed upon his destined victim with an air of ferocious joy, as he placed his hand upon his pallid brow, and felt the gentle moisture which already began to ooze from the sleeper's skin ; for our readers, doubtless, have already suspected that the draught which the leech had administered to Robert of Artois in the presence of the prior was nothing more than a powerful soporific, the wound he had received being anything but likely to cause his death, although from neglect and loss of blood it had occasioned considerable exhaustion.

"We must be brief," said Ezra, disturbing the old man's reverie of vengeance ; "day soon will dawn ; and it is not good men's eyes should gaze upon us bearing the body to the house—shall I raise him ? "

Abram made a sign of assent, and his companion soon removed the sleeper from his recumbent position ; and, with the assistance of the old man, was proceeding to envelop him in a cloak brought with them for the purpose, when a deep voice startled them. The curate had recollected that the body had been interred with several articles of value, which the prior, in the agitation of the moment, had either forgotten or not thought it worth while to remove ; amongst them a chain of gold and precious signet ring had attracted his avarice, and he was returning to the vault to secure them, when he was startled by the sight of the two Jews, whom he doubted not were there with the same intention. So servile was the respect and deference which all of their race paid to the humblest member of his sacred profession, so accustomed was he, in trampling upon them, to find an unresisting neck, that the idea of any possible danger to himself never once crossed his imagination.

"Dogs ! " he exclaimed ; " is it thus ye abuse the mercy of our holy Church, which suffers ye to draw your polluted breath in Christian lands in peace ? Violate the dead ! break open the sepulchre of a noble knight for the sake of the treasure he can no longer defend ! Alas ! alas ! what will not the thirst of gold lead men to ? " ·

" Especially priests," interrupted Ezra, in a cold, sneering tone ; " the reverend father measures the strength of others' conscience by the weakness of his own. It were a curious speculation to decide what brought him here."

The curate coloured with mingled shame and anger at the implied accusation, which a secret monitor whispered him was just ; still, as no proof existed of his intentions, he answered boldly, with the assumed confidence of insulted innocence :

" My motives are known to Heaven ; I parley not with unbelievers of the duties of mine office, which alone have brought me here. You will answer to the Church for this outrage on its laws—this robbery of the dead. Infidels, I arrest ye both.".

A low laugh, like the hiss of a serpent, rang through the vault as Ezra sprang upon the speaker, caught him in his giant arms, and forced him upon his knees beside the empty coffin ; then twining his long bony fingers in the hair of the priest, he kept him like an infant immovable in the position he had placed him in. For the first time the intruder's heart beat wildly, and he lost his haughty tone.

" What would you, masters ? " he cried, his cheek becoming paler as he spoke. " The crime may be atoned without the price of blood. Holy Church is not relentless, and a slight fine, perchance—"

"Ha, ha, ha ! a fine ! " exclaimed his captor. "The Christian dog prates as if he were in the presbytery, and we captives and bound before him. A fine ! how holy Church loves gold !—ha, ha ! a fine !—how much, how much ? "

"Mercy ! " exclaimed the curate, now seriously alarmed for his life, which, after such an outrage upon his person, he could no longer deem secure. "I'll be silent !—bind me by what oath you will—upon the Evangile, nay, on the consecrated Host itself ; only spare my life !—I'll show you," he added, "where the sacred vessels of the church are all concealed ; they are of gold—pure gold. Dogs ! you will not dare to shed a Christian's blood ? "

"Is it redder than a Jew's ? " demanded Ezra, still keeping him, despite his frantic struggles, on his knees. "Father," he added, addressing his companion in a tone of deep respect, "decide ; day will soon break. What shall be his fate ? "

"Death ! " said Abram, who had listened to the curate's offers of betraying the vessels of the church with contempt. " In the oath of a false priest there is no reliance ; in the heart of a coward mercy hath no dwelling. Once free he would break his vow of secrecy, and laugh at the credulous Jews as he consigned them to the flames."

"As thou art a man—as thou art human," shrieked the priest, " have pity ! "

"Am I a man ? " replied the Hebrew, in a low, stern voice. " Why am I hunted, then, like a vile beast of prey, by those who call themselves my fellow men ? E'en from his mother's womb, the Jew is made the scoff of a superstitious rabble, less brutal than their teachers ; his blood is thirsted for, e'en as the traveller lost in the desert thirsteth for the well. Ye have made earth no more a heritage for its once chosen people. Ye reckon us like herds, yet hold us in far less estimation ; ye rend the flesh from off our aching bones, doom, despoil us, beat us, rob us of our children and our wealth. In your Christian pride, ye trample us like potsherds 'neath your feet, yet, in the hour of vengeance, prate to us of humanity and mercy."

"Pity ! " murmured the fainting man, already half-dead with terror.

"Pity ! " iterated the Israelite, in a tone of scorn ; " were we in open day, and I grovelling like a worm beneath thy feet, what pity wouldst thou render me ? What would be thy answer to my prayers and tears ? Scoffs and bitter mockeries. And why ?— because chance made thee a Christian and me a Jew. Still it shall not be said that Abram, without necessity, was cruel. As gently as the shadow of the destroying angel's wing fell on the sleeping heathen's host, so death shall fall on thee. I sacrifice thy life not to my vengeance, but to my safety, priest."

The speaker drew from his vest the envenomed instrument with

which, on a previous occasion, he had menaced the esquire of
Robert of Artois, and with a firm hand inflicted a slight puncture
upon the neck of the kneeling man, immediately below the left
ear ; so small was the orifice that but a single drop of blood trickled
from the wound, although the effect was mortal. The head of the
priest fell gently upon his breast, as the hand of Ezra was withdrawn ; and, with a gentle sigh, the spirit fled from its earthly
tabernacle for ever.

"How shall we dispose of the Nazarene's body ? " demanded the
dwarf.

"I have bethought me," said his master. "Clothe him in the
garments of the sleeper, and place him in the empty sepulchre.
Should suspicion lead men to search the tomb, they will find, at
least, a mouldering corpse, and the ring and chain of Robert Artois
—his gown and cowl we must reduce to ashes."

" 'Tis well," exclaimed Ezra ; " but if the seekers come soon they
will never take the features of the fat priest for the stately face of
the Norman knight, although the colour of their hair and beards
are not unlike. How the craven proffered oaths and gold to save
his life ! I question if he would have hesitated to have thrown
his soul into the bargain."

"Silence ! " said Abram, in a tone of calm authority. "Sport
not with the dead ; we are no more its judges. As for the discovery thou pratest of, let but twelve hours elapse, and the eye
even of the mother who bore him would fail to recognise the
inmate of yon coffin. To thy work, Ezra, and perform it dili-
gently," he added ; "for it is a task in which I cannot aid thee ;
the corpse of an unbeliever would pollute the hand of a sacred
Levite."

The bodies of the living and the dead were quickly stripped by
the dwarf, and arrayed each in the other's clothes. The latter was
then lifted into the coffin from which the former had been so
recently removed. Although so lately deceased, traces of decom-
position already began to be visible upon the features of the priest ;
and it was with a feeling of perfect security that Ezra closed the
ponderous lid.

"Now raise the knight upon thy shoulders, and follow me,"
exclaimed the elder Israelite. "Once in the church, I will ex-
tinguish the torch ; darkness will best protect us."

Daylight had already begun to dawn when the two Hebrews,
unseen by mortal eyes, left the profaned sanctuary of St. Julian,
and regained the secure shelter of their lonely habitation.

Three days after the marriage of Ulrick and Mirvan, the two
bridegrooms were summoned, together with most of the Norman
and Saxon nobles, to attend a council to be held by Herbert de
Lozenga, at the episcopal palace, where matters of grave import

were to be discussed, affecting nothing less than the succession to
the Crown. By some means, the share which William of Normandy
had taken in the abduction of the two brides had got whispered
about—probably from some of the garrison of Filby ; and men's
minds were violently disposed against him. As soon as the
principal personages who had been summoned were assembled, the
prelate who presided exposed to them the villainy of the prince ;
his father's well-known disposition in his favour, contrary to the
rights of his elder brother Robert ; and concluded by demanding if
they were willing to assist in placing a tyrant on the throne who
had proved so reckless of their rights and honours, whose deceit
and cruelty were known to all, and whose reign could hardly fail
of proving destructive alike to Norman as to Saxon independence.

"Never, by Heaven ! " exclaimed Ulrick ; "let others bow a
vassal knee to this unknightly robber ; mine ne'er shall bend
before him. If England must own a foreign king, let him at least
be one whom primogeniture hath pointed out the Conqueror's
natural successor. The isle," he added, "is not a petty fief, to be
transferred at his caprice or pleasure. Robert of Normandy shall
be my sovereign, let who will else acknowledge William's title to
the crown. Nobles, it is for you to say if I have spoken well."

"You have," answered Mirvan and Odo of Caen, with one voice,
both equally excited as himself by the unmanly outrage which had
been offered to Matilda and Isabel. "Long live our valiant brother
in arms, and future king, Prince Robert of Normandy ! "

Edda and the rest of the nobles, entranced—the former by his
love for his grandson, and the latter by the example of two such
powerful leaders as Mirvan and Odo—joined in the shout ; and all
but Eborard, the wily prior of the Dominicans, added their voices
to the cry, which was enthusiastically repeated amid the clash of
swords, which the assembly waved above their heads in token of ·
adherence and fidelity to the cause of their future sovereign.

Robert, who was present, gracefully bowed his thanks. He
could, despite the natural familiarity of his manners, assume,
when occasion required it, both the language and the bearing
of a prince. His words were brief, but to the purpose. He
pledged himself—should he by their aid defeat the unnatural
disposition of his father in his brother's favour—to govern justly,
confirm the existing rights of the nobility, and look upon his
Norman and Saxon subjects but as children of the same great
family. When he had finished speaking, the shout again echoed
through the hall—" Long live Robert of Normandy ! "

"Words," said Herbert de Lozenga, rising as soon as the tumult
had subsided, "are but air, and leave no impress of their purport.
Let all here prove that they are men who dare maintain by acts the
resolution they have spoken. Here is a deed," he added, throwing
at the same time a parchment which he drew from his breast upon

the table, "by which we bind ourselves to venture our lives and fortunes, lands and honours, in the cause. I'll be the first to sign it ; and may Heaven reward me for the act, as I believe it to be just and holy ! "

No sooner had the prelate affixed his ·signature than the nobles crowded round the table, impatient which should be the first to follow his example ; even the prior, who saw no hope of escape, and who began to look on William's cause as hopeless, did as the rest ; George of Erpingham and Walter Tyrrel were the last to sign. As leaders of the forces of the bishop, they had both been summoned to the meeting. As soon as the ceremony was completed, Herbert de Lozenga folded the parchment and placed it in his bosom.

" Thanks, nobles, vavasours, and knights ! " exclaimed Robert, his eyes flashing with the anticipation of a crown. " It is to you that I shall owe my throne ; and, trust me, your future sovereign——"

" Our actual king ! " interrupted the prelate, sinking on his knee and kissing the speaker's hand. " Your royal father sleeps his last sleep. William the Conqueror, of all his vast possessions, retains but six feet of earth ; he expired ten days since at the monastery of St. Gervas. May God assoil his soul in peace."

So unexpected was the intelligence, that for a few moments those who heard it were mute with surprise. News did not then fly with the celerity of the present day ; none but the speaker and Robert suspected even the monarch's illness. As soon as they recovered themselves, every knee was bent to the earth, and one simultaneous cry arose of " God save the king ! "

" Sire," exclaimed Mirvan, "the present is the time for action, not for words. Might I presume to counsel you, with the dawn, surrounded by your faithful nobles, you must commence your march towards London. Your brother has many friends, active as he is ambitious. A single day's delay might prejudice your cause ; therefore, again I say, on to London.".

A smile passed between Herbert de Lozenga and the prince ; for no other, except his gaoler, was aware of the captivity of William, so faithfully had the secret of his arrest been kept by those who had undertaken its execution.

" Small danger from our brother," replied Robert, "since our good friend and faithful counsellor (bowing to the bishop) holds him in safe ward. We can arrange our differences without an appeal to arms. Where the lion's skin will not avail him," he added, " William can assume the fox's ; doubt not but he will listen to such reasons as we offer."

" And may I ask your highness," demanded Odo of Caen—for the kings of England did not, till a much later date, assume the title of majesty—" what terms you intend proposing to the prince ? "

"The plain fulfilment of our father's will," replied Robert, "simply substituting my name for his. England for the elder born, Normandy for the younger : they are not too hard, methinks, since both by right of primogeniture are mine."

"And what security will your highness exact," said Edda, "that he keep faith with you ?"

"His knightly oath," said the prince, "and my own good sword will prove sufficient pledges for his faith."

There was a pause, for not one present but was struck with the worthlessness of the first, and the little reliance which was to be placed upon the second part of the security. Thoughts dangerous to the captive's safety were passing in the minds of many, yet no one was found hardy enough to give utterance to the suggestions of his mind. Odo of Caen was the first to break the silence which oppressed them, and make himself the interpreter of the thoughts of all.

"Prince," he began, "there are men to whom oaths are as water or the changing wind—men whom no ties, however sacred, can hold—men whom the slightest breath of passion can induce to break their deep-sworn faith. William is one of these. A nation's peace, the safety of your friends, and the stability of the throne, demand a surer pledge than these."

"I understand," replied Robert, his cheek blanching as he spoke ; "you mean the tomb. But no, rather would I forego the crown itself, wander a simple knight the wide world through, seek fortune in the desert, than stain my hand in my unnatural brother's blood. True he has wronged me ; but the same womb bore us. True he would rob me of my birthright ; yet I have never read that Esau slew his brother. My hand would lack the strength to grasp the sceptre were it stained in William's blood. Think not of it more."

"It needs not, prince," said Walter Tyrrel, who already looked upon his captive's fortunes as for ever set, and who was anxious to render himself acceptable to the new monarch. "William is under my guard ; leave it to me, and he shall never cross your path again."

"Boy !" exclaimed the prince, "greatness is ever cursed by ready tools like thee ! Thou dost belie thy blood by such degrading service ; we had thoughts to have held thee near our person, and fostered thy career. This proffered baseness changes our intent. Retire from the council, sir ; nor presume to approach our presence until summoned. Father," he added, in a whisper to the bishop, "there is a curse upon our race ; the tiger's whelp, reared in the peaceful fold, betrays its lineage by its instinctive thirst for blood. Can the wild legend of our land be true ? Are we indeed Robert the Devil's brood ?"

Bowing lowly to conceal the rage and mortification but too visible upon his features, Walter Tyrrel left the apartment. A quiet smile of satisfaction played on the features of the prior of the Dominicans, as he did so, for he saw that the prince had made an implacable enemy, and that he himself had found a tool fitted for his purpose. " Wisely hast thou spoken, prince," said Herbert de Lozenga ; " for what blessing could attend a crown bought with a brother's blood ? But there are other means than oaths to bind this man—a means to draw the venom from his fangs, yet leave him still with life. Let him, in an assembly of the nobles, from my hands accept the priestly vows. No bishop then could crown him, no sword be drawn for his pretended rights. Once devoted to the altar, the Church would know well how to guard her own."

" By Rollo, priest, but thou hast hit the mark," exclaimed Robert, whose heart began to beat freely for the first time since the disposal . of his brother's person had been debated. " William will make a jovial monk, and many an abbey and fat benefice shall mark our loving favour."

A murmur of approbation arose amidst the nobles, who saw in the proposal of the prelate a bloodless solution of their difficulty. It was finally resolved that on the following day the prisoner should be brought before them, and compelled to conform himself to their decision, which the bishop undertook previously to make him acquainted with ; and with this understanding the council separated.

As Eborard crossed the cloisters on his way to his litter, he encountered Walter Tyrrel, who, still smarting under the reproof he had received, paced their deep shades, meditating schemes of vengeance. The wily churchman read his purpose in his knit brow and quick impatient step, and foresaw that his advances would be · gladly met.

" Methinks, sir knight," he whispered, " devotion like thine demands at least some courtesy ; even in its refusal, William had received its proffer better. Our new-made monarch must feel the crown securely on his brow ere he ventured to spurn the hand that might have rent it from him."

" That might have rent it from him ! " iterated the excited man ; " that will ! Father, I know thou lovest not this same Robert ; I marked thy hesitation when the bishop proposed the signing of the traitorous act. Set but thy foot to mine, and the withered leaf the wind makes sport of shall not prove more worthless."

" What meanst thou, son ? " demanded the prior, with an air of well-affected simplicity.

"Thou lovest not this would-be king—this Robert of Normandy ? "

" Certes, he hath proved himself, scant friend to me or to my order," replied the priest, with a shrug,

" That is as plain as words can say," resumed Tyrrel, " thou hatest him—so I do ; the lightning is not less dangerous because it slumbers in the thunder-cloud, nor thy hatred less to be feared

because veiled in outward calm and priestly unction. Wilt thou
join hands with me in this ? "

" I will," replied Eborard, in a voice so low that the impetuous
questioner caught the sense of his reply more from the look which
accompained it than the sound of the words. " Tell me," he added,
" how can I aid thee in the enterprise ?   Speak in all confidence ;
let there be faith, my son, between us."

" I am William's gaoler," answered the traitor, in the same
subdued tone.   " Hast thou two fleet steeds within thy stables ? "

" I have," said the priest, with a smile of intelligence, for he
began clearly to see Tyrrel's purpose ; "and they are both at thy
disposal ; better ne'er bore a knight unto the field ; kings might
mount them to do battle for their crowns."

" 'Tis well, father ! 'tis well ! Let them be waiting saddled at the
city gates. I will find horsemen for them both."

" When ? " demanded the churchman.

" At midnight ; we have scant time to lose."

The prior bowed his head in token of acquiescence, and requested
to know if the fugitives would require gold for their journey,
which he offered to supply them with, so anxious was he to secure
the success of a project on which his future fortunes hung. His
contentment increased when Tyrrel informed him that he had coin
enough.

" But, how—how," he demanded, " will you provide for his
escape ? All else seems easy after that."

" Leave it to me," replied the knight ; "long ere the dawn the
prince shall be upon the road to London. Lanfranc, the primate, is
his friend. The citizens will eagerly receive him. Once securely
king, doubt not but William's gratitude will find within the Church
a position more suited to thy services and zeal."

" Heaven knows best, my son," said his hearer, trying hard to
look humble and indifferent ; " we court not worldly honours, but
are content to be a humble watch-dog in the fold. Let us not waste
the time in vain discourse," he added, casting at the same time a
hasty glance to see if their conversation was observed, " lest evil
eyes behold us. Keep but thy purpose, and the horses shall not
fail thee. Farewell ! our Lady prosper thy intent ! "

With these words the two conspirators separated—the prior to
find his litter, and Walter Tyrrel to the tower where William of
Normandy, like a caged lion, fretted away the hours of his captivity.

He had not long regained his post, when Herbert de Lozenga
arrived to communicate to his prisoner the decision of his brother
and the nobles. His faithful marshal, George of Erpingham,
attended him.

" 'Tis well, sir knight," said the bishop, as Tyrrel rose and saluted
him ; " you keep good ward. Continue thy services, and the present .

cloud upon thy fortunes will pass away. How fares our prisoner? Impatient, doubtless, of his durance?"

"As a wolf caught in a springe, my lord; but I exchange few words with him. Curses and threats are sweetest words with him. My own temper is none of the most patient, and I avoid him, lest I should forget the respect due to his birth, as well as to his defenceless state; an he escape, let our new monarch look to it."

"Small fear of that," replied the prelate; "our towers are high, and you keep faithful guard. After to-morrow's evening, come to me in my oratory; I have much to speak with you upon, as well as reconcile you to your offended prince, in whose good favour, after all, you have a pleader whom you wot not of."

The knight merely bowed his acquiescence, and the speaker, with his companion, entered the prison.

"'Tis the last time," murmured Tyrrel to himself, "I shall be forced to wear the mask before him. When next we meet, my deeds shall make me known; but till that hour arrives, patience—patience." And once more he resumed his watch before the tower.

William was pacing his chamber with impatient strides when the churchman and his attendant entered: it was the first time of their meeting since the moment of his arrest. To one of his restless character, captivity was galling enough, but uncertainty was even worse than actual restraint. In the hours of his solitude he had pondered on its probable result, and formed a thousand schemes of vengeance on the man whose energy had baffled him; he longed for: yet feared the encounter, experience had taught him he had to deal with one with whom to resolve was to execute. He felt that he was too dangerous a captive to be lightly loosed. The prelate felt on his part that he had a difficult mission to fulfil: to bend an ambitious, proud, and stubborn mind to the resignation of its long-cherished hopes of rule and ambition. For a moment, therefore, they regarded each other in silence, measuring, like skilful wrestlers, each the other's strength. The passionate prisoner was the first to speak.

"So, my lord, you are come at last. I trust it is to implore our pardon for this strange outrage on your monarch's son. You have taken a strange way, methinks, to repay our royal father's favour, by holding his son a captive. Tremble at his wrath when he shall hear of it; his indignant hand will rend the mitre from thy brow, e'en though the Pontiff's self had placed it there."

"The vilest slave, the poorest serf," replied Herbert de Lozenga, unmoved by the prince's threats, "will never more start at the Conqueror's wrath or fear his frown; thy father sleeps his last sleep; the archangel's trump alone can awaken him."

"Dead!" exclaimed William, to whom the intelligence, in his present position, brought tenfold danger. "Dead! Where is thy

knee, sir priest ?   Forgettest thou that thou speakest to England's
king. or do I see a traitor ? "

"Traitor I am none. My knee hath already offered earthly
homage to its lawful sovereign, thy elder brother Robert. The
assembled nobles," added the churchman, " have confirmed my
voice ; in two days he marches on to London."

" To be crowned ! " shrieked William. " Priest of Belial ! 'tis
thou hast plotted this—my witless brother hath not brains to springe
a woodcock with. Tell me," he added fiercely, " what is the bribe
for which he bought thy soul ? Try if I cannot outbid him.
Was't gold—was't power ? for priests I know, love both. Tell me
thy price !—my ransacked kingdom shall be ground to pay it ; thy
voice in England shall be but second to mine own."

" Prince," interrupted his visitor, " it is already greater far than
thine. since by my mouth the king thy brother speaks."

" I say the traitor Robert Duke of Normandy ! " exclaimed the
prisoner, foaming with impotent passion, and striking his clenched
fist upon the table till the blood trickled from his knuckles ; then,
controlling himself with a violent effort, he added, " and what
would our loving brother with the fool his knavish tool hath
snared ? But I guess !—imprisoned monarchs seldom have long to
live."

" Unhappy man ! thy words are but the echoes of thine own evil
heart. Robert's voice was the first to spare thy life ; he would not
wear a crown bought with thy blood. Learn," he added, presenting
him with a paper, " upon what terms thou still mayst live, if not a
monarch, at least in honourable state.".

William eagerly perused the paper, and his cheek became
alternately red and pale, as rage or fear predominated, while he
did so. As he concluded, his passion broke all bounds ; he tore
the document into a thousand pieces, exclaiming as he did so :

" Accursed priest ! this is thy work. In every line I read thy
subtle malice. But thou shalt tear the quivering flesh from off
these bones with pincers—pour molten lead into my throbbing
veins—rend out my heart, ere I consent to pronounce the damning
vow. A priest ! Moloch shall be my god, and blood my consecration ; thy life shall be the first I offer at his shrine."

The infuriated man sprang upon the prelate, and, unarmed as he
was, would have strangled him or dashed his brains out against his
prison walls, had not George of Erpingham interposed his giant
strength between them. With his mailed hand he thrust him back,
and William, exhausted by his passions, sank upon a seat—his
hair erect, his eyes glaring upon the churchman like a foiled tiger
disappointed in its spring.

Herbert de Lozenga gazed on him with a mingled sentiment of
pity and contempt.

" Prince," he said, in a tone unmoved by anger, " thou hast heard

[ROBERT OF ARTOIS ATTACKED BY HIS MEN-AT-ARMS.]

thy doom. Twenty-four hours are given thee for reflection. That space elapsed, I resign thee to the charge of those who well know how to deal with natures such as thine. For thy attempt to lay hands upon the priest of the Most High, we scorn and pardon thee. Farewell! "

Without waiting a reply, the bishop, attended by his faithful marshal, quitted the tower.

" A priest ! " iterated William, as soon as he was alone ; " rather the dungeon or the grave. Fool ! to be thus caught. For every moment of my thraldom, a life should answer it, were I but once more free. The hoary villain is not to be bribed. Robert hath bought him ; body and soul he is his. Since my good angel hath deserted me, I call upon the fiends to aid me. Wretch that I am," he added, after a pause, " I am so lost that Lucifer himself would scorn to tempt me. No hope of freedom !—no loophole for escape ! —here and hereafter cursed!—undone for ever ! "

The captive sullenly dashed himself upon his couch, and gave himself up to the bitterness of despair. His reverie was not of long duration, for his solitude was broken by the entrance of Walter Tyrrel into his cell. At first he scarcely deigned to notice him ; suddenly the idea of tempting him flashed upon his mind, and starting from his recumbent position he abruptly demanded :

" Knight, art thou ambitious ? "

" Like most men," answered Tyrrel, coolly, " I seek to mend my fortune ; for, like your highness's, it has proved a scurvy one at present. Patience or time, I suppose, will better it ; if not, I must endure it."

" I'll better it," exclaimed William ; " satiate thy thirst with gold, thy pride with honour."

" It must be in the Church, then," answered the young man, carelessly, for it was no part of his plan to be too easily persuaded : " if rumour speaks rightly, prince, you are likely to possess scant other patronage, and I have little devotion for the cowl."

" With titles, boy," said the prisoner, sinking his voice almost to a whisper ; " the broadest earldom that our realm can yield, with wealth wrung from these traitors' blood. Knowest thou not that I am already king ? "

" I thought it was your elder brother, Robert. At least this morning, at the council, the nobles hailed·him so."

William winced at the reply, and even then mentally determined, should he succeed in winning his gaoler to his purpose, to repay him by long years of expectation and disappointed hopes for the pang it gave him. What to him was an oath more or less in the long catalogue of those already broken ?

" Can nothing move thee ? " he murmured.

" To what ? "

" To free thy monarch from the snare traitors have woven round

O 2

him—to accept the fortune which now woos thee to crown thy
name with honour—to place my foot upon the throne, where thou
shalt stand the nearest. Methinks," urged William, "an earldom
were no mean price e'en for so vast a favour ; what from my
brother canst thou hope for more ? "

" Perchance not half so much," replied Tyrrel ; " but then I risk
not life and honour. Besides, a prince's promise is so soon forgot."

" Shall I swear ? " exclaimed the captive, beginning at last to
comprehend the man with whom he had to deal; "propose the oath."

The young man did so ; and the prince eagerly repeated it,
binding himself by every saint to bestow the promised recompense
as soon as the crown should be securely his, and imprecating the
most fearful vengeance upon himself if he broke his oath to him.

"If I fail my promise," he concluded, "*may thy arrow let out
the perjured life-blood of my heart !*—may my days be but one long
agony of doubt !—may all good men execrate my name, and history
hold me to the scorn of future ages ! "

The triumphant Tyrrel sank upon his knee, and kissed the hand
the speaker held to him.

"Pardon me, sire, my doubts," he cried ; " but my future devotion shall alone for them. This very night I'll break your
chains ; true friends are watching eagerly to aid us."

" Name them," said the now joyous captive, who felt confident
that his escape was certain.

" The prior of the Dominicans."

" Good ! he may be trusted ; all churchman are not traitors."

" By his orders horses at midnight will be waiting for us at the
city gates. Long ere the day which was to seal your degradation
dawns, leagues shall divide you from your enemies. In three days,
at most, your highness may sleep in London, where the venerable
primate and your father's friends impatiently await you. Once
there——"

" My enemies shall feel the lion's wrath," interrupted William.
" I'll make their homes a desert—their names a scoff ; and thou
shalt be my instrument of vengeance ; like the faithful jackal,
thou shalt hunt down the quarry ; and we'll divide the victim's
spoil between us. Fear not, good Tyrrel," he added, familiarly
placing his hand upon the shoulder of the man in his heart he
already meant to deceive, "but there will be enough for both of
us. The headsman first, and confiscation after ! "

It was finally arranged that the knight should convey a suitable
disguise to the prince, who was not, however, to assume it till after
his evening meal, when all danger of observation from the men-at-
arms would cease, as after that hour they would have no pretext
for entering his apartment.

" And what mummer's mask am I to wear ? " demanded William,
when all was arranged, and Tyrrel was about to retire.

" A priest's."

" Good," he continued ; " 'tis like the eagle's feather on the shaft which wounds it. I'd like to trick the cunning bishop with a snare of his own skin. I'll wear my cowl sooner than my loving brother thinks, though not so long perhaps. Farewell. I have my instructions, and will follow them."

" Farewell, my liege," answered the traitor, who little thought that in aiding the escape of William he was marring his own proud · fortunes ; " when next we meet thou shalt be in fact, as well as right, a monarch."

" And thou a belted earl," said the tempter, graciously ; " the first and nearest to our throne."

With these words they separated—the youth to indulge in dreams of future greatness, the tyrant to meditate on schemes of future vengeance.

As the clock of the cathedral struck the hour of twelve the same night, a group of four men might be seen leading two well-appointed steeds towards the gate of St. Stephen's—then, as now, the direct road to London ; three were in the dress usually worn by the men-at-arms of that period ; the fourth, enveloped in an ample cloak and barret, might have been taken either for a noble in travelling costume or a priest. From the number of franklins and personages of note whom late events had assembled in the city, the departure of such a party even at so late an hour created no surprise to the warders—men selected from the burgher-guard—sleepy, fat-headed fellows, more inclined to drink their ale in peace than challenge for the pass-word three determined men who seemed both able and willing to dispute it.

" Thank Heaven ! " exclaimed the prior—for it was no other— as soon as they were about a bow-shot from the gate, " we are here at last. I trust our friends may arrive as safely. Bring the horses under the shadow of this tree," he added, pointing to an old oak, whose wide-spreading branches would have afforded obscurity to a much larger party ; " here we will wait the arrival of the fugitives. Holy Mother ! but this night's work has fatigued me."

The churchman seated himself upon the grass as he spoke, while the men secured the horses, and all awaited in silence the arrival of the prince and his companion. They had not long been thus occupied, when they were startled by a rustling in the branches above them. In an instant every one was on the alert ; the men at arms, with their arrows drawn to the head, ready to fire into the tree.

There was a pause, for the noise was not repeated.

" Waste not your shafts," said the prior ; " 'tis but an owl, or some bird whose rest we have disturbed. Hark ! "

" Whoo ! whoo ! " was heard distinctly from the foliage, followed by the shrill sharp cry peculiar to the obscene bird.

"I told you so," he continued; "three men-at-arms, and frightened by an owl!—ha! ha! ha!"

The speaker's raillery was cut short by the arrival of the two fugitives, who, dressed in the habits of monks, had contrived, through the treachery of Tyrrel, to pass unsuspected by the guard.

"Benedicite!" said the priest, as soon as he beheld them; "thank Heaven! they are arrived at last."

William and his companion threw off their disguise in silence, and appeared well armed in riding dresses underneath. The prince was the first to speak.

"Sir prior, we are your debtor; deeds, not words, must speak our thanks. Are these men to be relied on?"

"Body and soul, they are your highness's servants."

"'Tis well," replied the prince, as he mounted his horse; "let them attend us till we pass the outward post, when all danger for the moment ceases; and you, reverend father, accept our signet ring—it might betray its wearer, for not an officer in our realm but knows its impress; we will redeem it with a monarch's ransom. And now, my men," he added, "forward! If we pass unchallenged at the outward post, return to the good prior; if not, prove to the traitors you can use your swords. Adieu."

The two fugitives, preceded by the men-at-arms, advanced upon their way, leaving the churchman beneath the shadow of the oak, watching their progress with interest.

"He must succeed," murmured Eborard; "with less valour than his brother, he has ten times his cunning and perseverance; besides, the Primate loves him, and will respect the Conqueror's will. Once king, our haughty bishop may rue his traitorous zeal in Robert's cause. I'd give my life," he added, "but once to feel my foot upon his neck; he hath thwarted me at every turn. Life!" he added, "I'd almost give my hope of heaven."

"Agreed!" cried a voice from the centre of the oak—"agreed!"

Unnerved with terror, the blasphemer sank upon his knees, trying to mutter a prayer.

"*In nomine confiteor Dei!* Heaven have mercy upon me! Blessed St. Dominic, *ora pro me.*"

The invocation was interrupted by a scream of horror, as a figure, scarcely human in its proportions, dropped from the branches beside him, and seized him by the neck with a giant's grasp.

"Priest of Belial," whispered the dwarf—for it was no other than Ezra, who had been out to collect simples for his master, and had concealed himself in the tree on the approach of the party—"it is a compact. Thou art mine!"

At this moment, overcome with fear, the prior fainted.

In this state he was discovered by the men-at-arms, on their return. With some difficulty they recovered him from his swoon. But the ring—the prince's signet-ring—was gone!

CHAPTER XIII.

GREAT was the surprise and indignation of the nobles on the following morning, when, at the hour of their assembling, the flight of their captive, and the treacherous Tyrrel, was made known to them. Success, which before seemed certain, was once more reduced to the chance of civil war—a risk which many were anxious to avoid, whilst others secretly rejoiced at it, as a means of increasing their fortunes by the plunder and confiscations of their enemies' domains. Few, however, ventured to express either content or dissatisfaction at the probable result, for the principal leaders remained as firmly as ever united in the cause of the monarch whom they had unanimously acknowledged. But to Robert the intelligence was as a death-blow to his hopes ; the crown which he had grasped already seemed to elude him, and the share which Tyrrel had taken in his brother's escape deeply wounded him. The curse of his race, the hand of fatality, seemed to be upon him. Of the other members of the league, Herbert de Lozenga alone perhaps foresaw the probable downfall of their enterprise ; for he knew how popular, by his largess and courage, the fugitive had contrived to make himself with the army, to whom his competitor was comparatively unknown. The implicit obedience which the primate Lanfranc would be sure to pay to the last will of the Conqueror, by whom he had been raised to his elevated position, as well as his love for William, whom he had educated, and who had received the honour of knighthood at his hands, was another obstacle in their path ; and the mere fact of that prince being acknowledged and crowned by a prelate possessed of such influence in the kingdom, both from his high rank and virtues, together with the possession of the late king's treasures, would give him an immense advantage over his generous and less prudent rival. Still the prelate did not despair of retiring with his brother peers from the league with honour as well as safety ; for most of the nobles possessed estates in England as well as Normandy, and would naturally favour any arrangement which promised them security for their possessions in both countries ; their party was sufficiently powerful to be feared, and by remaining in arms, or by advancing towards London, they might probably secure by treaty a sufficient guarantee for their lives and liberties, as well as the confirmed investiture of their lands. With this clear view of their position, his object was to urge them to immediate action ; and his voice was the first which predominated above the confusion which the unexpected intelligence had caused.

" Hear me, most noble princes and lords," he cried ; " this is the hour for action, not for words ; firmness and promptitude will oft assure the triumph despair would resign as hopeless. Are we less unanimous or less determined than before ?—is our cause less just ? —or Robert's right to possess the crown less sacred ? "

" No ! " shouted the assembly, with one voice ; " Robert is our lawful king, and we swear never to own another whilst he lives."

" 'Tis well ! " resumed the speaker ; " leave words for women, then—deeds are for men ; and ours must answer for us. The *élite* of the army of the late king is still in France ; discontent is rife within the land ; the men of Kent bitterly resent the captivity of their earl, Odo, Bishop of Bayeux, the Conqueror's uterine brother. I have already sent trusty emissaries to inform them of our purpose, and doubt not but that they will rise to second us. , London, between two armies, must surrender. Hold we, then, our first resolve, and advance towards it ? "

" We do ! " was the cheerful cry of all ; and it was finally agreed that on the following morning they should commence their march —the young men eager to win fame and honour, the old ones to take advantage of events as they might arise. Just as the assembly was about to disperse, the door of the council chamber was thrown hastily open, and a stranger, clothed in complete armour, entered the hall, without saluting any of the astonished nobles ; he made his way to the spot where Robert was standing, and embraced him with a familiarity which nothing but equality of rank or the tie of blood could warrant.

The prince's first words explained the mystery of the stranger's want of ceremony.

" Welcome, my reverend uncle ! " he exclaimed, at the same time, according to the age, saluting him on the cheek. " By what good providence do we see you at liberty ? It is not often that our father's captives break their cage."

" By our faith, nephew," replied Odo of Bayeux,—for it was no other than the warlike prelate, whom the Conqueror had with great difficulty been prevailed upon, when dying, to release,—" but our brother's cage has proved a strong one. For the past, let us forget it. William, I trust, sleeps in peace, and all my enmity is buried with him ; but first," he added, " let me offer the homage of a subject to his sovereign, and then to affairs touching our mutual interests."

The speaker would have bent his knee in token of fealty, had not his nephew, whose hopes his presence had revived, gracefully prevented him, saying as he did so—

" The nephew can receive no homage from his uncle ; the king demands no pledge from one whose loyalty is so well assured. Besides, my lord," he added, " as a spiritual peer, it is not thus that you should do me service."

" True," replied the warlike churchman, with a smile ; " but 'tis always thus : whenever I have harness on my back I forget my priesthood, and assume the baron. See how gravely our brother of Norwich looks, as if to remind us of it. But come," he continued, " present me to your friends."

The shouts of "Long live the valiant Odo!" "Long live the valiant bishop!" echoed through the council chamber.

"Now then, to work," continued the prelate, as soon as the cries subsided; "let's see the muster-roll,—what nobles adhere to your standard; what friends you have to count upon; what enemies to crush, or to win over to your cause."

A few words made the speaker acquainted with the position of affairs, and the declaration by which the Norman and Saxon barons acknowledged Robert as their king, and pledged their lives and fortunes to support his claims, was submitted for his inspection by Herbert de Lozenga. He perused it eagerly, and with evident satisfaction.

"Ay!" he exclaimed, "this is something tangible. No vague promises, signifying nothing; no equivocation here. Lives and lands are engaged, and my unworthy name will be honoured by appearing in such goodly company."

Snatching a pen from the table, the speaker added his signature to the list, which he handed over to his brother bishop.

"When do we march towards London?" he demanded; "'tis there the battle must be fought and won."

"With the rising sun," replied the now hopeful Robert.

"Good! I will prepare for our reception there; I have friends amongst the greasy citizens. Find me, my lords, a trusty messenger; one with a soldier's eye and a statesman's head; the less likely to be recognised the better. He must be noble, for he will have to treat with nobles; brave, for the service is of danger; speaking Saxon as well as Norman tongue; for, in his mission, he must have speech with both."

Eborard, the prior of the Dominicans, although scarcely recovered from the fright he had received the previous evening, had, to avoid suspicion falling upon him for his share in the escape of William, contrived to be present; he saw that an excellent opportunity was at hand for serving the cause to which he was so deeply committed, could he obtain possession of the papers. Blandly, therefore, he proffered the services of his esquire, a creature devoted to his interest, to be the bearer of the important letters; vouching, at the same time, for his nobility, which was even more questionable than his fidelity. Perhaps there was something too eager in his manner of making the offer, or Odo of Bayeux knew too much of his character, for he refused it so drily that even the effrontery of Eborard did not allow him again to renew it. The concluding words of his refusal were even more significant:

"Churchmen, in the simplicity of their unworldly natures, are but poor judges of character, reverend prior; therefore, we will choose another messenger. Robert," he added, "let orders be given that no travellers be permitted to pass the city gates without a permission signed by some military chief on whom we can rely.

We must guard against treachery from within as from without ;—not that I suspect aught like treachery from any here."

The prior bit his lips, and resumed his seat in silence.

"I am less likely to be recognised," said Ulrick, "and, should the council deem me worthy of such trust, willing—nay, eager—to undertake the expedition, for I would fain do something to prove myself worthy of my place amongst you."

The warlike bishop eyed him for a few minutes as he would read his very soul. Experience had taught him that bitter lesson, learnt sooner or later in the world—suspicion ; but there was something so open in the offer, so modest in the way in which it was made, that he resolved at once to trust him. Some natures require no guarantee for their honour and fidelity, for God has imprinted truth upon their brow, and art can never imitate the signature. Ulrick was one of these.

"Be it so, young man," replied Odo. "I neither ask thy name nor birth, for something tells me that thy heart is nobler far than either. Short time for preparation waits thee ; within an hour thou must depart. Take such precautions as seem best to thee to travel unsuspected ; but remember it is an enterprise where prudence will avail thee more than courage, and wit protect thee better than thy sword."

Most present approved of the churchman's choice, for during the attack on Filby Castle they had witnessed the courage and cool presence of mind of the young lord of Stanfield.

"Farewell, my lords," said the young man as he quitted the assembly to bid adieu to Matilda and his mother ; "within the hour, I shall be ready for my departure."

"Had the guard of your prisoner, nephew," said Odo of Bayeux, "been confided to that young knight, instead of the worthless traitor who deceived you, our task might have been easier."

Robert heard the observation in silence, for there were circumstances which made the comparison between Ulrick and Tyrrel deeply painful to his nature.

The number of vassals which each noble could bring into the field was next gone into, and the line of march drawn out. Here Edda's knowledge of the country was of inestimable value, for he enabled them so to trace their route that all doubtful places or towns likely to be in possession of the enemy were avoided, the great object being to arrive before the walls of London with as little delay as possible. Their army was to be preceded by a proclamation in which Robert's claim to the crown, as eldest son of the Conqueror, would be duly set forth, and such promises of equal government held out, as would induce the oppressed Saxon population to hasten to his standard.

The council soon afterwards dispersed, the nobles to give orders for the departure of their troops, and arrange the order of march.

As Eborard mounted his litter at the palace gate, he whispered something to one of his attendants, who set off immediately towards the house of Abram, the Jew.

"So," exclaimed the prior, as soon as he was seated in his comfortable cell in the Dominican convent of the city, "my lord of Bayeux already doubts me—let him ; doubts are not proofs. The time will soon arrive when I may avow the step I have taken proudly to the world, and trample on my enemies. Robert, thy star is on the wane. William's is rising, and my fortune with it. Why loiters this cursed Jew?" he added, starting from his seat, and pacing the floor impatiently. "I must employ him as my messenger to London. Ulrick shall find friends whom he wots not of to meet him there. Robert of Artois' death shall yet be paid me at his hands."

At this moment, Abram was ushered into the apartment, and stood, bowing reverentially, before him. "So, infidel, thou art come," said the churchman. "1 have employment for thee, in which thou mayest win not only gold, but friends, so that thou executest faithfully the trust I shall confide in thee."

"Abram," said the old man meekly, "is the servant of his lord. Let the master speak, the slave hears but to obey. Is the reverend prior ill, the leech is ready with his drugs to cure him."

"Satan confound thee, unbeliever, with thy drugs and charms. I am for none of these ; thou must gird up thy loins, and journey for me even unto London."

"To London !" ejaculated the old man, with unfeigned astonishment. "What should the leech do there ?"

"That I will tell thee. Seek out the king, and deliver to him, word for word, my message. Tell him that his uncle, Odo of Bayeux, hath arrived, and that the rebellious nobles plot against his crown ; that the men of Kent are expected to rise in Robert's favour. Bid him look to Pevensey and Rochester—both."

"Alas ! my lord ; but these are fearful words to fall from lips like mine ; had not your reverend priorship better write ? "

"No, heathen," thundered the priest ; "I place my life in no man's hands. If thou art caught, stoned, burnt, or hanged, 'tis but a Jew the less ; for who would listen to his word against a Christian and a noble ? "

"True," said the leech, bitterly ; "the reverend priest speaks truly. The Hebrew's life is but as the twice-pressed grape, a thing fit to be trodden underfoot by every brutal clown or steel-clad noble. But how, please you, without a letter, am I to obtain an audience of the king ? They would spurn thy servant from his palace gate, e'en as an unclean beast from out the city walls."

" I will provide thee with a token that shall procure thee access ; but remember Ulrick, this new-found Earl of Stanfield as he calls himself, is the bearer of letters to those of their friends about the

Court. It is of the utmost consequence he should be secured. Use every diligence to arrive before him. It is well-known that thy people possess facilities for travel organised in the interests of their vile commerce. Say, dost thou understand me, Jew? and art thou willing to pleasure me in this?"

"My lord hath spoken," said Abram, bowing low, "and his servant hears but to obey his will."

"Tis well," answered the churchman; "so, on thy return, shalt thou find protection at our hand."

"Not for shekels of gold," replied the Hebrew, "or shekels of silver, will I consent to do this thing, but for thy favour."

"How can it serve thee?" demanded the prior, rejoiced to hear that his purse-strings were to remain undrawn.

"There is a bark lying in the harbour near," replied Abram, "which brought thee goodly wine from Rouen. Two of my kindred, who are tarrying with me, would fain return unto their native city, with sundry bales of merchandise—an order from thy hand, under thy seal, would secure their passage, and good treatment from the rude captain; this is the only guerdon I would ask in requital for my pains."

"Holy Mother!" exclaimed the prior, "but thou seemest well acquainted with our affairs. It seems our convent cannot import wine for the poor and sick, but a Jew's nose must scent it; besides," he added, willing to make the obligation greater than it really was, "it were an ill example for a Christian prelate to connive at a Jew's escape."

"Then seek some other messenger," replied the old man, firmly, "for thou hast heard the only conditions on which Abram will do thy bidding."

"Dog! this insolence to me! Dost thou not know that I can crush thee like a vile worm beneath my foot? The Church's arm, though slow to strike, is terrible when roused. Thou art too much honoured in our condescension; our confidence hath made thee bold. Let me but raise my voice against thee, and thou art lost."

"But thou never wilt raise it," coolly answered the old man.

The calm tone of his voice, so different from the usual tone of supplication with which those of his race addressed all who belonged to the Church, astonished the crafty prior, whose first impulse was to summon the assistance of his lay brothers, and consign him to one of the numerous prisons of the convent; but an instant's reflection taught him that the Jew must possess a surer guarantee for his personal safety than the mere confidence which had passed between them, ere he ventured to brave his wrath. It was, therefore, in an accent as free from anger as he could command, that he demanded why he should not raise it.

"Because, priest of Belial," said Abram, firmly, "it would be the signal of thy destruction. Hast thou forgot thy correspondence with thy vile nephew, Robert of Artois ? The letters are in my possession."

" Go on," said the priest, clenching his teeth with suppressed rage ; his eye glancing menacingly on the speaker.

" Remember, too, thy treachery last night. Were it but known that the prior of the Dominicans aided the flight of William of Normandy, and, churchman though he is, his life would be of as little purchase as the despised Jew's."

" And who would believe the Hebrew's word ? " demanded his hearer, with a sneer.

" None," replied Abram ; " but all would listen to his proofs— the nephew's letters, and the prince's ring."

" Sorcerer," shouted Eborard, starting from his seat ; " dost deal with fiends ? I'll have thee racked for this, rend the flesh from off thy unbelieving bones, bathe thee in molten fire, tear out thy accursed tongue. Fool ! idiot ! " he added " with such a secret to enter in these walls."

The firm glance and self-possession of the Hebrew during these fearful threats were not lost upon the speaker, who, in the very torrent of his wrath, calculated every chance affecting his own safety, which some secret presentiment seemed to assure him would be compromised by proceeding to extremities with the being who had ventured to defy him ; he hesitated, therefore, to give the signal which might lead to their mutual destruction ; they remained gazing on each other for awhile in silence.

" Hear me," at last replied Abram. " Thy crimes and my knowledge of them enable the despised Israelite and the haughty priest to treat as equals. I did not venture within these walls without good precaution for my safety. If I return not within the hour in safety to my dwelling, the letters which thou wotest of, and the prince's signet-ring, will be placed in the hands of Odo of Bayeux. Now, then, decide ; I speak no more."

In an instant the manner of Eborard changed. He felt that he was check-mated by the wily Jew, and he inwardly consoled himself for his present humiliation by anticipations of future vengeance when the success of William should render further temporising unnecessary.

" ' Tis well, Jew, at length I know the terms on which we treat as equals. Be it so ; but remember, that the least treachery on thy part will cost thee dear, for even should I fall I leave behind many who would avenge me. There," added the speaker, hastily writing the order to the captain, and sealing it with his seal, " there is the paper thou demandest for thy friends. See that the price be thy fidelity—thy mission faithfully accomplished, and we are quits."

" Thanks, most reverend prior," said Abram, bowing with his usual humility, " hast thou further orders for thy servant ? "

"None; thou knowest my message—see that it be delivered, or woe upon thy head."

The aged Israelite carefully folded the important paper, and placed it in a pouch in the inner lining of his garment. His dress was far less costly than the one we have described him as wearing in his house; instead of goodly cloth, his gaberdine was made of a threadbare stuff, patched in several places, and a plain cord, instead of the engraved silver girdle, bound it to his waist; yet, wretched as it was, probably an earl's fee would scarcely have purchased that miserable vestment, for gems of price were quilted for security within its folds, and the bond of many a noble for moneys lent sewn between the linings.

In Abram's way from the priory, the only remains of which at the present day is St. Andrew's Hall, where the greasy citizens of Norwich, in the days of its corporate corruption, fed upon the flesh-pots of Egypt, he had to pass that part of the city known as the Castle Ditches, being the space comprised between the inner and outer moats, and where the retainers of the nobles and the men-at-arms were in the habit of amusing themselves by wrestling, playing the game of quoits, or contending in feats of strength. For some time the old man made his way comparatively unmolested except by an occasional gibe or rude curse—insults to which he was too much accustomed to notice. At last he approached a party of soldiers, who had been playing for a wager at some game of agility, and who were clamorously urging upon the loser, a square-built, beetle-browed, ill-looking ruffian, to pay his loss.

"By St. Martin, masters!" he exclaimed, "but you are hard upon me; you cannot have more of a fox than his skin. St. Martin," he added, as he beheld the Jew approach, "never leaves his votaries in the lurch. Here comes my treasurer; now then, ye cormorants, ye shall be paid in full."

To seize on the person of Abram, and drag him into the midst of the circle, was the work of a moment; the feat was so dexterously accomplished that his companions hailed it with a laughing shout of approbation.

"What would ye, gentle masters?" demanded the old man, in his usual submissive tone.

"Money," replied the ruffian; "I have played on credit, and the saints have sent thee to pay my score."

"Money!" iterated the Jew; "and where should I obtain it? I have been despoiled of everything but the garments which I wear. The air I breathe is taxed, the light of heaven is taxed, my very prayers are taxed. Were you to rend the flesh from off my bones you could not wring a silver penny from me. I am poor."

The declaration was received with a shout of derision, as one of the pleasantest jests imaginable; the idea of a Jew being poor seemed to them so ludicrous, so accustomed were the brutal soldiery to such asseverations when they practised their unlicensed extortion upon them.

"We shall see," said the fellow, tightening his grasp upon his prisoner. "Were thy gold secreted in thy very heart, I know a trick to squeeze it forth. Be reasonable ; twelve silver pennies, and thou art free. Thou canst not object to that, in honour of the saint who hath sent thee to pay my debt."

"I have already told thee that I have no money. I am old, and in thy hands, weak, and cannot resist thee ; dispose of me as thou wilt, for when did Christian ever spare one of our persecuted race ? "

"He blasphemes ! " cried the fellows, who had gathered round, delighted at the sport of tormenting a Jew.

"Try the cord upon his thumbs," shouted one.

"Strip the unbeliever," said another, "and burn his greasy rags— the ashes will be worth the sifting."

The latter proposal seemed to hit their humour best, and, despite his feeble resistance, the gaberdine was nearly torn from off their victim's back, when they were arrested by the voice of Ulrick, who, on his way to the palace, to receive his letters of Odo of Bayeux, came suddenly upon him. As the party who attended him were numerously armed, the plunderers paused at his command.

"What would you do, my masters ? " he exclaimed. "Is it thus you show your courage, in despoiling an unarmed, aged man ? Shame on you—shame ! "

"He is a Jew," suddenly growled the fellow who had seized him, "and refuseth to pay, in honour of St. Martin, twelve silver pennies."

"And what right hast thou to force him ? Release thy hold upon his garment, or, by the saint whose name thou hast profaned, I'll crack thy casque, to teach thee mercy, knave ! "

This declaration was received with a murmur of discontent, not only from the ringleader, but by his companions, who were indignant that a Christian noble should interfere on behalf of an Israelite, and whose appetites were excited by the hope of plunder.

"Drag him along ! " cried one. " Bring him to the cathedral precincts ; no one will dare to interfere with us there."

"As thou art a knight," said Abram, in a supplicating tone, as the ruffians were dragging him away ; "for the honour of her who bore thee, leave me not in the hands of these rude men."

"Disperse the rabble ! " exclaimed Ulrick, to his followers. "What ! " he added, as their leader, who still held his grasp upon his prisoner, drew his sword to resist him, "art bent upon thy punishment ?—this, knave, to teach thee humanity, and this to remember Ulrick of Stanfield."

The indignant speaker made but two blows at the ruffian as he spoke. The first shivered the iron helmet on his brow ; the second inflicted a deep wound, which seamed his head from the temple to the jaw. His companions, seeing that the knight was in earnest, took to their heels; and the wounded man sullenly released his captive, who immediately threw himself at his protector's feet, blessing him for his humanity to one of the despised and persecuted race of Israel.

"Follow your companions," said Ulrick, pointing with his sword to the fellow he had wounded, and who was stanching his gashed cheek with the end of his sleeve; "and thank my mercy I do not consign thee to the care of my seneschal. A rope were a fitter instrument of punishment for a robber than a noble's sword. Begone! and, as you value life, beware how you cross my path again."

"Beware, sir knight," shouted the villain, when he had withdrawn out of the reach of the party, "how you cross mine! You have set your mark upon my face; mine shall be graven in your heart. Peter Norbeck never forgave an injury yet. We shall meet again to pay our scores."

"Follow him not," said Ulrick to his followers, who, indignant at the fellow's threats, were about to pursue him. "His head once healed, he will forget the fray: an he remember it, small matter."

"And now, noble sir," said Abram, who had arranged his torn garments, "let your valuer state at what price you set the old Jew's ransom; and poor as he is, he will beg from every brother of his tribe but he will pay it."

"Ransom," said Ulrick, in a tone of compassion; "and dost thou think, old man, I saved thee from yon ruffians, but to plunder thee myself? I should be then the greater robber. No! tell me but where thou livest, and two of my followers shall see thee safely to thy dwelling."

The Israelite listened to him in astonishment; so extraordinary did it appear to him that a Christian noble should render protection to one of his nation without extorting gold as the price of his service.

"Am I then free?" he demanded,

"Free as the air."

"And without ransom?"

"Without ransom."

Abram bowed to the ground before the young noble, and repeated his thanks, declining, at the same time, the escort that was proffered him. Perhaps he was fearful of attracting attention to his dwelling.

Ulrick, who was too enlightened to be entirely the slave of the barbarous, rude prejudice of the age, which regarded the Hebrews as a people accursed by God, and fit only to be oppressed by Christians, gazed on the venerable old man who had resumed his way, with interest and pity.

"It cannot be," he thought to himself—for he was too careful to shock the prejudice of the age by uttering the sentiment aloud—

[ULRICK DEFENDING HIMSELF AND GILBERT.]

"that Heaven intended man to be its avenger; Omnipotence needs not our finite strength to crush its enemies. See," he added, aloud, "the Jew returns; he hath thought better of our proffered escort."

Something had been cogitating in the old man's mind as he pursued his way. The being whose ruin he was commissioned to accomplish by the prior, by announcing his journey to London to William, had preserved him from the brutal outrage of the ruffians into whose hands he had fallen. Deeply as he had been wronged by Christians, his humanity was not quite changed to gall. He returned, therefore, on his steps, to warn him of his danger, and, if possible, provide him with a shield against it.

" Now, Israelite, what wouldst thou ? "

" I would speak with thee," said the old man, bowing servilely, "speak with thee, noble sir, alone."

Ulrick motioned his followers to retire. No sooner were they out of hearing, than Abram threw off the cringing manner which he had hitherto assumed, and spoke with the dignity and firmness of a prince addressing his equal—a tone which he maintained throughout their interview.

" Sir knight," he began, " I little thought ever to feel interest or care for one of Christian blood. Nay, frown not," he added ; "didst thou but know half the wrongs, the bitter mockeries, I have endured, thy anger would be less. Enough, I will serve thee. The journey you are about to take will be a dangerous one. The messenger of Odo of Bayeux would meet with little mercy at William's hands, were he discovered."

" Knowest thou," interrupted Ulrick, struck with surprise, " knowest thou thus much ? "

" More—much more than this," continued Abram. " A messenger already is commissioned to inform the prince of thy arrival, but for thy sake he shall not depart. I have the power, as well as will, to stay him. Where wilt thou lodge, supposing thou arrivest in safety at thy journey's end ? "

" At Whitefriars. I have letters from the bishop there."

" Then art thou lost. The prior is devoted to Prince William. He looks to be a bishop."

" With the Earl of Brittany then."

" Worse ; he would sell thee for a mess of pottage."

" At some hostel, then," added Ulrick, scarcely knowing where or what to say.

" They are filled with spies. No," continued the old man ; " thou hast served me for the sake of that common humanity which Christians would deny all of my race ; I, in my turn, will serve thee. Take these," he added, offering him a set of tablets, on which he rapidly traced something in Hebrew characters ; " it will provide thee with a secure retreat, where hatred would fail to find thee, and

power lack means to drag thee forth. Not an Israelite within the
realm but, at the sight of them, would count down gold at thy
necessity—will shelter thee within his dwelling."

"Who art thou, man of mystery?" demanded Ulrick ; "and
whence this power over thy peculiar people ? "

"Question not that," said Abram, "but use it for thy safety.
Should closer danger press thee, this ring will prove thy safeguard.
Farewell. And may that Being, who is alike the God of Jew and
Gentile, bless thee for thy kindness to my age."

There was something so truthful in the old man's voice, so honest
in its tone, that Ulrick doubted not, even for a moment, of his
sincerity and ability to serve him. He concealed the tablets, as a
precious gage of safety, in his vest, and gazed upon the ring, which
he still retained in his grasp.

"By every saint !" he exclaimed ; "but this is more mysterious
still—'tis William's signet."

With thoughtful mien he pursued his way to the palace, debating
in his mind whether to lay the singular gifts, and relate the interview, before the prelate, or keep silence upon the subject.

*   *   *   *   *

In a vaulted chamber in the house of Abram the Jew, the entrance
to which was so cunningly concealed as to defy detection, sat, or
rather was bound, in an iron chair, the gaunt form of Robert of Artois.
The wound which Rachel had inflicted was more dangerous in
appearance than in reality, and the skill of her father had quickly
caused it to heal. During his progress to convalescence the old man
had treated him with the tender solicitude of a parent. He had
preserved him, not for love, but vengeance ; for as soon as the cure
was complete he had removed him, whilst in a deep sleep, by the
aid of Ezra, from the apartment above, and securely bound him in
his seat of torture. The room in which the victim was confined was
a low, arched vault, built of unhewn stone, and lighted by an iron
cresset, suspended from the ceiling.

The first idea of Robert, on recovering from the stupor in which
he had been plunged, was that he was dead, and the gloomy cell his
assigned place of punishment ; for, before him was an object well
calculated to strike terror to a soul more firm than his. The Jewess,
embalmed by her father's skill, was seated on a species of tribune
before him—her dark hair, as when living, glittering with gems—
her eyes, glazed by death, fixed with a stony glare upon him. Vainly
he sought to shut out that fearful image ; if he closed his eyes it
presented itself but more vividly to his mental sight—there was a
species of fascination from which he could not fly. Memory presented
her as he first beheld her—young and unpolluted, innocent and happy,
till, like a serpent, he had left the trail of his destroying passions on
her young heart, and blighted its existence. There was something
too horrible for reason in this silent commune between the living

and the dead ; his mind began to wander ; at times he would entreat her to forgive him, then revile and curse her. Still the impassible accuser gazed upon him, unmoved alike by imprecation or by prayer. The countenance of Robert of Artois gradually became distorted by passion and terror ; Rachel's retained the cold expression of the dead. It is impossible to say how long the guilty man could have remained in this frightful solitude and lived ; his ravings already began to be incoherent, when Abram, with a case of instruments under his arm, entered the chamber of death.

"Dog ! " exclaimed the indignant noble, as soon as he beheld him, relieved from the worst apprehensions that he was dead. " What sorcery is this ? Why am I bound like a thing for sacrifice in this dark cavern, and what means this carrion here ? "

" It means," exclaimed the old man, with a passionate burst of grief, "that she was my child, and thou wert her destroyer. It means that she was betrayed, and that I am her avenger."

" Beware ! " shouted the captive, writhing with impotent rage ; " beware how thou attemptest my life. My uncle, the prior, will soon return to claim me ; his wrath will light a fire that will consume thee."

" He will return no more," calmly replied the Jew ; " he hath seen thee, as he believes, dead. Brantone, thy esquire, witnessed thy interment in the neighbouring church from which I have released thee, for not e'en the grave could shield thee from a hate like mine."

" What wilt thou do ? " demanded Robert, blanched with terror, when he saw how completely he was in the speaker's power.

" I'll tell thee," said Abram ; " I will not take thy life, for that were mercy, not revenge ; but I will so change thee, that e'en thy mother could not, were she living, recognise her child. A premature old age shall replace thy manly strength—a gift thou hast so oft abused ; the muscles of thy scornful brow and haughty cheek I will dissect away, till not one lineament remain of Robert of Artois. I'll change thy raven hair to grey, and pluck thy beard from off thy living face. Then, when thou art deformed in person as well as mind, when not one trace remains for men to know thee by, I'll send thee into the world to beg, to rot, to starve, to be the scoff of those who lately licked the dust from off thy feet. What thinkest thou, Christian—shall I not be revenged ? "

" Horrible ! " shrieked his prisoner. " Mercy ! Mercy ! "

" Ay," continued the old man, drawing a scalpel from his case of instruments, " such mercy as thou showedst to her. Writhe on, serpent," he added, " thou canst not escape me."

A groan of anguish broke from the unhappy man, as Abram plunged the instrument into his cheek, and began to remove the skin. Cries and supplications, mingled with threats and curses, were repeated, as with a firm hand and unmoved heart the avenger pursued his fearful task within the vault—the only witness the cold and passionless dead.

Day after day he returned to his victim, and relentlessly pursued his vengeance. By some corrosive preparation the beard was utterly destroyed, and the deep brown clustering hair thinned almost to baldness. As the Jew foretold, agony and terror turned it grey. At last, when the transformation was entirely accomplished, when the once haughty features of Robert of Artois, scared by a thousand minute cicatrices, were no longer to be recognised either by the eye of love or hate, Abram resolved to release him from his seat of pain ; the preparations for his own departure from England had long been secretly made. Again the powerful narcotic was administered, and the disfigured tyrant found himself, when he awoke from his deep slumber, reclining beneath a tree, not far from the castle of Ormsby, once his own domain ; he was clothed in rags, an oaken staff and wallet were on the ground beside him. Slowly he dragged his enfeebled steps towards the porch, where several men-at-arms were amusing themselves with Brantone, discussing the late siege of Filby Hold ; not an eye recognised in the wretched object before them their once haughty lord, and one, a fellow more surly than the rest, asked why he came prowling round the manor.

"Do you not know me ? " he demanded, in a trembling voice.

"Know thee ! " exclaimed Brantone. "No, fellow, the servitors of the prior of the Dominicans keep better company. Get thee to the convent. The reverend father bestows no alms here."

"The prior ! Do I dream ? " said Robert. "Methought this manor belonged to his once powerful nephew."

"Did belong," replied the men ; "but since our young lord's death, it hath been granted to his uncle."

A low groan was the unhappy man's only reply to the announcement.

"Lost ! " he murmured to himself—"lost for ever. The accursed Jew spoke truly. My own menials spurn me from my door."

As this moment an old hound, which had long been useless for the hunt, but which had once been his companion in many a gallant chase, approached, and began to whine and sniff the air uneasily around him.

"Look ! " observed Brantone, "if old Rollo does not seem to recognise him."

"Because," said Robert, dashing aside the indignant tear which the faithful animal's recognition had caused him to shed, "he is more faithful in his instinct than thou art in thy reason. Changed as I am, he knows his wretched master, Robert of Artois."

A shout of laughter followed the announcement.

"Master," said one, "ha, ha, ha ! The noble knight returned from Purgatory ! Ha, ha, ha ! "

"From a worse place," observed another, pointing to his scarred face. "Satan has left the mark of his claws ; he must have battled stoutly to have got back again."

"Peace," cried Brantone ; "don't you see the poor wretch is mad ? There," he added, throwing a small copper coin, "there is a mite for thee ; stoop for it, and begone."

The o'erfraught heart of his quondam master swelled bitterly at this last insult. Alms to be offered him at his own gate, by one of his own creatures, a thing whom but a few days before he could have crushed, was more than his haughty spirit could endure.

"Slave !" he exclaimed, "it was not thus thou didst promise to me when my mistaken pity saved thee from the gibbet to which thy life was forfeit, for plundering the abbey at Lisieux ; hast thou forgot thine oath of gratitude ?"

The loud laugh of the men, to whom the tale was imperfectly known, roused the anger of the esquire almost to madness, and catching up a quarterstaff which was near him, he would have felled the seeming beggar to the ground, had not the faithful hound sprung from his, by all but him, forgotten master's side, and pulled him to the ground. In an instant a dozen weapons were raised, and the brains of the faithful animal dashed out upon the spot.

"Villains ! you shall dearly pay for this !" exclaimed the excited Robert. "Deeply shall my poor hound's death be revenged !"

"Begone !" cried Brantone, rising from the earth. "I am a fool to listen or be angered at a madman's ravings. Use your staves," he added, sternly, to the men, "and drive the beggar forth."

The men-at-arms, eager to recover the good graces of the esquire, who was known to be high in favour with their new master, eagerly obeyed his commands, and, despite his curses and imprecations, drove the wanderer from the gate.

"God !" exclaimed Robert, as soon he was alone, "can this be real ? Is it not some hideous dream ? Rachel," he added, as the horror of his position flashed upon him in its bitter reality, "thou art fearfully avenged !"

Then commenced the real punishment of Robert of Artois.

CHAPTER XIV.

IT was near the hour of sunset, just before the guard for the night was set, that a traveller, dressed in the sober garb of a peaceful citizen, and mounted on a strong grey horse, which seemed more fitted for a belted knight than a humble trader, approached the barrier of Ludgate ; not, as now, in the very heart of the Metropolis, the busy nest of active industry, but one of the fortified entrances to the City, and connected by a low wall with the Barbican.

Cheapsyde, at the period of which we write, was a narrow street, far different from the Cheapside of the present day; quaintly-built houses, chiefly of timber, overshadowed the roadway with their rudely-carved projecting balconies, few of which were glazed— strong shutters of wood, raised or depressed with cords, serving the inhabitants to exclude both air and rain. As the buildings approached Cornhill they became more and more straggling, with gardens or patches of land between them. Sometimes a mansion of more goodly appearance than the rest might be seen a little removed from the wretched unpaved road, but more frequently the eye encountered only miserable huts inhabited by watermen and small traffickers, or families whose fortunes were as doubtful as their characters.

As Ulrick—for the traveller was no other than the disguised Lord of Stanfield— neared the gate, his steed attracted the attention of the men-at-arms, always ready to discuss the merits of a horse, or speculate upon the character of its rider. The warder—a grey-headed man, who still retained evidence of great personal strength, and whose keen blue eye, glancing from beneath an overhanging brow, would have prepossessed a physiognomist with any thing but an opinion in his favour—stood by, listening to them in silence.

"Marry," said one, "but our citizen is well mounted; I have seen a worse piece of flesh than that sold for a hundred marks; it seems of Flemish breed; perhaps its master is some foreign trader."

"Trader indeed!" observed a second; "where are his saddle-bags? He holds his seat more like a man accustomed to crack crowns than count them. There again! How well he reined him up over the broken ground! No, no; the rider of yon goodly steed has never been a trader."

The warder, who had been scrutinising the traveller, nodded his head with the air of a man who hears an opinion which coincides with his own, but continued his observation in silence.

"Welcome, my master," said the first speaker, as Ulrick reached the gate. "Art come to witness the coronation of our young King William? It takes place in two days. That steed would fetch a goodly price to figure in the pageant. Many a noble will appear worse mounted."

"Coronation!" repeated the traveller in evident surprise; "'tis rather sudden; it is but lately that I heard of his father's death. He is in haste, methinks, to grasp his crown."

"Traitors, 'tis whispered, disputed it with him," replied his questioner; "and the holy primate is resolved to make short work of it. Hast never heard of the king's elder brother, Prince Robert?"

"Not often," said Ulrick, trying to look indifferent; "princes and kings trouble me but little; I strive to make an honest living, and leave the great ones to settle their disputes."

"Thou art a trader, then?" demanded the warder, speaking for the first time.

The traveller merely bowed his head, so hateful to him was the subterfuge to which prudence compelled him to have recourse.

"And what dost thou deal in?"

"Steel, sir warder, steel."

"I thought so," drily observed the fellow, whose suspicions were excited, although but vaguely.

"An you lack a sword, good friend, I shall be happy to furnish you, and at a reasonable price," said Ulrick, willing to avoid further questions, which began to anoy him.

"Perhaps I may use the occasion," replied the warder. "I have long thoughts of cheapning one. Where shall I find you—in the city?"

"No, at the St. Dunstan, the patron saint of all good armourers," answered Ulrick, at the same time giving his horse the rein to continue his route. "Good night, my masters. I love not the late hour, and mine host of the jovial saint will be uneasy if I tarry longer."

The traveller with these words quietly resumed his way, much to the annoyance of the warder, who gladly would have detained him till the arrival of the officer and guard who were to relieve his post. Once or twice he had thought to have arrested him on his own authority; but the lack of warrant, and the idea that after all he might perhaps turn out to be some wealthy merchant, restrained him, for the City was extremely jealous of its privileges, and he was their immediate servant; still he determined not to lose sight of him, but set some one to dog his steps.

"Gilbert, Gilbert!" he exclaimed, directing the voice to the interior of the tower. Why, how the hound sleeps! Gilbert, I say! Ho! some of you, break your quarterstaff over his sleepy head!"

A shrill cry of pain from within announced that his brutal order had been complied with. A thin, pale, half-starved looking youth, of about seventeen, came from the guard-room, wiping the drops of blood which trickled down from his high and not unintellectual forehead. No tear, however, dimmed his bright blue eye, which shone from its caverned socket with almost unnatural lustre, indicative either of disease or insanity. Calmly the poor boy stood before his tyrant, who this time, either because he thought him sufficiently punished, or that time pressed, forbore to ill-use him further.

"Dost see yon traveller, hangdog?" he demanded, pointing to Ulrick.

"I do," replied the boy, meekly.

"Follow him—dog him to his home. Better lose thine eyes than lose the sight of him. When thou hast housed him, bring me word, fast as thy lazy limbs can carry thee."

"I will."

"Away, then," continued the ruffian, "and make good speed. If I find thou tarriest but one second I'll lash thee with my bow-string till I lay bare thy bones. Thou knowest me; do not trifle with my anger."

A slight and almost imperceptible shudder passed through the frame of Gilbert as he heard the threat. The next minute he was following the track of Ulrick, as he wound his way through the many intricacies of the crowded city.

It was not long before our hero perceived that he was watched; every time he turned his head he perceived the pale-visaged boy, whose glance instinctively shunned his, as if conscious of the degradation of his employment. As he approached Temple Bar considerable confusion was caused by a party of the City guard, who were escorting the civic authorities on their return from Westminster, where they had been to pay their homage to the new king, who had solemnly confirmed their charter, to attach them to his interests.

Ulrick saw that the occasion of avoiding his pursuer was too favourable to be lost: spurring his powerful horse, he dashed through the cavalcade, regardless of oaths and menaces, and quickly disappeared down one of the numerous lanes which led to the water side, by which means he avoided the Strand and the village of Charing, following the banks of the river till he arrived at Westminster, where he expected to find Anselm, abbot of Bec, in Normandy, a known partisan of Robert, to whom he was more especially addressed by Odo of Bayeux.

"Back, boy!" exclaimed one of the guard, rudely seizing Gilbert by the shoulders, as he was endeavouring to force a passage through their ranks to follow the horseman. "What will happen next, when traders take the crown of the causeway in the teeth of the City magistrates, and boys break through the City guard?"

"Pray let me pass," cried the youth, struggling to release himself from the speaker's grasp; my errand is of speed—you know not how much depends on my fulfilling it."

A loud laugh, accompanied by blows, was the only reply of the angry official, and the poor lad was thrust back until the procession had passed; when he had threaded the barrier Ulrick had disappeared.

Anselm, the abbot of Bec, who was afterwards destined to fill so important a niche in the history of his times, lodged with the prior of Westminster, to whom he was distantly related. In his manner he was cold and stately, concealing an ambition atoned for by great benevolence under a veil of self-possession. Perhaps in early life he met with one of those misfortunes which chill without freezing the heart; he had looked upon the world, and scorned its worthlessness. Deliberately he perused the missive of his brother prelate, glancing occasionally from the letter to the bearer, who met his gaze with that unembarrassed ease which only truth or long habit of dissimulation gives ; the scrutiny was apparently satisfactory.

"We meet, my lord, in strange times," he observed, "and your enterprise is one which only zeal and courage could undertake ; not that I venture to pronounce it hopeless. Many of the nobles prefer Robert's claim to William's ; but unfortunately the primate is against him. In two days the church will consecrate the usurper's rights ; Lanfranc will place the crown upon his head in the ancient abbey of St. Peter's."

"Have the nobles, then, no voice in his election ?" demanded Ulrick ; "for election it clearly is if the law of primogeniture be set aside. The barons of the Angles already have proclaimed his brother king, and even now, with Robert at their head, are on their march to London."

"Robert," said the churchman, "possesses many kingly qualities ; but he is rash as generous, and lacks the perseverance to assure the triumph of his cause. Who are his chief advisers ?"

"His uncle, Odo of Bayeux," replied our hero.

"Better in the field than at the council board," observed the priest. "Who next ?"

"Odo of Caen."

"A valiant knight. Proceed."

"Edda the Saxon, Herbert de Lozenga, the Earl of Norwich, with many chiefs and franklins of less note, and, last and least, myself."

"Good men, I doubt not," muttered Anselm, musing more to himself than addressing his visitor, "William de Warrenne, Roger of Shrewsbury, De Vere, and Neville, will, I doubt not, join him. Prince Henry, too justly offended at his father's will, might throw his influence in the scale—Hear me, sir knight," he added ; "I will see the men I speak of. Born no subject of this land—owing it no allegiance—I can securely do so. Visit me again to-morrow at the coming hour. Where art thou lodged ?—with secure friends, I trust."

Ulrick briefly informed him that he was a stranger in the capital, and had as yet to seek a lodging for the night.

"Imprudent," replied the churchman ; "tyranny is ever suspicious ; the City swarms with spies ; the very appearance of thy steed—for I noticed it from my casement—in a common hostelry would create inquiry. I will send it to the house of our order at Eltham. Leave it with me. Shouldst thou be compelled to fly, Kent must be thy hiding-place ; 'tis there the battle will be lost or won, for there lies Robert's strength."

Anselm's words were prophetic : it was in that fertile county, of which Odo of Bayeux was earl, that the struggle terminated which placed William Rufus on the throne of England.

"I would guard thee here," continued the abbot, kindly, "were I other than a guest, or did I deem it a safe hiding-place. Be careful of thy safety ; remember that prudence is sometimes better han courage. Farewell," he added ; " peace and security go with thee."

There was something so calculating, if not cold, in the churchman's manner that Ulrick scarcely knew what to think of him—his very caution seemed dictated more by prudence than regard ; still the high character he had received of him from those who sent him did not permit even for an instant a doubt of his good faith. " Perhaps," he thought, as he traversed the fields between the abbey and Charing, "it is but the coldness of the cloister." All men, he knew, possessed not the warm heart of his benefactor, whose nature was as genial as his own.

The unhappy Gilbert had vainly made his way along the crowded Strand, and from thence to the village of Charing, demanding of the passengers if they had encountered a citizen, whose person and steed he described. Some listened to him patiently ; others answered with a surly negative. All trace of the object of his pursuit had vanished, and what to do he knew not ; to return was out of the question. The brutal rage of his father-in-law—for such was the relationship between the warder and himself—increased, as it was sure to be, by disappointed avarice, was more than he dared encounter. He wandered for some time in the fields and open grounds between Charing and Westminster ; and at last, overcome with fatigue, seated himself beneath a tree, and reflected bitterly on his lonely, unprotected situation.

He had not been long thus occupied, before he was aroused by the lash of a bow-string vigorously applied to his shoulders ; and starting to his feet beheld, to his terror, the warder standing beside him. The disappointed ruffian, weary of waiting his return, had tracked him even there. " Cur," he exclaimed, repeating the blow, " is it for this I feed thee ? Is it thus my orders are obeyed ? Where hast thou left the man I bid thee watch ? "

Vainly Gilbert endeavoured to appease his wrath by relating the manner in which he had lost sight of him : the evil passion of the fellow was roused ; and, like the tiger, whose appetite for blood is increased by the first taste of it, so the terror and cries of the youth increased his persecutor's fury. " I have lost a fortune by thy heedlessness," he muttered between his clenched teeth. " I have seen Sir Walter Tyrrel, the newly appointed captain of the king's guard ; he recognised the rider from my description of his steed ; a price is on his head ; and thus to lose it !—Ay, shriek," he added ; " I'll show thee as little mercy as thou hast shown obedience."

It is impossible to say how long the enraged warder would have continued his cruel usage of his victim, had not Ulrick, who was returning from his visit to the abbot, chanced to pass the spot. Attracted by the cries of the boy, and disgusted with the cowardly conduct of the ruffian, whom in the twilight hour he failed to recognise, his first impulse was to interfere. Seizing him by the neck, he hurled him to a considerable distance from the tree, exclaiming as he did so, "Shame on thee thus to abuse thy strength ! The lash is fit but for the hound, not for a boy."

The first thought of the warder, on regaining his feet, was to attack the unceremonious speaker, whom he recognised at a glance ; but prudence, and the hope of gain, changed his purpose ; perhaps, too, the proof of strength which he had just received made him doubtful of the result, should he venture to encounter him ; he pretended, however, not to know him.

"Marry, master," he growled, "but you are ready with your hands, though I bear you no ill-will for that ; my temper is sometimes hotter than my reason. 'Tis the third time since Monday this disobedient boy hath given me the trouble to seek him. Let a drum but beat, or a banner wave, and presto ! there is no keeping him within the house. Come, Gilbert," he added, in a voice intended to be affectionate, "though knowest, if I am hasty of speech, and sometimes rough of hand, that at heart I am not an unkind father-in-law. Come," he added, in a low, peculiar tone, seeing that his victim hesitated, "I am not to be trifled with. Good night, sir," he continued, turning to his assailant ; "I bear you no ill blood ; but for the future be less ready with your hands."

Ulrick, who had quickly recognised both the speaker and the boy, was uneasy at the encounter, for he felt more convinced than ever that he had been dogged, and suspected that the scene he had just witnessed had merely been got up to detain him till assistance should arrive to secure his person. With a brief "good night," he turned coldly, therefore, from the mute supplicating look of Gilbert, which seemed to implore his protection, and directed his way towards Charing, turning from time to time a cautious glance to see if he were followed.

Scarcely was he out of earshot, than the warder whispered to his son-in-law, "Follow him—trail after him like a serpent on thy belly ;—lose sight of him again, and I'll rend the skin from off thy flesh. Raise thy head from time to time, that I may see the track."

The poor boy, his limbs still smarting with the chastisement he had received, threw himself, as he was bid, upon the ground, and glided after Ulrick, who, unable to distinguish the creeping form in the distance, pursued his way in the confidence that he had escaped them.

In his way to Westminster our hero had observed by the water side a quiet solitary house, where a bundle of straw hung out, denoting that entertainment might be had for man and beast : thither he had directed his steps, to secure his accommodation for the night.

"'Tis rather late," replied the host, eyeing him carefully, "for a respectable citizen, such as you seem to be, to seek his lodging ; but perhaps you are a stranger, a trader from distant parts, or——"

"I am," said Ulrick, "from a distant land, though not altogether a stranger in England. If the hour is too late to please you, I can seek elsewhere—a man with crowns in his pouch need never lack for shelter in a city like to London."

"Not so hasty, good master," quickly exclaimed the Boniface, in whose ear the word "crowns" tingled most musically ; "you might go farther and fare worse ; if we are careful whom we admit, it is that our house is honest ; were your gown quilted with nobles, you might sleep in surety here. Will it please you to sit here, or shall I serve you in the inner room ? "

Ulrick cast a glance upon the company, which consisted of one or two mendicant friars, several small traders, and three or four men whom it would have been impossible to place in any class, unless in that comprehensive one, cosmopolite. With a nod he signified to the host that he should prefer the inner room, where he ordered him to bring a flask of his best wine, and leave him undisturbed till supper time.

As the master of the house returned to the kitchen after serving his guest, a scowling figure, the cap carefully drawn over the brow, appeared at the outward door, and beckoned him out. It was the warder.

No sooner was Ulrick alone than his thoughts naturally reverted to his home and his young bride, whom he had left in the first hours of wedded happiness at the stern call of honour. Matilda, neither by tears, entreaties, nor sighs, had endeavoured to detain him ; for, in her gentle nature, even the passion of love was controlled by the sentiment of duty, and the resignation with which she endured the separation increased, if possible, her husband's admiration of her character and virtues. For some time he paced the floor of his lonely chamber, plunged in one of those delightful waking dreams in which youth cradles an unreal future ; wisely, perhaps, consoling itself for the turmoils, cares, deceits, trials. and disappointments of the present by the anticipations of happiness never to be realised. He was startled, at length, from this dreamy, reflective mood by a gentle tapping at the window ; at first he deemed it accident, and continued his solitary walk ; but its repetition soon became too frequent and too loud to admit of his remaining under the impression. Lowering the cord which held the shutter, he thrust his head into the night air to see who it was that had disturbed him.

"Silence, sir knight," whispered the trembling voice of Gilbert ; "you are beset like a tracked deer. The warder and myself have dogged you to your lair. He is gone to fetch the guard, and will be back within the hour. I am set to watch you here. For the sake of our dear Lady, fly, if you value life."

"And what, boy, makes thee take so great an interest in my favour?" coolly demanded Ulrick, who doubted whether the speaker's zeal in his service was not assumed to lure him from the protection of the house, so little did he think of the slight kindness he had shown him in saving him from his assailant.

"What makes me feel an interest!" iterated the youth. "Didst thou not defend me?"

"Granted."

"Speak for me with pity?"

"Well?"

"Well!" said the boy; "ah, 'tis plain you have always been beloved, have never missed the voice of kindness, or you would not ask that question. If you knew how crushed I had been in heart and spirit, how unused e'en to as much kindness as men would show a dog, you'd feel and understand the reason why I risk my life to serve you; though, perhaps," added the speaker, with a sigh, "it is so poor a thing that I should be a gainer by the loss."

There was a tone of sincerity, mingled with such utter hopelessness, in Gilbert's words, that, despite his resolution to be cautious, Ulrick felt convinced of the poor fellow's sincerity and purpose. Eager, like most generous natures, to atone for the pain his doubts had caused, he answered kindly:

"I believe thee, my good boy; forgive me that I wronged thy honesty by my suspicion. But tell me," he added, "whence comes the danger I must fear?"

"From the captain of the king's guard, to whom the warder described your steed and person. Perhaps, sir knight, you know him, for 'tis plain he recognises you?"

"How do you name him, boy?"

"Sir Walter Tyrrel. He hath promised gold to the warder if he succeeds in apprehending you."

The last doubt disappeared from Ulrick's mind; the name of Tyrrel was a fearful omen; for, although reared from childhood together by the good bishop, they had never loved each other. The open, warm heart of the young Lord of Stanfield had never found one affinity of feeling in his cold, calculating companion.

"Thou hast convinced me," he exclaimed, "of thy sincerity. In naming Sir Walter Tyrrel thou hast named my bitterest foe. Wait for a few moments, and I will rejoin thee."

The speaker was about to quit the window, when the voice of Gilbert again arrested him.

"Not by the door, sir knight—not by the door. My father-in-law and the host of the hostel are friends. He hath already put him on his guard. The outward door is fastened; you would be beset and overpowered. By the window—by the window, if you value life."

The advice appeared too reasonable to be neglected. The height was not very considerable to drop. Drawing his sword, which he

wore concealed beneath his dress, he held it in his teeth, so as to be
ready in case of treachery. He threw his legs over the low balus-
trade, and let himself fall upon the ground.

"Thank Heaven, you are safe."

"And thanks to thee, boy," replied Ulrick ; "for without thy
warning I had small chance of escaping them. There," he added,
offering Gilbert at the same time a gold piece, "is a token for thee.
Haste to thy home, and thy share in my deliverance may pass unsuspected."

The youth hesitated to take the money. The speaker thought
that he perhaps deemed it insufficient ; and, drawing another coin
from his pouch, of equal value with the first, offered them both.

"It is not gold, sir knight," sobbed the boy ; "it is not gold.
You bid me return to my home ; alas ! I have now no home. I
was set here to watch, and not to warn you. Farewell ! If you knew
the price at which I have paid my debt of gratitude, you would not
think so little of my heart that gold could recompense its devotion
to your service."

"Then come with me," said Ulrick, extending his hand, which
Gilbert joyfully seized and kissed. "I am but a fugitive myself ;
yet it shall go hard but I will protect thee. But first to provide for
our escape. Unchain the boat, and take the oars out of the others
beside it, to prevent their following us."

These orders were quickly executed. The oars were removed
from the two larger barks into a light skiff lying close to the water's
edge ; when Tyrrel, accompanied by the warder and two men-at-
arms, rushed down upon them. As soon as his father-in-law
perceived Gilbert, his rage knew no bounds. Once more the recompense seemed likely to escape him, through the treachery of his ill-
used victim, on whom, whatever might be the result of the adventure, he determined to be revenged. Drawing an arrow to the head,
he let fly the shaft ; and the devoted boy sank, wounded in the
chest, upon the shelving bank.

Ulrick, whose foot was upon the edge of the boat, might have
escaped without risking an encounter, could he have consented to
abandon his preserver—a baseness which, even for a moment, never
crossed his thoughts. To rush to the side of his wounded companion, and raise him on his left arm, whilst with his right he
defended their retreat, was but the work of a moment ; indeed, so
rapidly was the movement executed, that he had retreated several
paces before his assailants had recovered from their surprise.

"Yield !" exclaimed Tyrrel, rushing upon him with his two
followers ; for the warder had prudently run to the hostel to
summon the assistance of his friend the host. "Ulrick of Stanfield,
in the king's name, I arrest you !"

A blow from the quick sword of Ulrick was his only reply, as he
continued his retreat towards the bark, his face sternly turned

[ENCOUNTER BETWEEN ULRICK AND RICHARD OF LISIEUX.]

towards his assailants, his left arm still supporting the form of the
unconscious Gilbert. One of the men-at-arms had already received
a deep cut across the arm, which rendered it nearly useless, and the
second evinced but little zeal in approaching the keen blade of the
fugitive, which flashed like lightning round his head, and occasionally whizzed most unpleasantly in the ears of his enemy. Ulrick
and Tyrrel had the encounter nearly to themselves.

"Dogs!" exclaimed the latter, fearing the man he hated would
escape him, "must I do your duty? Upon him! take him alive if
possible, but, as you value your heads, suffer him not to escape."

Thus exhorted, the two fellows pressed yet nearer, when, by a
dexterous feint, Ulrick avoided the sword of his chief opponent,
and let fall his own upon his helmet. So tremendous was the blow,
that the straps of the head-piece gave way, and Tyrrel fell half
stunned to the ground. For Ulrick to place his foot upon his chest
to keep him there was the work of an instant.

"Back!" he cried, for the first time breaking silence, and holding
the point of his sword within an inch of the throat of his enemy;
"another step, and the blood of your leader dyes my blade."

The men hesitated between the desire of saving their captain and
the fear of punishment.

"Order them to throw aside their weapons," said Ulrick,
addressing his prostrate enemy.

"Never!" shouted Tyrrel, with a look of defiance.

The point of his conqueror's sword entered his throat about an
inch.

"Stay, stay!" he groaned; "if I command them to give up their
swords, wilt thou spare my life?"

"I will."

"By the honour of a knight?"

"By the honour of a knight," added Ulrick.

"Well then," said Tyrrel with a look of hate, "obey him! Throw
down your arms, I command you."

The men, who wished no better excuse than the orders of their
leader for relinquishing a contest of which they were both tired,
instantly obeyed, and cast their weapons half a bow-shot from them.

"Command them to retire a hundred paces from the shore,"
continued Ulrick, seeing that his first order was complied with.

"That thou mayst murder me!" shrieked the prostrate man,
writhing in mingled agony and shame beneath the foot of his
victorious foe.

"Carrion!" said the generous youth, pressing him yet more
firmly down; "the thought was worthy only thee. Decide! I speak
not twice."

Again the point of the sword approached the villain's throat.

The command was given, and, like the former, as promptly
executed. As soon as the men had retired the prescribed distance,

Ulrick released his enemy, first taking care to secure his sword. No sooner was his foot removed than Tyrrel rose doggedly from the ground. His rage was too deep for words—his humiliation too profound ever to be forgotten.

"For the sake of this poor boy," said Ulrick, after he had placed the wounded Gilbert in the boat, and was about to push of, I spare thy life ; but remember, Tyrrel, when next we meet, our strife is mortal."

"I will remember it," shouted the baffled traitor, shaking his clenched fist after the receding boat. "By Heavens ! " he muttered to himself, "my promised earldom could not give me half the joy as once to feel my feet upon thy neck."

The scene we have described had passed so rapidly, that by the time the warder had called the inmates of the hostel to his assistance, the boat which contained the fugitives had reached the middle of the stream, where the tide carried it down rapidly towards London-bridge.

"Follow them ! " shouted the ruffian ; "they have not escaped us yet."

The men rushed to the remaining boats, and found that every oar was gone ; curses loud and deep accompanied the discovery : meanwhile, the skiff pursued its way.

Ulrick's position was an embarrassing one : alone upon the water with his wounded companion, whom honour and humanity alike forbade him to desert ; no refuge near, no friend whom he could consult ; his liberty menaced at a moment when the gravest interests depended upon his activity and freedom. The recollection of his young bride pressed painfully upon him : what would be her fate and sufferings should he fall into the hands of his relentless enemy ? He was startled from his painful reverie by a deep groan from Gilbert ; the sound recalled him to himself. Abandoning the boat to the direction of the current, which bore it rapidly along, he approached the youth, and, with a gentle but firm hand, he drew the arrow from his breast, and felt considerably relieved when he beheld a gush of blood follow it ; for, like most knights of the age, he knew something of leechcraft, and was aware that the wounds which bled internally were the most dangerous. Opening his vest to tear a piece of linen to stanch the hurt, his fingers felt something hard ; mechanically he drew it forth, and beheld the tablets of the Jew. It seemed as if Providence, in the hour of his need, had brought them to his recollection ; for he remembered the words which accompanied the gift, though how to find the residence, at such an hour of the night, of any of the peculiar people, he knew not.

"How dost thou feel, boy ? " he demanded of his charge. "Art better ? "

"Much, much, sir knight," replied Gilbert, in a feeble tone,

" since you have withdrawn the arrow. I shall be strong soon, and able to assist you with the oar. Thank Heaven, you are not hurt."

" Knowest thou where we are ? "

" Upon the river."

" Knowest thou where reside the principal Jews of the city, merchants, or leeches ? " continued Ulrick.

" In Lombard-street, sir knight. Why dost thou ask ? "

" Because it is with one of them we must find refuge. My life is close beset ; my enemies will never think of searching for me there. Tell me," he added, " where must we land ? "

" There," said the boy, raising himself in the boat and pointing to a distant part of the bank ; " from thence, at the distance of a bow-shot, stands the house of Falk, of Cologne. Men say that he is good and charitable ; he is well skilled, too, in leechcraft. 'Tis said he cured the late king of the black fever, when all hope had failed him. But you will never gain shelter there."

" Why not, boy ? "

" He is too rich to need your gold. Men say he hath lent large sums to the king ; it may be to his interest to betray you ; and Jews, I've heard, would sell their souls to spite a Christian. Pray, go not there ! "

" It is our only hope," said Ulrick, with a sigh ; " persecution may have taught him mercy ; besides, you yourself say that he is good and charitable ; added to which, I have a means to secure his favour which something whispers me cannot fail of success."

Gilbert remained silent ; he was either too much exhausted, or felt too much respect and gratitude to his companion, to urge his objections further. Ulrick, as soon as they reached the shore, assisted him carefully from the boat, which, with his foot, he sent once more adrift, lest, being found near the spot where they had landed, it should set the blood-hounds on their track. The boy was so far recovered by the night breeze as to be able to walk, with the support of his protector's arm. Slowly they wound their way amid the various small craft drawn up on the shore, to be out of the reach of the tide and the empty barrels and pieces of timber scattered about, till they approached a narrow lane, inhabited chiefly by watermen, and which conducted to Lombard-street. Fortunately, from the lateness of the hour, there were few stragglers about to watch their progress ; a light might be seen occasionally through the crevices of the rude shutters, intimating that all the inhabitants of the place had not retired to rest. They proceeded without interruption, till they stood before the house they sought, the habitation of Falk, the richest merchant of his tribe. The house, though the most considerable in the street, presented, externally, but a poor appearance, it being entirely denuded of those quaintly carved attempts at ornament which already began to characterise the age. It was impossible, however, not to observe that the doors and shutters were framed with a careful attention to strength ; the latter, particularly, were so well joined together, that when closed not a single ray of light could penetrate from within or from without. Its master, like the rest of his nation, at the fierce period of which we write, although rich, enjoyed his wealth with fear and trembling ; for the populace,' taught to consider the once chosen people of God but as beings fit only to be hunted and persecuted, frequently attacked the dwellings of the Jews, veiling their appetite for plunder under the convenient cloak of fanaticism and religious pretext. It is astonishing how many of the descendants of the same ruffian populace may be found even at the present day—ay, and in high places, too, their savage and persecuting propensities only a little modified by the times in which they live.

The two fugitives, after looking carefully round them to see that they were unobserved, approached the door. Just as Ulrick was about to knock with the handle of his sword, it was unexpectedly opened, and a hand extended, which, grasping his, drew him and his companion into the house, a voice at the same time whispering : " You are late ; breathe not a word, but follow me."

"For a few minutes, Ulrick and his companion followed their mysterious guide in silence ; a thick cloth curtain, which screened a low arch, was drawn aside, and in an instant they found themselves in the midst of a brilliantly-lighted saloon. Lovely women, richly dressed, were seated upon cushions in the Oriental fashion ; high-browed, dark-bearded men, conversing in groups, standing beside them. It would be difficult to say which were the most surprised—the assembled Hebrews, or the two strangers so unexpectedly introduced among them. The women hastily let fall their veils, and their fathers and brothers, drawing their long knives—for swords were forbidden them—prepared to defend themselves from some expected outrage.

The guide, a youth, whose error had brought the two parties thus in contact, stood transfixed with anger and fear.

" Who art thou ? and what brings a Christian at this hour beneath my roof ? " demanded a tall, venerable-looking man, in a tone which proclaimed him to be the master of the house.

Ulrick placed the tablets in his hand, which the old man retired to read by the light of a silver lamp suspended from the ceiling in an inner recess of the apartment.

" What have I done ? " exclaimed the young Israelite whose heedlessness had occasioned the unexpected introduction ; " by my imprudence the Nazarene hath entered in the tent of my fathers."

The men, still grasping their knives, thronged round the intruders, their black eyes flashing in fearful wrath upon them. The terrified Gilbert clung to his companion, who in the midst of the menacing throng around them retained his calmness and usual presence of mind. He felt, from the manner in which they were hemmed in, that the least attempt at resistance would but provoke their fate. Several arms were already raised to strike, when the voice of the old man was heard as he issued from the recess, holding the tablets of Abram in his hands. "Harm them not," he cried. "Respect the guests of the high priest."

In an instant every hostile expression disappeared, and instead of being surrounded by ferocious faces, Ulrick and his companion found themselves amongst friends.

CHAPTER XV.

ULRICK and his companion were conducted to a well furnished apartment, provided with two couches, by their host, who, like most of his nation, possessed a considerable knowledge of surgery. The wound of Gilbert was carefully dressed, and the tired fugitives, after being refreshed, were left to their repose. Early in the morning the Jew visited them again, when our hero expressed to him their thanks.

"You owe me nothing," interrupted the old man ; "my house and services are freely yours ; he who hath served one so honoured of our nation hath a claim upon the gratitude of every Hebrew ; only point out the way in which it may be further useful to you. It seems that you are a personage of some note, for search hath been made in every hostel of the city, and severe penalties denounced against all who harbour you."

"And yet you, one of earth's persecuted race, venture to conceal me."

"I am accustomed to danger," resumed the old man, with a mournful smile, "and therefore almost indifferent to it. In childhood, when I ventured from my home to breathe the fresh air of heaven, I was hooted, beaten, and reviled by those of my own age. I bore it patiently, for I was but a sickly boy—so patiently that at last my persecutors got tired of tormenting me. My dawning manhood was but a series of dangers and humiliations. Three days after my first marriage the home of my wedded love was burnt and plundered, and my young bride, the idol of my soul, life's richest pearl, the descendant of a princely race—for the despised sons of Abram count names as lofty, Christian, as thine own—perished in the flames. The years which followed were a blank ; but I was avenged, fearfully avenged."

"Thy wrongs indeed were terrible. But how wert thou avenged ? " demanded Ulrick.

"By the captivity of the accursed city whose brutal rabble fired my peaceful home," sternly replied the Hebrew. "It was Jewish gold which armed the Conqueror's fleets—which paid his mercenary troops; the despised Jew forged the yoke destined for a nation's neck. William was but the agent of his wrath. Had I not procured him vast loans from amongst my people, his barks had never left the Norman shore; the very jewels of his ducal crown were pledged to me—his father's cup—all but his knightly sword."

"Is it possible?" demanded his hearer. "Could a being whom the world deemed so abject forge the fetters to enchain a country? Thou speakest truly, Jew: thou hast been fearfully avenged."

"And yet it has not shut out all humanity from my heart. Had Harold listened to my cry for justice, his bones had rested by the Confessor's. I pointed out the hands to him, red with my Sarah's blood, and asked for judgment; he refused me—why? Those hands were Christian. In his pride he proffered gold—gold!" added the old man, scornfully, "for the life of my young bride— gold to the man who could have counted treasure with him ten times o'er!"

"Thou hast suffered much!" exclaimed his guest, "and I marvel that, at the request e'en of thy dearest friend, thy door should open to a Christian. Should any of thy friends who witnessed my arrival here last night prove treacherous and denounce thee?"

"Fear not," said Falk, with a smile; "such are not the vices of our nation; persecution hath made us faithful to each other. There is not one of the vilest of our race who, on the sight of Abram's tablets, would not risk his life to shelter thee; besides, even the Red King's wrath would pause ere it reached me; he hath need of gold, is negotiating a loan amongst our people, and I am not the poorest of my tribe."

"Beware," said our hero, who felt deeply interested in the old man's story, "how you hazard your wealth on so poor a surety as William's faith; know you not that many of the nobles have already acknowledged Robert as their king?—that his uncle, the warlike Odo of Bayeux, is at the head of the confederacy?—that, in a few days, the army of his brother will besiege him in his capital? This pageant of a coronation will but render the tyrant's fall more signal; his reign will be a brief one."

"All," said the Jew; "I know it all; and can foresee the end as truly as though an angel whispered me."

"And that will be?"

"The downfall of your hopes. Robert hath courage, but not that dogged energy of purpose which wins and guards a crown; he is too much the bacchanal of the cup and kiss; his ally, Roger of Shrewsbury, is half won over. You smile," continued the speaker, "and wonder how the poor Jew should prate of such high matter; but learn that, if we have no voice at the council board of nations, our gold finds ears there. Yours will prove the phantom king, and mine the real one. But, tell me, how can I assist your present purpose?"

" By procuring me a safe disguise. I have friends whom I must speak with."

" The Abbot of Bec ? " demanded his mysterious host, with a smile. " Beware ! there is danger in the visit."

Ulrick started at the query, and a suspicion of the churchman's treachery glanced across his mind : how else could he reconcile the Jew's knowledge of his intentions ? Falk smiled at his suspicions, for he read them as clearly in his changing countenance as though he had given utterance to them.

" You wrong him," he said, replying to his guest's unspoken thoughts. " Anselm is incapable of treachery. He is the firm friend of Bishop Odo ; and, knowing that he is so, I guessed it was to him your letters were addressed. How do you propose to visit him ? "

" Dressed in the poorest garb your friendship can supply me with."

" Then you are sure to be detected. Suspicion is awakened ; and humble weeds are more likely to conceal a messenger than knightly armour or a courtly garb. If you go forth, do so like yourself."

" I have no armour," observed Ulrick, who saw at once the shrewdness of the advice, " and my good steed is sent to Eltham. It hath already once betrayed its master."

" I can supply you with both. When will you set forth ? "

" At the sunset hour. But my poor wounded boy," said our hero, pointing to Gilbert, who lay on his couch wondering what could be the subject of conversation between his protector and the Jew ; for they had both spoken in French, the common language of the higher classes at the time, and he understood only his rude mother Saxon.

" I will take care of him. As soon as he is strong enough I will provide him with the means to join you. Can I do more," demanded the Hebrew, " for the friend of the honoured Abram ? "

" Nothing," answered Ulrick, " but to accept his thanks for the generous hospitality thou hast accorded. Thou hast opened to me a new page in the history of mankind ; doubt not I will peruse it. For thine and Abram's sake, the Israelite shall henceforth be in deed, as well as in humanity, a brother to me. Despite the Church's dicta," added Ulrick, " reason tells me that Heaven never intended man to judge his fellow dust."

" In that I am repaid," said Falk. " Farewell ! Three hours before sunset the steed and armour shall be ready."

At the appointed time our hero, nobly mounted, and clad in steel a monarch might have envied, wearing his visor down, threaded his way through the City towards Westminster. Several times during his progress he encountered various portions of the royal guard, but none presumed to stop or question him. If, as he supposed, they were on the scent of the fugitive, his appearance was so different from what Tyrrel and the warder had described, that none could recognise him in the stately knight who slowly made his way through the crowded streets of the busy metropolis. He arrived without interruption at his destination, and once more stood face to face with the mitred Abbot of Bec.

" Welcome, sir knight," said the quiet, astute churchman ; " there has been hot quest after you. Tyrrel is seriously wounded, and the king furious at your escape ; you must have warm and true friends to shelter you, for they have done so at the peril of their lives. As you value your own," he added, " quit London instantly, for the city swarms with spies. A large reward is offered for your apprehension."

" Not with my errand unachieved."

"Leave that to me ; I am unsuspected," observed the abbot ; " your presence cannot advance the cause."

" But my letters, father ; my letters to the nobles."

" I will deliver them."

" I have friends, too, whom my absence——"

" May compromise," urged the priest, glancing uneasily around ; "soon as you quit the abbey, depart at once for Eltham ; there you will find your good steed waiting, together with letters, which I have forwarded you by a sure hand for our friends in Kent. You play a game for life, young man ; throw not a chance away, for you have crafty enemies upon the watch to seize it."

The advice was too reasonable to be neglected, and Ulrick saw that the cautious speaker had taken the precaution of forwarding his letters to Eltham, not to risk compromising either himself or friends, should their bearer unfortunately be taken. Hastily, therefore, bidding the priest adieu, he mounted his horse, determined, without further hesitation, to quit a spot which menaced him with so many dangers. Unfortunately, in the hurry of his departure, he neglected the precaution which alone had prevented his arrest in his progress through the city. He wore his visor up ; and the warder, whom he had so severely chastised the previous evening, and who, in the hope of encountering him, had been on the lookout with a party of his men the entire day, saw, and instantly recognised him. To seize his horse by the rein, and secure his sword, was but the work of a moment. He was so securely held, that resistance would have been as foolish as vain.

"What means this outrage, knaves ? " demanded Ulrick. " Do you take me for a thief, that you lay hands upon me in open day ? Beware that you have sure warrant for the deed ; it else may cost you dear."

" Warrant ! " exclaimed the warder, with a malicious grin. " The headsman shall be my warrant, since, ere nightfall, he will have to deal upon thee. By Saint Martin, to hear thee speak, one would think that coat of mail covered a belted earl, and not a scheming traitor. Away with him, my masters."

" And whither must I go ? " inquired their prisoner.

"To the Tower—his highness holds his court there. To think," added the fellow, with a laugh, "that silly head of thine should bring me fifty silver marks! They will buy plasters for the hard blows I got last night. Most of my debtors pay me one way or another—some with their coin, others with blood; but thou shalt pay with both."

"And thou shalt have more, knave, than thou dreamest of, an thou letst not go my rein. I tell thee, I bear a message from the king; at peril of your lives detain me."

"Ho, ho, ho!—which king?" shouted the men, to whom Ulrick's assertion appeared an excellent jest, so sure were they of his identity. "The King of the Saxons," as they contemptuously styled Robert, "or William the Red King?"

At this instant a party of the royal guard, headed by John of Montgomery, who was a secret partisan of the elder prince, whose cause he soon after openly espoused, approached the spot, and seeing a knight in rich armour, surrounded by several common men-at-arms, who evidently held him prisoner, halted to inquire the cause.

"The traitor who last night nearly slew Sir Walter Tyrrel!" shouted the warder, fearful lest the new-comers should interfere with his prisoner, and secure the merit of his capture to themselves.

"There is a reward of fifty marks upon his head," cried a second.

"Peace, fool!" growled the chief of Ulrick's captors, in an undertone; "do you want to have the bone snatched from between your teeth? You see, sir knight, that we have fairly taken him; our party is quite numerous enough to conduct him to the Tower."

"You, sir knight," said Ulrick, calmly, as soon as he could obtain a hearing, "doubtless will listen to reason. I know not whether these fellows are mad or drunk, or take me for another. I told them, as I tell you, that I came here on a message from the king. Question the men; they saw me quit the abbey—you know it is the residence of the venerable primate."

John of Montgomery shook his head. He was not deceived either by Ulrick's calmness or the equivocal truth he told of coming with a message from the king. His secret inclinations prompted him to release him; but prudence whispered that such a step might prove dangerous to himself. He was one of the few nobles with whom the Abbot of Bec had tampered, and he doubted not but in the knight before him he beheld the messenger of Robert to the priest.

"In times less doubtful than the present," he replied, "the word of a knight would be sufficient; but duty compels me to ask if you have no other proof?"

"None," said Ulrick, carelessly.

"No papers?"

"No."

" To be sure he has not," replied the warder, echoing his words ; "come, my masters, away with him."

" Back, churl ! " exclaimed the commander of the guard, regarding him sternly ; "it is not for a peasant to arrest a noble. Sir knight, I must demand your sword," he added, turning courteously to Ulrick ; "you are my prisoner. If your tale be true, your captivity will be but brief ; if not, I shall not ask excuse for performing an act of duty."

As Ulrick was about to yield himself a prisoner, he suddenly recollected the signet ring which Abram had given him. To draw his mailed glove from his hand, and hold it to Montgomery's sight, was but the impulse of a moment. The officer recognised it in an instant.

" By heavens ! " he cried ; " it is the king's own signet ring ! "

The confusion of the warder and his men may be more easily imagined than described ; like tigers who had missed their spring, they were about to sneak away, fearful of the consequence of their mistake, when the voice of their late captive arrested them.

" Secure those men."

The guard obeyed him in an instant.

" How is it your pleasure we should dispose of them ? " demanded their leader.

" To prison with them."

Montgomery waved his hand, and despite their protestations, they were dragged away, amid the sneers of the crowd who had collected round the spot, and who were delighted at the sight of the warder and his men being sent to prison. They had too often suffered from their brutality to pity them, but followed their escort, shouting and triumphing in their disgrace. In a few minutes Ulrick and the captain of the guard were left alone.

" And now," said the latter, "please you to give me the ring. I ask not too curiously how you obtained possession of it ; to me it is sufficient warrant for releasing you from the rude clutches of these men. Ride you to Eltham ? " he added, with a peculiar smile.

Our hero started, for the words conveyed a deeper knowledge of his movements than he suspected him possessed of. For a few moments they regarded each other in silence.

" Perhaps," slowly pronounced Ulrick, at last drawing the signet from his finger and giving it.

" Then ride quickly," continued his questioner. " There you may chance to find a steed and friends ; every hour you rest in London may bring those less easy to be satisfied by your story than myself. Farewell ! sir knight ; perhaps when next we meet we may meet as friends."

Waving their hands as a signal of adieu, the two knights separated ; Ulrick to cross the neighbouring ferry on his way to the rendezvous designated by the worthy abbot, and Montgomery to relate the history of his capture, and justify his share in his release by returning William his lost signet-ring.

Our hero had journeyed several miles before he perceived that he was followed by a young fellow dressed in the ordinary travelling costume of the times, who rode a light horse, whose active pace enabled him to keep up with his own good steed, encumbered as it was by the weight of a rider armed *cap-a-pie*. Turn which way he would, still the rider pursued the same route ; once, to avoid the persevering horseman, he made a considerable detour by a wood which took him a winding distance from the main road towards Croydon ; but, faithful as his shadow, his pursuer followed him— stopped when he stopped, and resumed his way as soon as he gave his steed the rein.

Although Ulrick felt little uneasiness at the idea of a single enemy, still he was annoyed at being so perseveringly tracked, and determined to ascertain at once the purpose of the traveller, whose route, by some caprice, seemed so exactly to tally with his own.

Emerging from the wood, he turned an acute angle of the road, and reined his horse to await the arrival of the fellow, who could not possibly ascertain whether he had pursued his way or not till he was close upon him. The *ruse* succeeded, for, in a few minutes he heard the quick, light step of the horse. Wheeling his own round, he met the rider face to face. It was a lonely, retired spot, fit for an encounter ; to avoid him was impossible.

The fellow who had so closely dogged him proved to be a young man about three-and-twenty ; a light pointed beard, rather inclined to red, adorned his chin, and connected it, by a few straggling silky hairs, with his moustache ; his air, despite the simplicity of his dress, was. martial ; and he rode his horse with the air of a man accustomed alike to war or to the chase.

Ulrick was the first to speak.

" It seems, friend, that we ride the same way ; whither are you bound ? "

" That is a question," replied the stranger, " which a prudent man scarce cares to answer."

" Still it must be answered," said our hero, " if we are to remain at peace. I suffer no man to dog my steps."

" Nor I any man to question mine, whether my errand be of pleasure or caprice, business or danger. Ride on, sir knight," continued the young man, with a quiet smile ; " we shall soon see if our affairs or inclinations lead us the same way."

There was an easy, half-mocking tone in the speaker's voice which jarred upon Ulrick's ear, not that there was anything in the words at which he could fairly take offence ; still it annoyed him. Pointing to the two roads which diverged from the corner of the wood, and fixing his eye sternly upon the intruder, who seemed more amused than frightened by the encounter, he said :

" It is my pleasure to ride alone ; choose your way."

" And mine to ride in company," coolly answered his tormentor. " The society of so brave a knight is a safeguard to a poor citizen. It is your own fault that we have come in contact ; I was content with the protection of your shadow."

Fully convinced that he was followed by some spy or agent of the tyrant's, the Lord of Stanfield drew his sword, determined at once to end the matter, for he doubted not but the speaker only waited their arrival in some village, or an encounter with some of the partisans of William who patrolled the country, to order his arrest. A glance of haughty surprise, more than fear, passed over his tormentor's countenance at the action, and he quietly observed that he was unarmed—an assertion which, in appearance at least, was true, since neither sword nor weapon of any kind was visible upon his person ; he seemed totally unarmed.

" I cannot raise my sword," exclaimed Ulrick, petulantly, as soon as he was convinced of the fact, " upon an unarmed man, whatever may be his intentions, be he spy or enemy."

" Of course you can't," coolly answered the horseman, " so you may as well sheathe it again. It would be murder ! Besides, if our roads should prove the same, why not pursue them in good fellowship together ? "

" Because it is my pleasure to be alone."

" An unsocial humour that, and savours more of the cloister than the camp."

The fugitive started at the speech, and asked himself, could the strange horseman know him, or was it but one of those random shafts which shrewdness or hazard sometimes wing ? Whichever it might be, he felt that it was more necessary than ever to separate from his obtrusive companion, whom he once more sternly bade to choose his way, as he was resolved to ride alone.

" What if it leads to Eltham ?—would you wish me to arrive there before you ? "

Ere Ulrick could reply, another horseman, well armed and powerfully mounted, dashed round the corner of the wood, and seizing the bridle of the stranger's horse, commanded him in peremptory but respectful tone to follow him.

" To my grave as soon," replied the young man. " Villain ! let go my rein ! Quick, sir knight ! your sword !—lend me your sword ! "

Ulrick, who deemed the pretended arrest a new pretext to detain him, set spurs to his horse, and had already gained a short distance from the scene, when the sound of his own name arrested his attention. Involuntarily he wheeled round to listen—it was repeated louder than before.

" Ulrick of Stanfield ! Craven, false knight ! is it thus you fulfil your vow of chivalry to aid the unarmed and defenceless ? Thy blazon will be stained for ever."

The language of the stranger, together with the mingled tones of entreaty and indignation in his voice, convinced our hero that, whatever might have been the young man's object in pursuing him, he was at least no spy. A few seconds brought him to the spot where the last-comer was still dragging the steed and his prisoner after him.

"By what authority do you arrest this young man?" he demanded.

"By one not lightly to be disputed," replied the knight, for such his golden spurs proclaimed him—"the king's!"

"Produce it, then."

"Fool! dost think a belted knight requires other warrant than his sword? Mine shall always answer for its master's deeds to all who dare to question them! This, to teach thee a lesson of more caution."

Holding the rein of his prisoner's steed in his left hand, the speaker made a dash at Ulrick, from whose well-tempered helmet the blow of his sword glanced as from a block of adamant. In the fierce encounter which ensued he had ample occasion to prove the value of the Jew's gift—the armour, weapon, and horse were admirable. Both knights were masters of their weapons, which flashed with fearful celerity, describing fiery segments round each other's heads. Their steeds seemed to take part in the struggle; so firmly were their riders seated, that one mind appeared to animate them.

The blows of his opponent—and they were rained both thick and heavily on Ulrick's armour—tried its strength, but made little impression; whilst, on the contrary, the red blood followed in several places the stroke of his own good sword. Several times they retreated to short distances to draw breath, which they had no sooner recovered than, wheeling round, they returned again to the assault. Although the life-stream damasked the well-polished mail of the aggressor, his strength was by no means exhausted; and our hero, who was apprehensive of the arrival of succour, felt the necessity of finishing with him. Relying on the training of his steed, the third time they renewed the encounter, instead meeting the shock, he dexterously avoided it by passing to the right, striking a furious blow with his long weapon as he did so on his opponent's helmet; so well was it directed, that the steel clasps which united it with the neck-piece were cut asunder, and a severe wound inflicted. The wearer's head sank upon his breast, for one of the principal arteries was severed, and in a few seconds he fell, exhausted by rapid loss of blood, upon the ground. By the time his enemy had alighted all was over—the strong man was a corpse.

"A knightly blow, and well struck," exclaimed the young stranger. "I took thee from the first to be a man of courage. 'Tis well for both of us that we are not deceived. But mount thy steed, and let us hasten onward ; but first reach me yon traitor's sword—perchance," he added, "I may have occasion for it yet."

There was too much reason in the advice not to be followed ; the victor remounted, and for a few minutes rode silently with the stranger whom he had rescued by his side.

"How didst thou learn my name ? " he at last demanded.

"I know the names of most men," drily answered the horseman. "Methinks you were in no haste to claim it."

"Indeed," said Ulrick ; "then perhaps you can favour me with the name of my opponent ? "

"Perhaps ; enough for the present that he was as brave a soldier, and as unscrupulous a villain, as ever followed banner to the field. Many a knight whose hold might else have blazed, and many a mother who else had mourned her dishonoured child, may thank thy arm. His last course on earth is run. But come," added the speaker, "let us understand each other. Ride we to Eltham ? "

"We do."

"In fellowship ? "

"In fellowship," said Ulrick ; "but tell me what is thy name ? "

"Henry," replied his companion, "for the lack of a nobler ; my father gave me little else beside. So call me simply Henry, or Henry the simple—which you will ; I am no stickler for ceremony —it irks me."

"So it would seem," replied our traveller, who began to be rather amused than angry with the fellow's humour. "May a man, without being thought too curious, demand how you became acquainted with his name ? By our Lady of the Rood, it came most opportunely to thy tongue ; perhaps some starling whispered it ? "

"By my faith," said the young man, "it was more like a raven than a starling ; there was blood upon his beak."

"And his name ? "

Henry, as the stranger called himself, shrugged his shoulders, and looked at him with a peculiar smile, as much as to inform the questioner that that was his secret ; but seeing a frown upon Ulrick's brow, and probably reflecting that want of confidence was but a poor return for the service he had received, he answered frankly that Sir Walter Tyrrel had first told it to him—a piece of intelligence which caused his companion to regard him once more with suspicion.

"Tyrrel ! " he exclaimed ; "why, he is my bitterest enemy."

"Save one," drily added the strange horseman.

"And that is 'the king,' as William of Normandy hath styled himself."

"Ay," said Henry ; "and as, to-morrow, Lanfranc will crown him. The fellow whose throat you so cleverly cut brought me an invitation to the ceremony ; his method of delivering it was a rough one, so I declined it."

[DEATH OF HERBERT DE LOZENGA.]

B

The easy, familiar tone of the speaker puzzled our hero, who was at a loss to understand the rank of his companion, and his avowed connection with Walter Tyrrel. Had his purpose been unfriendly, nothing would have been more unlikely than his owning it; besides, he was, till Ulrick gave him the dead man's sword, unarmed, and every step their horses took lessened the distance between them and danger.

"Thou art a riddle!" he cried, speaking as much to his own thoughts as to Henry. "And thou no sphinx to solve me. Have a little patience; and in time, like the serpent's tail in the emblem of eternity, the puzzle will unfold itself. Thou seest," he added, "I have dealt with bookcraft in my time—though more, perchance, with men; but with thy cloister-breeding thou canst understand me."

"Perhaps," replied Ulrick, secretly annoyed at the increased mystification to which he was being subjected.

"I tell thee that thou shalt, then. Let that content thee," resumed the speaker; "only I bide my time. And now tell me, sir knight of Stanfield—how dost thou like the strange companion fortune hath sent thee?"

"So well," said the party he addressed, "that I will put no more interrogations, lest, knowing thee better, I should like thee less."

"Frankly spoken; there is something fresh in truth; I know the sound, although it is so seldom in my short life that I have heard it spoken. At Eltham the riddle shall be explained."

"At Eltham be it," answered Ulrick.

A short ride brought the travellers to the priory of White Friars, a dependency on the rich abbey of Bec, in Normandy. It was situated near the village of Eltham, in one of those secluded, quiet, sunny nooks which the monks of old so loved, and so well knew how to select, and which in no country are more frequently found than in merry England. It was one of those spots where silent sanctity might build its cell, or the broken passions of humanity, shipwrecked on the sea of life, seek and find repose. The evening hour; the stately heron, winging its solitary way to the distant wood; the glorious sunset, whose last rays, lingering like a lover's kiss, gilded the slender pinnacle of the church,—were all in harmony, forming a soft, dreamy picture, which the horsemen completed.

On their arrival, they were immediately conducted to the apartment of the prior, a stately-looking personage, who received them alone, and who hastened to inform Ulrick that his steed, and the promised letters from his brother Anselm, had already arrived; at the same time informing him that a lodging was already prepared for him for the night within the walls.

"And where am I to lodge?" demanded the stranger, in a half-petulant tone, displeased perhaps at being overlooked by the lordly

R 2

churchman; "is there no room for me, good father, in your pious rookery?"

The priest answered haughtily that a cell should be prepared for him near his master. He was evidently offended by the irreverent tone of the speaker, whom he took for an esquire or attendant upon the person of his visitor.

"A cell!" iterated Henry; "well, a cell be it. We will do penance for our sins, since the hospitality of our host so limits our entertainment; but when last we hunted in this neighbourhood, if our memory fails not, we were better lodged; 'tis true we were not then a fugitive."

The prior started from his seat, and approaching the stranger, overwhelmed him with excuses for not having at once recognised him; adding, that he must reproach the Lord of Stanfield for neglecting to inform him that his walls were graced by the presence of such an honoured guest."

"Faith," said the young man, laughingly, "you must grant the good knight absolution, then; for he dreams as little that his troublesome companion is the youngest son of the Conqueror, as you, holy father, did yourself."

"Prince Henry!" exclaimed Ulrick, in astonishment, at the same time bending the knee.

"Ay," said his highness, "Henry the simple, as men call me, though perhaps, after all, I have more wit than my scoffing brother dreams, whose fraternal love was so disinterested he could not bear me from his own safe keeping. My lodging is already furnished in the Tower; but, like a wilful youth, I preferred my liberty or Robert's guardianship to his. Tut, man," he added, "never kneel to me; I am as poor, nay poorer than thyself. Our father's love, of all his vast possessions left us but one poor hold in Normandy, and a remembrance upon his treasurer, to be paid when we can get it."

There was something so frank and soldier-like in Henry's manner, that our hero felt instantly at his ease; for, after all, he had only taken such precautions at their first meeting as necessary prudence and his safety dictated. The young prince explained that it was by the advice of Anselm he had quitted London to join himself to Robert's fortunes, and that he had recognised Ulrick's person from having been a concealed witness of his first interview with the abbot.

"And who was the traitor?" demanded our hero, "who would have forced your highness back?"

"Richard of Lisieux, our brother's pander, tool, and executioner. William will miss him sorely when there is some act which fears the light of heaven to be accomplished. Stanfield," he added, kindly taking his protector by the hand, "we owe thee a debt of gratitude for that good blow; it removed a stumbling-block from out my path—a bloodhound from my track. Few persons live to tell the tale of their captivity whom that bad man has guarded."

It was finally arranged that no notice should be taken to the community either of the arrival or of the high rank of the prior's guests, who both supped in his apartment, and soon afterwards, fatigued with the events of the day, retired to rest, each throwing himself upon his pallet ready dressed, in order to be prepared in case of danger or surprise.

The prince and Ulrick had not been long sleeping when they were roused by their host, who, attended by Father Segsil—an aged Saxon monk, who of the community alone possessed his confidence—entered their cell.

"Rouse, sir knight!" he exclaimed ; "in less than an hour the enemy will be upon us. They must not find you here ; Jesu Maria ! they would burn our convent with as little ceremony as a burgher's hold."

"And whence comes this intelligence, good prior ? " demanded Henry, starting from his couch. "Would it had tarried some two or three hours later ; I was indulged by Mistress Fancy with a dream too glorious ever to be realised. I should like to have revelled in it some few hours longer.

"The intelligence," replied their host, paying little attention to the latter part of the prince's speech, "is from brother Segsil," pointing as he spoke to his companion, who stood regarding Henry with a look in which hate and interest were strangely mingled.

"May he not be mistaken ? " demanded Ulrick.

"Father Segsil is never mistaken," replied the prior ; "in an hour the satellites of William will be here."

"Hath any messenger arrived at the convent ? "

"No."

"May not the good father be mistaken in his intelligence ? "

"Father Segsil is never mistaken," repeated their host, gravely ; "his warnings are not to be neglected."

"Why, then," said Prince Henry, laughing, "we must e'en obey them, as our fathers did the oracles of old, blindly and in confidence. Forgive me, holy man," he added, turning to the aged monk, whose dark eyes were still fixed immovably upon him, "if I am somewhat more sceptic than the prior here ; perchance it is the fault of unclerkly breeding."

"Shall I convince thee ? " demanded the old man, in a tone which seemed to echo from a sepulchre.

"Faith ! I demand no better," replied the young man, extending his left palm, which the monk thrust contemptuously aside ; and seizing his right hand firmly, fixed the prince's attention by the intense expression of his gaze.

"Thy dream shall yet be realised, proud boy—the crown of England waits thee."

The prince started ; that which at first he had treated as a jest became serious, for the monk had indeed interpreted his vision rightly. The flush of hope and surprise suffused his brow as he demanded of the soothsayer :

" When ? "

" When the Red King sleeps his last sleep—when the blood of the Conqueror's favourite son hath gladdened the oppressed soil of England, and bid her children hope for peaceful days. Then," added the old man, " the crown thou hast so often dreamt of shall be thine."

" But shall I keep as well as win it ? " demanded Henry, who, although less influenced by the superstition of the age, could not avoid placing confidence in the man who had so singularly interpreted his dream.

" That will depend upon thy marriage," replied Father Segsil. " If thou art fortunate enough to win a bride of the royal Saxon blood, thou shalt die king of England ; if not, the curse of thy race will overtake thee. Now, then, away ! I speak of the future to thee no more."

" Tell me but this : shall we meet again ? " demanded Henry.

" If thou art wise enough to follow my counsel, yes. At the proudest moment of thy life, if not when the last trumpet summons earth together, I'll meet thee face to face. Farewell."

" Hast thou no good fortune, father, to predict to me ? " said Ulrick.

The old man gazed mournfully upon him, and shook his head, muttering to himself :

" Saxon—Saxon ; I read it in his open brow and bright blue eye. Thou hast asked the old priest for a prediction—better have sought his blessing ; but since the choice is made, take it and begone—a career of honour, an unstained faith, a soldier's laurel, but a broken heart. Once more I charge thee," he added, impatiently, " to begone—ride for your lives. Once past the bridge, you may slack the rein—no living thing will ever cross it afterwards."

The confident tone of the monk's voice, and the implicit faith which the prior placed in his intelligence, no matter how mysteriously obtained, decided the young men at once to depart. Hastening to the stables, they found their horses ready saddled, and after a *benedicite* from the prior and his companion, resumed their journey, Ulrick leading his grey steed by a loose rein with him.

Scarcely had they passed the bridge, a short mile from the convent, and which connected the high banks of a deep ravine, too steep for any horse to climb, too wide to leap, when the wooden fabric burst into a brilliant flame, which dark figures were seen feeding with bundles of straw and faggots. The monk's prediction came to their recollection—living thing never crossed it more.

CHAPTER XVI.

THE morning after Ulrick's departure from Norwich, Robert of Normandy, at the head of a considerable body of troops and the nobles who acknowledged his authority, marched from the city. Herbert de Lozenga, whose experience was of so much value in the council, accompanied him in quality of chancellor, that prelate having consented to retain his office at the. entreaty of the new monarch. Edith and her daughter-in-law retired to Stanfield, which, removed as it was from the scene of war, a small party of vassals was sufficient to defend. The bride of Mirvan was their only guest ; and there, in the antique oratory of the countess, they offered up their united prayers for the absent warriors' safety.

The prior of the Dominicans, who had accompanied the confiding monarch to the gate of St. Stephen on his march, had returned to his convent, and was walking in his stately garden, which extended from the church (now St. Andrew's Hall) to the water side, speculating in thoughtful mood upon the future, and not feeling perfectly in security touching the past. The absence of the curate of St. Julian's alarmed him, although few, he thought, could blame him for having extended the rites of Christian burial to a knight so valiant as Robert of Artois, and his own relative besides. The principal cause of his uneasiness arose from the Jew, who had so strangely possessed himself of the prince's signet-ring, and in whose hands the papers found upon his nephew might be turned to dangerous account. Twice had he sent to the house of Abram ; it was empty, not a trace of any living being remained. He had found, too, upon inquiry, that the vessel to whose captain he had given the leech the letter had sailed for Rouen, having taken several passengers with him.

"Let but William triumph—and he can scarcely fail to do so," he muttered to himself—"and I may laugh at enemies, open or concealed."

"Perhaps ! " exclaimed a voice, so near him that the words were almost spoken in his ear. Eborard started, and beheld a pale, attenuated being, meanly clad, regarding him with a fixed look. His forehead was high and bald, his face marked with a thousand minute scars, which gave it a most ghastly appearance, and his limbs seemed to sink under him from sickness or want.

"And who art thou, fellow ? " demanded the prior, with a haughty stare of surprise, "who darest so boldly answer to our thoughts, and how gaindst thou entrance here ? "

"By the old way ! " replied the strange intruder, whom our readers have already, no doubt, recognised as Robert of Artois.

"The old way ! " iterated the puzzled churchman ; "what old way ? "

" The secret door behind the statue of St. Dominic in the cloisters," replied the stranger, for such he appeared to his uncle, " where you once heard a strange confession, father, and performed a stranger deed.".

" And what was that ? " demanded Eborard, still more and more amazed.

" The marriage of a Christian with a Jewess."

" Hush ! " exclaimed the astonished prior, turning pale at the words, which had been spoken loudly, for the mere whisper of such a sacrilege would have been sufficient to subject him to the censure of the Church ; and, if proved, to deposition from the high rank he held within its pale.

" Even as you please," said the mysterious man : " I wish not to offend you."

" How didst thou learn the fearful secret ? "

" Because I witnessed it," replied his tormentor, whose object was to work upon the fears of his reverend uncle ; for he knew him too well to expect much pity or generosity at his hands should he make himself known to him. " Added to which, I have the fact attested under the hand and seal of Robert of Artois."

" Where is it ? " eagerly demanded the priest, who felt how necessary to his safety it was to possess himself of such an important document. " Hast it with thee ? "

" It were a wise trick that ! " exclaimed his nephew, " to bring my gage of safety to the enemy's camp ! No, no, sir priest, 1 am not to be caught in such a springe ; the paper is in secure hands, who will transfer it to the primate should aught like ill occur to me.".

" Thinkest thou," stammered Eborard, " that I am capable of——? "

" Every thing," interrupted the wretched man ; " nay, frown not, priest, nor raise thine eyes in pious mockery to Heaven, to attest the innocence thou hast long since lost ; enough for me, I know thee," he added ; " know thee better than the confession ever yet revealed thee—better even than thou knowest thyself. Now let us deal together."

" What wouldst thou—gold ? " demanded the terrified churchman, who inwardly cursed himself that he had ever yielded to the passionate menaces and entreaties of his nephew, and performed the sacred rite between him and Rachel—the only condition on which the haughty Jewess consented to be his ; for, although she placed no faith in the ceremony herself, she thought it might bind him.

" I would," laconically answered Robert.

" What sum ? "

" As much as will defray the expense of a knightly suit of armour and a good steed—say two thousand marks : thou seest 1 am moderate to begin with."

" Two thousand devils," groaned the prior ; " where should I find so vast a sum ? Dost take our poor priory for a bishop's see ? An I were to count you half the sum, the brotherhood would keep a twelvemonth's Lent."

"Take it, then, from the treasure which thy nephew confided to thy care," said his disfigured creditor ; "ten thousand chances if ever he returns from Purgatory to claim it at your hands."

"What treasure ?" faltered Eborard.

"The twenty thousand marks in gold," sternly replied Robert ; "to say nothing of the vessels of gold and silver torn from many an outraged shrine. The money, quick, at once ; for I am sick of parleying with thee ; and, now I think on't," he added, "make it three thousand marks—it will save trouble for us both."

Eborard thought it best to comply with the demands of his unwelcome visitor at once, lest they should rise as he disputed them ; he felt he was in his power, and had no resource left but to obey. His secret, whilst confined to his own breast, was his slave ; in the possession of another, it became his master, and he submitted to its chains. Motioning to Robert to follow him to his cell, he counted down the gold to him with a heavy heart ; for, like most worldly natures, he clung to the yellow dross ; it was an idol which in his selfish breast had replaced the purer image of his God.

"There !" he exclaimed, as the last glittering piece fell from his reluctant fingers ; "I trust thou art satisfied."

"For the present," coolly replied his nephew, pouching the coin. "Farewell. Perhaps we may one day meet again."

"The paper—the confession of Robert of Artois ?" demanded Eborard, with an imploring look, which showed the importance he placed on the possession of it. "When shall it be mine ?" .

"Never," said his creditor, "till I am paid in full. Fear not—it is in safe hands ; I am not likely to slay the goose which lays such golden eggs. Sleep in peace till next thou hearest from me ; that is," he added. "if a soul so black as thine can sleep. Hast any message to William of Normandy?—for in three days I trust to join him. There is work to do in which I may be useful."

"None," sighed the prior ; "at least none which thou canst bear."

"I have no other means to gain access to him," resumed his tormentor, with a smile—the first which, since his fearful punishment, had been seen upon his pale, disfigured countenance. "Adieu, most pious father," he added, with a sneer. "I do not ask thy benediction, lest it should turn to curses on my head."

"Adieu," said the priest, as he left the cell ; "and may all the plagues of Egypt go along with thee ! Who can this ruffian be," he murmured, " who thus holds my destiny in his rude hands ? Can it be some agent of the accursed Jew ? No matter who, I am in his toils ; and resistance, like regret, is equally in vain."

In the manner in which Robert of Artois had approached his

uncle, he had shown a true appreciation of his character. If he
had revealed himself, ten to one he had not been believed. Besides,
in his own person, the crafty prior might have defied him, for he
could not have denounced him for the sacrilege he had committed
in marrying him to Rachel without implicating himself—a thing
most anxiously to be avoided. He had suffered as few men have
suffered, and the effect produced within his mind was as great as
the change upon his person ; but whether for good or evil, time
alone can tell.

Concealing his gold carefully upon his person, he passed the city
gates, having first provided himself with a good steed, which he
bought of a Saxon peasant, who had most probably stolen it from
some straggler of Prince Robert's army, for the price at which he
sold it was a vile one.

"Now, then, for London," muttered Robert of Artois, when he
was fairly on his journey. "Like a shadow of the past, I will appear
amongst them ; like a voice from the tomb, I will croak my
predictions in their ear. There is one being left in the world who
still, perchance, may love me ; let me seek him out ; and then as
destiny or inclination hereafter may decide."

As William, two days after his coronation, was leaving his capital
to march to the encounter of his brother, who, by the advice of his
counsellors, had thrown himself into Kent, he was accosted by a
knight, sheathed in a plain black coat of mail, who demanded an
audience in private. There was something in the tone of the
speaker's voice which told the Red King he was no stranger to him ;
and despite the remonstrances of his attendants, whom he commanded to ride apart, the favour was accorded. Long and earnest
was the conversation which ensued, the monarch frequently
expressing by his gestures both interest and surprise. At last, at
his request, the stranger raised his visor, and disclosed the features
of his favourite, Robert of Artois ; but so changed, as we have
described, that but for the unanswerable proofs of his identity,
which from former passages between them he had been enabled to
adduce, and the strange tale of his metamorphosis which he had
related, his master never could have credited his assertion.

"This is indeed the poetry of vengeance," exclaimed the king, in
a voice almost of pity ; for there were still, when his evil passions
were not roused, some traces of humanity in him ; but fear not,
Robert, thou shalt have ample means of paying back the Jew thy
debt with interest. My lords," he added, beckoning his suite to
approach, "henceforth this noble stranger is attached to our person ;
for the present, it is his pleasure that his name and rank should be
concealed. Know him, then, but as William's friend, and the Black
Knight. The time, I trust, will soon arrive when we may grace
him with a nobler name, the one he hath so long and faithfully
borne ; till that hour arrives it is our pleasure that none question

him of the past. Forward, my friends," he added, at the same time
setting spurs to his impatient steed ; "forward to Kent."

It is far from our intention to trace the course of the civil war
which ensued, with varying success, between the two brothers :
history hath more faithful chroniclers than we can presume to be.
William—as crafty as Robert was generous and rash—contrived
to engage the affections of his Saxon subjects by liberal concessions
in their favour. They were now so thoroughly subdued, that few
longer aspired to the recovery of their ancient liberties, but were
content with the promised mitigation of the iron rule of their
Norman princes. The Red King at last contrived to detach Roger,
Earl of Shrewsbury, from his brother's interests, who, with his
powerful fleet, prevented the arrival of succours which the con-
federates expected from Normandy ; thus place after place fell into
his hands, and despite the devotion of Odo of Bayeux, Ulrick, and
the few nobles who still adhered to a falling cause, Pevensey Castle
alone held out for Robert.

It had for some time been besieged in vain ; the great natural
strength of its position rendered it almost impossible to be
taken except by famine. Changing, therefore, his often foiled plan
of assault into a blockade, William set down to besiege it in due
form.

In the various battles which had been fought our hero had twice
preserved the life of Robert, who repaid him by an attachment as
sincere as he was capable of entertaining. Often would he, when
walking with him on the ramparts, indulging in familiar conversation, express his regret that Heaven had not blessed him with such
a son. "I feel," added the unhappy prince, "that then I should
have something worth living for." It was evident that some secret
sorrow prompted this regret ; but Ulrick possessed too much
delicacy to seek his confidence on the only point where he seemed
disposed to be reserved.

It was on a similar occasion, when the realmless monarch, who
for a considerable time had been silently occupied in watching the
night fires of the enemy, whose forces encircled the last spot of
ground which owned his authority in England, turned suddenly
round to his companion, and breaking silence, exclaimed :

"I am weary of being cooped up like a wild fox in my den.
What thinkest thou, Ulrick—are we not strong enough to lead a
sortie from the keep ? My sword is getting rusty for lack of use,
and I feel the gall within my heart is rising daily to my lips ; a
bout might cure me of this folly, or end it, perchance, at once.
'Tis but the hour of ten ; by midnight all might be prepared."

The Lord of Stanfield, whose absence from Matilda made the
monotony of his existence but more drear, eagerly caught at the
proposal, and they were descending the ramparts to give the orders
necessary to carry it into effect, when they encountered the

venerable Edda and Herbert de Lozenga, who were both hurrying
to a lone watch-tower at a distant angle of the castle. The prince
informed them of the project he had just conceived, which the
prelate listened to with a reproving air, for although a man of peace,
he saw at once that, even if successful, it would be attended with
no ultimate advantage.

"You hear our pleasure doubtingly, my lord," said Robert, in a
half-offended tone.

"I may question its wisdom, sire," replied Herbert, "without
presuming to censure it. Our only hope is that succours from
France or Normandy may arrive ; but for your unhappy quarrel
with my Lord of Shrewsbury, they had been here ere this. Wait
but a little and——"

"I'll wait no longer !" replied the monarch sternly ; then added,
for he saw that his manner had given pain, "Yet still am thankful
for your prudent counsel. Truth is, my lord, I am weary of this
world of treachery and disappointment. The brightest gems in
England's crown could not console me longer for the absence of
green fields and a merry chase. I must do something to break my
thrall, lest in very spleen I turn upon myself and devour my own
heart. France—pshaw ! by Rollo, but our brother the other side of
the Manche has had good reason, long ere this, to leave us to our
fate. William has found the way to grease the Frenchman's palm ;
I have no hope from France."

"But I have, sire," quietly observed the bishop ; "brighter than
ever."

"You have received letters, then, my lord ? " observed Ulrick,
eagerly.

"No."

"Nor message ? " added Robert.

"None. I see," said the prelate, with a smile, "this mystery
displeases you. Deign to come with me, sire ; if there be treason,
it shall be explained. Trust me it is no dangerous one ; for the
noble Edda and myself, together with a few poor monks, are the
sole conspirators."

With these words the speaker resumed his way, followed by the
aged Saxon and the two warriors ; not a word was spoken till they
arrived at the tower we have already mentioned.

"Now, then, for the conspiracy !" exclaimed Herbert, lighting a
lamp, and placing it in one of the loopholes of the battlement ; "it
will soon be answered."

Robert saw to his surprise that a similar light, in a few seconds,
made its appearance in the window of a belfry attached to a small
convent, removed about a bow-shot from the line of the enemy's
camp.

"It is already answered," said Edda ; "the intelligence is good."

By placing the lamps in different positions, questions were asked and the responses made—a system of telegraphing which lasted about twenty minutes ; at the end of which time the prelate, turning with a smiling face to Robert, informed him despatches had arrived from France.

"And their contents, my lord ?" hastily demanded the prince.

"In ten days succour will arrive, winds and the will of Heaven permitting," answered Herbert.

"Is't sure ?"

"Most certain."

"Still will I forth to-night. I feel an impulse not to be controlled. The fierce spirit of the founder of my race is on me," added the prince ; "it is an omen presages me success. Within the hour, the moon will set. Let the soldiers arm themselves with flax and torches ; bring flasks of oil to pour upon the tents. By Rollo's sword ! Pevensey shall witness a blaze this night to light up its old towers ! See to it, Stanfield."

Ulrick eagerly withdrew to prepare the men for the night's work, which he doubted not would be warm and bloody ; for, whatever might be Robert's defects as a leader, want of courage was not one ; though, unfortunately, it was of that reckless kind which, however valuable in an individual soldier, is little to be desired in a chief.

The bishop remained silent ; he saw no good could result from the attempt, but knew that it would be useless to oppose it further, for Robert had sworn by the oath of his race—the only pledge which the princes of his name were never known to violate. The experienced Edda also disapproved of the expedition.

"You, my good father," resumed the prince, "will summon our council, and impart the intelligence. You have no need of my weak head to aid you ; whatever your wisdom may decide upon, Robert is always ready to approve."

"Always ?" demanded Herbert, perhaps rather maliciously.

"Always, unless it cross my previous resolution. Farewell," he added ; "wait but an hour longer on the ramparts, and you shall see a blaze, old friend, to cheer your drooping spirits : the camp of my rebel brother shall feed the flame."

The party had scarcely left the ramparts when a figure, which had been hid by one of the huge embrasures of the battlements, stepped from its place of concealment into the bright moonlight, and throwing aside the cloak which enshrouded him, discovered the person of a man-at-arms, who had evidently been a spy upon their conversation. A deep red cicatrice extending from the temple to the jaw identified Peter Norbeck, the ruffian from whose brutality, our readers will recollect, Ulrick had saved Abram the Jew, and who had vowed vengeance for the chastisement his insolence and cruelty so well had merited. With a smile of mingled satisfaction and hatred he drew an arrow from his quiver, and shot it towards a low mound lying between the castle and the enemy's camp, and remained for a few minutes leaning on his bow to watch the result. A low flame from some kindled brushwood told the traitor that his intelligence had been received ; and he left the ramparts to return to his abandoned guard, muttering as he went—" I have kept my word. Norbeck's oath of vengeance hath never yet been broken."

The intended sortie from the castle was betrayed.

Robert of Normandy and his chosen band had halted about half a mile from William's camp, to give final instructions for the assault. The spot was a long avenue of aged oaks, opening on the plain, where the tents of the enemy were clearly to be seen in the pale moonlight. Some of the men were carrying dry furze and combustible matter, which they had hastily collected for the occasion ; others were whispering together, calculating the plunder which would probably be found in the tents of the Red King and his nobles, whilst the principal leaders of their own party were bidding adieu to Herbert de Lozenga and Edda, who had accompanied the expedition thus far on its way.

" Be not too rash !" exclaimed the warlike prelate ; " your enemies are numerous, and should they rally after their first surprise, must overwhelm you. Remember, Ulrick, you have now a being whose existence hangs on yours ; remember that your life is pledged deeply to her, as to your country, and that one rash act——"

A deep groan from the speaker interrupted the conclusion of his caution, as he sank mortally wounded by an arrow which some unseen hand had winged. The aged Edda caught him as he fell.

" Treason !" shouted Robert of Normandy and the knights, who witnessed with horror the cowardly assassination ; " we are beset ! To arms ! to arms ! "

A party of William's followers, who had been planted in ambush, rushed from their concealment in the forest ; Tyrrel headed them, urged on by the double motive of hatred to Ulrick and the desire to distinguish himself in the cause upon whose success his promised earldom depended. Many of Robert's men-at-arms, encumbered by the brushwood and materials they had gathered, died ere they could draw their weapons ; others fled. The principal object of the enemy seemed to be to secure the person of the prince, whom Odo of Caen, and his namesake of Bayeux, and several knights, stoutly defended, reckless of their own lives, provided they preserved that of the unfortunate monarch to whom they had sworn allegiance. As brave as he was rash and inconsiderate, Robert for awhile resisted every attempt to reconduct him to the fortress ; but with each moment's delay the danger which menaced him and his devoted defenders increased. Bands of dark, fierce-looking mercenaries were beginning to form in compact bodies round them ; the one headed by Tyrrel had already taken the party in the flank, so as to cut off their retreat. Ulrick, who had vainly attempted to rally the fugitives, saw the danger, and, at the head of a dozen of his Saxon followers, threw himself between his friends and the enemy to defeat it. Here the battle raged most fiercely ; the sword of Ulrick did fearful execution ; each sweep left a gap in the compact Norman ranks, which their overwhelming numbers alone enabled them to fill up. The rival leader fought with all the desperate courage of humbled pride, ambition, and unslaked hate.

"Save the king !" shouted our hero, who saw that he and his gallant band would uselessly be sacrificed, unless immediate advantage were taken of their devotion to retreat to Pevensey, for longer resistance was impossible.

"Down with the traitors !" echoed Tyrrel, who felt like a famished tiger when he sees his prey escaping him. "Five hundred marks for this boaster's head ! —a thousand for the person of Prince Robert ! "

Animated by the hope of reward, again the mercenaries rushed on the faithful few ; but though they were again repulsed by the calm courage with which they were encountered, another such attack must needs be fatal. Half of Ulrick's little band had bit the dust, and two were wounded. Again, therefore, he shouted with increased energy and desperation to save the king and to retreat to Pevensey.

Robert, who had resisted every persuasion of those around him to retreat, no sooner heard the voice of Tyrrel offering a thousand marks for his person, than he became a changed man. Flinging away his broken brand, he turned to those near him, saying in a husky voice ;

"The sin of our youth hath found us. The day is against us. On, friends, to Pevensey !—'tis our last hope."

It is doubtful whether the devoted courage of the Lord of Stanfield could have secured them from falling into the hands of the enemy, had not a party, headed by Mirvan, sallied from the castle to assist them, for the shouts of the combatants had been heard through the stillness of the night upon the battlements, and the garrison judged their friends had been surprised.

Even thus supported, their retreat was with difficulty accomplished ; they rushed pell-mell into the courtyard ; and so close was the pursuit, that the drawbridge, which was raised the instant they had passed, let several of the enemy into the deep moat as it rose, for their feet were already upon it : the arrows of the men-at-arms upon the watch-tower soon despatched them.

"Where is the bishop ? " demanded William de Warrenne.

"Dead "' groaned Robert.

"And Ulrick ? " said Mirvan, anxiously looking round.

"Dead or a prisoner, too."

That night there was scant revelry in the beleaguered fortress of Pevensey.

The following morning the warder brought notice that a gibbet was being erected within bow-shot of the walls, the ground around it was kept by a numerous body of archers, and that the troops of William were assembling in vast numbers in order to be present at an execution of more solemnity than usual.

Mirvan heard the intelligence with dismay, for his fear but too rightly foreboded that it was for Ulrick, for the companion of his youth, the friend of his heart, the husband of Matilda. Half-frantic with grief and indignation, he imparted his suspicions to Prince Henry, who immediately conducted him to his brother's chamber, where the council was already assembled.

The chiefs were debating on the propriety of holding out to the last, or at least till the promised aid from France should arrive; their position, though wearying, was anything but desperate. Pevensey was strongly garrisoned, well-provisioned, and, except from treachery within, might long protract its surrender. Robert sat listening to the debate more like an unconcerned spectator than a king whose crown and life were perchance at issue. His heart was crushed; from some secret cause the conduct of Tyrrel deeply affected him; and the probable fate of Ulrick, who had so generously devoted himself to insure his safety, weighed deeply on his spirits. Mirvan's tale roused him from his apathy.

"What!" he exclaimed, starting from his chair, "the gibbet for the bravest knight that ever drew his sword in honour's cause? Perish thus ignominiously for my sake?—never, never! Decide, my lords, upon some means to save him. My crown— my life— whatever my cruel brother will, to ransom him; but cursed be my name, and stained my shield, if Ulrick perish, and through fault of mine!"

Odo of Bayeux, although deeply grieved at Ulrick's misfortune, contemplated no such sacrifice to save him. His own ambitious projects, which aimed at nothing less than the Papacy, demanded that his favourite nephew should be king; and to advance his views one step, he would have bartered a hundred lives, and thought the attainment of it cheaply paid. He proposed, therefore, that a herald should be sent to William's camp, offering ransom for the prisoner, and declaring that, in the event of any outrage being offered to his life, his friends would fearfully retaliate upon all of the opposite party who might fall into their hands.

Robert heard the proposal with undisguised contempt; he knew too well the ferocious disposition of his brother to suppose for one moment that any consideration of humanity could influence him. The rest of the council approved of the idea, Mirvan alone excepted.

Whilst the debate was going on, the realmless king took up a pen, and amused himself by writing, occasionally listening to what the various speakers urged. Without showing his letter to any one, he carefully sealed it with his private signet, and placing it in the hands of Mirvan, whispered him:

[WILLIAM RUFUS TAKING THE OATH.]

"Take it to William's camp ; let a herald and a flag of truce precede you. I know the price of your brother's life, and, vast as it is, I am prepared to pay it. Away ! before these selfish men suspect and seek to thwart our purpose."

Mirvan kissed the hand of the generous, but rash and feeble, prince ; he half-suspected the sacrifice he was about to offer to the shrine of friendship and honour, and quitted the room in silence.

"Where goes my Lord of Norwich ? " demanded Bishop Odo, looking anxiously after him ; "I trust, fair nephew, you have no secrets from your friends—proved friends—such as we are ? "

This was too direct a question to be evaded ; from any other than so near a relative Robert would have answered haughtily, and perhaps even so to him had not his soul been oppressed with the bitterness of its sorrows and disappointments. It was one of those moments when we feel the insufficiency of worldly grandeur—when the phantoms of the past, like mournful shadows, obscure the interests and passions of the present—when pride appears as ashes, power as worthless, and the heart thirsts to indulge in those sympa-thies which adorn and dignify humanity—sympathies which form the perfect part of an imperfect whole—the mortal signs of an immortal spirit.

" I can treat with my brother better," he answered, to his uncle, "than through my council, for we have long understood and known each other."

"This is folly—spleen ! " exclaimed the prelate ; " the very mad-ness of misgoverned judgment ! Wouldst fling a sceptre from thy head as t'were a spinster's distaff ? "

"Perhaps," carelessly replied Robert ; "especially if the toy encumbered me."

" Recall the messenger ; this must be prevented."

Odo and several of the knights advanced towards the door, when the prince with great dignity placed himself between them, still holding in his hand the pen with which he had written to his unnatural brother. Possessed of great mobility of character, the outrage to his rank had roused him ; the fierce passion of his race was upon him, and his eyes flashed with ill-suppressed indignation. In an instant the sadness of his heart had passed away.

"Is this your deference," he uttered sternly, "to your sovereign's will—this, my lords, your loyalty to the monarch you have sworn allegiance to ? Remember," he added, "but one scratch of this pen "—here the speaker dashed it from him as he spoke—" and William is your lawful king ; and you, instead of loyal nobles, become a herd of vile conspirators,—your lands given to confiscation, your heads the axe's forfeit prey. Advance one step to recall my messenger, and I declare my abdication, proclaim my brother king, without one stipulation for your lives and honours ; and well you know the tender William's mercy ! As it is, whatever our own fate, yours shall be cared for ; whatever our own sacrifice, your lands shall remain secure."

The members of the council gazed upon each other in surprise and consternation. The dilemma was too serious a one to be trifled with ; they felt that without the prince they were but a band of conspirators, without hope of mercy. Before they could recover themselves, the fall of the portcullis announced that Mirvan had departed with the herald, when all thoughts of opposition ceased ; for they would have been as useless as dangerous. Robert listened coldly to their protestations of respect and submission, and waved them haughtily from his presence.

" My poor brother," exclaimed Prince Henry, taking him kindly by the hand as soon as they were left alone, " is this sacrifice indeed worth making ? Remember that a crown once lost is seldom e'er regained. Reflect, it is not yet too late."

" I have reflected," answered Robert, calmly.

" My heart would burst were it longer prisoned here, shut up with mere lip loyalty, petty jealousies, and vile ambitions. Besides, I long for the green woods again ; I am sick of human faces, and want to look on nature, to talk with her in her deep recesses. Her silent voice will pour no odious flatteries in my ear, waken no storm of passions in my heart. I would forget the past, and all that can remind me of it," he added ; " its vain regrets, its broken hopes, its worm which never dies. Woman's love hath palled upon my lip, man's treachery left but a sepulchre within my heart. I have found but one being constant, in friendship devoted, generous, true ; he hath sacrificed himself for me ; he shall not perish if my crown can save him."

It was while labouring under feelings bitter as these that the unhappy prince, a few years later, sold his duchy of Normandy to the rapacious William for the contemptible sum of ten thousand marks, and engaged but a band of adventurous followers in the Crusades, which Peter the Hermit so successfully preached throughout the principal countries of Europe. But we are anticipating events ; it is time that our readers returned to Ulrick, whom we left contending with his old enemy, Tyrrel, to protect the retreat of his friend and sovereign, the unfortunate but generous Robert.

Opposed to overwhelming odds, it was the object of our hero to sell his life dearly rather than be taken, for he well knew the fate which would await him at the hands of William and his worthy minion ; but, despite his frantic courage, and the numbers which fell beneath his weapon, he was at last surrounded and disarmed. The large reward which the leader of his enemies offered for securing him alive tempted many of the men-at-arms to risk their own lives in securing him. Tyrrel's joy knew no bounds when he beheld the being whose superiority he had always hated a helpless prisoner before him ; every epithet which insulting cowardice could apply to vanquished heroism did he lavish on his captive, who bore it with that calm, silent contempt which often strikes deeper in the breasts of the unworthy than scorn or loud reproaches. When brought before William and his nobles in the tent of the former, his demeanour was cold and dignified ; and when that tyrant, with a refinement of cruelty, condemned him to the gibbet, although his cheek might blanch, his glance was as free and his mien as erect as ever. So favourable was the impression, that even his enemies thought it hard that so noble a knight should be so unnecessarily degraded. Some interceded for him, but in vain ; the Red King affected to despise the history of his birth, and condemned him as a mere peasant to the shameful tree.

"It is the crime, and not the scaffold, which dishonours," answered Ulrick, proudly, as he heard his doom. "All true hearts, fierce prince, will judge thy judgment, and infamy will brand thy memory with it."

Wounded and bleeding as he was, he was hurried from the tyrant's presence, and cast into a dungeon till the coming morning ; then to be again led forth, to meet his doom.

As we have described, the gibbet was erected within bow-shot of the castle, and most of William's troops were on the ground ; the Red King and his favourites arrived soon after to see our hero die. The coward heart of Tyrrel beat high with gratified revenge ; he anticipated with ferocious joy each pang, and revelled in the idea of the agonies which such an ignominious death would cause his victim's proud and gallant spirit.

At the foot of the fatal tree stood a fellow clothed in a crimson shirt, which descended nearly to his ankles ; his sleeves were rolled up to the shoulder, displaying his coarse, muscular arms ; he was, perhaps, the least excited spectator of the scene. He was coolly occupied in selecting a coil of rope from a number near him, and twisting it into a slip-noose—the occupation proclaimed the executioner.

"Now, marshal," exclaimed William, turning to Sir Richard Whetstone, "how long are we to wait ? Hath not the shaveling trussed the fellow for the gibbet yet, or must we lose the morning chase to wait the good father's pleasure ? "

" Be not impatient," replied the knight, in deep disgust ; " your victim, sir, is ready."

Many of the nobles beheld with equal indignation the execution of a man whom they had so often encountered in the battle-field, whose courage had been the theme of even the common soldier's tongue, and whose enmity to Tyrrel they thought justified by that unworthy favourite's insolence and presumption. Several of them had solicited William in his favour : he had sternly refused to listen to their prayer, or change the unknightly nature of his death.

"Ha, ha, ha!" shouted Tyrrel, as soon as Ulrick reached the fatal spot, "I thought his vaunted courage would abandon him at last. See how pale the traitor is!"

"With loss of blood, then," coolly answered Ulrick; "but, coward, I parley not with thee. Once more I do protest, for the honour of my knighthood, against the degrading nature of my death, which only a mind framed like a tyrant's could have conceived, or men lost to honour execute. Now then I am ready to meet my fate as becomes a Christian and a noble."

"As a traitor and a felon!" shouted Tyrrel.

"Away with him to the gibbet!—fit end for the vile peasant!"

So disgusted was Roger of Shrewsbury with Tyrrel's conduct, that he dashed his mailed glove in the villain's face, exclaiming as he did so:

"Cur! another such a word, and I'll rend thy fawning, lying tongue from out thy mouth. For his treasons, his judges best can answer for their judgment; but peasant he is none: and I proclaim him liar, craven, and forsworn—aye," he added, fixing his eyes upon William—" e'en though he wore a crown—who dares to brand him one! His death is a murder, not an execution!"

A murmur of approbation from the nobles 'near, who were equally disgusted with the speaker, warned William that he was treading upon dangerous ground; still, in the bitterness of his hatred, he determined to persevere. Tyrrel, pale and subdued by the noble scorn and haughty glance of so powerful a noble as Roger of Shrewsbury, withdrew behind his master.

"Proceed with the execution," exclaimed the impatient monarch; "let us end this scene."

Ulrick, despite his courage and lofty resolution, turned pale as the minister of shame approached him; it was not death he feared—it was dishonour. Ere, however, the ruffian could lay a hand upon him, Mirvan, his horse covered with foam, followed by the herald whom he had outridden, galloped on the ground; and, advancing to the Red King, placed his brother's letter in his hand, who turned alternately pale and red with emotion as he perused it.

"What are your orders, sire?" demanded Whetstone, kindly hoping that something favourable to Ulrick had occurred.

"Suspend the execution," said William, with ill-concealed rage.

"Your highness!" exclaimed Tyrrel, fearful lest his victim should escape.

"Back, sir knight," cried his master, haughtily, and not unwilling to mortify him; "this is beyond your sphere. Guard your prisoner, marshal, but treat him well. Let us," he added, turning to the principal nobles near him, "in to council."

Whetstone cut his prisoner's cords, and in an instant Ulrick and Mirvan were locked in each other's embrace; whilst Tyrrel stood confounded and abashed at the strange termination of the scene.

CHAPTER XVII.

DURING the following morning a spacious pavilion, destined for the meeting of the royal brothers, was erected on the plain, at an equal distance from the camp of the Red King and the beleaguered fortress. There, for the first time since the Conqueror's death, the two princes were to meet, and articles of peace be debated between them. The position of William, though thus far victorious, was anything but sure. The crown sat but loosely on his brow ; to bind it there securely he was obliged to make concessions, at which his haughty soul revolted, to the nobles and clergy, many of whom, with all his condescensions, were but coldly satisfied.

Robert, although reduced to the strong castle of Pevensey, possessed a moral strength in his alliance with the French king, which the adherence of Lanfranc and the barons barely balanced in his rival's cause ; added to which, the promised aid from France might still arrive, and turn the tide of fortune in his favour. The usurper was too keen a gamester not to calculate every chance ; like most heartless men, he was capable of sacrificing even his resentments to his interests, and hence the order to suspend the execution of our hero ; for the generous Robert, in his letter, expressly declared that all attempts at negotiation would be vain if a single hair of Ulrick's head were touched.

Many loiterers, attracted by the coming interview, were lingering round the spot ; amongst others, Tyrrel and Robert of Artois, whom we shall henceforth designate by the name he bore in the camp, that of the Black Knight. The mystery which attached to his person—his intimacy with the king, as well as the cold habitual reserve of his manner, which forbad all attempts at approach—made him an object of curiosity with many, and of a superstitious dread with others. Tyrrel, however, only saw in him a dangerous rival in his master's favour ; he was jealous of his importance, and anxious to find some clue to his secret as a means of supplanting him, the first step to which he naturally thought would be to bring about a certain degree of intimacy : the present was too good an occasion to be thrown away.

" *Bon jour*, sir knight ! " he exclaimed, in a careless, off-handed tone, as he advanced towards the spot where the object of his speculation was standing, gazing with a dreamy look upon the various preparations.

The Black Knight simply bowed his head without replying, but Tyrrel was not to be so put off.

" So," he continued, "our campaign is nearly over. Robert, though a foolish prince, is at least a generous master, since he resigns his crown to save his favourite's life."

" A sacrifice till now unheard of," replied the party addressed, " in the history of princes. Their memory, like water, retains no trace of the absent object once reflected there. The most devoted service, in their eyes, is but a duty scantily paid ; their promises are as unstable as the winds, with which their favour changes."

"You, at least," said Tyrrel, "have no reason to complain, since your favour with the king exceeds the proudest nobles ; his confidence in you is as unbounded as your merits. Many envy the Chevalier Noir—since it is his pleasure only to be known as such—his hold on William's friendship."

"Perhaps fools often take mere tinsel for pure gold," answered the Black Knight, carelessly ; "but you," he added, "ought to be equally satisfied. The services you have rendered Rufus are deep and many : first you released him from prison ; conducted him to London to be crowned ; detected the correspondence of his enemies ; and since you recovered from the wounds received on the occasion, have done good service in the wars. These, sir knight," he added, sarcastically, "are claims a prince like William never can forget, e'en were his memory shorter than his love."

"And you might add," muttered Tyrrel, who began to feel anything but satisfied at the delay in his promised earldom, "that through my agency the plans of the besieged have all been known and frustrated—witness last night's attack. Peter Norbeck is a useful agent in the fortress of our enemies."

The name of Peter Norbeck seemed to excite the surprise of his companion, for it was connected with certain passages of his life to which he had long lost the clue ; it was, therefore, no longer in the light bantering tone which he had assumed, but in accents of deep and undisguised interest, that he demanded if he alluded to a Norman man-at-arms who was formerly in the City guard.

"No," resumed the speaker ; "but to his brother, whom the bastard of Stanfield punished for trying to squeeze a vile Jew's purse of a few silver pennies. The fellow hates, as such men only hate, with the ferocity of a bloodhound, as well as its determination. I have found him a faithful agent, perhaps because the prey we hunted was the same. The man you inquire after is his brother, now one of the warders of the City who first detected Ulrick's mission to the rebels."

"Is he with one of the companies who have followed Rufus to the wars ?" demanded the Black Knight.

"There is the very man," exclaimed Tyrrel, pointing to the warder, who, with several of his companions, was lounging about to watch the proceedings ; "he is my go-between with his brother."

Without a word of adieu, or thanks for the information, his questioner, turned upon his heel, and proceeded directly, with his usual measured tread, towards the spot where the group were standing. Laying his mailed hand upon the ruffian's shoulder, he simply pronounced the words, "Follow me," and without waiting to see if he was obeyed, directed his steps towards the neighbouring wood, conscious that his authority was such, from his influenco with William, that men even of a much higher rank would reflect twice ere they ventured to dispute it. The warder followed with the instinctive obedience of a hound at the call of its master. The Black Knight was held in a sort of mysterious terror by all, a feeling to which the ghastly expression of his countenance—now scarcely human—not a little contributed.

As soon as they reached an open sward, bounded by a running brook, where the brushwood and grass were too low to give shelter to an eavesdrooper, the foremost paused, and waited till the man whom he had so long been anxious to find stood before him face to face.

" Is your name Norbeck ? " he demanded.

" It is, sir knight," answered the fellow, respectfully, at the same time feeling uneasy, although he knew not why, at the strange conference which he foresaw was about to take place between them.

" Formerly of the Cityguard ? "

" And now one of its warders," added the fellow, hoping to create a favourable impression by the announcement of the responsible office with which he was intrusted.

" To whom," continued his questioner, " sixteen years since, a male child was intrusted by a noble knight, together with a large sum of money—the boy to be brought up as your wife's, by a former marriage ; the gold to be employed for his support and future establishment in life ? "

" The same," faltered the man, his uneasiness and astonishment increasing at every question.

" Doth that boy still live ? "

" He does."

" And where ? "

" Marry, that is more than I can tell," replied the warder ; " 'tis months since I beheld him. He was always a wayward, stubborn brat, even as a child ; as he grew up, I had hard lines with him. The traitor who should have swung this day upon the gibbet can tell you, perhaps, more of his whereabouts than I can, since he it was who took him from me. I'd give the heaviest coin in my purse but to lay hands on him again."

" Why so ? " demanded the Black Knight, a shade of haughty displeasure rendering his features still more repulsive than even their unnatural transformation had made them.

" Why so ? " iterated the ruffian ; " why, because is it not natural I should wish to find the runaway again ? But may I ask, noble sir, why you feel so interested in his story ? Perhaps he is known to you ? "

" Ask me nothing," sternly replied his questioner ; " but as thou valuest that neck of thine, answer truly ; think not to deceive me, for I can detect the lie on falsehood's quivering lip—read it in the shifting glance or hesitating speech. I have dealt too long with men to be easily deceived, and despise them too much to pardon their treachery lightly. Tell me," he added, drawing his sword, " how the boy's fate became mixed up with the knight of Stanfield's ; and remember that thy first lie will prove thy last—I warn not twice ! "

Finding that it would be dangerous to prevaricate, and ignorant whether the knight's motives to the boy were of good or evil, but trusting to the latter, the warder, without much disguise, described all that had passed between both Gilbert and himself, even to the beating and wounding of the former, and his rescue by Ulrick from his hands. Had the wretch, when he related the lashing with the bow-string, caught the flash of the fierce vindictive eyes fixed upon him, he would have read his doom as plainly as if voice had spoken it. When he had finished, he stood with a half-doubtful, half-confident air before his mysterious judge.

"And thou hast told me all ? " demanded the Black Knight.

"All," said the ruffian, anxiously ; " I trust, noble sir, that you are satisfied."

" I were difficult to please an I were not satisfied," answered his questioner, sarcastically ; "thou hast proved thyself a faithful guardian—a most kind one. Thou mightest have slain the boy, and yet thou only gavest the lash ; as men correct a hound at fault, a restive steed, or base-born serf. There," he added, bitterly, taking a handful of coin from the pouch suspended at his girdle ; " there is the first proof how much I am satisfied with thee ; anon, thou shalt have another more lasting than the present : I am one who always pays his debts."

As the speaker poured the money into the warder's greedy palm, he dropped, apparently by accident, several of the pieces upon the ground ; in stooping to pick them up, the head of the fellow was bent to the earth, leaving an opening about two inches wide between his helmet and rough coat of mail, which left the back part of his neck totally defenceless. Before his fingers could grasp the first coin, the long heavy blade of the Black Knight's sword descended with the rapidity of a flash of lightning upon the mark, and the head of the ruffian rolled at the feet of his executioner.

" Carrion ! " exclaimed the assassin ; " if, indeed, he merited the name of such ; the headsman should have dealt with thee, and not a noble's sword ; thou art but too honoured to fall by hands like mine."

Spurning the gory head, whose eyeballs were still rolling in their sockets, contemptuously from him, he was about to quit the spot, when he observed a packet of papers in the belt of the being whose crimes he had so fearfully punished : to secure and read them was the work of a few minutes. Surprise and indignation were visible on his countenance as he did so.

"Fratricide as well as usurper," he murmured, "this crime, at least, shall be prevented ; if I cannot recall the past, at least I will endeavour to atone it."

With these words the unhappy man directed his steps towards the scene of meeting.

At a preconcerted signal, the royal brothers, each attended by six nobles totally unarmed, set out for the place of rendezvous ; the men-at-arms, fity in number, who escorted them, halted by agreement at a hundred paces on either side of the tent. In the train of William were Lanfranc, the primate ; Roger of Shrewsbury, Aubrey de Vere, and three barons of less note. With Robert came the Earl of Norwich, Edda the Saxon, William de Warrenne, and three Norman vavasours, who still remained firm to his cause. The party of Robert were the first to enter the tent ; the prince preceded his friends a few paces, leaning on the arm of Mirvan, with whom he was engaged in deep conversation.

"Had my son proved worthy of his name." said the unhappy prince, "my hand should have withered ere I set my seal to such a treaty ; as it is, with me the secret dies, since I alone possess the proofs of his legitimacy and birth."

Had not the speaker's attention been occupied by the sudden blast of the trumpet which announced the arrival of William, they must have heard the rustling between the inner lining and outward canvas of the tent, occasioned by the retreating steps of one who had overheard the prince's confidence. It was the traitor Tyrrel.

"He comes," said Robert, advancing to the altar erected in the centre of the pavilion ; "one struggle, and 'tis past."

At this moment William Rufus and his party entered. The heavy draperies of the pavilion were let down, and the two monarchs and their councillors were shut from the gaze of the men-at-arms without. Prince Henry had declined being present at the interview : either he doubted the Red King's faith, or he disapproved of the sacrifice which his brother Robert was about to make. Cunning beyond his years, he veiled beneath an appearance of lighthearted reckless humour schemes of ambition which the prophecy—for such he considered it—of the Saxon monk at Eltham had engraved too deeply on his heart ever to be effaced. Whilst the conference was taking place, he remained with the escort at a distance, laughing and chatting with the officers who commanded it.

"There they go," he exclaimed, as the parties entered the tent ; "the vulture and falcon are at roost together. We shall soon have no better sport than to hunt the red deer in the forest, gentles ; that is, if our kind brother of the red poll leaves us the liberty to do so."

"If your grace has a doubt upon the subject," observed the young noble to whom the observation was addressed, "I should advise the air of Normandy—there, at least, you may hunt in security."

" Perhaps ! " said a deep voice near them. The speakers turned and beheld the Black Knight, whose person they had become too familiar with during the late struggle not to recognise. With his usual quiet step he had approached them almost unperceived.

" Back, sir knight ! " exclaimed the prince. " Know you not it is forbidden by the terms of the truce for either party of the escort to approach the other ? "

" I belong not to the escort," replied the intruder ; " my errand is to place this packet in the hands of Henry of Normandy." The knight held out the papers he had taken from the belt of the warder as he spoke, and disappeared almost as suddenly as he had presented himself.

The prince perused the letters so mysteriously conveyed to him, and although they contained nothing less than matters touching his life, not a frown or gesture of surprise betrayed the deep emotion which the perusal of them occasioned. Trained early to the wiles and intrigues of courts, he was perfectly master of himself, and while he read the hearts of others, guarded the secrets of his own like a sealed book.

To those who knew the fiery, impatient character of Robert, it was a matter of surprise that he discussed the proposed articles of the treaty with his brother so calmly ; by it he accepted his father's will, and gave up all claim to the crown of England, contenting himself with his hereditary duchy of Normandy. The only points on which he was inflexible was the safety of Ulrick, and the personal security both of life and lands of his adherents. On these no arguments could move him, and William, who saw that the primate and the nobles of his party not only coincided in the reasonableness of the terms, but were prepared to support his brother in insisting on them, was forced, though with an ill grace, to yield. Lanfranc drew up the treaty, to which the rival princes and barons set their names and seals, both brothers swearing on the altar to observe it.

" Stay," said Robert, as William, with a cold sarcastic smile upon his face, was about to quit the altar, " thou hast sworn on the Evangile—swear also by the oath of our race to keep good faith with me. Thou knowest the tradition of our house—thou knowest the fearful curse which hangs o'er him who breaks it."

" What I have sworn I have sworn ! " exclaimed William, turning pale ; for, superstitious as he was cruel, he knew that the required oath would deprive him of his cherished scheme of vengeance. " Why doubt my faith, or tax it further ? "

" Why ? " iterated Robert ; " because I know that oaths are like water with thee. Didst thou not swear to our mother at the abbey of Caen never to prejudice thy elder brother's right ? The crown thou hast obtained by perjury best can answer how thou hast observed thy oath. Didst thou not swear to prove a loving brother

to her youngest Henry, and hast thou not sought his life ? Thy
oath on the Evangile ! " he added ; "as soon would I trust the
inconstant wind or fickle waves as such an oath from thee. Speak,
lords, have I not reason ? "

" You have," replied the primate and peers, who began to feel
regret at the part they had taken, and were anxious to make the
treaty a lasting one between the princes—a step to which their
interests impelled them, for most held possessions in Normandy as
well as England, possessions which, in all probability, they would
lose should war again break out between the brothers.

" Still the Norman hesitated, for vengeance was almost as dear to
him as ambition ; vainly he gazed upon those who had placed him
on the throne for encouragement in his refusal ; cold, stern glances
met him on every face, and he felt that delay might prove
dangerous even to his crown and life.

" Swear ! " exclaimed the united nobles, unanimously, several of
his own party advancing towards Robert.

" Be it so," muttered the tyrant, furiously ; "propose the oath."

" By the bones of Rollo," said his brother, impressively, " you
swear never to attempt aught against the life, liberty, and honour of
Ulrick of Stanfield—to restore him instantly to freedom—in return
for the unreserved surrender of my crown—and to hold all who
have supported my rights scatheless in honours, lives, and lands."

" I swear it," repeated William, faintly, " by the bones of
Rollo."

" And may the curse of your race," added his brother—" of him
men call the Devil's Son, whose couch of fire not all the prayers of
Holy Church or blood of Heaven's blest martyrs e'er can quench, be
yours if e'er you break your oath ! "

All present shuddered as Rufus repeated the fearful imprecation ;
for not one but firmly believed that the soul of the common
ancestor of the two princes was to remain, according to his compact
with Satan, in hell till one of his descendants, by breaking the
oath of his race, should release it.

" Now, then," said Robert," " take the crown, and may it prove
to thee of thorns. Care and suspicion haunt thy pillow—poison
the wine-cup in thy hour of mirth—pall e'en the kiss of beauty on
thy lip ! Reign in terror—haunted by shadows—heartless, friendless, and alone ! "

William, despite the natural hardihood of his nature, shrank at
the well-merited malediction of a brother whom he had so
treacherously supplanted in his birthright, and left the tent with
his train in gloomy silence ; leaving Robert to await the arrival of
the rescued prisoner, according to the terms of the treaty to be
immediately set at liberty. As the monarch left the pavilion,
Tyrrel, impatient to impart the important secret he had so basely
obtained, arrested his steps, and demanded a moment's audience ;

his look and bearing indicated that it was for a communication too
pressing to be refused.

"Prince," said Edda, addressing the now crownless king, who
still remained standing by the altar where Rufus had pronounced
the fearful oath, "the joy I feel at the certitude of again embracing
my grandson will hardly repay the sorrow which I experience at
this most generous sacrifice, fatal alike for thee and for my country ;
history will chronicle the heroic deed long after the icy hand of
Death hath effaced its record from the hearts of those who witnessed
it."

"It has been greater, old man, than thou wotst of," said Robert,
kindly ; "but let it pass : all of my race are not alike ungrateful.
In my path through life I have sown affections and gathered tares ;
love hath been blighted, honours lost, ambition crushed ; e'en in
that corner of my heart," he added, bitterly, "where I had garnered
up a hope for age, the mildew of treachery and deceit hath found
me."

All were impressed with the deep melancholy of the speaker's
voice, and listened in respectful silence.

About half an hour after William's departure the curtains of the
pavilion were once more raised. Edda and Mirvan advanced to
meet their liberated friend ; but found, to their surprise, that,
instead of Ulrick, it was the primate, with Roger of Shrewsbury and
Tyrrel, who entered the tent.

"Where is the Lord of Stanfield ? " demanded Robert impatiently.

"A prisoner," replied Tyrrel, with an air of triumph and
malicious satisfaction.

"By whose orders ? "

"The king's."

"What ! " exclaimed the indignant prince, "hath William already
broken the oath of his race ? This baseness is unworthy even of
him. And you," he added, addressing Lanfranc, "priest of the
Most High, primate of England, witness of this perjury, you
announce it to me ! Shame ! oh ! shame."

"The king," said the churchman haughtily, "hath broken no
oath ; he took it but conditionally."

"Conditionally ! " repeated all the nobles present.

"That his brother," resumed the speaker, "made an unreserved
surrender of the crown. Hath he done so ?—can he do so ? "

"Why not ? " demanded the prince, with a look of surprise.

"Because thou hast a son, to whom thy rights devolve—if rights
thou hast," replied Tyrrel impatiently. "Deny it not ; I heard
the avowal from thine own lips almost within the hour."

Robert turned deadly pale ; it was clear to all that his very heart
was torn with rage, with contempt, with deep and bitter emotions.
Fixing his eyes upon the speaker with so singular an expression
that even the bold traitor was awed by it, he murmured :

"And thou heardest this?"

"I did."

"Where?"

"Behind the curtains of the tent. More," added Tyrrel, "that thou alone possessed the proofs of thy son's legitimacy and birth."

"Dishonoured villain!" exclaimed the prince, with a burst of passion. "First perjury to thy benefactor, who confided his prisoner to thy ward, and now dishonour to thy knighthood by meanly descending to be a spy. But I waste words," he added, using a violent effort to recover himself; "I'll speak with thee anon. First for the archbishop—what would our perjured brother?"

"That," said Lanfranc, "which alone can render the oath of William binding, and enable you to fulfil your stipulations in the treaty of the unreserved surrender of the crown—the proofs of your son's birth."

"What if I refuse?" said Robert.

"Your minion dies!" answered Tyrrel, with a look of exultation —"hangs on the gibbet, from which, by a trick, you would have rescued him—hangs like a dog, unless his master saves him."

It was sad to see the look of loathing and disgust with which the prince turned from him to address the primate.

"And what proof have I," he said, "if I consent to leave my son without a name, to sacrifice his birthright to my brother's fears by the surrender of these proofs, that your monarch will keep faith with me?"

"William's fearful oath," replied the prelate, "which then becomes a surety, and mine; for by my priestly vow I swear," and the speaker kissed his golden cross as he spoke, "if he keep not faith with thee, this voice, which proclaimed him king, shall launch the thunders of the Church upon his head—this hand, which anointed him, shall sign his deposition. Robert of Normandy," he added, "may trust the faith of one who never broke his vow to God, to friend, or enemy."

"As friend or enemy I trust thee," said the prince, drawing at the same time a parchment, with the seals of his mother, the Queen Matilda, the Archbishop of Rouen, and Onfroy, Marshal of Normandy, from his breast. "Take the proofs; from this hour forth I am a childless man; the retribution is complete."

The hand of the archbishop trembled as he received the important document. Devoted as he was to the interests of the Red King, he could not behold without emotion the sacrifice— accomplished, as it were, against nature—wrung by treachery from a generous, noble heart.

"Let it console thee, prince," he said, "that this deed has secured a nation's peace and a true friend's safety. Within the instant Ulrick of Stanfield shall be free. Farewell! Would we had earlier met, or been for ever strangers!"

Motioning to Tyrrel to remain, the primate quitted the pavilion
to bear Rufus the proofs he was so impatient to obtain.

No sooner had Lanfranc departed than Robert recovered his
usual self-possession and serenity. Without deigning to cast a
glance either of reproach or hate upon the man who had so
unscrupulously betrayed him, he began to give directions for his
approaching departure for Normandy, where Mirvan, whose chief
possessions lay there, as well as those of his young bride, proposed
to accompany him.

"I cannot," he exclaimed, "bow the knee and profess lip loyalty
to a sovereign I despise. My heart would wither in its own deceit.
Let William," he added, "confiscate my English fief—my father's
lands and father's honours shall content me."

"Which shall not be lessened by our favour," said his prince,
embracing him. "Normandy hath forests as wide as any England
boasts, to chase the red deer in, and hearts as true to welcome
thee."

"Old as I am, I, too, would with thee, prince," added Edda,
"were I not planted to the soil like some aged oak. Uproot me,
and those who live beneath my shade must perish too."

Again the curtains of the tent were raised, and this time his
impatient friends were not doomed to disappointment, for the lord
of Stanfield entered at liberty. His first impulse was to bend the
knee to Robert, whose generous sacrifice had deeply touched his
grateful nature ; the prince welcomed him with a sad, but friendly
smile, wishing internally, as he gazed upon him, that Heaven had
blessed him with a son like Ulrick. Tyrrel looked upon the scene
with an affectation of scorn and triumph.

"Robert, my sovereign," said our hero, "what hast thou done to
preserve my worthless life ?—widowed this wretched kingdom of
its happiness, bartered thy birthright, sacrificed thy son, all—all for
me ?"

"Bartered them freely," interrupted Robert, "since I have
preserved my friend, rewarded virtue in its noblest form, and
punished vice and measureless ambition. Ere I depart," he added,
"from the realm no longer mine, I have a debt to pay. Leave us,
my lords ; leave Ulrick and myself with Walter Tyrrel alone within
the tent ; anon we will rejoin you on the road to Pevensey."

The command was instantly obeyed, the prince and the two young
men alone remained within the tent. Tyrrel's first impulse was to
lay his hand upon his sword, for although the speaker and the
knight of Stanfield were both unarmed, his suspicious nature fore-
bode treachery.

"Touch not thy sword, young man," exclaimed Robert, mournfully.
"It is not with such weapons I would punish thee. By Heaven,
my sister's honour, or my father's bones, are not more sacred to me
than thy life."

[GILBERT PROTECTING HESTER FROM THE MONK.]

T

"Punish me?" faltered Tyrrel, lost in amazement at the prince's tone and manner.

"Ay, with words which shall pierce deeper than my sword! fall like a coal of fire upon thy head! gnaw like a serpent's fang within thy heart!—if indeed," added the speaker, contemptuously, "reptiles have hearts."

"Rail on, prince!" exclaimed Tyrrel, with an affected laugh; "I can forgive a baffled gamester's spleen; my promised earldom shall console me for a few sharp words."

"Can it console thee for a crown?" sternly demanded Robert. The young man started from the pillar of the tent, against which he had been carelessly leaning; a light from heaven or hell broke on his astonished mind; for the first time he suspected that which, if true, would indeed, to a soul like his, be the most fearful punishment his treachery and ambition could receive! Twice he essayed to speak, but the voice remained choked within his throat.

"A crown!" at last he hoarsely murmured.

"Ay, a crown!" repeated the prince; "ambition's dream; fortune's last gift to reckless, daring minds.—Ulrick," he said, passionately, "I have been a man of pride and sin, but still of unstained honour. I gloried in the blazon of my house, the power of my race, the fame of my forefathers, their hundred victories by land and sea; judge, then, how deep the pang which rends this heart when I proclaim that man of infamy and shame—that thing I loathe and spit upon—my son, the legitimate heir of my proud name, the inheritor by birthright of Normandy and England."

The guilty man crushed as by the voice of a denouncing angel, sank overwhelmed upon his knees; deeply as Ulrick despised, he could not gaze upon his humiliation without pity.

"Fool!" continued the excited father, with yet greater vehemence, "go bend the knee to him who should have been thy subject—for whose hollow promise thou hast lost a throne; go cringe and fawn to beg the earldom bought with a crown, and beg for it in vain. Tread, a thing scorned and abhorred, upon the soil which should have called thee master; die as thou hast lived, without a name, self-disinherited!"

"Not without a name," faltered Tyrrel, rising from his knee; "thy son can never lack a name."

"And who will give it thee when I disown thee?—the kind uncle," added Robert, with a sneer, "whose abject tool thou hast become, and into whose hands, like an obedient hound, thou didst resign the only proof of thy high lineage? Never more shall the secret pass these lips;—fool! I but tell it thee to be thy punishment."

"Is thy justice so implacable?" replied the wretched man; "does no sentiment of nature speak within thee at least to acknowledge me thy son?"

"My son a landless beggar?—never, never."

T 2

"Normandy is still within thy gift," urged Tyrrel, for so we must continue to designate him.

"But never shall be thine!" interrupted his father, sternly. "Set but a foot in it, and I will place thee in a cage where thou shalt fret against the bars in vain. Reptile! thou art completely crushed. Hint but to William of thy birth, his jealousy will doom thee dead. By thine own arts is every hope defeated. The only witness of thy birth, the venerable guardian of thy youth, is dead—slain, I too justly fear, by thy unnatural hand."

"Then I am lost!" murmured the conscience-stricken culprit in a low voice to himself.

"Lost and accursed!" added his justly-incensed parent, "both here and hereafter! Instead of the fond heritage of a father's love, receive his malediction! I curse thee in the name of the long-cherished hopes and affection thou hast blighted! May no child e'er live to honour thee—no voice of love or duty smooth thy dying pillow! May the shadow of the greatness thou hast lost haunt thee like an avenging spirit—the secret of thy birth fester like a serpent's fang in thy vile, treacherous, proud, ambitious heart! May the death-hope which whispers peace to the repentant sinner's soul fail thee in thy last hour of need! May thy grave remain unhonoured by a human tear—shunned as a spot accursed by every foot! False knight and perjured friend, degenerate son and most unnatural traitor, farewell for ever!"

The wretched man, crushed by the fearful weight of a father's malediction, so terribly pronounced, rushed from the tent as if fiends pursued him—the avenging words echoing in his ears as he fled. More like a spectre than a human being, he passed the guards and officers who surrounded William's tent, and, dashing aside the silken curtains, entered the inclosure. It was fortunate, perhaps, for the monarch that he was absent. All that Tyrrel found there were the ashes and half-melted seals of the fatal parchment, the proof of his high birth. The sight still further increased his fury, and, foaming like a maniac with impotent rage and shame, he hastily left the spot.

The broken-hearted Robert remained, after the departure of the son whom he had so fearfully cursed and justly disowned, a prey to terrible excitement. In the midst of a life of reckless dissipation, he had long counted on the moment when the Conqueror's death would have enabled him to acknowledge him; for, though not of royal birth, his mother had been noble. It was some time ere Ulrick could bring his chafed spirit to something like composure; but all his entreaties to induce him to recall his malediction were in vain.

"Never! never!" he impatiently replied, dashing, at the same time, as if ashamed of human weakness, a tear from his burning cheek. "Words wrung from a heart bruised like mine can never be recalled. 'Tis past for ever; the last hope of my life is gone, and nothing now remains but a few years of madness, folly, the wine-cup, and the revel—the battle-field, or pilgrim's staff—an heirless name, and childless sepulchre."

"He may repent, and yet atone the past," urged our hero, willing to calm him further, by giving utterance to a hope he was far from entertaining ; for none knew so well as he how radically bad was the nature, how engrafted the vices, of the being for whom he pleaded. His words, however, produced an effect the very opposite of his intent ; the more he pleaded, the more obstinate the outraged prince became ; and he finally extorted from Ulrick, before they left the tent, a solemn vow never to reveal the secret of what had passed, or the mystery of Tyrrel's birth, save at his express command. The oath was reluctantly taken, but faithfully kept. They afterwards rejoined their friends, and returned to Pevensey.

As the train crossed the drawbridge Prince Henry encountered the warder's brother, Peter Norbeck, who, by an affectation of blunt humour and open speech, had gradually wormed himself into his favour ; indeed, so much so, that, from a simple man-at-arms, he had promoted him to a post amongst his personal attendants ; little dreaming that, in so doing, he was but walking blindly into the net which his enemies had spread.

"Ah, good Peter ! " exclaimed the young prince as soon as he beheld him ; "I have employment for thee. Send Bras de Fer, the executioner, to my chamber ; I would speak with him."

"With Bras de Fer ! " echoed Norbeck, turning pale ; for conscience whispered that it might be for himself the services of that hated functionary were about to be required.

"With Bras de Fer," repeated Henry with a loud laugh, slapping him at the same time familiarly on the shoulder. "Why, how the fellow stares ! Go you before, and fix me a noose in the carved oaken beam in the great hall. And see that the cord be strong ; for," added the speaker in a tone of confidence which might have deceived a more suspicious nature than Peter's, "within an hour a greater weight of treachery and crime than thy honest nature can suppose must swing there."

"Fear not, your grace," replied the ruffian, perfectly reassured by the prince's manner on his own account ; "the cord shall be strong enough to hang the fattest monk in merry England, where, as men say, the holy crows are fattest."

Had the speaker seen the cold, satirical smile which Henry sent after him as he departed on his errand, he would have gone less cheerfully on his way.

Within the hour the prince, attended by a dozen men-at-arms and the executioner, entered the hall, where Peter Norbeck, mounted on the summit of a ladder, had already strung the fatal cord. Bras de Fer eyed the preparations critically, and nodded approval.

"I think it will do, your grace," exclaimed Peter, admiring his own skill.

"I trust it will," replied the prince sarcastically ; "but Bras de Fer had better try it."

The functionary, who had previously received his instructions, began to ascend the ladder, as if to try the strength of the cord, according to Henry's orders. Peter, to make way for him, mounted still higher, and thereby facilitated the purpose of the hangman.

"Perhaps I had better have descended ? " he observed.

"Not at all necessary," replied his companion, with a smile of quiet humour ; for he seemed to enjoy the joke exceedingly ; "indeed, I could not very well do without you."

"You will find it firm," said Peter, catching at the rope and placing it in the hands of Bras de Fer, who assured him it would answer the purpose extremely well. "How do you make the knot ? "

"That is a secret. Most men are bunglers at the knot ; but, as you are not a likely man to betray confidence," continued the hangman, "I don't mind showing you. You perceive, on turning the rope twice thus, you allow the noose to run, but not to slip ; once formed, you pass it round the neck of your subject thus."

Suiting the action to the words, the speaker quickly placed the fatal cord around the throat of Peter Norbeck, who sat listening with unsuspicious gravity, deeply interested in his explanations.

"What next ? " he demanded.

"Why, the next thing we do," replied Bras de Fer, "is, perhaps, the most delicate touch of our craft—the most difficult point of all. Passing our arms thus, we pinion our man, and, springing with him from the ladder, launch our handiwork into eternity."

The executioner, who had gradually got his victim in the requisite position, sprang with him from the ladder as he spoke. Sliding down the convulsed body of the criminal, he dropped to the ground, leaving Peter Norbeck swinging in the air, much to the amusement of the men-at-arms, who had watched the whole proceeding as an excellent jest.

"Cast the carrion into the moat," said Henry, as he quitted the hall when the death-struggle was over. "Such be the fate of every cowardly assassin—the doom of every traitor."

The letters which the Black Knight had placed within his hand proved that the wretched Norbeck had undertaken, for a bribe of two hundred marks, to poison him that very evening at the banquet.

CHAPTER XVIII.

"FAREWELL to England!" exclaimed Robert of Normandy, as he entered the bark at Rye destined to bear him from the land whose crown he had so singularly lost. "I leave thee with regret, for thou hast been the scene of many a gallant hope, of many a daring deed. Farewell, my friends," he added ; "should England grow distasteful to you, remember that while Robert hath a home in Normandy, he hath a heart to share it with you. Give no fresh cause of umbrage to him who is now your king, and you are safe. William's fears will prove sufficient safeguard. He may break his vow to God, his brother, and his people, but never will he dare to violate the fearful oath of his unhappy, fated race."

Ulrick was the last whom the exiled prince embraced, exclaiming as he did so :

"Adieu, thou noble heart ! How different had been my fate had pitying Heaven but blest me with a son as true, as worthy of my love, as thou art ! Living or dead, in exile or on a throne, Robert will rest thy debtor."

Odo of Bayeux and Prince Henry, who accompanied their nephew and brother to his duchy, embraced in turn their companions in arms, who, according to the stipulations, were immediately to separate, each at the head of the remnant of his followers, to return to his respective home. Edda, our hero, and Mirvan were still at the head of a considerable number of vassals— the imposing appearance which they presented, together with the safe-conduct of William, prevented their being attacked by any of the disbanded soldiery who roamed the country, plundering the weak and frequently exacting ransom from the strong.

On a bier, in the centre of their march, was borne the body of the venerable Herbert de Lozenga, so foully slain by an assassin's hand, arrayed in his episcopal robes, his face calm as a sleeping prophet's. The body of the murdered prelate was preceded by twelve priests from the neighbouring monasteries, who sang at intervals the Litany of the Dead. Ulrick followed it bareheaded and unarmed. The kind old man had been to him as a father, and he mourned him like a son. In his pious gratitude, he had had the corpse embalmed, and intended to entomb it in the magnificent cathedral his munificence had built. There, in the centre of the choir, before the high altar, may still be seen the resting-place of the Chancellor of William the Conqueror and first Bishop of Norwich, Herbert de Lozenga ; all his predecessors, as well as himself up to the year 1094, having borne the title of Bishop of Thetford only.

On the arrival of the funeral train in the city, both people and clergy came forth in crowds to meet it ; all united to pay the last act of homage to their pastor, whose benevolence had been unbounded, as his life had been holy and useful. Even his successor,

Eborard, the worthless prior of the Dominicans, whom William, much to the discontent of the primate, had named to the vacant see, joined in the procession. Such is the homage which triumphant vice is sometimes bound to pay to virtue.

Those only who have felt the pangs of separation from the being whom they love—the agony of doubt, of hope, and fear, which imagination causes in the anxious heart—can picture the meeting between Ulrick and his bride, who now gave visible promise of becoming a mother, and forging by the holy claims of maternity a yet more indissoluble tie around her husband's heart. Edith too—the once more happy Edith—embraced her son, her Edward's living image, and in the gladness of the present hour forgot the tears and trials of the past. Amongst the first to welcome him was Gilbert, the poor boy whom he had left wounded behind him in his flight from London, under the hospitable care of the rich Jew, Falk of Cologne. Four months' absence had so improved his appearance that his benefactor could scarcely recognise him ; his anxious, terrified look had given place to one of modest confidence ; his attenuated cheeks glowed with recovered health ; his step had become elastic, and his spirits light. Still, in the midst of his joy—and it was almost childish—at again meeting with the first being who had ever shown pity or interest in his welfare a cloud of doubt obscured his open brow ; something remained to be told which he feared might change his protector's smiles to frowns.

"Welcome, my faithful boy !" exclaimed Ulrick, raising him from his knee. "Beshrew me, but I should often have borne a lighter heart had I but known thou wert well housed at Stanfield. How didst thou find thy route hither—did the Jew direct thee ? "

" Not the Jew," faltered Gilbert, " but his daughter Hester, who tended me, watched over my sick-couch, ministered like an angel to my sufferings. O, my lord ! if indeed the sight of your poor Gilbert gives you pleasure, it is to her care alone you owe it, for my heart was all but broken when you returned no more."

" Indeed ! " replied our hero, smiling at what he deemed the boy's grateful enthusiasm ; " it seems the pretty infidel made good use of her time, and traced her image on thy young heart while within her power."

" Pardon me, my lord," said Gilbert, blushing, " but Hester is, or rather soon will be, a Christian."

" Indeed ! " answered Ulrick, thoughtfully. " Of this we must speak further ; meanwhile, welcome, dear boy, to Stanfield."

It needed all the influence both of his mother and Matilda to restrain our hero's anger when they informed him that the beautiful Jewess Hester had not only left her father's roof with Gilbert, but was actually at that very moment an inmate of the Hall. His first impression was that the wounded youth had availed himself of her father's hospitality to seduce her from the paths of innocence ; still there was something so childish in his look, so frank in his nature, that his mother's words easily induced him to discard it.

"You wrong them," said Edith, calmly ; "if they love, it is as angels love—earthly passion hath not yet left its stain on their unsullied hearts. The maid is truly Christian ; truth from the lips of a poor sick boy hath reached her soul, and Heaven, which smiles not always on the churchman's homily or scholar's page, hath worked its will through him. See her, Ulrick," she added ; "question her ere you decide to scare the young-fledged soul upon Redemption's threshold back from its place of rest ; see her, and be convinced."

Matilda, seeing the impression which his mother's words had produced upon her husband, without waiting for his reply, raised the silver call to her lips—the signal agreed upon for Hester to enter. It was impossible not to be struck with the beauty and childish grace of her manners as she did so. Bending the knee, before he was aware of her intent, she raised his hand to her lips and kissed it. Such was the homage which in her father's house she had been accustomed to pay to the elders and chief men of her people.

"They tell me, Hester," said Ulrick, raising her kindly as he spoke, "that thou hast left thy father's house to become a Christian —is this thing so ?"

"It is," replied the maiden, modestly" ; else had I not abandoned my father in his age, or the sisters of my blood."

"And what hath wrought this change ? Why wouldst thou leave the faith of thy father and thy nation ?"

"Because I found it," said Hester, speaking in the phraseology of the East, which, from her childhood, she had been accustomed to, "as barren as the sea of my own distant land, whose waters never yet were ruffled by the sea-bird's wing ; because I found in it observances without devotion, a body without a soul."

"And what hast thou found in Christianity ?" demaded our hero, struck with the impressive earnestness of her manner and peculiar expression of thought.

"Love," replied the Jewess, with a modest blush ; "love, with which creation teems ; love, which at every step proclaims the work of an Almighty Hand ; love, which makes suffering joy, and persecution peace ; love, which is God, since God alone is perfect love. Not all the Temple's awful pomp," she added ; "the name, at which nations trembled as they read, graved on the high priest's mitred brow—speak the Divinity like those plain words, ' Love one another."

"And Gilbert taught thee thus much of Christian faith ?"

"Taught me," said Hester, "and taught me not ; I felt as if I but remembered it like some forgotten air which memory hath treasured in its cell. The note-key struck, and all the gushing melody returned."

"Hast thou no other love?" asked Ulrick.

"For my father and my sisters, yes," replied the maiden, her eyes suffused with tears at the recollection that her absence had clouded the joy of their once happy home.

"And none for Gilbert?"

"For Gilbert?" repeated the maiden, with a look of innocent, childish surprise, so pure that our hero almost blushed to have asked the question. "Oh, yes, I love him as I love all things of God; I love him as our great father loved the dove which brought the branch of peace; love him as the faithful friend who guided my footsteps here; as a brother," she added, gravely—for the first time, perhaps, comprehending the drift of the question. "Hester will never love him less or more."

"Would that the venerable Herbert lived!" exclaimed Ulrick; "his pure soul would best direct and understand thee; mine is unequal to the task. Remain, Hester, with the kindred spirits of my wife and mother: they will instruct and love thee. Soon as thou art prepared, the Church's rites shall welcome her stray dove back to its longing bosom."

Peaceful that night was the slumber of the Jewess; the last cloud, as she imagined, between her and happiness had disappeared; she dreamt not of the trials by which Heaven would test her fortitude ere it crowned her triumph by making her its own.

Early the following morning, Ulrick encountered Gilbert on the ramparts; the poor youth, scarcely aware of the nature of his feelings towards the beautiful being whose destiny had become so strangely mixed with his, was listening beneath her window to the hymn into which her morning prayer broke forth:

"I have seen the Lord's might in the fair evening star—
In the bright worlds of light He hath scattered afar;
Not more wondrous are these as a proof of His power,
Than the insect whose home is the bright-tinted flower.

I have heard the Lord's voice in the thunder's loud sound,
When the lightning's red flash scattered terror around;
But His dread will is spoken as plain as in these,
When borne on the delicate voice of the breeze.

Oh! there is not a thing that hath being or life,
From the emmet's small form, to the ocean's wild strife;
Not a leaf on the shrub, or a sweet-scented flower,
But are emblems alike of His goodness and power.

I have seen the fierce waves by the tempest's breath thrown—
Man left on the billow to struggle alone—
And felt that each creature was safe in His hand
On the mad foaming sea, as when cradled on land."

"Rash boy!" said our hero, pityingly; "thou art drinking of the draught that will but increase thy thirst. Tell me, dreamer,"

he added, " what I can do best to show my gratitude for thy past
service."

" Gratitude ! " echoed Gilbert. " Ah ! now you jest, my lord.
What debt can you owe to the wretched being whom your bounty
rescued from a slavery worse than death ? Besides, what more can
I desire than to remain near you—to watch and tend you—live for
your use—die in your service ? "

" Dreams, boy, dreams ! " replied Ulrick, who saw that Gilbert's
was a character which mingling in the world alone could form, and
which, permitted to vegetate in peaceful solitude, would lose even
the little energy it possessed. " The purposes of a life may not be
wasted for a caprice like this ; fortune hath many roads to
greatness, and the courageous heart cannot fail to find one."

" I am without ambition," sighed the youth.

" A cloister, then, perchance, would suit thee better ? "

Gilbert started ; for a monastic life was the very last of which he
had been dreaming. His kind protector feared that his love for
the fair Jewess would prove hopeless. Hers was one of those
pure, visionary natures which seldom descend to earthly love, but
exhale themselves away in the retirement of the convent or the cell
of the desert ; and he was anxious to plunge him into the active
realities of life, in order to make him forget its dreams—too often
the most difficult and painful task for youth.

" A cloister ! " echoed Gilbert ; " never ! never ! My heart was
never framed for solitude. Do not send me from you," he added ;
" all my hopes and affections are garnered here. It would break
my heart to part with them."

" This is madness, folly, boy," answered Ulrick.

" I must be the physician of thy mind as well as the protector of
thy fortunes. In three days I will give thee letters to Robert
Duke of Normandy ; for my sake he will cherish thee 'neath his
wing. There thou mayst achieve a name a soul like Hester's may
be proud to love. At the present hour her heart is wedded to her
faith alone ; it knows no other rival."

" In three days ? " sighed the youth.

" In three days," repeated our hero, turning away, unable to
resist the pleading look which Gilbert directed towards him.

" In three days," repeated the boy, as he plunged into the
neighbouring wood, " I shall again be desolate. Fool, to think
that earth produced one flower of happiness for a wretch like me !
Ungenerous Ulrick ! " he added, at the same time throwing himself
upon a low bank under one of those great oaks beneath which,
perchance, the soldiers of Cæsar had often halted, or the Druid
celebrated his mysterious rites ; " blessed himself in all that love
can yield, little he recks of the poor peasant youth, whose gratitude
is perchance a burden to him. Why send me from him ? What
need have I to seek a name ? "

"Thou hast a proud one, boy—as proud as his whom thou namest thy protector," exclaimed a deep voice near him. "But thou must prove thyself worthy of it ere thou darest to claim it."

Gilbert started from his seat; absorbed in his sorrow, he had not marked, when he threw himself upon the bank, that a stranger, dressed in a pilgrim's russet garb, his cowl drawn over his features, was already seated beneath the shadow of the gnarled tree.

"What knowest thou of my name or me, father?" demanded the astonished youth.

"More than thou knowest of thyself," replied the stranger; "for that past, which is to thee a volume sealed, my eyes can read."

"The page would be a sad one," said Gilbert carelessly; for he deemed the pilgrim sporting with him.

"It may be a glad one soon."

"Father," said the young man, "'tis plain thou knowest but little of me or my fortunes: thy science hath deceived thee. My birth is humble as thy russet gown; my name ignoble; my life hath hitherto been wretched—useless. Sport with me no more; I am too sad for jesting."

"And I too pressed for time," replied the stranger, whom our readers have no doubt already suspected to be no other than Robert of Artois. "Answer me this: dost thou not bear a red cross deeply printed on thy breast—near to thy heart?"

"I do," exclaimed Gilbert, feeling, for the first time, deeply interested in the pilgrim's question. "From infancy I have observed the mark; and once, when I asked my father how it came there, he answered me with blows, and bade me keep my peace."

"Vile slave!" muttered the stranger; "but his debt is paid. Tell me, boy, did no secret loathing of thy heart—no impulse whisper thee—the warder was not thy father?"

"I knew," said the young man, "he was but my step-father."

"Thy step-father!" repeated the pilgrim contemptuously. "He never saw thy mother; her proud heart would have spurned him like a cur, had such a being raised his eyes e'en to the dust she trod on."

"Maud, then, was not my parent!" exclaimed Gilbert, "Thank Heaven for that! Stranger, thou hast removed a weight from this bruised heart. The heavy blow, the taunting speech, the bitter gibe, were doubly bitter when I reflected 'twas a mother dealt them. But tell, in mercy tell me, who were my parents? Live they yet?"

"Thy mother sleeps the sleep of all; thy father lives, though men believe him dead. A fate as strange as cruel, and merciless as just, obliges him to walk the earth like some unburied shadow: but fear not thou; his crime leaves no dishonour on his name; thou yet mayst proudly bear it. It shall go hard but the hope lost to himself he will achieve for thee."

"His name! his name!"

"Merit it, boy, and thou shalt learn it," replied the pilgrim ; "for the present hour, farewell. Let what has passed remain a secret, locked in thy breast like the first impulse of thy boyish love. Thou knowest the ruin called the Druid's Cell ? Should danger threaten or misfortune reach thee, seek me there ; for, poor and abject as the world may deem me, I may not lack the means to save or serve thee."

Ere Gilbert could recover his astonishment the speaker disappeared within the wood, leaving the bewildered youth in doubt whether what he had heard was real or but the vision of some waking dream.

Bitterly did the poor monks and clergy regret the loss of their venerable superior, Herbert de Lozenga, whose rule had been of love. His successor's, the unworthy Eborard, proved of iron ; for, conscious that he was regarded with dislike, if not contempt, he avenged himself by the annoyance with which petty tyranny torments the spirits it cannot subdue. Short as had been his reign, the chapter had already appealed against his vexations, harsh encroachments on their privileges, to the primate, whose power alone could stand between them and the haughty bishop. Reckless as Eborard was, he trembled at the name of Lanfranc, whose indignation at his appointment had been openly expressed, and whose authority, for a canonical fault, could even yet depose him, despite the protection and favour of the king. He had just heard from one of his creatures of the proceedings of the monks, and was pacing his chamber in rage and vexation, when an attendant entered to inform him that a stranger, meanly clad, desired admittance to his presence.

"I have no humour to listen to strangers or intruders ! " exclaimed the impatient prelate ; " I am pestered enough with the stiff-necked brotherhood, whose spirit I must either bend or break. Send him to the prior or the almoner ; and to teach thee, brother, discretion for the future, I forbid thee for the rest of the week to appear in refectory during the evening meal."

" But the stranger, reverend father," urged the dismayed lay brother, " has letters of importance, as he says. I told him how difficult you were of access, but he would take no denial ; he said they were from the king."

"The king ! Imbecile, admit him instantly ! And for thy want of sense," added Eborard, " in detaining this messenger from the king, add to thy penance a midnight vigil to our Lady ; pray to her to teach thee common sense, and grant me patience to bear with thee."

" Now, fellow," said Eborard, as Falk of Cologne humbly bent before him, " what is thy will with us ? Have we misunderstood thy message ? Dost thou indeed bring letters from the king ? Or was it but a *ruse* to gain admittance to our presence ? "

Bowing low, the aged Israelite, who seemed worn with grief as well as travel, presented a slip of parchment, sealed with the royal signet. In it the monarch recommended the bearer to the bishop, urging him to obtain for him, by every means, possession of his daughter, deluded from her home by the esquire of the lord of Stanfield.

"He must be rich," thought the prelate to himself, "to have obtained such a missive from the Red King."

"How can I serve thee?" demanded the bishop, after having carefully perused the letter.

"By restoring to me my child," replied the Jew. "Thou art a judge as well as high-priest of thy people. Thy laws forbid all intercourse between the children of our nation. Hester hath been deluded from me by a wounded snake, which in my pity I had sheltered. A shame hath fallen upon Israel; desolation is upon my hearth—sorrow on my grey hairs, for the child of my age hath dishonoured them."

"Thinkest thou," demanded Eborard, eager, in his hatred, to involve Ulrick in the censures of the Church, "that this boy—this esquire—is but the cloak for some more artful villain? That his master, the lord of Stanfield——"

"Never saw my child," interrupted Falk; "at least not till she had abandoned the home of her fathers. In my desolation I will utter no injustice, lest the Lord of Israel confound me in His wrath. Till this serpent Gilbert poured his venom in her ear, Nazarene never gazed upon her face. I had garnered her like my life's pearl, in secret. My care was for her, my toil for her, my prayer for her. Perchance," he added, bitterly, "I had made an idol in my heart, and the God of my fathers hath punished me for my wickedness."

"Why seek, then, to regain her?" said the churchman, coldly.

"Because she is my child," answered the Jew; "and merciless as the Christian's law hath been to us—persecuted, reviled, outraged, and degraded as we have been—the iron finger of oppression hath not effaced all trace of humanity from my breast. Because when the last trumpet shall sound, and the scattered race of Israel shall assemble in the valley of Jehoshaphat before the judgment-seat of the Most High, I would exclaim, 'Thanks, Lord, the children which thou gavest are all with Thee!'"

"Should she turn Christian?"

"Horror!" shrieked the Hebrew; "rather would I behold her dead than turned unto the strange God of the Christian. Pardon me!" he exclaimed, as he marked the haughty frown on the bishop's brow; "I know it is a great thing I demand—an unheard-of thing—for a Jew to exercise his natural right over his rebellious child, for an Israelite to find justice against a Christian; but if I am poor in prayers," he added, "I am rich in that the Church

prizes more than the empty triumph of an infant convert. I am
rich in gold. Name what ransom, sum, mulct, or offering—call it
what you will—you please ; were it the last shekel of my house,
I'd count it freely—restore me but my child."

The passionate grief with which Falk pronounced these last
words made little impression upon the obdurate heart to which
they were addressed : but his offers of gold were more favourably
received ; for Eborard was one of those in whom the yellow idol
Mammon had long replaced the purer image of the Deity ; his
dreams were of gold ; his very prayers, if the ignoble aspirations
of such a thing of clay merit the name, were all of gold. Belus
had found in him a ready worshipper, for his statue was of gold.
One rival passion, whose existence he dreamt not of, lay dormant
in his heart ; its sleep had been profound, its waking was destined
to be fearful.

" Thou speakest truly, Jew," said the bishop, after a pause, in
which he had mentally calculated how much he could wring out
of him ; " it is a great thing which thou demandest ; still, as the
Church is merciful, and the king befriends thee, I may perchance
stand thy stead in this ; but thine alms for such a favour——"

" Shall content e'en thee," said Falk, eagerly ; " I am no niggard
to cheapen when 'tis my flesh and blood I would redeem ; name
the sum at which I may secure the Church's silence, and thy
powerful aid."

" What thinkest thou of a thousand marks of gold ? " demanded
Eborard.

" 'Tis a large sum, but yet it shall be paid," answered Falk—
" paid were it the last coin I possess. Place but my child once
more beneath my care, and the gold," he added, with a sigh, " is
yours."

" Think not, Jew," said the churchman, " that I consent to this
for mine own gain. Thy gold is for the poor. Penance and
prayer must atone my share in this, if indeed the maid be truly
Christian."

" I know ! I know ! " impatiently interrupted the old man,
fearful lest the prelate should demand an extra sum as a solace for
his conscience ; which, however, he shrewdly valued at its true
price. " Fear not that the Israelite misjudges thy condescension.
When wilt thou secure the wretched girl ? "

" This very day our precept shall be issued forth," said Eborard ;
" and the gold——"

" Be counted to thee," replied Falk, " when Hester is restored
unto her father. Farewell, my lord. To-morrow the poor Hebrew
will once more kiss the dust before thy sacred presence."

With these words the dignitary and the despised Jew parted—
the former to issue his mandate for the arrest of Hester, the latter
to seek a lodging with one of his nation in the city.

That same evening Ulrick was seated in the oratory of his mother, listening to Matilda, who was instructing the young and beautiful neophite in the creed of her new faith. There was something so pure, so innocent, so free from every taint of earth, in the character and enthusiastic devotion of the maiden, that her protectress began to regard her almost with a sister's love. Added to which, the pious work in which she was occupied was, according to the spirit of the age, so meritorious in the eyes of the Church, that it assured paradise to those who successfully completed it.

"But why," urged Matilda to Hester's wish of retiring to a convent as soon as she had been received into the Church, "why quit the world? It hath duties as sacred as the cloister. Besides," she added with a smile, "poor Gilbert's love merits some pity."

A blush suffused the cheek of the fair Jewess, and she was about to reply to her, when the subject of their conversation rushed into the oratory, exclaiming:

"Save her, my lord! They come to drag the victim forth to sacrifice; they would tear her alike from heaven and you; the soldiers of the Church demand their prey."

Ere Ulrick could reply, the curtain which screened the entrance to the oratory was drawn aside, and a tall, ferocious-looking monk, followed by an officer who bore the new bishop's arms embroidered on his vest, and a party of men-at-arms, unceremoniously entered the apartment. Indignant at the sight, Gilbert half-drew his sword, and in his enthusiasm blood would have doubtless been shed, had not the hand of our hero restrained him. Matilda, offended at the intrusion, and alarmed for the safety of her *protégée*, half encircled her with her arm, and regarded the men with an inquiring but disdainful glance. The priest read from the parchment which he held in his hand a citation for Hester to appear before the bishop and the ecclesiastical court, to answer to the charge of having fled with a Christian; a crime," added the fellow, "abhorrent both to God and man, and punished by the Church with death."

As soon as he had concluded, the civil officer advanced to arrest her.

"My dream—my dream!" exclaimed the Jewess, fixing her beautiful eyes on high, and every feature glowing with the most exalted enthusiasm. as if already she beheld the martyr's crown. "The wolf hath broke the fold; the tiger hath tracked the fawn. The words of my vision are realised—'If thou wouldst indeed be Christian, learn to suffer, for to suffer is to love.' I am ready; whither must I go?"

"To prison!" replied the officer, moved, despite himself, at the sight of so much beauty and courage; although, in the fulfilment of his office, he advanced to secure her person as he spoke.

[HESTER RESCUED FROM THE VIOLENCE OF EBOHARD.]

" Back ! " said Ulrick, sternly ; " is Stanfield Hold a brigand's den, that thus your master violates the laws of courtesy, and seizes on my guest ? The maid is Christian."

" Let her prove it," replied the priest ; " but till she does she is our prisoner."

Ulrick regarded him with a smile of cold contempt. Terrible as was the power of the Church, he knew that it had its limits ; but had it been ten times more despotic, he would have blushed to have resigned an innocent, unoffending being at its summons, who had no friend save himself.

" I will be warrant for the maid's appearance," answered our hero ; " till then Stanfield is her home, and I am her protector."

" What if we resist ? " demanded the monk.

" My vassals shall scourge ye to the boundaries of my lands. Hence ! " he added : " pollute my home no longer ; lest I forget your office in its errand, and crush ye like vipers 'neath my feet ! Gilbert, haste to the seneschal ; call out the guard, and bid them hurl these intruders into the moat, if, in three minutes, Stanfield is not clear of them."

Scarcely had the command escaped his lips than the youth had quitted the apartment.

" Beware, sir knight ! " exclaimed the monk, as he retreated ; " the Church's arm is iron—it will crush thee."

" Better be crushed by it than live its slave," said Ulrick. "Away ! and tempt not my patience further ! "

" Not for me ! " exclaimed Hester—" not for me this coil ! What were my worthless life to one moment's danger unto thee or thine ? Besides," she added, " the fate my vision told must be fulfilled. Sir officer, I am your prisoner, and will follow you."

" Never," interrupted Matilda, " will I resign you to the charge of that ferocious man. If danger threatens, courage must meet it ; if persecution comes, patience must bear it ; if death awaits us, innocence shall welcome it."

At this moment the seneschal and men, conducted by Gilbert, entered the oratory ; and the baffled messengers of priestly tyranny, venting curses, withdrew, to inform their employer of the failure of their mission.

Early on the following morning, as Eborard was considering how best to accomplish his designs, and secure not only the person of the Jewess, but involve Ulrick in the censure of the Church, he was informed that a female demanded to see him. Finding, on inquiry, that she was young and beautiful, he gave orders to admit her—for, churchman though he was, he was not insensible to the charms of a red lip or flashing eye. Much to his annoyance, the prior, whose cold, stately manner towards him not all his courtesy and blandishments could change, entered his apartment at the same moment as his visitor.

" Welcome reverend brother ! Benedicite, fair daughter !" he
exclaimed, addressing each of them. " We will but hear the worthy
prior's pleasure, and attend your will."

" Hear it now, my lord !" exclaimed the female, bending her
knee, and at the same time throwing back her veil, which discovered
features of such uncommon loveliness, that Eborard felt the warm
blood rushing to his heart with most unpriestly violence. " I am
your prisoner—the Jewess, Hester, whom you seek."

The prior devoutly crossed himself ; for, although a kind, he was
a superstitious man. His superior remained gazing upon her with
flushed brow and trembling pulse. For the first time' in his life he
felt subjugated by the influence of beauty. Often as it had crossed
his path before, it had never touched his heart.

" Is it possible ? Art thou," he demanded, " the Jewess whom
the lord of Stanfield insolently refused to our behest ? 'Tis well
he hath thought better of it ere our wrath had crushed him."

" The knight of Stanfield sheltered me not as a Jewess, but as a
Christian, reverend father."

" Now, praised be our Lady !" exclaimed the prior, with a
benevolent smile ; " the lost sheep of Zion returned to the fold,
and a soul is won. Thou art a Christian, maiden ? "

" In all but name," replied Hester, modestly.

" And hath Ulrick," demanded the prior, in a tone of disappointment, " sent thee here to plead thy cause alone ? "

" He knows not of my coming," said the maiden. " Visions had
warned me· of approaching danger. Could I behold my kind
protector suffer through his zeal for me ? That were indeed to prove
myself unworthy of the name I bear in heart.'

" Remove her," said the prelate to the attendant lay brothers,
who appeared upon his summons.

" Where ? " demanded the prior. " To the convent of St.
Mary ? "

" No," replied the bishop, sternly, "to· he palace prison."

Despite the prior's intercession, the maiden was conducted to the
prison ; and the good man, whose interference had been haughtily
rebuked by his superior, with a thoughtful mien returned to his cell
within the cloister.

Gilbert remembered the advice which the recluse had given him,
to seek him in the hour of danger or adversity ; and on the arrest
of Hester, he sought him in his retreat, and summoned him, with
all the energy of despair, to fulfil his promise.

" Follow !" exclaimed the unknown, moved to compassion at the
distress of the only being who still possessed a claim upon his
affections ; " it is not exactly the destiny I would choose for thee,
but since Heaven hath willed it so, I will not vainly seek to thwart
its purpose."

An hour's walk brought them to the palace-gate of the haughty

Eborard, where, despite their entreaties, threats, and despair, they were refused admittance by the prelate's guard, who advised them to apply to the almoner, or to come on the following Friday, which was dole-day. As they were returning, disheartened, fortunately they encountered the worthy prior, who listened with pity to Gilbert's tale, and felt his interest in the fate of the fair Jewess augmented by the artless story of her conversion.

"Hast thou courage, boy," he demanded, "to ride to London, and demand an audience of the primate?"

"To death," said Gilbert, eagerly, "in such a cause."

"'Tis well," resumed the churchman. "I will give thee a letter which will secure thee an audience of Lanfranc. Tell thy tale with the honest simplicity thou hast told it me, and doubt not the result."

"And I," replied the recluse, "will arm him with a weapon to depose and crush this mitred tyrant, whose sacerdoce is a blasphemy—whose religion hypocrisy."

The good prior's letter was speedily written; and that very day Gilbert, bearing a packet from his mysterious friend as well as the priest's missive, started for London.

CHAPTER XIX.

IN his anxiety to ascertain the fate of his *protégé*, Ulrick had several times presented himself at the palace of the new bishop to solicit an audience, but without success; the haughty churchman refused to see him, and he returned on each occasion to the inquiring Matilda the bearer of fresh disappointment and disquietude. Short as had been Hester's residence at Stanfield, she had acquired not only the love of its generous owners, but the esteem and admiration of all its inmates. Her youth and beauty, no less than fervent piety and unfeigned humility, had won her friends. The poor whom she had solaced, the wounded she had tended, were all unanimous in their praise of her gentleness and patience; and many openly declared that, should the haughty prelate seek to wrong her, crowns should be broken and swords drawn in her defence. Meanwhile the recluse, as the Black Knight was now called, did not remain idle.

If the conduct of Eborard appeared inexplicable to the friends of the Jewess, it was still more so to the brethren of the convent and his own immediate household. Since he beheld his prisoner, his character seemed entirely changed; he no longer occupied himself in tormenting his clergy, or inventing fresh means of curtailing their privileges. Even his schemes of ambition for awhile were laid at rest; letters remained unanswered; decrees, long meditated, postponed; and his revenues unaudited. In the solemn offices of the Church, the episcopal throne was frequently vacant, and the hours which should have been devoted to the services of his God were passed, to the astonishment of all, in visits to his prisoner, whose chamber was guarded by several of his minions whom he had brought with him from his priory, and on whose unscrupulous fidelity he could rely. The inmates of the convent were debarred all access to her.

The younger monks observed, too, with significant smiles, the attention which he paid to the adornment of his person ; gems of price, contrary to the canons of the Church, glittered on his fingers, and his hair and beard were perfumed. His table, to the great scandal of the prior, was served with the choicest wines, and he indulged in the excitement of the cup more like some reckless soldier than the sober inmate of the cloister.·

The truth was, Eborard loved—if indeed the impious sentiment which could make him forget his vow to God and priestly rank merits the name—madly, wildly loved.

Ardent piety alone can reconcile men to the cloister, or the deepest sentiment of religion wed them to the priesthood. Eborard's union with the Church had been one of interest and ambition only. It is not, therefore, to be wondered at that the cold barriers which prudence and calculating hypocrisy, had raised melted like wax before the breath of human passion.

Love in the virtuous, well-governed heart is a pure, gentle stream, fertilising and refreshing all that it embraces ; in the unholy breast it is a torrent, whose pathway is destruction and desolation.

It was on the fifth morning after the departure of Gilbert for London that Falk of Cologne, after much entreaty, succeeded in obtaining an audience of the bishop, whose intentions, although far from guessing the truth, he began vaguely to suspect. The prelate received him with his usual haughty indifference ; indeed, he would have scarcely deigned to dissemble with the Jew, but for the letter which he had been the bearer of from the king. To his demand for his daughter, he replied that, great as was his inclination to serve him, he could not forget the duty he owed to his high station and the laws of the Church ; but that in a few days, after he had again consulted the chapter on the subject, he might perhaps be enabled to restore her to him.

" Perhaps ! " iterated the Jew, eying him keenly, for he was no stranger to the character which Eborard bore ; " there was no ' perhaps' when first we spoke ; then all was clear and well defined. Have I," continued the agitated father, " but withdrawn my child from one peril to expose her to the worst extreme of fate ? Nay, bend not, priest," he added, " thy haughty brows on me. While Rufus has need of gold, I bear a charmed life beyond thy malice to assail. Give me my daughter, or I will appeal unto the primate.

Little as he loves our persecuted race, he loves still less the priest who holds his vows as feathers in the balance of his evil passions." With difficulty the prelate restrained the scornful defiance which rose upon his lips, but prudence bade him dissemble ; he more than half-suspected that complaints sufficiently serious had already been made to the stern Lanfranc against him, and he trembled at the idea of an additional charge ; for, as legate of the Pope as well as Archbishop of Canterbury, the zealous primate was in all matters of ecclesiastical discipline his all but irresponsible judge ; besides which, he knew him already to be prepossessed against him.

" I pardon thee, rash man," he answered, trying to assume the tone of injured innocence, " thy vile, injurious suspicion ; it proves how little thou knowest of Holy Church, or its much-slandered ministers. In thy headlong passion appeal unto the primate. I am prepared to meet the charge, and surrender him my prisoner. For me, perchance, it were the safest step, for my brethren already wonder at the clemency I have shown to a daughter of thy unbelieving race ; but, remember, once in his power, not e'en the king's authority can tear her from it ; and if his justice dooms her to the stake, blame thyself, not me."

" The stake ! " shrieked Falk, his cheek blanching at the word. " No, no—impossible ! Though priests, ye are men. Ye cannot have forgotten the mothers who bore you, the sisters who shared your love—all is not stone in your cold, selfish hearts. The stake ! and for a child ! " he added. " It is too horrible even for Christian cruelty."

" She hath fled, and with a Christian," said the prelate, coldly ; ●" such is the Church's law."

" Accursed be that law ! " exclaimed the Hebrew, still more and more excited ; " for 'tis of Moloch's creed. Devils alone could frame it ; no men, save those who have renounced the ties of nature, be found to execute it."

" This in our presence, Jew ? Thou blasphemest."

" Hear me," continued the aged Israelite : " I know the key-stone to your hearts ; 'tis gold—the yellow idol at whose shrine your souls are daily sacrificed. Yield me my daughter back unstained, unharmed, and I will sate your avaricious thirst, though I count down the last shekel of my wealth, and wander forth the beggar of my tribe."

" It cannot be," answered Eborard, his impious passion struggling against his cupidity ; " all I dare do I will—unseemly haste would compromise myself— in a few days perchance."

" A few days ! " interrupted Falk, sternly ; "and what in a few days will my daughter be to me ? A degraded thing ; abject as violence and brutal lust can make her. Deny it not—the lie would blister on thy lip ; a father's fears can pierce the shallow veil of

thy deceit. Man," he added throwing himself upon his knees, "if
our creeds be different, our natures are the same ; our loves and
hates, impulses, hopes, and fears, all spring from the same source.
Beggar me, and I will bless thee ; restore to me the child of my
age, and at the judgment-seat of the Most High the Jew will not
accuse thee."

"Thou hast my answer ; lay it to thy reason, not thy passion.
In five days thy daughter shall be free, and Heaven pardon thee
thy unjust suspicions."

"Enough," said the supplicant, with an unnatural calmness ; "I'll
trust its justice further than thy mercy. Farewell, sir priest ; thou
hast yet to learn that if the Hebrew be slow to strike, his aim is
but the surer."

Without further reverence or word the speaker quitted the
apartment.

"There is some spell upon me," exclaimed the guilty man, as
soon as he was alone—"a spell which drags me to perdition. It is
no longer the cool blood which circles in my veins, but the
volcano's burning lava. The image of this girl pursues me at the
altar, in my dreams ; my prayers are of her, my thoughts of her,
my being is of her. Vainly I fly from restless vigils to a more
restless couch. Fever is in my sleep, and mocking kisses sear my
eager lips. I will possess her," he added, " e'en though my forfeit
soul should be the purchase of a moment's bliss."

For a few moments he continued to pace the rush-strewn floor,
and then, as if struck by a sudden thought, raised the silver call to
his lips, and sounded twice. The signal brought Robert of Artois'
former squire, Brantone, to his presence. His new master had
already proved his usefulness, and hesitated not to trust him. •
Beckoning him to the window where he stood, he pointed out to
him the retreating figure of his visitor, who was seen slowly winding his way across St. Martin's Plain. The fellow's eye followed
him with the sagacious look of the bloodhound. Instinctively he
guessed what was expected from him.

"Seest thou yon man ?" demanded the prelate, pointing to the Jew.
" I do, my lord."

"Wouldst know him again ?"

"From a thousand," said Brantone ; "it is not the first time I
have seen him. For days he has been lingering round the palace,
and twice asked an audience of the prior."

"Did he obtain it ?" eagerly inquired Eborard, whom the intelligence confirmed in his fearful purpose.

"No, my lord ; I took upon myself to drive him forth."

"And thou didst well," observed his master, with a smile ; " but
he had done better who had silenced his slanderous tongue for
ever. Thou wert speaking to me lately," he added, " of the lands
of Carrow—part of the fief of thy late master."

"True," eagerly interrupted Brantone.

"Come to me in two days," slowly continued Eberard, with a look of peculiar meaning ; "and we will speak yet further on the subject. I am not one of those ungrateful masters who forget faithful service. Am I understood ?"

"Perfectly," replied the esquire, with a look of intelligence. "As for yon infidel, rest satisfied, my lord, in this world he shall cross your path no more."

"I seek not to understand thy meaning," said the churchman ; for he was a hypocrite even with the instruments of his crimes ; "'tis true he hath menaced me—outraged my honour by his vile suspicions—threatened to denounce me," he added, bitterly, "to the primate ; but, as a Christian, I forgive him. Do thou the same. Farewell."

"Umph !" muttered Brantone, as he retired from his master's presence ; "such forgiveness is like that of the Bishop of Beauvais to the thief who stole his cup; he pardoned him the robbery, but burnt him for the sacrilege. Heaven keep me from such pardons as churchmen give !"

"The crime indeed is fearful !" exclaimed the prior, who, with an agitated step, was pacing the cloisters of the cathedral, accompanied by a venerable ecclesiastic, one of the members of the chapter, and our old acquaintance the recluse, during the Jew and the esquire's interview with his superior. "Heard Christian men ever of such wickedness ? It is enough to make the very saints tremble in their shrines, and his pious predecessor rise from his tomb to shame him ; unholy love in an anointed bishop of the Church !—a sin indeed hath fallen on our house."

"Why not at once arrest him ?" demanded the youngest of his companions ; "the evidence is clear."

"Because," said the dignitary, "he is canonically our superior, and we are bound by oath to obey him in all lawful things. The primate only is his judge ; without him we can do nothing. Would to our Lady he were come !"

"Should he in his madness offer violence to the innocent object of his lust ?" observed the aged monk.

"Fear not that," replied the recluse ; "I am bound by no vow of obedience : should he attempt it, I would rush from the place of concealment where I so long have watched, and strangle him with as little remorse as I would crush a serpent beneath my foot."

Both the prior and his companion crossed themselves in horror at the idea of such a necessity.

"Such a deed fits not a Christian man," said the former ; "remember that, however unworthy, he is still a priest, and that no layman's hand may touch him. But, hush," he added, as Brantone entered the cloisters ; "there goes the bloodhound whose

fearful errand we have overheard. Heaven forfend that the life of
the wretched Jew should fall a prey to his vile master's treachery!"
  "Deep as is my cause of hatred to the accursed race, I will at
least preserve the old Jew," whispered the disfigured man, "and
baulk yon villain's purpose. The lord of Stanfield owes him a debt
of gratitude, for the Jew once preserved his life."
  "Have you the means of communicating with him?" demanded
the prior.
  "I have."
  "Is he still within the city?"
  "In the city and on the watch," replied the recluse; "he is not
one of those to sit contented by the ingle-side whilst danger
threatens a hair of those he loves. We may trust the Jew's safety
with confidence to him."
  The letter was written and despatched. That very night Brantone was an inmate of the deepest dungeon of Stanfield Hold; his
schemes of villainy for a while were baffled.
  In the morning of the day previous to which Falk, according to
Eborard's promise, was to receive his daughter, two Carmelite friars
arrived at the convent, and demanded hospitality for the night—a
request which the prior, to whom such matters were generally re-
ferred, instantly accorded. There was nothing in the manner of
their reception to convey the idea that the strangers were other
than they seemed; yet all the brotherhood appeared to feel that a
deeply observant eye was upon them. The stately demeanour of
the elder chilled as well as awed them. The service of the day
was performed with more than usual attention on the part of all;
and when at night the prior, in the absence of the bishop,
gave the usual benediction, the monks retired to their cells with a
vague impression that some event of moment threatened their
house. The elder ones, who were members of the chapter, were
seen about an hour afterwards, when all was silent in the cloisters,
to glide singly with stealthy tread and thoughtful brow into the
apartment of the prior.
  That very night the worthless prelate had resolved to accomplish
his design. The fever of his blood, excited by the wine-cup had
mounted to his brain, and in the gratification of his unholy passion
he was prepared to violate alike the laws of God and man—the
sanctity of his order, and the innocence he should have guarded.
  The great bell of the cathedral tolled the hour of midnight as he
rose from the table where he had been carousing in solitary sin,
and directed his steps towards the tower where his prisoner was
confined.
  The chamber of Hester was a long-disused oratory, of an
octagonal form, each side containing an arch quaintly carved in
stone. In the one opposite to the door an altar formerly stood, but
the steps which led to it, together with the crucifix, carved in the

wall itself, remained; the former having, perhaps, been too cumbrous to be removed. To the left of the entrance was a strongly-grated window, which by day alone gave light to the apartment. The arch facing it had formerly conducted to another recess, in which most probably a similar window had been situated; but it was now blocked by a solid screen of coarse oak panel-work, on which some faint attempts at ornament had carelessly been traced. A lamp, suspended from the ceiling by an iron chain, shed a feeble light upon the kneeling person of the fair Jewess, whose pale cheek and sunken eye showed the mental torture to which she had been subjected by her impious persecutor. But if the maiden's eye was hollow, its brightness was not dimmed. In her enthusiastic nature she regarded the trials to which she was exposed as sent to test her faith, for which she would have sacrificed her innocent blood with joy, and like the Christian virgins in the first ages of the Church, have hailed the martyr's crown as the proudest boon which Heaven could bestow.

Still, despite her courage, and the confidence which she felt in her delivery, even though it should prove by death, from the loathsome offers of her persecutor, the human portion of her nature trembled as the door of her prison opened, and the excited Eborard, still under the influence of wine, entered the apartment. Having first secured the door, he placed his torch upon the ground, and for a few moments surveyed his victim in silence. It was a picture angels might have wept to witness: a priest of the Most High meditating sin, and purity unarmed, except by prayer. The priest was the first to break the silence.

"Maiden," he murmured, in a voice thick with emotion, "the hour has arrived which decides the fate of both of us. Why didst thou cross my path? Till I beheld thee my dreams were but of ambition—my days of calm content. I have appealed to reason, and reason fleeth from me; religion mocks my prayer. Grant me thy love, and all that wealth can purchase, hope desire, or man achieve, are thine."

"All?" replied the Jewess scornfully; "all save Heaven."

"We will make earth our heaven," replied Eborard. "Our paradise shall rival Eden's bowers—its fierce delights fall with reviving freshness on thy heart, truer than the dull, placid dream which angels dream. Hast thou no pity in thy nature? Can a form so framed for love enshrine a heart of stone? Name but the price at which I may attain thee, I'll ransack earth to find it. This heart, so cold to all, hath now become love's glowing temple, and thou the idol of its shrine. Thou art my life—my destiny! I live but in thy smile. Be merciful."

"Be merciful unto thyself," replied Hester, "and cast this hateful passion like a leprous garment from thee. What have I done, that thou shouldst strive to scare my unfledged soul from its salvation?

Why seek to change the light of my young days to darkness so profound no after ray of hope can pierce it? Thou art a teacher of thy people, a shepherd of thy fold; lead not the steps of innocence astray; act not like the fell wolf unto thy charge. God," she added "let not this man's wickedness shake my new-born faith! let not e'en his triumph make me doubt Thee! Save me from him, and him from his weak self!"

"Thou prayest in vain," said the apostate with increasing resolution; "not Heaven itself can save thee! I tell thee, maid, thou wert created mine, ages before this world was framed—twin stars, loving in heaven, and at last, in time's fulness, born on earth in form of frail humanity. With restless love I've sought the sacred partner of my soul. Beauty's light hath beamed athwart my path, but never touched my heart; music's voice wanted thy breath to give it melody. I cannot live but in thy presence. Thou wert not, sure, created to destroy me, or, if thou wert," he added with increased excitement, at the same time seizing her by the arm, and attempting to enfold her in his accursed embrace, "the same bolt shall crush us both; but ere it falls thou shalt be mine!"

"Release me!" shrieked the trembling girl, vainly attempting to free herself from his passionate hold. "I am but a child; think on thy priestly vow! . . . Hath Heaven no aid? or are its thunders silent?"

"This is coyness," whispered Eborard; "soon wilt thou laugh at these old prejudices, and thank love's teacher for the gentle violence which woos thee to thy happiness. These struggles," he added, tearing aside the veil which shrouded her virgin form, "do but accelerate my triumph."

The wretched girl strove with almost superhuman strength against the attempts of the apostate priest, whose excitement increased with every convulsion of her graceful form. Placing his hand upon her waist, he endeavoured to pollute her lips with his detested kiss. Horror gave additional force to her frantic efforts; and, thrusting him from her, she sprang upon the steps beneath the crucifix. Clasping the sacred emblem as her last refuge, she exclaimed, in a voice which woke the silent echoes of her dungeon:

"Priest of God! darest thou brave thy Master?"

For a few moments the wretched man was appalled. With the trustful confidence of an infant clinging to its parent, Hester embraced the crucifix; her eyes lit with the enthusiasm of faith—her dishevelled tresses veiling the bosom whose modest covering the rude hand of her persecutor had torn aside.

"Ay, even there," cried Eborard, the dark passions of his evil nature doubly inflamed by the contest, and disappointed—"even there will I claim thee. If Heaven hath thunders, let it strike and save thee."

"It hath!" exclaimed a solemn voice, whose deep tones transfixed the guilty wretch with terror, as he was about to drag his victim from her last protection; "Heaven hath heard, and by its servant answers thee."

At the same instant the rude oak panelling was drawn aside—being, in fact, a concealed door, whose existence was known only to the prior—and Lanfranc, the primate, attended by the members of the chapter, Ulrick, and Gilbert, all of whom had been concealed witnesses of the impious scene, entered the apartment. The stern brow of the prelate was dark with horror and indignation at the sacrilege he had heard, the profanation which had been attempted.

"Saved! saved!" said the Jewess, in a voice of enthusiastic gratitude, as she sank upon her knees. "In Heaven hath been my trust, and Heaven hath not deserted me."

"Lost! lost!" murmured Eborard, slowly recovering from his surprise, and not daring to meet the primate's indignant gaze; "the Arm I braved hath struck me down at last."

In an instant Ulric and Gilbert were at the side of Hester, whom they raised from her attitude of thanksgiving. At the sight of her friends, the energy which had so well sustained her through the fearful scene gave way, and, drooping her head upon the manly breast of her protector, she wept as sisters weep upon a brother's bosom. Meanwhile, four of the monks secured the person of the apostate superior.

"Wretch!" said Lanfranc, advancing to Eborard, and tearing the golden chain and cross, the emblems of his episcopal rank, from his unworthy neck; "as legate of the Pope, I here degrade thee; deprive thee of all authority and jurisdiction in the now widowed Church; suspend thee from all priestly functions. Away with him to prison."

"Thou art mine enemy," replied the wretched man, recovering some portion of his former audacity, "and leagued with these, the rebel inmates of my convent, to destroy me. I appeal from thee unto the king."

The prior and monks listened with horror and astonishment to the accusation, mixed with some uneasiness, for they well knew his influence with the monarch, whose interference might still screen his unworthy favourite, and impose him on them; but they knew not the character of the primate, who listened to the culprit unmoved.

"And what canst thou urge," demanded Lanfranc, pointing to Hester, "against the maiden's accusation?"

"That she is an infidel—her oath against a Christian prelate will not be believed."

"What to these witnesses, the members of thy chapter?"

"That they are mine enemies, who have rebelled against me," answered the unblushing apostate.

" And to me ? " continued the primate, willing to see how far his infamy would lead him ; "what canst thou urge against my oath ? "

" Thy well-known opposition to my consecration—thy insolent remonstrances with the king," replied the prisoner, hope once more beginning to dawn within his subtle mind. " Fallen as thou thinkest me, William will not forget the service I have rendered him. His powerful hand will find the means, despite thy enmity, to raise me."

"Fool ! " said the archbishop, calmly, " thou dost but precipitate thy doom. Nor king nor prince shall ever judge between us. As primate, already have I suspended thee from every priestly function ; as legate, I excommunicate thee ; I cast thee forth from out the living Church—cancel thy share in its inheritance. Appeal," he added; "to thy unworthy master : see if his arm be strong enough to break the curse of Rome, or cancel the sentence which I here pronounce." *

All present listened to the denunciations of the speaker with a sacred terror, so universal was the dread of excommunication in that unenlightened age. Men whispered it with fear and trembling, shrinking from the unhappy wretch on whom it fell, as from a pestilence whose slightest contact was pollution—a living corpse doomed to eternal death.

The guilty Eborard, overwhelmed and crushed by the last act of the stern justice of Lanfranc, felt that every hope indeed was gone, and permitted himself to be dragged unresistingly away by those who but an hour since had trembled at his frown.

"Approach, poor girl," said the primate, addressing Hester, who still clung to Ulrick, as to a brother's side ; " nay, fear not, maiden— all are not wolves who guard the fold. If our voice be stern in judgments on the guilty, it is rich in blessings on a soul like thine. I bless thee ! " added the old man, laying his hand upon her head, as she knelt, trembling with awe and gratitude, at his feet ; " I bless thee out of Zion. Angels have watched thy heart to guard its purity, and blessed martyrs smiled upon thy triumph. The Church shall receive thee, stray one, to its bosom, e'en as a mother welcomes her lost child. These hands shall pour the regenerating waters of baptism upon thine innocent head ; and never shall they be raised in prayer or benediction, but thou, fair child, shalt be remembered."

The heart of Hester was too full of gratitude to Heaven to permit her tongue to express her thankfulness ; but the warm tear which fell upon the venerable hand which had been extended in blessings over her spoke to the prelate's heart more eloquently than e'en her lips had done.

It was morning ere the rescued convert, escorted by Ulrick and the now happy Gilbert, returned to Stanfield, where Hester was

---

* The unworthy successor of Herbert de Lozenga was really deposed by the Pope, though not exactly in the manner related.

received both by Edith and Matilda with the expression of the warmest love. Again and again was the wondrous tale of her deliverance repeated, and the youth called upon to explain his share in it. It seems that on perusing the letters of which he was the bearer, both from the prior and the mysterious recluse, the primate at once proposed to accompany the messenger to Norwich, to witness with his own eyes the truth of the fearful accusation placed within his hands. The rest is easily understood. Lanfranc and Gilbert were the two Carmelite friars who had claimed hospitality at the convent, and whose arrival had so impressed the community; for the simple russet gown could not veil the prelate's stately form, or dim the lustre of his searching eye. The members of the chapter alone were entrusted with the secret of his presence; and by them the arrangements were planned which led to Eborard's detection, even in the moment when it seemed least possible to those who calculate not that the ways of Heaven are unlike the ways of man.

On applying on the following morning for an interview with Eborard, Falk was conducted to the presence of the archbishop, who explained to him that his daughter was no longer a prisoner, and that in two days he should himself receive her into the bosom of the Church. The unhappy man, overwhelmed with the intelligence, to him ten thousand times more terrible than death, withdrew, like one stunned, from the primate's presence. He saw too well the stern, sincere character of the speaker to tempt him by that universal key to the human heart, gold; for in Lanfranc's heart it was but dust, when weighed against the triumph of his church, or the redemption of a human soul.

"A Christian!" muttered the Hebrew to himself, as he directed his steps across the plain of St. Martin on his way to the city. "The curse never fell upon my house till now. Our blood hath been shed like water, but it was the sacrifice of faith; our gold hath been wrung from us by torture, oppression, and the rack; but now the richest pearl is taken from us—the fairest flower is torn from Judah's stem. Our name will become a by-word on our nation's lips—a scorn, a shame to Israel! Never!" he added, bitterly. "If the degenerate girl can thus forget her duty to her kindred and her father, he will not forget his oath to Israel's God, or that he is a judge and elder of his people."

Full of this stern resolution, he directed his steps towards the market-place, where, by the corner of the church, dwelt a dealer in drugs, one of his own peculiar race. Hassack was known, not only to the city, but all the country round, for his curious skill in herbs and simples. Many a greedy heir had sought his aid; and the parent whose length of days was a check upon his wild career slumbered in peace: the unfaithful wife removed the jealous husband, the perjured lover the victim of his passions. Unscrupulous, and caring for nought but gold, the amassing of which formed the only pleasure of his withered heart, Hassack's skill was at the disposition of all who could gratify his ruling passion. So crude were the tests which science at that time possessed, that the detection of poison was almost impossible ; and the poisoner pursued his guilty trade, suspected, but in safety—too many great ones whom he had served being bound to interest themselves in his protection. Just as Falk reached the dingy, wretched-looking spot where the poisoner retailed his drugs and nostrums, he encountered the recluse, to whom he had formerly been known, having in his days of extravagance and pride frequently advanced him money upon his knightly bond. Fortunately the change which Abram's vengeance had wrought in him precluded the possibility of a recognition ; the pale, agitated countenance of the Jew excited his attention ; and crossing to the old stone pulpit, near which, in Catholic times, the priests and monks used to address their flocks, and the proclamations of the city authorities were made, he hid himself behind one of the heavy pillars, to watch his proceedings, which an instinctive feeling told him were dangerous to the life of Hester, and consequently to the happiness of Gilbert. After half an hour's converse, the old man quitted the den, the character of whose owner was well known to the observant spy, who marked the sigh of deep-drawn agony which broke from the bosom of the wretched father as he passed him. As soon as he was out of sight, the recluse, in his turn, entered the house of Hassack. At first the conversation between him and its master was violent, but the Jew's tone of defiance gradually subsided to one of deference, and at last to entreaty. For once he had found his master.

    *   *   *   *   *   *

Lights were blazing on the high altar of Norwich Cathedral, and the font was decked with earliest flowers of spring, on the morning of the day which was to receive the fair Hester into the bosom of the Church, which put forth on the occasion that imposing pomp which no ritual has ever equalled either in grandeur or sublimity.

Despite the silence which had been observed respecting the sacrilegious conduct of the unworthy Eborard—and the silence of the cloister is proverbial—strange rumours, connecting his name with that of the youthful Jewess, were rife amongst the people—rumours which the absence of the suspended prelate from the service at which the primate had twice publicly officiated only tended to confirm. At an early hour the vast aisles were crowded by the curious citizens and their buxom wives and daughters. Many of the latter had heard wonderful descriptions of the neophyte's beauty, and most of them came, womanlike, to criticise and to compare. A few, and but a few, came for the nobler purpose of joining in the hymn of triumph for a soul redeemed from error.

[DEATH OF THE RED KING.]

Amongst the crowd of spectators was an aged man, bent more by sorrow than by age, whose compressed lips and blanched cheek gave but faint indications of the fearful struggle passing in his breast—a struggle which rent his very heartstrings with its anguish, maddened his reeling brain, and whispered him despair. Disguised in the loose gown and hood then commonly worn by the superior class of citizens, the miserable Falk—for it was no other than the father of the convert—had been one of the first to enter the church, where the discovery of his presence would probably have caused his death. He had seen with a bitter smile the decoration of the font—to him the altar of sacrifice, and remained to await the completion of the rite which was to sever him for ever, as he thought, from the child of his age, and bring shame and humiliation upon his name and race.

The procession at last approached : first came four boys clothed in long white rochets, tossing the silver censers from side to side, filling the air with costly perfumes ; then a monk bearing the primate's cross ; after him the priests and brothers of the community, headed by the prior holding his staff of office. A shade of sorrow was on the good man's brow, for he thought on the dishonour which the Church had received in the crimes of his late unworthy superior. Lanfranc, adorned with the insignia of his high office, closed the procession, walking under a canopy borne by four knights. As the prelate proceeded along the aisles, he scattered his benedictions on the kneeling crowd, which rose and sank like an undulating wave as he approached and passed them. But the principal object of all eyes was the fair convert, who clothed in white and veiled by drapery, was led by her sponsors, Ulrick and Matilda, towards the sacred font. Gilbert watched her approach with the same delight with which an infant might, in the early ages of creation, ere sin had drawn its curtain between men and the bright beings of another world, have watched an angel's steps. His heart was almost too full for breathing, his happiness far too great for words ; yet a few moments, and Hester, his boyhood's hope, his earliest dream of love, would become a partaker of the same faith—the same hope as himself. The recluse, who felt a deeper interest in the proceedings of the day than any yet suspected, watched his excited looks, and, for reasons best known unto himself, determined not to lose sight of him.

The venerable primate had already poured the regenerating waters, and pronounced the words whose might opens the gates of the lost inheritance of Adam to his fallen race, when a loud cry startled the more distant spectators. Hester was seen to sink into the arms of Matilda and Isabel, who with her husband had graced the solemnity with their presence. At first they thought that the young Christian, overcome by her emotions, had fainted ; but the increased agitation of those around her, and the astonishment of

X 2

the priests, many of whom in their zeal were disposed to cry "A miracle!" soon convinced them that something far more singular had happened. The voice of Matilda at last was heard distinctly to exclaim, in accents of anguish and terror :

"Alas! she is dying—she is dying!"

"Dying!" re-echoed the crowd, impatiently pressing nearer to obtain a view of what was passing.

"Dying!" shrieked Gilbert, thrusting those who stood between him and Hester aside ; "let me once more behold her, that her image may be impressed on my young heart—its first and latest idol."

Despite the resistance of the crowd, the agitated youth broke through the compact mass, and rushed into the circle which, overwhelmed with grief and horror, surrounded the apparently dying Hester. The wreath of flowers and veil had been removed from her fair brow, and her long dark tresses, damp with the regenerating stream, contrasted fearfully with her pale cheek ; her eyes were closed, and large tears hung on their soft silken fringes. As the innocent child lay with her head pillowed upon Matilda's gentle breast, she looked like Purity expiring in the arms of Religion.

"'Tis past!" exclaimed Lanfranc, signing the cross over the unconscious girl ; "Heaven has claimed its own."

"She is not dead," murmured Gilbert, his voice choked with the deep agony which consumed him. "Cold as she was to earthly passion, she could not leave me without one look for memory to treasure in its cell—one word, to break at once the heart her gentle nature was too merciful to crush, and leave to linger in an unpitying world. Hester," he added, taking her hand, and fixing his despairing eyes upon her already rigid features, "hear the voice of my agony, the cry of my broken hope. A look, a word, a sign for the poor boy whose love was like the love which angels feel—on whose dull path no future ray of happiness may shine."

It seemed as if the sound of his voice had arrested her pure soul for a moment in its flight, or that its guardian spirit, with a human tear, permitted it one moment to return to grant the boon he asked. As if waking from a heavy sleep, Hester opened once more her veiled eyes, and cast on the speaker a glance such as a dying sister might bestow upon an only brother—a glance where the sorrow of parting, where piety and love were unstained by human passion or regret.

As the maid sank with all the rigidity of death into the arms which supported her, the primate motioned to his attendants to remove the fanatic Gilbert from the church—an office which they accomplished with firmness, but with kindness, closing the gates to prevent his return.

The unhappy youth plunged into the wood which lay between

the cathedral and the river. Despair was in his heart, and madness in his eye ; but there was one who read his purpose—his guardian genius hovered near him. The recluse, who had followed him from the church, was hard upon his footsteps.

Another yet more wretched being left the cathedral at the same instant as Gilbert—the unhappy Falk whose bigotry had, as our readers have doubtless long ere this suspected, plotted the death of his daughter at the very moment of her conversion. The claims of his nation and abandoned faith to vengeance were even to his morbid mind completely satisfied ; but now a new avenger, the father, awoke within him—nature spoke with a voice which neither sophistry, anger, nor superstition could silence. Hester was his only girl—had been the light of his solitude—the pupil of his leisure hours ; and he loved her as all men love the thing they teach —as old men love the children of their age.

The priests had already commenced the Litanies for the Dead, when the calm voice of Lanfranc, who had recovered his usual composure, interrupted them.

"Not the prayer of intercession, brothers, but the hymn of triumph. Heaven hath taken the maiden to itself ere sin or human passion had time to sully with their breath the seal of redemption upon her unpolluted brow ; we have seen an angel wing its flight to heaven, claiming its new-won heritage, and not a sinner trusting for pardon, part doubtful on its way. Bear her to the church, strew flowers before her, as for its virgin bride, and raise the song of joy."

In the enthusiasm of the moment, the young maidens who had come to witness the ceremony of Hester's admission into the Christian pale raised the inanimate body in their arms, and bore it to the high altar, before which a bier had been hastily arranged ; others strewed flowers, as the primate directed, in their way ; while the attendant clergy raised the solemn song with which the Church marks its rejoicings and consecrates its triumphs :

> " *Te Deum Laudamus Te,*
> Rejoice and raise the grateful strain,
> Heaven from earth a soul shall gain,
> Scatter the incense round.
> Salvation's news to Israel tell,
> The Church's note of triumph swell,
> And the pealing anthem sound.

> " *Te Deum Laudamus Te,*
> She comes, she comes; lost Judah's child,
> No more from Thee and Heaven exiled,
> We bear before Thy shrine.
> 'Tis done—life's early threshold past,
> The Hebrew maid redeemed at last,
> Is sealed for ever thine."

The multitude joined in the strain ; and the service, which was begun in the baptismal rite, ended with the dirge for the dead. At a late hour in the evening, at the request of Hester's protector, the body was removed to Stanfield, to be placed in the ancient vault of the old chapel, where Ulrick and Matilda were in the habit of offering up their daily supplications for the repose of their murdered fathers' souls. After the service they had retired to the oratory, as usual, indulging in that deep communion which hearts devoted to each other alone can know, when Gilbert, his eyes excited by hope, his lips quivering with eager emotion, followed by the recluse, entered the apartment.

CHAPTER XX.

ULRICK and Matilda were both startled at the appearance of Gilbert; the excitement, the wild look of happiness, amounting almost to insanity, which glistened in his eyes; his eager words cut short and broken by the deep emotion under which he laboured whilst endeavouring to unfold the secret which had caused him such tumultuous joy, that reason was almost shaken on its seated throne. Finding it impossible to explain himself, he sank upon his knee, and caught the hand of Matilda in his, exclaiming as he did so: "Heaven hath not yet claimed its own! Lady, she lives! Our angel lives to gladden earth with virtues all her own—lives to give sunlight to my path, and waken music once more to my ear."

"Alas!" said Matilda, in a voice of pity, "he is mad; grief hath distraught him. Poor boy! poor boy!"

Ulrick inclined to the same opinion as his wife. He looked first at Gilbert, then at the recluse, whom he recognised, despite his disguise, as the mysterious Black Knight he had so frequently seen during his own imprisonment in the camp of Rufus, and whose influence with the king he was no stranger to; indeed, from the unearthly character of his features, the once handsome Robert of Artois was now a being whom, having encountered, it was all but impossible to forget.

"He is not mad," replied the intruder, in answer to Ulrick's inquiring look. "Heaven, to permit me to atone for many crimes, has enabled me to perform one good act. Hester, the Jewess, indeed no longer exists; but Mary, the Christian, sleepeth."

Mary was the name the fair convert had received in baptism.

"Sleepeth!" repeated Matilda, in a voice which trembled between hope and incredulity.

"Sleepeth!" iterated the recluse. "I wonder not, lady, at thy incredulity; but her fate is not more wondrous than my own. Aware, from cruel experience, how bitter is the hatred, how undying the vengeance of her race, I have permitted the seeming triumph of her father's purpose to secure her safety: he and all the

world, except her friends, must deem her dead ; but to them—to
the true hearts that love her—I again repeat, the maiden lives."
   " Explain this mystery," said Ulrick ; "if thy words be sooth,
more welcome sounds ne'er fell upon mine ear."
   " You all," resumed the narrator, " know Hassack, the Jew, who
vends his nostrums in the market-place ? "
   " We do ! " impatiently answered his excited listeners.
   " Also his fearful skill in poisons and such drugs as minister to
the worst of passions ? "
   " By reputation well."
   " And I, perchance, by evil, sad experience. The day previous
to Hester's baptism," continued the recluse, " I encountered her
distracted father ; e'en my seared heart could pity him, for I read
the storm of human passion raging in his heart ; bigotry contending with paternal love—vengeance with pity—the cry of
nature with the voice of hate ; 'twas the mind's agony, more lasting
than the body's pain, leaving scars deeper than vulgar eyes can
read—burning, although unseen. I traced him to the house of the
vile mediciner—saw him with trembling hand count down his
gold—instinctively I guessed it was the price of blood."
   " His child's ! " exclaimed Matilda. "Impossible ! Jew though
he be, thou wrongest him."
   " So judge the pure in heart, lady," resumed the speaker ; " but
so judge not those whom crime or sad necessity hath forced to
watch the hearts of others—to trace deceit lurking beneath the
brow of seeming frankness—falsehood peeping through the mask
of truth—the voice of cruelty with mercy's accents burning on its
lips. Reason tells us what men should be ; bitter experience shows
us what they are. What followed proves I judged the Jew and his
rash purpose rightly."
   There was a tone of sarcasm and subdued passion in the voice of
the recluse, which startled the ear of Matilda ; she felt confident
that she had heard its sound before : it woke an echo in her heart
at which memory trembled but was confused, for not one feature
of the wretched man could she recall to mind. Fixing her eyes
upon him almost with a look of terror, she involuntarily exclaimed :
   " Surely we have met before."
   The seared brow of her ancient persecutor flushed as he had
heard an accusing angel s voice ; but his repentance was too sincere
to equivocate or deny the truth. Feeling that the time for re-
vealing himself had not yet arrived, he contented himself by
simply admitting that they had.
   " When and where ? " demanded the lady, with increased interest
and curiosity.
   " That, too, ere I quit this land for ever, thou shalt learn : this
present hour permit me to proceed. On Falk's departure from the

poisoner's den I entered. It matters little to my story by what means I forced him to confess the purpose of the old man's visit; enough, he did confess it. It was to bribe him to prepare a liquid which, mixed with the water in the sacred font, would cause the death of all upon whose brow 'twas sprinkled."

"Villain ! " cried Gilbert—"unnatural mônster ! E'en at the gate of heaven to sacrifice his child ! "

"Why not have denounced the fearful sacrilege ?" demanded Ulrick, who, with the horror-stricken Edith and Matilda, listened with anxious heart for the conclusion of his tale.

"Denounced him ?" repeated the recluse. "Little dost thou know the fearful race. For good or ill they far surpass the dogged bloodhound in unwearying patience ; the snake is not more subtle in its windings, the tiger more ferocious in its spring. I was born noble as the noblest in my land, was honoured, rich in lands and friends, possessed a form the eye of beauty had not always loathed to gaze upon. In evil hour I wronged an aged Jew—a thing," he added, fiercely, "whom, in my pride of strength, I could have crushed like a vile worm beneath my feet—whose life, to human thinking, was a reed within my iron hand ; and yet he vanquished me."

"Vanquished thee ! " repeated Ulrick, in a tone of incredulity.

"Vanquished and judged me. Not, indeed, with knightly arms, but more than devilish cunning ; deprived me of my very name—robbed me of the rights I drew e'en from my mother's womb—tore from my seared and blistered front the seal of individuality which God had stamped upon my brow—made me the wretch I am."

"Fearful man ! " shrieked Matilda, " I know thee now—know why my heart trembled at thy voice—my nature shuddered at thy presence. Ulrick, it is——"

"My father, lady," interrupted Gilbert, clasping her robe, "my father ! "

The agitation of the poor youth, his imploring glance, and the recollection that he had saved the life of Ulrick, sealed the secret upon her lips ; though how her ancient persecutor could be the parent of the speaker was a mystery she could scarcely comprehend.

"What means this strange terror," demanded Ulrick, "and still stranger recognition ? However evil," he added, addressing the recluse, "I know that thou art capable of good, for thy timely warning saved Prince Henry's life."

"Then for that one good act," said Matilda, " question him no more ; if he hath deeply sinned he hath been sorely punished. Unhappy man ! " she added, " Heaven forgive thee ; I never will accuse thee at its bar."

"Thanks, lady, thanks, for thy most generous pardon," replied the repentant man, at the same time gracefully bending his knee before her ; "it will lighten the anguish of remorse in many a

bitter hour. But concealment comes too late. Ulrick of Stanfield,"
he added, rising as he spoke, and speaking in a firm and almost
haughty tone, "thou seest a man whom friends and kindred alike
deem dead—a man whose dirge Holy Church hath long since sung—
whose heritage his greedy heirs have ta'en—a man who, pandering
to a tyrant's lust, would have aided Rufus to deprive thee of thy
fair bride. I need not say the wreck of Robert of Artois stands
unarmed before thee."

For a few moments there was a powerful struggle in Ulrick's
breast. The man who had caused him so much fearful misery
stood before him. The idea of injuring an unarmed man never
for an instant presented itself to his imagination ; but when he
reflected upon his wrongs, twice did he feel tempted to bid him
arm himself, and meet him knightly in the field ; but each time he
encountered Gilbert's pleading look and Matilda's forgiving smile.
The better principle of his nature prevailed. He could not crush
a heart already torn and bruised.

"Robert," he exclaimed, "friendship there can never be : let
there be peace between us, however great thy crimes. Thou hast
truly spoken—they have been fearfully avenged. This boy,"
pointing to Gilbert, "whom thou callest thy son, shall be a bond
of mutual forbearance between us. On with the tale this strange
discovery broke."

"Enough ! " resumed Robert, as we must call him. "I had the
means to compel the poisoner to my purpose. The nature of the
drug was changed, and a mixture prepared which caused the
appearance of death only. From the opening of the cathedral
doors I watched the arrival of each comer. Despite his disguise, I
recognised the Jew, saw him stealthily pour into the font the
means, as he thought, of vengeance on his child. You know the
rest."

"Let us haste," said Matilda, "to the vault ; should the poor
child awake amid the horrors of the charnel-house, reason might
totter on its throne."

"Fear not for that," observed the preserver of Hester ; "since I
alone possess the power to wake her."

He drew from his vest a small box filled with a pungent aromatic
as he spoke.

"Come, father," cried Gilbert, impatiently, "to the vault—the
vault."

"Caution, boy," said Robert, calmly ; "for we have to contend
with those who know no scruple where their vengeance is concerned ; the hatred of her race would reach the maiden e'en at the
altar's foot, should they once suspect her life has been preserved.
Can you," he added, addressing Ulrick, "answer for the caution of
all within these walls ? "

"All," replied our hero ; "there is not one in Stanfield but loves the maiden for her gentleness and virtue ; but as already the shades of night draw on, it were better, perchance, to wait till the house-hold are retired to rest ere we descend into the chapel. For a few days Hester can remain concealed within my wife's apartments ; none can enter unbidden there ; we can afterwards consult the means of safety—now our first step must be to rescue her."

Ulrick's proposition was too reasonable to be rejected ; and, despite the impatient eagerness of Gilbert and the anxiety of Matilda, the party remained within the antique oratory waiting the hour of midnight. Never did the tardy foot of Time advance more slowly than to the excited watchers. At last the turret-clock struck the hour, and our hero and Robert of Artois, each taking a waxen torch from the iron sconces in the walls, prepared to descend.

The chapel of Stanfield was a low, irregular building of unhewn stone, of even greater antiquity than the hall itself, its architecture being of the earliest Saxon age. Rude stone coffins, containing the ashes of many of its ancient lords, from their ponderous size more resembling tombs than sarcophagi, were ranged in the aisles, in deep recesses cut within the walls. The one in which Hester had been inclosed was in a niche nearest to the altar. Over it frowned the image of some long-forgotten saint :

> Carved in grey stone and cunning work,
> The labour of some rustic sculptor's hand.

As the party entered the quaint old edifice, their torches flashed upon the salient points of the building, lighting the massive shrines with a dim, religious light, which brought them into a faint relief, and cast broad, deep shadows, such as Rembrandt would have loved, upon the roughly-jointed pavement. In fact, the scene was one equally suited for the poet or the painter :

> Regardless of the night's dull gloom,
> They cast around a curious gaze
> On low broad arch and massive tomb
> Seen by the red light's flickering rays.
> Saints in sculptured stone were there,
> Whose spirits in the noiseless air
>   Watched o'er the sacred pile.
> At this perchance the world may deem
> My words a visionary dream,
>   Philosophy may smile.
> But if communion e'er be given
> With beings less of earth than heaven,
>   'Tis in some lone hour, when
> The relics of long ages past,
> The shadows o'er the rapt soul cast,
>   Our thoughts are spirits then.

" How still and solemn is the night ! " whispered Matilda, who, despite her husband's entreaty, had insisted on accompanying them upon their expedition ; " not a breath of air sighs through the vaults of the old chapel. The very echoes of our footsteps fall noiseless as the feet of Time upon eternity's dull sand. Yet here sleeps one," she added, advancing from the entrance of the chapel, where, with the rest of the party, she had paused to contemplate the scene, and, pointing to the tomb of Hester, "whom, living or dead, his breath cannot corrupt, whose nobler essence his scythe cannot destroy, for her mortal covering was no more to Hester than the casket to the gem it guards and holds."

"True!" exclaimed the recluse; "and from this bed of death— this living tomb, replete with life and beauty, shall arise creation's masterpiece—pure, lovely woman. Whilst all is silent, let us hasten to hurl back the ponderous stone, and wake her back to life and its warm ties—its tears, humanities, and tendernesses—if possible, to love."

As pale as monumental marble, Gilbert was standing by the tomb; life and passion seemed to have deserted his cold cheek; his heart was too full for words—one would have broken it; a tear would have been a blessing, and yet he could not weep. Rooted he stood, like a statue, by the spot—animation and life suspended in the deep struggles of doubt and hope.

"Aid me," said Ulrick, drawing from his vest a bar of iron, which he had brought with him for the purpose, and at the same time placing his torch in the hands of Matilda; "should the poor girl awake within her tomb, it were too much for reason; aid me to lift the stone."

By the repeated efforts of the speaker and the recluse—for Gilbert remained perfectly incapable of rendering the least assistance—the ponderous lid of the coffin was at length removed, and the fair form of the inmate met their gaze. Her countenance was as calm as that of an angel sleeping. The flowers with which affection had strewed her resting-place were still unfaded. Her hand, Matilda thought, grasped the silver crucifix, which the primate himself had placed upon her breast, as if to press the image of her Saviour nearer to her heart. Stooping, she imprinted a kiss upon the sleeper's brow, and felt, as she did so, more than a dawn of hope, for a gentle moisture, different from the cold, clammy dew of death, remained upon her lips.

At the sight of the being whom he so tenderly, passionately, though hopelessly, loved, the spell which had bound the senses of Gilbert was broken. With a loud cry he flung himself at the foot of the coffin, and called upon her, with a thousand endearing expressions, to awake and gladden those who loved her by her presence.

"Wake, Hester!" he exclaimed, "that earth may once more gladden in thy smile. Wake, and save me from the living death which existence without hope or love must bring. Wake," he continued, in a strain of yet deeper passion, "though but to

enshrine thy beauty in a cloister. I still might hover round thy
home, as restless spirits pine around Eden's gates. Wake," he
added, with a cry of despair, seeing that his adjurations were unanswered, " e'en though it be to smile upon another, to break the
heart whose idol thou hast been, and whose last words shall bless
thee."

" Patience, Gilbert," said Ulrick, laying his hand kindly upon his
shoulder ; " prayers and tears are for the dead, and Hester, I trust,
is living. See, her brow is unchanged, the rose upon her lips
unfaded ; be firm, and wait with patience."

" She'll wake no more," groaned the excited boy ; " Death is too
greedy of his prey to resign so fair a victim—heaven too proud of
such a conquest to yield back the brightest angel of its virgin choir.
Father," he added, wildly, " thou hast deceived me—broken alike
thy faith and my torn heart ; for this is death—not sleep—not
sleep."

The recluse, deeply moved by his son's agitation, drew from his
vest a small silver box, which he carefully opened, and poured a
portion of its highly aromatic contents upon a sponge, So powerful
was the perfume that the chapel was filled with the sweet odour.
Placing the sponge in the hand of Gilbert, he said :

" Apply it to her brow and nostrils : the subtle essence will
evaporise the foul drug which holds the maiden in this lethargy.
Be firm ; trust to thy father's word—he will not fail thee, boy."

Eagerly did his son receive the precious gift, and kneeling by
the side of the fair girl, applied it, as he was directed, to her brow
and nostrils. The effect was slow but curious ; no sooner did the
essence come in contact with the spots where the poisoned water
had fallen, than a thin vapour was distinctly seen to arise from the
sleeper's skin, a profuse perspiration followed, and, to the inex-
pressible joy of all, a deep-drawn sigh proved that the breath of
life was not extinct within her form.

" Thank Heaven ! " whispered Matilda, who had watched the
process with intense interest as well as hope, " she breathes." Had
not a flood of tears come to her relief, she must have fainted, so
violent had been her emotion.

At last, to the frantic delight of Gilbert, Hester slowly opened
her eyes, but as if overcome by the light of the torches round the
coffin, or oppressed by the soporific influence of the drug, heavily
closed them again ; her lips moved twice—nothing but inarticulate
sounds, however, broke from them.

" Hush," said Ulrick, " she would speak—there again," he added,
at the second effort.

" Gilbert ! " faintly murmured the waking girl, again opening
her eyes, and fixing them upon the youth.

" She speaks ! " he shrieked, starting from his knees and raising
her in his arms. " Heaven hath heard its wretched creature's

prayer—the cry of his lone agony—the voice of his bruised heart. God ! " he added, "dares the impious wretch who doubted of Thy mercy, dares he thank Thee ? "

Matilda received the scarcely awakened girl within her arms from Gilbert, who reluctantly resigned her ; so greedy did he feel of the privilege of once more supporting her weak, trembling form, that he felt jealous of resigning it even to one of her own sex.

"Let us quit this gloomy place," said Matilda, in her turn resigning the precious burthen to her husband's stalwart arm. "Bear her to my chamber ; she is cold—but half-recovered still. I and my women are the best nurses now."'

The proposal was too rational to be opposed even by Gilbert, who entreated, however, to be permitted to kiss her hand ere Ulrick bore her from the chapel. He had the happiness of again hearing her murmur his name as she was carried from him—a circumstance which neither Matilda nor her husband failed to remark.

On the following day, when Gilbert was admitted to the presence of Hester, he observed with joy the faint blush of pleasure which suffused her cheek as he entered the chamber. Our readers will remember the effort which she made at the moment of her supposed death to open her sealed eyes—the look she had cast upon him—the half-murmured expression of his name. The cry of his despairing love had waked an echo in her heart never heard till then, and the same name had been the first word her lips pronounced when recalled from the living tomb to which she had been consigned. Living it might indeed be called, for, although animation had been suspended, consciousness had all the while remained. She remembered the death-dirge which had been chanted over her, had felt the warm tears of Matilda as she imprinted the parting kiss upon her brow, and endured for four-and-twenty hours all the terrors of the grave ; felt, in anticipation, the earthworm preying on her beating heart. Vain had been all her efforts either to move or speak ; the drug was too potent for her will to break ; every faculty seemed changed to stone ; she felt like a living statue imprisoned in a rock.

In the desolation of her loneliness the memory of Gilbert had returned to her—his boyish but devoted love—the agony of his parting look—and the first feelings of love engendered in her heart, as it faintly beat within its sepulchre. Many days had not elapsed before the ardent youth obtained from her the confession that she was content to live for him ; that gratitude had given birth to a yet warmer passion.

How sweet, how exciting is the sensation when first the lip of woman tells us we are beloved ! The soul expands, it merges into a new existence. The flowers appear more fragrant to the sense ; earth seems full of music, we hear its melodies in every murmuring wind or babbling brook, catch beauty from the stars, revel in nature's harmonies, and find a shrine in every nook and dell. Pity the heart can feel the spell but once ! Other and fairer lips may breathe the words again, but they will never fall so sweetly on the ear as when man hears them first.

For days Gilbert was plunged in this intoxicating bliss. When driven.from the chamber by Matilda's anxious care, he wandered in the umbrageous woods of Stanfield, told to the trees his tale of happiness, or whispered it to every running stream. Hester was soon sufficiently recovered to share his walks ; and often at the evening hour, deeply veiled, accompanied by Ulrick and Matilda, she would venture forth to catch fresh health from the pure breeze of heaven.

The lord of Stanfield felt it to be his duty to inform the venerable primate, whom the proceedings which necessarily followed Eborard's deposition detained in the city, of the wonderful recovery of Mary ; for it is by her Christian name that we shall henceforth designate the beautiful convert. The good man listened with astonishment to the strange tale, with indulgent kindness to the history of her love. Stern only to himself, his heart was not insensible to the happiness of others ; and after a long interview with Robert of Artois, in which that unhappy man revealed to him, under the seal of confession, the secret of Gilbert's birth, Lanfranc not only gave his approbation to the marriage, but offered himself to visit Stanfield, and secretly to celebrate the rite. Addressing himself to Ulrick, as he bade him farewell, he said :

" Heaven, it seems, hath designed them for each other, and mine shall not be the voice to part them. Go," he added ; " in five days I will meet you at your ancestral home. There shall their love be consecrated by the Church's blessing ; that done, let them quit England, and for ever. The unnatural fury of her father, should he discover that his child yet lives, may else prove fatal to her, despite a husband's watchful care and love."

It were needless to describe the ectasy of Gilbert or the blushes of Mary, when they heard the primate's decision : the first was wild with joy, the latter calm in the deep sentiment of her happiness—a happiness she was too pure a child of nature to conceal, too artless to deny—a happiness which their friends witnessed with a joy but second to their own.

Our readers may remember that on the retirement of Robert of Normandy from England, Mirvan, whose principal possessions, as well as those of his bride, were situated in that country, resolved to follow him, being too much disgusted with William's tyranny to accept him as his sovereign. With the consent of both princes he succeeded in exchanging his English fiefs for estates of equal value in the land of his fathers, whither it was his intention to sail as soon as Ralph de Gael, his successor as governor of the city, should arrive. Under his protection it was decided that Gilbert and his young bride should retire to Normandy, where, with the wealth which Robert of Artois had rescued from his unworthy uncle, they could live in happiness, if not in splendour. Fain would Ulrick and Matilda have accompanied them ; but they were bound to England by other ties and other claims. Edith and the venerable Edda still lived to claim their care.

The day at last arrived which was to unite the youthful lovers in those indissoluble bonds which death alone can break. Faithful to his promise, the venerable Lanfranc arrived at Stanfield ; the chapel was secretly prepared, and at midnight, in the presence of Ulrick and Matilda, the nuptial benediction was pronounced.

Three days afterwards the happy pair sailed under the protection of Mirvan and Isabel for Normandy, their future home of love and happiness. The letters which their kind protector furnished them with for the duke insured them a princely welcome, and Gilbert gradually rose to offices of trust and honour. As the party were assembled on the Denes at Yarmouth, watching the arrival of the boat which was to convey them to their ship, the happy bridegroom was made aware that his separation from his father was to be eternal. To all his remonstrances the repentant Robert of Artois answered that his resolution was fixed, and that his future days, under the approbation of the primate, were devoted to his God alone.

" Go, my children," he added, "and if the blessing of a guilty man may weigh with Heaven, mine shall fall like its soft dews upon your innocent heads ! Whether in the cloister's shade or the far-distant plains of Palestine, my last thoughts will be of you ; my latest prayers be yours ! Farewell ! Pray that at the judgment-seat of the Most High we all may meet again ! "

There is nothing more painful to the heart than the bitter task of bidding adieu to those we love ; linger over it as we will, the fatal word must at last be spoken. Happily the agony it occasions is seldom lasting, or o'ercharged nature would succumb beneath the pain. Still it was long, very long, ere the sundered friends forgot the anguish of that sad hour. Mary clung to Ulrick and Matilda, with all the passionate grief which an infant feels when separated from the parents who have loved it. The former was at last obliged to untwine her arms from the agitated Matilda's neck, and place her in the boat, where, on the shoulder of her equally affectionate Gilbert, her sorrow gradually exhausted itself in tears and prayers for the generous beings who had so warmly sheltered and protected her.

As the vessel receded from their view the primate bestowed his benediction on the exiles ; it accompanied them on their journey over the deep waters, even to the country of their future home : the good man's prayers were heard in heaven.

Three months after the scene we have endeavoured to describe
Matilda became a mother, and the joy which she and Ulrick both
felt as they clasped their infant daughter to their breasts blunted
the edge of their regret. The aged Edda lived long enough to
hold the little stranger at the font : perhaps, in the secret wishes of
his heart, he would rather it had been a boy ; but as its parents
were both young enough to be the authors of a numerous race, he
concealed his disappointment, and expired in the arms of his
grandson—blessing him and the infant shoot whose graceful
maturity he was not destined to witness. Seven years afterwards
a second daughter completed the domestic happiness of our hero,
who welcomed it with as fond a smile as though it had been a son
destined to bear to distant time the noble name and manly virtues
of his father.

Robert had acted wisely in exacting from his brother William
the oath of his race with regard to the safety of the lord of
Stanfield. Although frequently urged by his unworthy minion
Tyrrel—whose hatred of Ulrick since the dreadful interview in the
tent had, if possible, increased—to exert the regal power to oppress
him, the king remained faithful to his vow ; the fearful penalty
which he superstitiously believed attached to its violation he dared
not brave. Securely seated on the throne, he even permitted the
return of his younger brother, Prince Henry, to England, where he
doled out to him at intervals the, scanty appanage which the
Conqueror had left him.

Rufus had reigned about eight years, when the death of Lanfranc
rendered the primacy vacant ; an occasion which the greedy
monarch eagerly seized for retaining its revenues in his hands, as
he had already done those of several other vacant bishoprics ; but
falling into a dangerous sickness, he was seized with remorse, and
the clergy representing to him that he was in danger of eternal
perdition if he did not make atonement, he sent for Anselm, abbot
of Bec, who, our readers will remember, had been one of his
brother's most devoted partisans. The churchman, on his arrival,
humbly refused the dignity—fell upon his knees, and entreated
the king to change his purpose, and when he found the monarch
resolved, kept his hand so closed that it required considerable
violence to force him to receive the insignia of his spiritual office ;
but once within his grasp, he held it firmly—and William had more
than one occasion to repent the choice he had made, for the new
prelate was as courageous as he was incorruptible ; in short, for
once the tyrant had found his master. Anselm's reputation for
sanctity and humility was too great for even the regal authority to
venture to assail him.

In the midst of his career William had often experienced one
bitter pang—the thought that on his death-bed his brother Robert,
whom he detested, or Henry, who was equally the object of his

[MARRIAGE OF HENRY WITH THE SAXON PRINCESS.]

aversion, would succeed him. He resolved, therefore, to marry, and secure, if possible, a direct successor to his crown. By means of spies, he discovered that his younger brother frequently visited the convent at Rumsey, where the Princess Matilda, daughter of Malcolm, the third king of Scotland, resided, under the protection of her aunt, the abbess Christina. Although, during the lifetime of her uncle and brothers, Matilda was not the heiress of the Saxon line, still she was dear to the nation on account of her connection with it. Her lover—for such Prince Henry in secret was—had never forgotten the prediction of the aged monk, Father Segsil, at Croydon. Ambition had tempted him in his first visit to the convent ; but the virtues and beauty of the recluse soon inspired him with a purer motive, and he loved—truly, passionately loved. Nor was it long ere he won from the fair girl's lips the confession that he was beloved again. We may imagine, therefore, his fury and despair when Tyrrel, with a malicious smile, announced to him his brother's intentions of proceeding to the convent, and to give England a queen in the person of the Saxon princess. Deeply as he felt wounded, both in love and in ambition, by the intelligence, he was too much a courtier to give his enemy the triumph of perceiving that the shaft had reached him, and he parried the thrust by demanding, in his turn, when the king was to bestow on him the so long promised earldom, which his services merited. This was a sore subject with the traitor, and he winced beneath the thrust. Despite all that he had done (and his services to William had been as varied as they were unscrupulous) the recompense was as distant as ever. The monarch still put him off with promises ; nay, seemed to take a malicious pleasure in exciting his hopes only to disappoint them. Indeed, his intention in this respect was frequently so apparent, that the traitor often questioned whether the secret of his birth was not even known or guessed at by the tyrant, and the suspicion but added to his shame and disappointment.

"William will find," said Tyrrel, with a scowl, "that even my loyalty may be urged too far. He hath broken promise and oath with me ; and yet the latter," he added, with a peculiar smile, " was a strange one."

" It would have been stranger," observed Prince Henry, " had he kept it. Humph ! " he added, as he turned upon his heel and left the knight, " that fellow might be useful ; he hath a conscience as pliant as a courtier's back."

That very night the unhappy lover sought an interview with Anselm ; an achievement of no common danger, for since the recovery of his health the Red King's remorse had disappeared, and he bitterly regretted that ever he had been induced to bestow the primacy upon a character so cold and so unyielding as Anselm. Since their dispute, the episcopal palace had been continually surrounded with spies ; and those nobles were sure of being visited with their monarch's displeasure who either visited or entertained relations of amity with its master. It was not, therefore, without reason that the prince took the precaution of disguising himself in a monk's gown and capuchin to obtain access to him. Cold as Anselm was, he was not incapable of friendship. He had not forgotten the previous visits of Henry to Westminster, when he was only Abbot of Bec, and he received him again, if not with warmth, at least with cordiality, and listened to his tale with deep interest.

"What!" exclaimed the primate, when Henry had related his tale; "wed with a nun professed! Is William mad? or does he dream the Church's thunders slumber in our hand? There must be some deceit in this; he never dares attempt it."

"You mistake, venerable father," sighed the anxious lover; "Matilda is not a nun: she has only worn the veil as a protection in these lawless times, when even the altar can scarce protect its own. Her lips as yet have breathed no vow which sunders her for ever from the world."

"Then am I powerless!" exclaimed the churchman. "Had she been wedded to the altar, I would have snatched her from a hundred kings; but, as it is, Rufus may claim her person: he is the guardian of every orphan in the realm."

"But still," said Henry, and then paused.

"Still what?" demanded Anselm, fixing his eyes upon the hesitating speaker.

"The Church may claim her still. Who is to know her vow is yet unspoken, if you assert it is? Pardon me, holy father," he added, sinking on his knee as he marked the frown on the prelate's brow; "but despair hath made me mad. I love the fair Matilda, not with the rash impulse of a lawless love, but truly, nobly, with a passion worthy her name and mine. Again," he added, "my tyrant brother threatens to cross my path. He hath despoiled me, and I have borne it patiently; plotted against my life, and I have forgiven him; but let him touch my love, my heart's first hope, my manhood's prize, and I will beard him in his strength. Like himself, I have the blood of the same fiend-begotten ancestor within my veins. Let him beware how he arouses it."

"This is the very frenzy of despair. Hast thou forgot he is thy king as well as brother?" demanded Anselm. "But perchance it is ambition leads thee to seek the Saxon princess's hand. Her name, in the event of William's death, would pave her husband's pathway to the throne. And I have not now to learn that Henry of Normandy aspires to the crown."

"At present he aspires only to the love of the fair Matilda," answered the young man.

"And I will aid thee!" exclaimed Anselm, after a pause, during which he had well scrutinised the features of his visitor—"when does Rufus start for Rumsey?"

"With the dawn. With him to will is to perform. He knows no procrastination in the search of interest or pleasure."

" I will place a bar between him and his hopes," resumed the primate, "which, powerful as he is, he cannot break. Farewell, and thank thy fortunes for this visit ; it hath saved the maiden from the tiger's fangs. No words—I know the gratitude of princes. I will save Matilda for her own sake as well as thine."

That very night the archbishop, attended only by a slender train, left the metropolis, and directed his way towards the convent where the princess, unconscious of her danger, resided, in her holy, calm retirement.

On the second day after his departure, William, attended by a numerous suite of nobles and retainers, entered the small town of Rumsey. With a refinement of cruelty which only a heart like his would have been capable of, Prince Henry was forced to be of the party. The only hope of the unhappy lover was in the promise which Anselm had made. Although he could not foresee the means, he doubted not of the power of the holy man to perform his word, for his influence was scarcely second to that of the Red King himself.

On arriving at the front of the convent, they found the gates closely barred ; nor was it till the third summons of the herald, who demanded admittance in the name of the monarch, that the venerable and noble abbess condescended to make her appearance at the gate. Proud of her royal birth, and still more of her spiritual authority, the aged Christina demanded, in a cold, calm tone, the cause of the king's visit to her humble cell ; for so, in the mock humility of the age, she designated the truly magnificent establishment over which she had so long and honourably presided.

" I come to claim my ward," impatiently exclaimed the tyrant— "the Saxon princess, Matilda, who hath too long been lost in the obscurity of the cloister—to place her in a sphere where the homage due alike unto her birth and matchless beauty shall encircle her— in a word, good mother, to place her on the throne to which she is so nearly allied in blood."

" Matilda is the bride of Heaven," answered the abbess, " and earthly love, e'en though a monarch's, were a sacrilege too fearful to be dwelt on. Retire, then, prince, and leave the house of God to its poor inmates, who ask but liberty to pray for the welfare of their country and the salvation of their souls in solitude and silence. Again I do repeat it, Matilda is professed."

" 'Tis false," said the infuriated Rufus ; " none of your holy trickery with me, your pious mummery, and holy cant! Give entrance to the convent, or by my father's soul, I'll batter the sacred rookery down ! Fit fate for such a nest of treason and rebellion !."

"The will of Heaven be done !" exclaimed the aged abbess.

"Come, then, and, if thou darest, rend the Church's bride e'en from the nuptial altar ; but beware," she added, sternly, "the curse of the saint from whose embrace you tear her. Weak as my voice is, it shall yet be heard in heaven for vengeance on the sacrilege and crime. Unbar the gates," she added to her attendants, "and let the monarch enter."

Without deigning an obeisance to the tyrant, the venerable speaker retired from the gate, and in a few minutes the ponderous doors of the church were flung wide, and Rufus and his nobles entered.

The scene which met their view was well calculated to impress the superstitious nobles with awe. As they advanced slowly down the centre aisle, in every stall of the choir was seated the immovable form of a veiled nun. The superior had resumed her seat upon her abbatial throne, close to the high altar, which blazed with a hundred lighted tapers ; clouds of rich incense filled the air, and partially obscured the group of priests who officiated before the sacred shrine. In the centre of them might be perceived the kneeling form of the young princess, divested of her rich attire, and robed in the simple habit of a nun ; a long tress of her golden hair, lately severed from her fair head, lay upon the altar ; and as William and his train gained the centre of the church, the black veil held by the officiating priest descended like a cloud upon her head. The heart of the unhappy Henry failed him at the sight ; it seemed the knell of hope.

"What trickery is this?" demanded William, his cheek and brow flushed with rage at the sight. "Where is the Saxon princess, the niece of Edgar Atheling?"

"Dead !" replied the abbess ; "the princess Matilda lives no more."

"Dead !" echoed the king and nobles.

"Dead," resumed the abbess, "to the world ; she is a nun professed. Raise, sisters, the hymn to invoke the blessing of the Most High upon the sacrifice."

In obedience to the command of their superior, the nuns had commenced the "Veni Creator" before the disappointed king, had recovered himself sufficiently to interrupt them. His harsh discordant voice was soon, however, heard above the choral strain of the trembling cloistered maids.

"And who," he exclaimed, "without my license, hath dared to do this? Bear witness all," he added, "the rites are not yet complete ; that, without my sanction, they are invalid. Matilda is destined to a throne ; she is my ward, and thus I claim my right."

The speaker strode to the rails of the altar, which he burst recklessly open, and advanced to seize the trembling girl, who clung to the sanctuary for protection. Already had his rude hands grasped her veil, when the deep voice of the primate, whose presence he had not perceived amongst the crowd of priests, arrested the impious act; he started at the sound; the hiss of a serpent had been more grateful in his ear.

" 'Tis well, prince," said the churchman; "is not the measure of thy iniquity yet full? Thou hast widowed the Church of her bishops; applied to ambition and ungodly waste the revenues of the sequestered sees, the patrimony of heaven and the poor; and now, to complete thy guilt, thou comest with armed men and sinful violence to rend the spotless bride of Christ from His insulted altar. Back," he added, "ere the justice of offended Deity levels the thunder of its wrath against thee; back, ere I place thy realm in interdict, and breathe on thee, and all that aid thy evil passions, the sentence of the Church."

At the sound of Anselm's voice the most devoted followers of Rufus drew back; they knew too well his stern, unbending nature and vast influence with the people, from his reputed sanctity, to brave him. The Red King alone maintained 'his ground, and confronted the courageous primate.

" I will at once appoint bishops to the vacant sees!" he exclaimed, trusting to bribe Anselm to acquiescence by the promise; "restore the revenues!"

" Back," repeated the archbishop, sternly.

" Yield on the point of the investitures," he added.

" Back," continued the unmoved prelate.

" Confirm the Church's liberties."

" Back," iterated the churchman, who knew too well the character of the monarch to trust his promises, or be deceived by them into a dereliction of his duty.

Seeing that his commands were not obeyed, the archbishop advanced to the altar, and taking in his hands the legatine cross, held it up slowly before the people: every knee, except William's, was bent in the church at the sight. Then followed a breathless pause, for all guessed the fearful words about to follow.

" Let all who would not share in the excommunication," he continued, "pass the threshold of the church. If a single armed foot but cross the sacred line an inch, a breadth, a hair, on him and on his race I breathe the curse of Heaven."

" What!" exclaimed William, as he saw the nobles slowly quit the church, "will you desert me at yon shaveling's bidding? Salisbury, Mortimer, Warrenne! is this your loyalty? Traitors!" he added, when he saw that all but himself had passed the limit prescribed by the primate, "your lands shall pay the forfeit of this treason."

" We will not war against the Church!" exclaimed the nobles. "Our lands were won by our good swords; our swords shall still maintain them. Thou art the king, but he is the archbishop."

" He is a traitor!" hoarsely muttered the king, at the same time laying his hand upon his sword.

"Strike!" said the prelate, "and crown my pilgrimage with the martyr's glorious crown; strike, and deluge the shrine of God with blood: strike and set the seal of death upon thy guilty soul. Lo!" he added, snatching the veil of Matilda from his grasp, " I defy thee; king as thou art, I thrust thee forth from out the sacred precincts. Armed with the Church's banner, I oppose thee—drive thee like a fierce wolf from out the sacred fold."

The instant William drew his sword the horror-stricken nobles cried out "Sacrilege!" and had rushed into the church, had not the previous command of the archbishop restrained them.

William, subdued by the firmness of his enemy, and alarmed at the spirit displayed by his hitherto obsequious barons, recoiled as the prelate advanced, and retreated backwards till he had passed the threshold, Anselm following him all the while under the protection of his cross. As soon as the royal intruder was expelled, the primate with his own hands closed the gates, and the choir burst forth spontaneously in a hymn of triumph.

In an irritated mood, the baffled tyrant returned to London, and immediately afterwards, attended only by Tyrrel and a few of his immediate followers, started for the New Forest, created by the devastation of his father, to indulge in the pleasures of the chase.

On the third morning after his arrival, at an early hour, he left Winchester, accompanied by William de Bretuil, Tyrrel, and others, for the hunt. Fortunately for the fair fame of his brother, Prince Henry on that fatal day remained in Winchester, or a share in the death of the tyrant had doubtless been attributed to him.

Rufus, like all the princes of his line, was extremely jealous of his prerogatives in hunting. Volumes might be filled with the cruelties inflicted by the Norman sovereigns upon the transgressors of the game-laws. The chase was their ruling passion, and Tyrrel shared in the instincts of his race. In a sylvan glade of the forest he had stricken a royal deer, which was so designated from the number of branches on its antlers; his foot was already upon the neck of the palpitating victim—the knife in his hand ready to give the *coup de grâce*, when a horseman broke through the intervening brushwood. It was Rufus, whose evil genius had sent him to be a witness of the act.

"Villain!" he exclaimed, "it is a royal hart. What insolence is this?—e'en in our very presence to strike our prize!"

Tyrrel murmured something about not having counted the number of branches on its antlers.

"I'll teach thee how to count!" interrupted the furious monarch. "By heavens, it is a hart of grease fit for a king to chase! A prison may teach thee better manners, knave. Should the hound be served before its master?"

Stung by the insult, and alarmed at the menaces of the tyrant, who had never been known to pardon an offence against the forest laws, Tyrrel became desperate. The consciousness of high birth and merited degradation—of William's broken promises, had engendered a flood of venom in his heart, which wanted but one added drop to make it overflow. That drop the last words of Rufus gave. "Hound!" iterated Tyrrel. "Hear! 'Tis thou who art the hound, and I thy master. Remember thy oath—'*May the keenest arrow in thy quiver pierce my perjured heart if I break faith with thee.*' The faith hath been broken, and the hour of vengeance hath at last arrived."

"Traitor!" said Rufus, half-drawing his sword.

"Traitor to thy teeth!" exclaimed Tyrrel, as he fixed the fatal arrow to his bow. "Know 'tis thy injured brother Robert's son who strikes—whose avenging arrow rids England of her tyrant, and peoples hell with another of his fated race."

That very night the body of the Red King was conveyed to Winchester in a common cart by a peasant family named Purkiss, who had found it in the forest, and the guilty Tyrrel sailed in a fishing boat from the land where his birth entitled him to reign.

CHAPTER XXI.

ON hearing of the death of his brother, Prince Henry felt that the moment had arrived for the realisation of his long cherished and deeply meditated schemes of ambition. His first step was to hasten to the episcopal palace in Winchester, and secure the treasures of the late king—an act which he successfully accomplished, despite the remonstrances of their keeper, De Breteuil, who frankly told him that they were the property of his legitimate sovereign and elder brother Robert. The impetuous prince drew his sword, and menaced him with death in the event of his resisting him ; and being backed by a considerable number of barons, whom he had gained over to his cause, that faithful officer was compelled to yield. Two days afterwards, feeling himself sufficiently strong, Henry threw off the mask, and proclaimed himself king ; his elder brother's absence from the kingdom materially facilitated his obtaining possession of the crown. Thus the rights of Robert were a second time set aside by the successful usurpation of the younger princes. After a short struggle, during which that unfortunate man displayed his usual reckless courage and inconsistency, a compromise was entered into, chiefly by the influence of the primate Anselm. The elder brother resumed his duchy of Normandy, and acknowledged Henry as king, on condition that the latter paid him a considerable pension annually.

Ulrick had been amongst the first of the few nobles who joined the standard of the legitimate monarch, and the very last to counsel his abdication of his rights—a conduct which, when the

struggle had terminated, did him no injury in the friendship of
Henry, who, of all his brother's partisans, excepted the lord of
Stanfield alone from feeling the weight of his resentment, and
even invited him to be present at his nuptials with the Princess
Matilda, which, as soon as the peace was concluded, he prepared to
celebrate with all due pomp at Westminster.

A council of prelates had been previously held by Anselm, who
declared before them that the vow taken by the Saxon maiden had
only been conditional, as a means of protecting her from the
tyranny of the late king. The reasons were found valid, and
Matilda pronounced at liberty to marry by the unanimous
judgment of the assembly.

The abbey church was crowded by nobles and their high-born
dames, who vied with each other in the cumbrous magnificence of
their costume. Despite the censures of the Church (and the
primate had fulminated them loud and frequently) against the prevailing fashion of the day—the long-toed shoes, looped with silver,
and not unfrequently golden, chains to the knee—the wearers of
these forbidden ornaments were numerous and bold : the occasion
of displaying their preposterous finery was too tempting to be lost,
but the most prudent took care to draw back from the circle
which surrounded the archbishop, whose inflexibility they well
knew and dreaded. This ridiculous mode lasted nearly two
centuries, despite the prohibition of the Church, which even in the
plenitude of its power, when its thunders could crush a throne,
found them impotent against a fashion. Such are the anomalies of
poor, weak human nature.

The shouts of the people, who were transported at the idea of the
descendant of their ancient monarchs sharing the Conqueror's
throne, announced the arrival of Henry and his bride, who soon
afterwards entered the church, followed by the abbess of Rumsey,
the aged Princess Christina, Ulrick, Matilda, and a stately train of
chivalry and beauty. As the bridal procession moved towards the
high altar, where Anselm, attended by his suffragan bishops,
stood ready to perform the rite, Ulrick's thoughts naturally
reverted to the aged monk at Croydon, who had prophesied to
Henry his high fortune, and its continuance, provided he married
in the royal Saxon line ; nor did he fail to remember the prediction touching his own fate—"a life of unblemished honour, but a
broken heart." "Let it come," he murmured to himself ; "provided
it spare those I love, I fear not the bolt myself."

He was soon, however, diverted from such sombre thoughts by
the commencement of the ceremony.

The archbishop had scarcely pronounced the first words of the
service, when a loud voice from the back of the altar commanded
him to forbear. In an instant all was confusion ; men gazed upon
each other, and with inquiring eyes seemed to demand the cause of

such unseemly interruption. The superstitious trembled, for the sound evidently came from the shrine of St. Edward the Confessor, whose canonised bones rested behind the altar. After a few moments' pause, during which Henry endeavoured to reassure his trembling bride, just as Anselm was about to recommence the ceremony, the command was repeated in a still louder tone than before, and the tall, stately form of Father Segsil, the aged monk of Croydon, was seen slowly advancing from the tomb of the sainted king, whose name was still so dear to every Saxon heart. Though clad merely in the ample, flowing, dark robe of his order, prelates and nobles were alike impressed with awe at his appearance. A long silver beard fell in waving masses upon his breast, his features, though sharp with age and vigil, retained traces of former beauty as well as dignity ; bright blue eyes flashed from beneath a lofty brow, such as the divine Angelo in after years gave to the prophet Moses. Time, as loth to touch perfection, had laid his hand most gently upon him ; his noble form was but slightly bent with the weight of a hundred years ; and as he slowly advanced, guiding his steps with a simple staff, all involuntarily made way for him, till he stood before the altar, confronting Henry and the archbishop.

Fixing a searching glance upon the bridegroom, he demanded in a tone in which a monarch might have addressed his vassal, or the priest of Jove proclaimed his antique oracle to some expectant worshipper :

" Dost thou remember me, O king ? "

Henry, who was too much impressed by the sudden apparition to reply, bowed his head in token of his recognition of the speaker, whom, from his vast age, he had long since considered as numbered with the dead.

" All I foretold thee is accomplished," resumed the old man : " the Red King sleeps within his grave, and thou art king."

" Most true, good father," replied the monarch, who had quickly recovered from his surprise.

" I told thee, prince, that we should meet again—meet at the proudest moment of thy life—and I have kept my word. But if this marriage," added the monk, " is indeed to bind the Norman and the Saxon race in the strong chain of love—to heal the wounds of mutual hate, and give a long divided country peace—no voice but mine must celebrate the rite. It is for this that I have lived. This one act accomplished, I have done with life, and all its waking dreams."

" Art mad, my brother ? " exclaimed the archbishop, indignant that a simple monk should interfere with his high office. " Who art thou that, at thy bidding, England's primate should resign his functions ?—speak ! I love not priests who deal in mysteries."

With a faint smile, Father Segsil approached the angry prelate,

and whispered a single word into his ear ; the effect was electrical.

Anselm started, and regarded the old man with an air of mingled
awe, astonishment, and respect. Bowing his head in acquiescence,
he took from one of the attendant bishops his consecrated stole,
and placed it with his own hands around the neck of the aged
man ; saying, as he did so :

" It is most just. The will of Heaven be done."

Henry and his bride were both too much struck by the lofty bearing
of Father Segsil and the sudden act of the archbishop, to offer the
least opposition. On a motion of the old man's hand they knelt
before him, whilst with a firm voice, which sounded through the
lofty aisles of the church like an echo from the grave, he
pronounced the nuptial benediction. At the conclusion of the
ceremony he laid his hand upon the head of the youthful queen,
and blessed her even as a father might have blessed his child.

" Thou daughter of a hundred kings ! " he cried ; " yet a few
moments, and the voice which blesses thee shall be heard no more
on earth, but it shall rise before the throne of the Most High, to
implore His mercies upon thee and on thy people. Protect thy
oppressed country ; be thou a refuge to the weak—a hope to the
despairing ; so shall men bless thy name on earth, and angels write
it in the Book of Life in heaven. So shall thy race—no, no," he
murmured, as, overcome by some sudden emotion, he sank into
the arms of those around him. " Dark ! dark ! The spirit hath
passed from me. I can see no more."

" He is dying ! " exclaimed Anselm, who had placed his finger
upon the pulse of the aged monk ; " his race is run."

" Hast thou no blessing, no gift for me ? " demanded Henry,
bending his knee, and catching the hand of the expiring man,
whose sudden death, after the accomplishment of the events he
had so singularly foretold, struck him with religious awe and
astonishment.

" I have," faintly replied Father Segsil, opening with an effort
his nearly closed eyes. " Where is St. Edward's crown ? "

" Upon my brow," answered the king.

" And where his sceptre ? " he resumed, in a still weaker tone.

" I bear it in my hand."

" All," murmured the old man to himself, " all but the ring are
there—St. Edward's ring, the matchless gem, graved with the holy
cross. St. George, who won the ruby stone in Palestine, predicted
it should ne'er be worn except by England's kings. Where," he
added, speaking in a still louder tone to the Norman prince, " where
is the coronation ring of England's monarchs ? "

" Lost ! " exclaimed the abbot of Westminster, who, from his
office, was guardian of the regalia ; " lost on the field of Hastings.
It is well known the Saxon monarch wore it in the battle ; it hath

never since been found, despite the recompense the Conqueror offered, the search his soldiers made."

Father Segsil, with an effort which seemed far beyond his expiring strength, raised himself from the arms of those who supported him, and gazed with an expression of mingled benevolence and dignity upon the youthful sovereign at his feet. Thrusting his hand into his bosom, he slowly drew from it the long-lost gem, and placed it with a mournful smile on Henry's finger, whispering as he did so :

"Now thou indeed art king ! " and, exhausted by the effort, he fell back into the arms of those who were near him—a corpse. The young queen and her aunt, the aged abbess Christina, sank upon their knees and offered up their prayers for the dead.

"This is indeed a precious gift," said Henry, pointing to the ring and addressing the archbishop. "The good monk hath been its faithful guardian. He was a holy man," he added : "he foretold our succession to the crown—our marriage with Matilda. Bury him, my lord, like a prophet and a saint."

"Bury him like a king," replied the primate, "for such, in truth, he was."

"A king ! " repeated Henry and the nobles who were near.

"A king," iterated Anselm. "God hath miraculously prolonged his days beyond the usual span. But I repeat, the voice which all heard pronounce upon our monarch and his queen the nuptial benediction was the voice of Harold the Saxon king, so long thought slain upon the field of Hastings. Peace to his memory—honour to the brave and the unfortunate ! "

This strange discovery accounted for the interest the monk had taken in the marriage of Henry and Matilda. It was afterwards fully confirmed by documents left by the preceding abbot of Croydon, to whom the defeated monarch, immediately after the battle of Hastings, had made himself known, and by whose advice he had devoted himself to the Church.

The obsequies of the aged prince were privately, but regally, celebrated by night, in the church where he had resigned his latest breath, his last resting place being at the foot of the holy Confessor's tomb, and known but to the few who assisted at his interment, and to whom the secret was confided.

Immediately after the marriage of Henry, Ulrick returned to Stanfield. All hope of throwing off the yoke of the Norman race was abandoned on the union of the princess Matilda, whom the people loved for her charities and many virtues, as well as for her Saxon descent, and prayed that she might be the mother of a race of monarchs to succeed her—a prayer destined to disappointment, as she died without issue many years before Henry, who, soon after her death, married again, in the hopes of an heir, but was equally doomed to hope in vain.

Ethra, Ulrick's eldest-born, was at the age of sixteen a tall, graceful, capricious, wayward girl ; in her Madonna-like beauty she more resembled her grandmother, the once beautiful Edith, than either her father or Matilda. From her earliest childhood she had betrayed a strange passion for solitude, and frequently had alarmed her anxious parents and terrified her attendants by escaping from them to bury herself in the deepest recesses of the surrounding forests, where the distracted Ulrick had, on more than one occasion, found her seated by some babbling brook, singing to the murmuring waters, or couched, like a young fawn, within a mossy dell or flowery nook, weaving wild garlands of the simple flowers which grew around her. The sight of her innocent amusement and infantine beauty would arrest the reproof upon her father's lips. How was it possible to scold the fairy being whose musical laugh at the sight of him rang through the woodland glade ? Ofttimes the words of anger were checked by a shower of kisses ; for, despite her wild temper and strange taste for solitude, she loved her father with all the deep affection of her thoughtful nature ; her heart clung to his as the graceful ivy clings around the majestic oak. She was proud of his courage and manly strength—proud of his fame, and the devotion of the Saxon race, who looked upon him as their protector—proud that he was her father.

Finding it impossible to restrain this peculiar disposition in his child, Ulrick resolved, as far as possible, to provide for her safety ; for which purpose he trained two young bloodhounds, who gradually became so much attached to their fairy charge that they followed her in all her wanderings, stopped when she stayed, guarded her whilst she slept, and, with the wonderful instinct of their nature, permitted no one who was a stranger on the domain to approach her person. Ethra loved her savage, wild companions ; for savage they truly were to all but her. Often, in sport, would she try to baffle their peculiar powers of tracking out those they sought, by concealing herself within the cleft of a rock, or climbing into the leafy branches of some lofty tree. The faithful animals seemed to understand and enjoy the sport. Aided by their exquisite scent, they invariably found her, and bayed with joy at the discovery. Some of the aged servants of the household predicted that no good could possibly arise from this strange companionship ; and the old chaplain remembered a prophecy said to have been written by a former lord of Stanfield, which ran thus :

> Woe to our house, when the maiden and hound
> A home in the halls of the stranger hath found ;
> The raven and owl shall inhabit it then,
> And the wolf and the fox make its turrets their den.

Our hero, although far from superstitious, could not avoid being struck by the singularity of the prediction, which he commanded to be carefully concealed from his wife, threatening with his severe displeasure any who should reveal it to her—a prohibition which caused the domestics but to repeat it the more frequently amongst themselves, till at last they became persuaded that their young mistress was the being whose evil fortune was to bring the long-predicted desolation upon the house of her fathers. They shook their heads ominously when the maiden and her dogs passed by them, and not infrequently signed the cross, or dropped a bead to Heaven for her safety ; for, strange and capricious as was her disposition, all who knew her felt themselves impelled to love her.

. It was on a fine morning in September that the young heiress, clad in her simple dress of white, crossed the drawbridge, attended by her faithful followers, Thor and Woden ; for so they had been named,,in honour of their pure Saxon blood. The warder shook his head as they passed him, and whispered to the seneschal his fears that the dreaded prediction was not far from its fulfilment—a confidence which the officer returned by informing him that death-lights had been seen in the chapel, a sure sign of misfortune to their master's race. The deep bay of the bloodhounds, and the joyous laugh of their charge, were soon lost in the recesses of the forest into which they plunged. Their cry startled the timid fawn from its secret lair and roused the antlered stag to direct its flight far from the nut-brown woods of Stanfield. The thoughtless, happy girl was making her way through the intricacies of the underwood—now recalling the dogs from the scent of the flying deer, now urging them on—when the animals suddenly uttered a deep growl, and darted down a narrow path which led to a fountain known by the name of the Druid's Well. Ethra imme-diately followed, fearful lest her companions, so ferocious to all but her, should attack some traveller, or peasant hastening to his labours. On reaching the spot she discovered the hounds both crouching, as if to spring upon an aged woman, who had evidently climbed the low projecting rock on which she stood for safety. Although dressed in mean attire, there was an air of dignity in her manner which struck the beholder with respect. Her foot was firmly planted, and a sort of staff, with a long knife at the end, such as might be used for cutting water plants, was grasped in her right hand, ready to strike her assailants in case they should approach her.

"Down, Woden—down, Thor !" cried the maiden, rushing between the excited dogs and the object of their attack ; "down, I say ! Do not fear, good mother," she added ; "they are obedient to my voice, and will not harm you."

"Do I look as if I feared them ?" exclaimed the woman, in a harsh voice. "It is long, very long, since I feared aught of earth, and I might add of Heaven ; the first can take from me nothing but life, and the latter is too merciful to harm me."

The woman descended as she spoke, and fixed a curious glance upon the fair girl who had so opportunely appeared to rescue her ; for, despite her weapon and the courage with which she might have used it, the two dogs, who lay whining and crouching at their mistress's feet, would doubtless have torn her in pieces but for her interference.

"You are a stranger, mother, in these parts," said the maiden, meeting her glance with a look as bold and searching as her own. "If you have lost your way, I will guide you ; if you are in distress, follow me to the castle, and I will relieve you. One good, at least, results from my strange wandering propensities—they lead me frequently to the succour of my fellow-creatures."

"Thou art, then, the daughter of Ulrick of Stanfield," exclaimed the woman ; "she whom the superstitious peasants call the Forest Fairy ? Thy beauty well deserves the name—thy goodness even more so than thy beauty. Farewell ! I have no need of human guidance—human help. I dare not longer stay, lest, as I gaze upon thee, and read thy fate, my heart should feel once more the throb of sympathy and pity."

"And what will be my fate ? " demanded Ethra, whose curiosity was excited, but not her fears.

"Canst thou bear to listen to it ? " said the stranger, peering at her from beneath her bushy brows.

"I can bear much," answered the maiden, proudly. "Armed in my innocence, I have never yet experienced fear, though I have passed the lone hours in the forest, and marked the lengthening shadows creep silently upon my path—have felt the lightning's kiss upon my cheek, yet hath it never harmed me. While innocent, I laugh at fear."

"But when innocence hath left thee ! " interrupted the woman, with a bitter laugh.

"I first must cease to be," replied Ethra, with offended dignity ; "thou ravest of things impossible, good mother."

"I thought so once," shrieked the hag ; "but, like thee, I was deceived. Hear me, proud daughter of a still prouder line. Thou hast asked to know thy fate, and I will not deny thee. Thou shalt love and be beloved, be won and scorned, be injured and avenged. Thou art in the toils : fly as thou wilt, thou canst not escape thy doom ; for there is one upon thy track who never yet spared woman in his lust, or man in his revenge. Farewell ! Perchance, when thy fate shall be accomplished, we may meet again."

The speaker had no sooner concluded her prediction than she plunged into the thick underwood which grew around the borders of the well, and disappeared ere the astonished Ethra could detain her. The two dogs, who had watched her with suspicion, sprang

[ULRICK APPEALING TO HIS COUNTRYMEN.]

z

forward, and would have followed her, had not their mistress once more restrained them. The affectionate brutes looked wistfully into her face, as if to ask the reason why she forbad them to follow the instinct of their nature, which told them the object of their fury was dangerous to their mistress's happiness and peace.

"She is mad!" exclaimed the maiden, seating herself close to the well; "and I were as mad as she is to heed her strange predictions. I must keep more at home, and check this rambling disposition, fitting the daughter of some village serf, but not the heiress of the lord of Stanfield."

Whilst thus seated indulging in her many fancies, her eye was attracted by a water-lily which floated on the well, almost within reach of her arm from the projecting piece of rock on which she sat. Bending to secure the flower, whose beauty pleased her, the maiden overbalanced herself and fell. The pool was deep and dangerous; and despite the efforts of her faithful hounds, who leaped in and supported her, she must have perished but for the arrival of a stranger, who, seeing that the dogs were incapable of dragging their burden over the species of natural parapet formed by the rock, hastened to assist them by leaning over the water where the barrier was lowest. The sagacious animals swam with their inanimate mistress directly towards him. Catching her by the arm, he drew her forth, and, laying the insensible form upon the grass, busily occupied himself in endeavouring to restore her. Relieved from the weight which they had for a considerable time sustained, Woden and Thor soon contrived to release themselves from their watery prison by leaping over the rock. Jealous, as they generally were, of the approach of strangers near their charge, they seemed to feel that in the present crisis he was a friend, and they aided the exertions of the young hunter—for such the preserver of Ethra, by his costume, seemed to be— by licking the hands and face of the inanimate girl, occasionally howling piteously in evidence of their distress.

After chafing her hands and forehead for a considerable time the young man applied a small silver flask to her lips; and observed with pleasure, after swallowing a few drops of the rich cordial it contained, that the object of his care heaved a deep sigh, and half-opened her eyes, which, overcome with languor, she immediately closed again.

"How beautiful!" exclaimed the stranger, gazing upon her with sudden and passionate admiration; "could I, ere life returns, snatch from her lips one kiss, memory should treasure it with those golden hours which, like the oases in the desert, cheer life's pilgrim on his dreary way."

Ardent as was the speaker's admiration of beauty, and reckless as were the means by which he gratified it, the very helplessness of Ethra protected her from further outrage than the burning kiss

z 2

which he imprinted on her lips, and which many of my fair
readers may feel inclined to think he had fairly earned by the
service he had rendered in dragging her out of the water—only it
was not quite generous to pay himself ; one kiss bestowed is worth
a thousand stolen ones.

The impression upon the still, half-conscious girl was electrical ;
a tremulous agitation ran through every limb, and a faint blush
instantly suffused her features.

"Where am I ? " she murmured.

"In safety, lady," replied her preserver—"guarded by one who
would give his worthless life a thousand times ere danger should
approach you, or sorrow blight one smile upon thy brow. But tell
me," he added—for he had noticed the golden girdle and bracelets,
the badges of her high rank—"whom have I had the happiness of
serving ? "

"I am the daughter of the lord of Stanfield," said the maiden,
casting down her eyes, for she felt uneasy beneath his gaze.

Had she seen the frown upon the inquirer's brow, as she
announced her lineage, Ethra might have been spared the long
corroding sorrow of after years—for it was a frown of bitterest,
deepest hate, black as a thunder-cloud, but transient as the
lightning's flash. Recovering himself, he demanded in the same
bland voice :

"And you have lost your attendants in the forest ? "

"These are my attendants," replied Ethra, with a blush, as, for
the first time, the impropriety of her rambling disposition was
forced upon her. "Thor and Woden are faithful guardians ;
besides," she added, "on our own domain, surrounded by the serfs
and vassals of our house, what should I have to fear ? "

"Fear ! " exclaimed the hunter ; "who that wears human form
could harm thee ? No, lady, thou art as safe within the forest
shade as within thy father's halls : thy beauty and thy innocence
protect thee."

Ethra started from the bank upon which the stranger had placed
her ; the word innocence had recalled to her mind the hag's
prediction. She felt, she knew not why, that it would be wiser to
end the scene at once. Gracefully thanking him for the service he
had rendered her, she asked him his name, that her father might
know whom to thank for the preservation of his child.

"My name," said the young man, with well-acted humility, "is
too obscure to dwell upon the lord of Stanfield's memory ; nor is it
from his hands I seek reward. One thought of the wandering
hunter, lady, when you pass this spot, one kind recollection of his
services, and they are over-paid."

Gracefully bending the knee, he kissed the hand which the
maiden extended to him, and disappeared up the winding
pathway which conducted from the dell.

Ethra remained for several minutes fixed to the spot, absorbed in her reflections ; the kiss which the bold stranger had impressed upon her lips when he thought her insensible shocked her delicacy, but haunted her imagination ; the deep but respectful admiration with which he regarded her, the service he had rendered her, all created in her heart an interest for the stranger dangerous to her peace.

" I wonder," she whispered to herself, as slowly she directed her way from the Druid's Well, " if ever we shall meet again. I fear that he will think me ungrateful, for I but coldly thanked him."

It was in this pensive mood that Ethra arrived at Stanfield. On her way the gambols of her faithful companions had been unheeded, or repressed with an impatient word. With a light step, she regained her chamber, and changed her still soiled, damp dress, for fresh attire. Resolving to conceal her adventure from her parents, the excuse for so doing was the fear of distressing them by an account of the danger she had run ; the reason must be sought in those instincts with which love baffles the wisdom of experience. Ethra already contemplated meeting with the preserver of her life again ; the relation of her adventure might prevent it, and hence her silence. I need not inform my readers that already the maiden loved.

It was not long before the meeting of Ethra and her lover—for such the stranger soon became—was an event of daily occurrence. It were needless to repeat the arguments by which he won from his destined victim the promise of concealment of their passion ; persuasion is sweet from the lips of those we love, and the young heiress was, despite her high birth, but a mere child of nature. What to her were the distinctions of rank or country in the being to whom she had given her affections ? His land became her land, his God became her God. Once, and once only, she had pressed him for his name—the reply struck horror to her heart.

" Ask it not, dearest ; it is proscribed in the halls of Stanfield. Sooner would thy proud father see thee dead than the bride of thy Norman lover. He hates alike my name and lineage."

" You wrong him," exclaimed Ethra, weeping—" I am sure you wrong him. Ulrick hates none but the cruel and depraved. Is not my mother, too, of Norman blood ? And think you he would hate the race from which she springs ? Of all your countrymen, I know but one of whom he speaks with anger or disdain."

" And that one ? " demanded the stranger.

" Is Ralph de Gael, the cruel constable of the king within the Angles. Men say he hath a demon's heart shrined in a glorious form. His name is famed for cruelties. How many outraged maidens mourn the hour he ever crossed their path ! how many desolated homes hath not his fierce vengeance made ! " •

"And yet," observed her lover, with a peculiar smile, "you do not seem to fear him."

"I," replied the maiden, "am too high a mark for his fierce, lawless passion. He fears as well as hates my father, whose influence with the people would raise a storm to overwhelm him, should he dare to lift his eyes to a daughter of his house. Besides," she added, "I have never seen him."

It were useless to follow the subtle windings by which Ralph de Gael—for the stranger was no other than the dreaded Norman—entwined himself like a venomous snake around the pure heart of the fair girl, whom, from the first moment he beheld her, he destined to become his victim. With a refinement of wickedness, he resolved not only that her love should lead her to abandon her home, but that it should be made the means of destruction upon those she left behind. Of all the nobles in the Angles, Ulrick alone had dared to brave his tyranny, and protect the weaker vavasours and merchants from his exactions; he had even on more than one occasion appealed from his decision to the king, who, anxious to conciliate the support of one so powerful with his nation as our hero, had done prompt justice to his complaint : hence the bitter hatred which the unworthy tyrant felt ; and the triumph of inflicting a death-blow to the happiness of the man he feared was dearer to him than even the gratification of his selfish passion.

By degrees he led the wretched girl to contemplate the crime, at which at first she shuddered, with a lenient eye, and finally to consent to abandon her home to become his wife ; trusting, as many have trusted, to the honour of a villain, and to time and natural affection, to reconcile her offended parents to her choice. Could she have seen the real aim of the monster's project, she would have shrunk with horror from his words as from a demon's whisper ; but the poison was veiled by flowers, and the unwary victim fell.

Stanfield, like most of the mansions of the time, was well fortified and guarded—prepared to resist every attack from open force, and only to be taken by treachery or surprise. At sunset, the drawbridge was every evening regularly raised, nor ever permitted to be lowered, except by the command of the lord of the hold himself. The most accessible part of the hall was at the back, near the chapel, where a small postern, which was never fastened till a late hour, gave ingress to the building. Persuaded by the treacherous Ralph, Ethra, whose feelings had been worked on by his tears and despair, whose enthusiastic nature had lent itself to the excitement of the life of love and happiness which in glowing colours his eloquent tongue depicted, consented to secure the keys and fly with him. The night was fixed for the event ; he promised to come alone : we shall see how the false craven kept his word.

The last light had long disappeared from the towers of the hall, and every inmate save one retired to rest, when a party of men were seen to steal one by one from the neighbouring forest, and approach the moat at the back of the hall. Four of them launched a small boat, which they carried with them, upon the stream ; and their leader, clad no longer in his hunting garb, but cased in knightly steel, entered the frail bark, and directed it towards the fatal postern where the unhappy Ethra had promised to await him. Finding the postern open, he beckoned to two of his followers to pass over before he penetrated into the interior in order to seek his victim. Cautiously he traversed the great hall, attended by his minions, whom he directed to lower the drawbridge and admit the rest of his destroying band.

Scarcely was the order accomplished, when Ethra, who, with a touch of her better nature, had lingered to kiss her sleeping sister, and breathe a parting prayer at the door which led to her mother's chamber, descended the great staircase and entered the apartment. The villain flew to meet her and enfold her in his serpent embrace. "What means these men ? " whispered the trembling girl, terror-struck at the sight of a numerous band in possession of her ancient home. "What do they here ?—hast thou deceived me ? "

"They are here to protect our flight. Come," urged the impatient tyrant, "time is too precious to be lost. Should thy father wake, blood might be shed—the blood of him thou lovest—and all our hopes destroyed."

At this moment one of the men who had been stationed at the bridge entered the hall, and addressing Ralph de Gael by his title, told him to decide quickly, for that a light had been seen in one of the turrets, and that doubtless some of the inmates were alarmed.

"Ralph de Gael ! " shrieked the unhappy girl ; "then I am lost ! Hear me," she added, sinking on her knees : "let me be the only victim—trample on my heart—satiate thy hatred in my tears ; but spare the authors of my being—spare my innocent sister. God ! " she continued, convulsively, "betrayed, and through me ! "

Without a word the triumphant tyrant seized her in his arms, and giving her to his esquire, told him to remove her from the scene—an order which, despite her shrieks and struggles, he was preparing to obey, when the frantic girl burst from him, and seizing the cord which communicated with the alarm-bell, rang a peal which startled the unconscious sleepers from their rest.

"Monsters ! " she cried, "they shall not be butchered in their sleep. Ho ! Ulrick, to the rescue !—arm, arm !—the foe, the foe ! The Norman is upon us ! "

"Curses upon her fury ! " exclaimed Ralph, seizing her a second time, and placing her in the hands of a party of his men, who this time succeeded in bearing her over the drawbridge ; "away with her. Now, then," he added to his men, as the sound of their

·horses' hoofs assured him he was obeyed, "fire the castle; fire it on every side; let not one escape to tell the tale of Ralph de Gael's vengeance."

The alarm which Ethra in her despair had sounded unfortunately came too late. As fast as the men-at-arms descended they were butchered by their cowardly assailants, who from their place of ambush shot them off at their ease. Ulrick raged like a lion from tower to tower; every step of ground his enemies gained upon him was bought with blood. His position was a fearful one. A sea of flames—for the enormous oaken rafters of the hall had taken fire—waved over his head; and the shrieks of the women, mingled with the groans of the wounded and dying, added to the horror of the scene. Our unhappy hero was fiercely contending with Ralph de Gael and two of his esquires, when the voice of Matilda fell upon his ear. With a cry of agony, which burst from the deepest recess of his heart, he cast away his sword, and rushed up the burning staircase. The father and the husband only lived within him—the warrior was extinct. As he reached the corridor, which led to his mother and Matilda's apartment, a burning mass of wood and stone fell from the ceiling, and barred his further passage. Vainly, with his naked hands, he tossed the blazing beams aside, till the seared flesh fell from his fingers. The barrier was too solid to be removed by his single strength, and the wretched man heard the last shrieks of his adored wife and mother as the crumbling roof fell with the crash of thunder upon that part of the building where they slept. Ulrick, in his despair, would have leaped into the blazing gulf, and shared in the destruction of those most dear to him, had not a new interest in life been suddenly awakened. His youngest child, the lovely Myrra, a girl about eight years old, had, in the first terror of the alarm, hastened from the chamber where she slept, and thus escaped the fearful death of her mother and the Countess Edith. To raise her in his arms, to clasp her to his aching breast, was the impulse of an instant; he felt that, wretched as he was, life had still one tie for which he wished to live; and catching up a blazing brand, he directed his steps to the chapel, from whence a vaulted passage, could he but once obtain the entrance to it, conducted to a place of safety. As a son, a parent, and a husband, our hero had been sufficiently tried that night; and Heaven, which had permitted the crimes of that fearful hour for its own wise purposes, preserved him to avenge them. The fugitive, with his weeping burden, reached the place of concealment in silence and in safety, when the last tower of the once stately hold of Stanfield had fallen a prey to the devouring flames, and nothing remained of the abode of hospitality and virtue but a smouldering mass of ruin.

Ralph de Gael, attended by his followers loaded with plunder, returned to Norwich. Good men cursed them on their way, and

even the lawless and the vicious thanked Heaven that their souls
at least were free from such a deed. The rage and indignation of
the Saxon nobles was deep and loud ; but, in losing Ulrick,
unfortunately, they had lost the only leader upon whom they could
rely. The triumphant oppressor loudly proclaimed that he had
proofs of a meditated rebellion in his hands—called upon the
Norman barons to join him with their vassals, provisioned his
strong hold, Norwich Castle—a fortress almost impregnable before
the invention of artillery—and prepared to act vigorously upon the
defensive. Thus weeks and even months passed away, and Ulrick's
most ardent friends, who all believed him dead, agreed to await
the return of the king from Normandy, whither he had gone to
invade the duchy of his gallant but unfortunate brother.

It was long, very long, ere the unhappy Ethra, whose existence
her betrayer carefully guarded as a secret from all, recovered from
the raging fever into which the events of that fearful night had
plunged her. Youth and care ultimately prevailed, and the poor
girl, the shadow of her former self, was at last pronounced free
from danger ; it is true, that with time her health, and even the
beauty for which she had been remarkable, gradually returned,
but her mind remained partially obscured, nor was it till years
afterwards that it recovered the full vigour and energy of its early
tone. Weakened, as she was, in spirit as well as body—friendless,
and in the power of an unprincipled villain, whom, despite his
crimes, she still loved—those who know the human heart will
wonder little that Ethra, won by his prayers and tears, his oaths of
penitence and eternal love, consented to become his in the presence
of a few friends in whom he could confide. The marriage rites
were celebrated. It was neither to her birth nor virtues the
unhappy girl was indebted for the consideration which made her
his wife instead of mistress, but to his thirst for her possessions.
The heiress of Stanfield was too rich a prize to be permitted to
escape him, or to be obtained by other means than marriage.

The wedding feast was cold and solitary, as Ralph and his chosen
friends caroused in the great hall of the castle. The golden cup
was in his hands as he was about to pledge his guests. The
pride of successful villainy flashed in his eye, and seemed to say,
"World ! I may brave thee now ; " when a herald, wearing the
Royal arms upon his vest, entered his presence unannounced, and
summoned him in the name of his liege lord to appear before his
Court in ten days to answer for the crimes of murder and treason.

"And who is my accuser ? " he demanded, with a haughty
smile.

"Ulrick of Stanfield," replied the herald in a solemn voice.

The cup fell from the villain's hand untasted, and the unhappy
Ethra was borne senseless to her chamber.

CHAPTER XXII.

AFTER the unhappy lord of Stanfield the most powerful chief of the Angles was Arad, a noble whose large possessions and high military reputation gave him a merited influence with the warlike and still but half-subdued Saxon race. To him, as to his surest friend, Ulrick fled on the destruction of his once happy home, and was, with his infant Myrra—the only living pledge, as he believed, of his Matilda's love—secretly received and sheltered until the raging fever, brought on by bodily as well as mental suffering, yielded to time and the devoted care by which he was surrounded. All but his host believed him dead. The poor wept for him, the good lamented him, and none but the wicked triumphed in his fall. The generous Arad felt the wrongs of the suffering man as keenly as though the brand of the Norman savage had desolated his own hearth ; and in the indignation of his honest nature would have summoned his countrymen to arms to avenge them, had not the precautions of the tyrant in proclaiming the pretended conspiracy, and calling upon the great vassals of the Crown for aid, deprived him of every chance of doing so with success. The rough nature of the old franklin frequently melted as he listened to the wild ravings of his guest calling with the most endearing epithets upon his murdered wife and eldest born, and reproaching them for their delay in coming to soothe him in his agony. At such moments his host would bring the little Myrra, and place her in her distracted father's arms. True to nature's instinct, even in the most violent paroxysms of his grief Ulrick recognised his child. Comparative calmness would gradually succeed to frenzy, and burning tears and passionate kisses relieve his o'erfraught heart. Sometimes he would rave of the monk of Croydon, who had predicted his unhappy destiny, and adjure him by the double name of priest and king to revoke his fearful prophecy ; demanding, with almost infantine simplicity, what crime he had committed to merit such a fate. As time, however, rolled on, these outbreaks of excitement became less frequent : a calm deep melancholy succeeded to the fever of his heart and brain, and if his tears unconsciously fell upon his slumbering child, they were tears which soothed, and not inflamed, his sorrows. Well was it for Ralph de Gael that the existence of the unhappy Ethra was unsuspected beyond the limits of his castle ; for the knowledge of her being in the hands of his enemy would have restored to the bereaved father the energy of action which slumbered but was not extinct. His horror and indignation would have been like the volcano's wrath, or the destroying angel's breath. As it was, he decided, before he attempted to rouse his friends to arms, and plunge his beloved country in all the miseries of civil war, to appeal to Henry's justice for redress ; and, not till that should fail, to draw the sword to avenge his private wrongs. As soon, therefore, as the monarch's return from his expedition in Normandy was known, Ulrick once more directed his pilgrim steps towards London. How different were his feelings from those which animated him on his first journey ! He was then the happy husband of an adoring wife ; full of the confidence of youth—its hopes and bright imaginings—where were they now ? Buried in the ashes of his once peaceful home ; extinct for ever in an unhallowed grave. As the solitary wanderer passed along, bowed and changed by sorrow, friends and foes, as they gazed upon his pale cheek and emaciated form, failed to recognise the once gallant lord of Stanfield.

The result of his appeal to the king did not belie the opinion which Ulrick had formed of Henry's gratitude to the preserver of his life ; both the monarch and his queen listened with indignation and interest to the story of his sorrows. A herald was instantly despatched to Norwich to summon Ralph de Gael to answer for his crimes before the Royal presence. The citation, as our readers may remember, fell like a thunder-clap upon the assassin at the impious banquet which he gave to celebrate his nuptials with the unhappy Ethra, whose ill-requited love had been the means of bringing desolation upon the home of her youth and all who loved her, and whose crime was destined to be yet fearfully avenged.

Ralph de Gael was not a man to remain idle under the accusation which remained suspended over him ; he was too much accustomed to mix in the political intrigues of the day, too well acquainted with courts and courtiers, not to know that a falling favourite has seldom friends. Many of his countrymen had envied him his influence with Henry, and the almost independent command which the monarch had entrusted to him. He felt that an instant and complete justification of the crimes he had committed could alone prevent his fall, and he resolved to recoil from no means, no matter how odious, to clear himself in the eyes of his sovereign—a point only to be accomplished by forging proofs of the pretended conspiracy of the oppressed Saxons to throw off the yoke of their Norman masters ; for he well knew that to alarm Henry for the security of his crown, and the nobles for the safety of their ill-acquired possessions in England, was to assure himself of oblivion for the past, and full indemnity for the future, for any act of tyranny or spoliation his avarice or licentious passion might lead him to commit.

Like most of the great religious establishments of the age, the monks of the cathedral were celebrated for the beauty of their illuminated manuscripts and the skill of the laborious writers, who spent their lives in multiplying those precious works of art which at the present day form the pride of collectors and the glory of our libraries. Amongst the brothers the most renowned

for his skill was a certain Father Onfroy, a man whose time was
equally devoted to religion and the exercise of his pencil.
Although not many years professed, none knew his name or
country, or the reasons which had driven him from the world :
the charitable attributed his retirement to sorrows ; those who
envied his renown as an illuminator darkly hinted that it was
caused by crime—an opinion which his unsocial disposition and
reserved manner, to say nothing of the care with which on all
occasions he wore his capuchin over his features, gradually
obtained credence. His labours were incessant ; he seemed to fly
to them as to a shelter from himself, or as a penance rather than
an occupation. His hours were equally divided between prayer
and the exercise of his voluntary labour ; the only relaxation
which he permitted himself was an occasional evening walk upon
the banks of the quiet river which bounded the domain of his
convent.

Two days after the arrival of the herald at the castle the solitary
was missing. Great search was made by order of the prior and
chapter ; the stream was dragged for miles, rewards offered, but all
in vain ; before the unhappy man again saw the light of heaven
years were fated to elapse.

As my readers have doubtless surmised, Father Onfroy had been
secretly carried off, and was a prisoner in the castle, to serve the
guilty purposes of Ralph de Gael, who hesitated at no means,
however vile, which were likely to insure his safety.

Amongst the many spoils of Stanfield Hall which the midnight
marauders had carried off, was a chest of deeds, charters, and
letters, the latter chiefly in the handwriting of Ulrick, sent by him
to his anxious wife during the siege of Pevensey. These were sufficient for the tyrant's purpose. He doubted not but that by threats
and promises he could so work upon the hopes and terrors of his
skilful prisoner, that he should forge him proofs of a conspiracy in
a writing so like to Ulrick's that even the affectionate wife to
whom the models were addressed would have pronounced them
genuine. In this, however, he calculated erroneously. Father
Onfroy rejected the proposition with indignation ; nor was it till
the torture had been twice employed that he consented to lend his
assistance to the fraud, which was to be the signal of our hero's
further ruin.

"It will not thrive with thee, Ralph de Gael ! " exclaimed the
monk, as with a trembling hand he gave his gaoler a list of the
materials necessary to tinge the paper, and give an appearance of
age to the forgeries ; "it will not thrive with thee. Like thee, I
have been a man of violence and blood ; but Heaven hath smitten
me, as it will smite thee in the pride of thy security, the triumph
of thy guilt. Repent ere repentance comes too late."

Under the threat of the torture, which de Gael was even obliged to repeat, the monk at length completed his odious task, and the proofs damning to Ulrick's fame were at last in the hands of his bitter enemy. True, they were forgeries ; but who was to detect them, whilst the only living witness was a captive, consigned, despite his employer's oath to the contrary, to the deepest dungeon of Norwich Castle ?

The morning at last dawned on which Ralph de Gael was to meet his accuser face to face, in the presence of the king and council. The courtiers frowned or turned their backs upon him as he traversed the court-yard of the Tower, where Henry held his court. In the certitude of his triumph, the villain met their silent reproach with a brow as haughty as their own, for he well knew that his safety depended not upon their favour.

" Weather-cocks ! " he muttered to himself ; " in an hour you will fawn upon the man whom now ye affect to despise, and whose favour ye so long have envied. My safety depends upon myself, not on such weak instruments."

With a firm step he ascended the stairs conducting to the privy chamber, and found himself confronted with his outraged victim and the sovereign whose confidence he had so unworthily abused. It required all our hero's firmness to endure the presence of the man whose crimes had widowed his heart of happiness, and made his home a desert.

Reckless as the Norman nobles generally were in their schemes of oppressing the unhappy Saxons, there was a point at which even their fierce license stopped. The midnight surprise and wholesale slaughter of Stanfield filled even their stern natures with horror ; added to which, Matilda was of their race, the daughter of one of the oldest of their companions in arms, related by blood to many. And it was evident, from the cold greeting with which many returned his salutation to the assembly, that most were disposed against him.

" We command you, Ralph de Gael," said Henry, " to answer to a charge which, if true, will leave a stain upon the Norman name which not your worthless blood can wipe away—to answer for midnight robbery and murder ; for assailing, like some midnight thief, cowardly and in disguise, the castle of a faithful subject, giving his house to flames, his heart to desolation. Ulrick of Stanfield," he added, turning to the accuser, " produce your charge."

All eyes were turned upon our hero, who, with a countenance flushed with emotion, and a heart lacerated by memory, related the destruction of his home and the loss of his wife and child. " Face to face," he added, with an expression of scorn beneath which De Gael writhed, " the villain dared not meet me. His craven heart, like some vile thief's, bold only 'neath the veil of night, shrank at the thought of manly open combat, where knightly swords, and not the assassin's steel, decide men's quarrels. He hated too, as

well as feared me ; for my voice, as all here know, was ever raised
against his exactions and oppressions ; my home the shelter of his
victims."

"Go on," said the accused, with a sarcastic sneer ; "anon I'll
answer thee."

"Not for my home destroyed," resumed Ulrick, with a burst of
natural eloquence, "not for the plundered treasures of my house ;
but for those dearer treasures of the heart—those ties no wealth
can purchase or after-life renew,—for my murdered mother, wife,
and child, I call for justice on him ; I demand it in the name of
the monarch whose confidence he hath abused, and the blest spirits
whose voices long ere this have been raised against him at the bar
of Heaven. If he fails to clear himself, I demand judgment, a
felon's judgment, on his accursed head ; if he dispute my charge,
the knightly combat in the lists against him."

All were surprised at the cool effrontery with which Ralph de
Gael listened to the overwhelming accusation against him, and
rose to refute it. Taking a packet of letters from his bosom, he
threw them on the council-board, saying, with a haughty tone,
"There lies my justification ; let my accuser dispute it, if he can.
For the loss of the innocents who were dear to him, I mourn ; but,
statesmen and soldiers, you, noble lords, can well understand the
stern necessity which, when the kingdom was in peril, led me to
draw the sword. Read, and be convinced."

"What means the traitor ? " demanded Ulrick, whose astonishment was only equalled by the king's.

"Are these" said the wily Norman, pointing to the letters,
"your handwriting ? "

"Certainly," answered our hero, slightly glancing over the well
imitated superscription, "the hand is mine ; but what wouldst
thou infer from that ? "

"You hear," exclaimed the triumphant villain, "he hath
acknowledged them ! Read, noble lords, the proofs of his vile
treason ; a plot to sacrifice each Norman noble in his hold—to
drive us from the land our swords have won, not by open fight,
but by assassination. The means are well contrived, the scheme is
deeply laid. Now ask me why I crushed the serpent in its very
den ; why I gave to offended Justice's sword the plotting murderers
of your wives and children. Those papers are my answer."

Ulrick, overwhelmed with horror, heard one by one the artful
forgeries read. Their author had well calculated on the interests
and passions of his judges, the most influential of whom were
singled out by name, as the first victims of the intended outbreak.

The indignation of Henry was as unbounded as his interest for
the injured Saxon had been sincere.

"What answer," he demanded "makes the lord of Stanfield to
these proofs against him ?."

"That they are forgeries!" exclaimed Ulrick, recovering his self-possession, "mean, cowardly, forgeries. My life disproves them; and my sword shall wring confession from my accuser's lips, let but the king grant the combat."

"It may not be," said the chancellor, rising; "the Saxon already hath avowed the writing his. What faith can be placed upon his truth who, in the same breath, owns and disowns his acts as interest and his safety prompts him? The sword only may be appealed to," he added, "where material proofs are wanting; but we have evidence which leaves no doubt upon the mind of Justice—the traitor's own confession."

"Hear me, lords," interrupted Ulrick, "not for my life—sorrows have made it worthless; but for my honour, that nobler part of man which not the tomb can hold or time destroy. I do protest my innocence. The very frankness with which I owned those letters might have convinced you they were forgeries. Compare my character with my accuser's. Would he who stoops to murder shrink from lying? Would the midnight thief hesitate at any act, however vile, to screen his worthless life? My own and my outraged country's cause," he added, "might drive me to draw the sword; but to become an assassin, never, never. The thought was worthy only of the fiend whose soul conceived it; mine scorns and rejects the cowardly accusation."

"You hear him," said his accuser, with a cold, satisfied smile; "the traitor half-avows his treason. But I have one proof more; a witness none will venture to dispute—one on whose testimony I place my life and honour. Prince," he continued, in well-affected humility, "do thou decide between us; to thee the writing of this man is known; thy clerkly knowledge cannot be deceived—do thou decide between us."

The piece of flattery was well-timed; for Henry was vain of the title which men already gave him of "Beauclerc," in allusion to his skill in letters. Bending over the papers, the monarch perused them attentively, and a shade of sorrow and regret passed over his brow as the last fell from his hands.

"On my kingly word," he exclaimed with a sigh, "I do pronounce them real."

"Enough!" said the chancellor, a haughty Norman, devoted to the interests of his countrymen, and, like most hackneyed statesmen, ever ready to judge the worst of human nature. "We can no longer hesitate; the constable is fully justified in all that he hath done—the Saxon is the traitor. Sire," he added in an under-tone to his still hesitating sovereign, "no weakness now; private friendship must not trifle with the safety of a crown, the honour of a nation. The culprit must to prison. Leave him to the council. The rack may wring from him the confession of his crimes, the names of his accomplices."

Henry shuddered ; for it was not without a struggle that he
resolved to consign the preserver of his life to the tender mercies
of his nobles.   Despite the apparent proofs, something whispered
him that our hero might be innocent ; but policy commanded alike
the suppression of his feelings and the concealment of his opinion.
Bowing his head in token of assent, without bestowing a parting
glance upon Ulrick, he quitted the council-chamber to inform the
queen of the unexpected turn which the accusation had taken ; for
the Saxon princess, whose influence over him was unbounded, felt
deeply for the wrongs of her outraged countryman, whose gallant
bearing had won her good opinion, and whose treachery it was
difficult to persuade her to believe.

"No !" exclaimed the generous woman, when Henry related to
her De Gael's charge, and the proofs by which he had supported
it ; "let who will pronounce him guilty, I cannot believe it.
Truth dwells on the unhappy Ulrick's tongue ; his life belies the
deed : I would almost pledge my own that he is innocent !"

"Matilda," said her husband gravely, "thou judgest warmly.
Thou, too, art a Saxon."

"Have I loved thee less?" replied his wife, turning her blue
eyes upon him reproachfully.

Not for an instant could the affectionate prince endure the look ;
folding his arms around her, he imprinted a kiss on her fair, open
brow, and begged, with all a lover's earnestness, to be forgiven.

"I fain would think like you," he said ; "but proofs are strong
against him.   Were I convinced of his innocence—nay, had I but
a doubt that he is guilty—despite the council and the angry peers,
I'd interpose and save him."

"And you will save him, Henry," said the queen.   "You owe
him life for life : remember, even if guilty, he preserved yours.
What would be your remorse—your future agony and shame—if
time should prove him guiltless ?"

"Perhaps," whispered the monarch, "there is a way to save him.
We will think more of this ; and trust me, love, the Saxon Ulrick
shall not fare the worse for thy sweet prayer and good opinion of
him."

On the departure of Henry from the council-chamber the
unfortunate lord of Stanfield had been removed, by command of
the haughty chancellor, to one of the subterranean dungeons
beneath the White Tower, close to the water-passage known by the
name of the Traitor's Gate.   Too proud to descend to reproaches
or entreaties—too hopeless to offer further vindication, our hero
suffered himself to be conveyed to his damp cell in silence.   To
him death had no terrors ; for his heart was already ashes, and, but
for the stain upon his name, he could have contemplated his
approaching fate, if not with joy, at least with resignation.   Even
in his prison his heart beat lighter than his accuser's ; for, despite

[THE CONFESSION AND THE PARDON.]

his momentary triumph, something whispered to De Gael that truth would yet be heard; and even while listening to the congratulations of the courtiers who once more flocked around him, and the compliments of the members of the council, his spirit sank within him. The coldness of the queen during the evening banquet to which he was invited was remarked by all; she shuddered visibly as his lips pressed her reluctantly extended hand; and it was clear to all, however the king and nobles might esteem his truth, that Matilda's heart was enlisted in the cause of her unhappy countryman.

At an early hour her majesty quitted the circle, and her departure was followed by an encouraging smile from her husband, who remained, however, for some time after her, in deep conversation with William de Neville, the aged Constable of the Tower, a man whose fidelity to his prince was above all suspicion, and on whom Henry looked as on a second father.

"I'll do it, sire," whispered the old man, hesitatingly; "but 'tis against my judgment. Heaven grant we both repent not of it; but be it as you will."

As the knight concluded his remonstrance, he bowed and left the presence. With his departure a weight seemed to be removed from Henry's soul. Calling for a cup of wine, he drained it to the dregs in honour of his queen, and many a gallant lip and heart responded to the pledge.

Whilst the banquet in the great hall was at its height—for the Tower, at the period of our tale, was both a fortress and a palace—two persons, closely disguised, were threading the cold, damp passages which conducted to the prison of our hero. One was the aged Constable, to whom alone the clue was confided of the various secret entrances and means of egress from the prison, used more frequently for purposes of tyranny and death than freedom to the unfortunate and innocent. His companion was the generous queen, whose prayers and tears had won from Henry the liberty of his prisoner.

On entering the dungeon, they found our hero sleeping on the ground as calmly as an infant sleeps upon its mother's breast. The Constable was surprised, for it was not often that his captives slept.

"And can this man be guilty?" whispered Matilda to her companion, as she gazed upon Ulrick's placid features. Such, believe me, is not the sleep of those whose waking thoughts are of murder and of treason. I should like to compare the Saxon's slumbers with those of his accuser."

"'Tis hard to judge," replied the knight; "for who can read the heart of man?—it is a mystery even to the angels nearest the throne of God. He who framed alone can comprehend it. But time presses; morning must not dawn upon our enterprise and see

A A 2

it unaccomplished. 'Tis strange," he added, with a smile, "that William de Neville, who bore the Conqueror's standard at Hastings, should be aiding a Saxon to escape from Norman justice !—few would believe it."

"Say, rather," replied his companion, "aiding thy king to pay his debt of gratitude. Yon sleeper saved his life, and all of Rolla's race are not alike ungrateful."

"Enough, 'tis Henry's will," observed the old man ; "that hath ever been my law. What ho !" he added, in a louder tone, "Ulrick, sir knight, awake."

The sleeping man slowly opened his eyes, not with that sudden start with which unquiet guilt springs from its restless couch, but with the composure which a fearless conscience gives.

"What would you ?" he exclaimed. "Hath the night passed so soon ? Well, I am ready."

"Ready for what ?" demanded the Constable, with a look of surprise.

"For aught which pleases Heaven," replied Ulrick ; "for beyond the tortures and the cruelties with which man goads his fellows, I behold the spirit's triumph and the freed soul's emancipation, plains of eternal light and waving palms ; long-silent voices whisper in mine ear, ' Welcome at last to peace.' "

"To liberty as well !" exclaimed Matilda, raising her veil. "The path is free, the dungeon door unbarred. Away at once. Use fortune while thou mayst."

"The queen !" said the astonished prisoner, gracefully bending his knee ; "what errand brings an angel's presence to this dreary dungeon ? "

"To pay the debt thy grateful monarch owes—to set thee free," replied the generous woman ; "to preserve a father for his helpless child, an avenger for the outraged Saxon honour."

Ulrick's natural hesitation to fly and leave a branded name behind him was overruled by the allusion to his infant Myrra, and the hope of one day returning to prove his innocence and avenge his murdered race. He suffered himself, therefore, to be conducted by the aged constable to the boat which by Henry's orders waited at the Tower-stairs to convey him to Normandy, where he soon afterwards joined a band of Crusaders on their march to Palestine ; where, in knightly action under the burning sun of Syria, he endeavoured for a while to forget the wrongs and sorrows which drove him from his native land.

With Ulrick's disappearance the last barrier to the triumph of the infamous Ralph de Gael was removed ; for whatever might be Henry's secret opinion of his services, and the truth of the conspiracy which he had alleged against the Saxons, he was too politic to express it; seeing that it was firmly believed by the great Norman barons, to whom he was chiefly indebted for his crown, and whom (such was their power) it might have been dangerous to offend.

    *   *   *   *   *   *

Ten years had elapsed since our hero's departure from England, during which period the oppression and tyranny of the worthless governor of the Angles had risen beyond human forbearance. The eyes of the suffering people, vavasours and franklins, were, in the absence of Ulrick, all turned towards Arad, whose watchful prudence had hitherto defeated every attempt to surprise or to subdue him. Men's minds were in this unsettled state when it became gradually whispered that midnight assemblies were being held on Monkshold Heath, and in the Druid's cave at Whitlingham, in which many of the inhabitants of the city joined. These rumours were not long in reaching the ears of the suspicious Ralph, whose spies were everywhere, and he provisioned the stronghold of Norwich Castle in expectation of the approaching outbreak.

Amongst the few national festivals which the oppressed Saxons still continued to celebrate was the anniversary of St. Edward, on which occasion the elder nobles met to exchange the courtesies of life, and the younger ones and commons to indulge in knightly sports, archery, wrestling, and quarter-staff—exercises in which few peoples could excel them. Arad, attended by a more numerous train than usual, was one of the last to reach the heath where the assembly was held. The spot marked out was an undulating plain broken by hills, now forming part of the inclosed lands of Thorpe, extending from the chapel of St. William in the wood down to the river's bank. The arrival of the man whom the oppressed Saxons looked upon as their leader was hailed with shouts of joy, and " Long live the valiant Arad," and " Success to the Lord of Ormsby," echoed far and near.

The aged chief was attended by his only son and heir Edward, and his nephew Ethwold of the Rath, a young man to whom he had been guardian.

It was observed that the young men were unremitting in their attentions to a fair girl who rode in the midst of the train, and who was received by the more aged Saxons with tokens of affection and respect. The maiden was no other than Myrra, who, from the period of her father's exile, had shared the home and paternal love of Arad, and whom rumour had long since assigned as the destined bride of either his son or nephew, for both the young men loved her, and hence the looks of jealous rivalry which occasionally passed between them ; but the open-hearted, generous Edward was evidently the favoured lover. A shade of sadness passed over the features of the exile's daughter as she returned the greetings of her friends, for to her the projected outbreak was no secret, and she knew not how soon the home of her adoption might be made a

desert, and the friends who had protected her reduced, like her
gallant father, to misery and exile.

As the day proceeded, the people noted with great satisfaction
that one by one their leaders slowly retired to the depths of the
wood which skirted the place of their assembly, to deliberate, they
fondly trusted, on the means of redressing the wrongs beneath
which they groaned, and throwing off a yoke as humiliating as it
was burthensome to them. Let it not be imagined that all the
nobles and franklins who were present at what might not inappro-
priately be called the council of the Angles were unanimous in
their views. Some were restrained by their doubts of success, or
the more worldly consideration of personal security; others were
content to live on any terms, however vile or degrading.

Considerable uneasiness existed amongst the wavering and timid
at the presence of a tall war-worn pilgrim, who stood by Arad's
side, and to whom alone, of all the assembly, he seemed personally
known. The red cross on his shoulder denoted he had served in
Palestine; and the golden spurs upon his heels vouched for his
knightly rank. Some whispered that he was a spy, a supposition
instantly rejected by those who gazed upon his gallant bearing, and
the evident recognition of him by their brother nobles.

The business of the day was opened by Arad, who, in a speech
replete with energy, drew their attention to the condition of their
unhappy country, to the continued oppressions of Ralph de Gael,
and the little hope of redress at the hands of the monarch, who,
since the death of his Saxon queen, Matilda, had given himself
entirely up to his Norman ministers and councillors. "Are we,"
continued the aged chief, "once more to draw the sword for Saxon
independence, or yield our necks, without one further effort, to the
debasing yoke our masters place upon us? Shall we decide to live
as freemen, or to die as slaves?"

There was a pause. The assembly felt the importance of the
reply they were called upon to make, and remained silent. Ethwold
of the Rath, the speaker's nephew, was the first to break it. Though
not naturally a coward, he was selfish. Hitherto the brand of the
Conqueror had not assailed his hearth—added to which, the importance which his rival cousin would obtain in Myrra's eyes,
should the insurrection prove successful, at once determined him.
Briefly and confidently he spoke of the hopelessness, the madness
of the attempt, and called upon the meeting to disperse, ere the
knowledge of their designs should give their rulers fresh pretext
for further spoliation.

With a triumphant smile Ethwold remarked the effect his speech
produced. Many of the vavasours and petty nobles were retiring,
when the deep-toned voice of the pilgrim arrested their ignoble
purpose.

"Men!" he exclaimed, dashing into the midst of them. "Can

ye be men, and tamely thus resign all chance of freedom ? Are ye so debased, ye cast the sword aside and kiss your chains ? Prove yourselves worthy of your fathers' fame, and free your daughters from the Norman's lust. Your future sons, drawing the love of freedom from their mothers' breasts, nobly shall defend the rights their fathers bled to win, the stream of life with nobler impulse beat, and one brave deed regenerate our race."

Few as were the impassioned words of the speaker, they found an echo in the hearts even of those who wavered. Men crowded around him—the young with enthusiasm, the old in admiration. But Ethwold was not a man to be easily silenced : he was one of those who, if not eloquent, at least are plausible.

"Who is this stranger," he demanded, "who takes upon him to give lessons unto men and nobles ? Beware," he added, "lest this seeming zeal should hide a traitor."

"Traitor !" repeated the pilgrim. "England! my own, my father's land, have I for thee wandered o'er Asia's burning sands, or froze amid the horrors of the North, thus to be branded with traitor's name ? Hear me, Saxons," he continued, "'tis not the first time ye have hung upon my words, or followed my broad pennon to the field. Exiled for freedom and my country's rights, for years I wandered 'neath a burning sun, yet felt it not—the fire was in my brain ; oft o'er the pathless deserts of the East my steps have strayed—the simoom harmed me not ; in storm, in danger, in the battle's heat, I courted death in vain. Once, when Despair usurped fair Reason's throne, I gained the craggy mountain's topmost height, and would have plunged into the abyss beneath, but at that moment some spirit whispered 'England might be free !' My heart, my sword, were all my country's claim, and Ulrick would not rob her of her right."

The shout of the astonished Saxons at the announcement of their banished hero's name rang far and wide. Many a gallant heart beat with admiration at the sight of him, and eager hands were stretched to welcome him. In the midst of their enthusiasm, however, a voice was heard at whose sound all gave way. The youthful Myrra had heard her father's name. Gliding like a spirit of light and beauty through the circle which surrounded him, she sank upon her knees, her voice shaking with emotion : all she could find strength to utter was :

"Your blessing—your blessing, father—for your long-parted child."

As the stern warrior gazed upon the kneeling seraph at his feet, the thoughts of other days and other ties came over him. Placing his hand upon her head, he answered, while tears coursed each other down his manly cheek :

"Sweet as the dew which fell on Israel's race my blessing rest upon thee, thou only blossom of my marriage bed the hand of tyranny hath spared me. Look on her, chiefs," he added, addressing the franklins, who had respectfully drawn back not to intrude upon so sacred a meeting; "say, should a form like this give birth to slaves? should beauties rare as these become the Norman's prey? Here, on the hills where free your father's trod, I call upon you, in the sacred name of freedom—call you to burst wide your bonds —cast back to earth the fetters which enthral you—renounce the oppressor's yoke, and rise erect and free as God and nature's chartered laws have made you."

One wild enthusiastic cry for liberty was the result of the appeal ; men drew their s.vords, and swore no longer to hold their lives at their masters' pleasures; even Ethwold, carried away by the feelings of the moment, joined in the shout for war.

"Noble Ulrick," he exclaimed, "forgive me. I knew not the nature my suspicions wronged. Let Myrra's hand become the pledge of unity between us; my fortune and my friends will then be thine ; my vassals know no other leader, my inexperienced years no other guide."

It needed not the pale cheek of Myrra, or the ill-suppressed indignation of the youthful Edward, whose imploring eyes were fixed on Ulrick, to induce his generous nature how to decide. Drawing the trembling girl yet nearer to his heart, as if to shield her even from the outrage of such a proposition, her father answered with a bitterness and scorn to which in other years his lips were strangers :

"Yield her to thee ! Consign her pure and spotless to thy arms ! Rather would I strike her to my feet ! rather behold her perish in the pile in which her sister fell, than yield her beauties to a willing slave ! Go," he added, with an expression of, if possible, increased contempt,—"go, count thy gold, and view thy hoards increase ! Breed sons to swell thy Norman master's train, and daughters to be victims of their lust ! Go, live securely, but thy nation's scorn ! "

Slowly, and with a look of unutterable hate, Ethwold withdrew from the assembly, the eyes of which were turned reproachfully upon him. Curses were on his lip, yet he spake them not. Revenge, like a vulture, was gnawing at his heart ; and he resolved, even at the sacrifice of those who shared his blood, it should be gratified.

The same day saw him closeted with Ralph de Gael, to whom, however, with the usual cunning of his nature, he only half-confided the danger which threatened him : spoke of the meditated rising of the Saxons; but forbore to name Ulrick as their chief, promising, however, to deliver him into the hands of a party of his men, provided he might retain his daughter as his sole reward. The double traitor was in some degree forced to this ; for, without the aid of the Norman soldiers, he knew it would be impossible to complete the outrage he meditated, as he well knew no Saxon could be found to lay a hand upon the lord of Stanfield—such was the influence of his name—the love which his gallant fame and devotion to his country had inspired. The compact was accepted, the necessary force placed at his disposal, and Ethwold retired from the castle bound to the bidding of his master like a worthless hound.

The name of Ulrick, and the shouts which welcomed it, spread far and near amongst the excited Saxons. The games were rapidly broken up, and the serfs and peasants burst in upon the circle hitherto reserved for their masters; all were eager once more to gaze upon the man whose name had been the watchword of their youth, whose arm the protection of their homes, and whose memory in their grateful hearts had survived even his services. In the enthusiasm of the moment all distinction of rank was forgotten, and it became necessary, men were so mingled together, for the leaders to retire to mature their plans ere the news of Ulrick's return should be noised abroad—a secret which, after the public recognition of his person, could not be long concealed. In the hurried council which followed, it was decided that the exile should at once proceed to Stanfield to raise the ancient vassals of his house, who, writhing under the exactions of their new master, would rise to a man, and strike for their ancient lord and freedom.

That very evening, near the old cross where the road divided from Cotessey to Wynmondham, an aged woman, leaning on an oaken staff, might have been seen watching the setting sun, whose last rays kissed the graceful spire of the cathedral, and crowned with a flood of golden light its splendid pinnacles; her quick, restless eye was directed to a copse of stunted beech and brushwood near, from which a steel-clad Norman man-at-arms might occasionally be seen peeping, casting down the road impatient glances, such as the hungry wolf might cast upon its loitering prey.

"Ay," muttered the old woman, resuming her occupation of gathering herbs, "wait; he will not tarry long. The noble stag and timid fawn are both within the toils. First, the mother," she added, counting with her fingers, "then the wife and eldest born, and now the sire, and the last shoot of his doomed, blighted race. Blood will be shed. I feel—I scent it. I saw the corpse-lights flitter in the ruins of Stanfield—a sure token of death in its lordly line. He comes, the victim to the sacrifice—the eagle to the archer's aim."

At this moment Ethwold and several of his followers left their ambush to secrete themselves behind the cross, in order that they might secure their prey between two nets, and so cut off all chance of escape.

"What dost thou here, wretched hag?" exclaimed the haughty Saxon. "Away! we want no spy upon our deeds. Hence, ere my archers lash thee with their bow-strings till the flesh falls from thy accursed bones."

"There needs small wit to guess the deed," replied the beldame, sharply, "when Saxon joins with Norman to oppress his country. Hell is sure to register it, and Heaven to punish it."

A laugh from the men-at-arms stung the traitor at whom the bitter sneer was levelled. Striking the speaker with the back of his weapon brutally over the temple, he once more bade her begone.

"Ethwold," screamed the hag, in a voice rendered painfully sharp by passion, as she wiped the blood which trickled down her haggard features, "thou art a doomed man! Saxon and Norman shall alike reject thee; the gallows-tree shall end thy vile career; the pie shall chatter on thy fleshless skull, and the winds whistle through thy unburied bones. Craven and traitor, the curse of her whose words ne'er fall to earth be on thee! Thou hast struck a woman; by a woman's hand thy fate shall be accomplished."

Ere the astonished Ethwold could give orders to secure her, the hag had fled into the wood, whose intricate windings forbade all hope of a pursuit.

It was with bitter, sad reflections that Ulrick and his daughter, whose tears had drawn from her father a reluctant permission to accompany him to Stanfield, approached the once happy home of love and childhood. A thousand recollections rose in the mind of each as they remarked the well remembered cross which divided the two domains. Both, as by a mutual impulse, reined their steeds to repeat an Ave! for the safe conclusion of their journey. The action was too favourable for the intentions of the ambushed ruffians to escape their notice. In an instant the travellers were surrounded, and the male rider disarmed.

"What would you, masters?" he exclaimed, taking them for robbers, "gold? I have but little, and to that ye are freely welcome. What," he added, seeing that they were about to bind his arms, "would ye offer violence to a pilgrim of the Cross?"

"Ethwold!" shrieked Myrra, as the eyes of the triumphant villain encountered hers, "betrayed! betrayed!"

At the name of the perjured Saxon, the fearful truth flashed at once in all its horror upon the mind of the unhappy father. Bursting with a frantic effort from the men-at-arms who held him, he sprang upon the traitor, whose life, unarmed though the indignant Ulrick was, would have fallen a just sacrifice, had not numbers overpowered him.

"It is accomplished," murmured our hero to himself; "man may not struggle with his destiny."

There was something so calm and dignified in the resignation of their captive, so touching in the tears and the affectionate caresses of his fair child, that even the rude Normans felt moved, and conducted them to the city with respect and silence.

Ethwold, to avoid being seen with the party, and his treason to his countrymen thereby at once made known, lingered behind, triumphing in the anticipated possession of the high-minded girl who had rejected him, and the despair of his rival cousin, whom he hated.

"Now, then," he exclaimed, "I can meet scorn with scorn and hate with hate. Ulrick dishonoured me before my nation; the scaffold soon will claim him. Myrra preferred the boyish love of a mere stripling to my fervent vows—ha! ha! ha! Soon shall she sue and learn to wait my smiles, come at my beck, and tremble at my frown. I'll break her haughty spirit," he added, "and find more pleasure in the task than e'en her love could yield me."

"You must be brief, then," whispered a voice near him, "for your courtship will prove but short."

He started, and found the hag whom he had so brutally treated grinning maliciously at his side. The first impulse of the haughty franklin was to repeat the chastisement; but on a motion of her hand, he was disarmed by a dozen wretched-looking men, who had crept through the underwood and gradually surrounded him, and who immediately hurried him from the high road into the depth of the forest.

"Dogs!" he exclaimed, as one of them drew from his vest a rope, "would you bind me?"

"Ay," replied the hag; "bind thee where Satan's hand alone shall loose thee—where thy crimes long since should have consigned thee—to the gallows-tree!"

"Thou darest not, woman," he answered. "Knowest thou who I am? Slaves! I will rack ye limb from limb for this. Hear me," he added, seriously alarmed for his safety, for one of the ruffians had already made a noose at one end of the cord, and advanced with the intention of placing it round his neck, "I am rich; I'll buy my life with gold—gold, which is the master-key to pleasure—gold, which will purchase wine and beauty—all that men's hearts desire, all that their wishes can frame."

"All but thy life!" screamed the woman; "for couldst thou coin the earth in gold, and count it down before me, I'd trample on thy offer. Do you hesitate?" continued the fury, observing that some of the outlaws were pondering on the Saxon's offer. "Fools! would the man who sold his country e'er keep faith with you? Obey me, or I break all ties between us—denounce ye to your Norman tyrants' mercies, and leave ye to your fate."

The outlaws, who were dependent on the hag for the necessary supplies of food, and whose influence over them was still further increased by her skill in wounds, not unfrequently called into requisition in the hazardous life they led, hesitated no longer. Despite his yells and frantic struggles, Ethwold was attached to

the fatal tree. As soon as the men retired he caught with his
unbound hands to the branch to which he was suspended, and for
a few moments procrastinated his fate.

"A priest, a priest!" he shrieked. "Let me not perish body
and soul. Save me, woman, and I will be thy slave, thy hound;
chain me in the deep centre of the earth, feed me on carrion, use
me as a footstool, spare my life, but for repentance."

"Ha, ha, ha! how the hang-dog howls!"

"Mercy! mercy!"

"The pie shall chatter on thy fleshless skull!" repeated the fury.

"But for one hour to pray."

"The winds shall whistle through thy fleshless bones!" she
added.

"No hope—no hope!"

"None!" exclaimed the aged woman, sternly. "My word is
kept; thou hast struck a woman, and a woman's hand consigns thee
to thy doom."

Raising her long staff, she struck the struggling wretch upon his
hands till the repeated blows forced him to let go his desperate
hold, but not till bruised bones and mangled flesh had lost all
power of supporting him. He fell with a heavy jerk, and, after a
few convulsive struggles, Ethwold, the betrayer of his country,
swung a corpse; cut off in the moment of his triumph by the agency
of a weak creature, whom in his strength he could have crushed,
and whom in the wantonness of his power he had treated cruelly.

CHAPTER XXIII.

RALPH DE GAEL paced the great hall of the castle, impatiently
awaiting the arrival of his prisoners. Had he been aware who the
redoubted leader was, he would hardly have entrusted to a
subordinate the task of securing his person; for, despite the number
of years which had elapsed since the exile of our hero, conscience
—that busy monitor—at times whispered in his ear that Ulrick
might return to exact fearful retribution for his murdered wife, his
desolated home, and outraged honour; and the thought would
poison the wine-cup and arrest the smile upon his lip. Prudence
had prevented his ever making public his marriage with the guilty,
the unhappy Ethra; the greater parts of the estates of Stanfield had
become his by confiscation, and the knowledge of his union with
the child of the man whom he had so cruelly persecuted could have
answered no other purpose than to cover his name with additional
infamy. The betrayer and betrayed lived still: her remarkable
beauty, which even sorrow and remorse had failed to touch, held
the tyrant in a bond which habitude had contributed to rivet; for,

although his infidelities were frequent, they were carefully concealed from the eyes of his injured wife.

" Where stay the loiterers ? " he demanded of an esquire who at a respectful distance awaited his commands. " Night hath already fallen. Can the Saxon have escaped me ? Who leads the men ? "

" Herbert," replied the officer. " A cool head, my lord, and a still better sword."

" I know his qualities," interrupted the impatient Norman, who loved not to hear the praise even of the instruments most faithful to his crimes. " Let the torturers be summoned. I'll wring confession from the Saxon's lips. No mercy, no weakness now. The cord and axe shall be each rebel's doom. I'll crush the traitors like a nest of vipers 'neath my iron heel."

The warders, however, cut short his threats by announcing the arrival of his prisoners, who were instantly conducted by their captors to his presence. Ulrick, although heavily chained, still supported the steps of his fair child; his paternal arm encircled her waist, half-veiling her form in the folds of his dark mantle. Time and the burning sun of Syria had so changed him, that even the eye of hate, whose glance is often keener than that of love, failed to recognise him. His step was erect, in the conscious integrity of his life and the dignity of his nature ; his eye, like that of an imprisoned eagle, shrank not from the gaze of his captor, which, on the contrary, gradually quailed beneath its glance.

" Who art thou ? " said Ralph de Gael, in a much less haughty tone than he usually assumed towards his victims, for the bearing of the soldier of the Cross had involuntarily awed him.

" A Saxon," was the reply.

" Humph ! I guessed as much," interrupted the Norman, " from thy insolent bearing. What else ? "

" Thy foe ! " added Ulrick, sternly, "thy deadly foe. Mine is no common hate. I tell thee, Ralph de Gael, were we both struggling on the wave, with but one plank between us and eternity, my hand should dash that plank aside rather than float with thee."

" Father, father ! " whispered Myrra, alarmed at the effect his words produced upon the astonished tyrant, " patience, patience for mine and for thy country's sake."

" Indeed ! " exclaimed the surprised Norman, for it was not often that such words had fallen upon his ears, more used to prayers and supplications than reproaches from his victims ; and what cause ? "

" What cause ! " iterated our hero, approaching him ; "have I not told thee that I am a Saxon ; and canst thou ask the cause ? Look well around thee ; view the groaning earth, which once teemed plenty to her children's toil, made wild and barren 'neath the Norman sway ; view well the happy homes, the antique

towers, in which of old the Saxon lived and ruled, now desolate
beneath the Norman brand.　Dost thou still ask the cause?"—and
here the expression of the captive's eye, as he repeated the question,
was like the forked lightning's point, or the concentrated glance of
the fierce basilisk.　"Again look forth, and view our offspring,
children of our blood, fettered like slaves to pamper up your pride,
or made the victims of their tyrants' lust.　Our country lost, our
homes profaned, our trampled liberties, our broken hearts—all, all
proclaim the cause."

For a few moments Ralph de Gael remained pale with rage, and
speechless from the mere impotence of passion.　There was a tone,
too, in the speaker's voice which jarred upon his soul like the
return in manhood's years of childhood's half-remembered terror.
He felt convinced that he and his prisoner had met before ; but
memory, so changed was his victim, failed to whisper where.　His
pride was galled at the proud glance beneath which his own had
quailed.

"Fool!" he at last replied ; " ours is the right of conquest ;
victory places the yoke upon your necks, and justifies our sway."

"Nothing can justify a tyrant's sway," answered the prisoner
calmly.　"Freedom is man's inalienable right, stamped by the
Godhead on his form when he went forth creation's chartered lord.
Nor conquest's law, nor deed on vellum sealed, nor e'en man's
own assent, can ratify its loss.　Though ages more than e'er the
world has seen had passed since first your fetters bound us down,
yet from the moment that we spurned our chain, and felt our
rights, humanity's lost charter was restored.　Wretch!" he added,
"the measure of thy cruelties is full—a people rise in their
indignant strength—despite thy guards, thy crouching slaves, their
justice yet shall reach thee!　When thou shalt see this bloodstained
hold, the seat of thy dark tyranny and crime, a prey to flames—
when frantic fear shall prey upon thy heart, and wild remorse call
Heaven in vain for mercy, think on the wrongs of Ulrick, and
despair."

"Ulrick!" repeated Ralph aloud.　His cheek blanched as he
beheld the secret terror of his life before him ; then muttering to
himself, he uttered, " 'Twas instinct, then, which made me shudder
as I looked upon him."

"Wretch!" echoed his victim, "where is the home thy sword
hath made a desert?—the wife thy bloodhounds hunted to the
grave?—the child that perished in the blazing pile?　Deep in the
grave I may forget my wrongs ; but whilst one spark of waking
life remains, 'twill be employed in precious, dear revenge.　Off,
vile chains!" he added, "more terrible than death.　Oh! for the
lightning's arm to strike thee!"

"The unhappy man became so excited by the recollection of his
wrongs that, unarmed as he was, he rushed upon the destroyer of

his happiness, and raising his chains as a weapon above his head, doubtless would have inflicted a summary vengeance upon the tyrant, had not his guards restrained him. One more zealous than the rest held the point of his sword at the throat of the fallen Saxon, and waited but a nod or look from his unworthy chief to strike—a sign which would most probably have been given, had not Myrra, alarmed for her father's life, forgot the natural timidity of her nature and the horror which the name of her enemy inspired. Kneeling at the Norman's feet, she even clasped his hand, nay, bathed it with her tears, and implored him by every sentiment of pity and humanity to spare a being whose heart his cruelties had already crushed, whose brain was maddened by the memory of his sorrows. It would have been impossible for any one, even less the slave than Ralph de Gael of beauty, to gaze unmoved upon so fair a suppliant;—her ripening form, like the swelling bud of the fragrant rose, gave delicious promise of its bursting beauties ; her blue eyes, like sapphires, gemmed in tears, were turned imploringly upon him ; while from her prostrate position his licentious eye caught the rich contour of her heaving bosom. It was long since he had gazed on aught so fair, so fresh, so beautiful ; and the heart of the voluptuary throbbed with an emotion to which it had been for years a stranger.

"Rise !" exclaimed Ulrick, who beheld with a sickening sensation the looks of lawless admiration which the Norman cast upon the innocent dove trembling within his clutches. "Plead not to him for mercy, lest from the tomb thy mother's shade indignant rise and curse the child who bends to the destroyer of her race. Thinkst thou," he added, "I could value life as that man's loathsome gift ? "

"Fear not," said the tyrant ; "thou shalt have thy wish— the trial first, and then the headsman's office. Away with him to a dungeon ! Guard him, fellows, as you would your lives ; your heads are on your faith."

"To a dungeon ! " replied Ulrick ; "even there my spirit still can scorn thee. Come, Myrra," he added, opening his fettered arms to receive his terror-stricken child ; "even in a prison a father's heart can shield thee—a father's breast pillow thy innocent head."

"Not so ! " exclaimed Ralph, with a sardonic smile ; " it were a stain upon our chivalry to consign so fair a prisoner to so foul a den ; our castle hath a bower more suited to her beauty and her years."

"No, no ! " shrieked Myrra ; for as he spoke a nameless terror struck upon her heart. "My father's dungeon, the scaffold, or the grave—anywhere with him. I dare not—will not—quit my father's side."

Despite her tears and entreaties, despite the desperate efforts of her distracted father, the unhappy girl was torn from his protecting arms, and placed by the guards in the hands of their chief, whose admiration of her beauty was, if possible, increased by the charm of its sorrows, and who listened to Ulrick's frantic curse with a triumphant laugh.

At a wave of his hand the captive was dragged by overwhelming numbers to his dungeon, and the helpless Myrra left in the power of the object of her terror.

It is impossible to say, in the excitement of the moment, to what excess his passions might have hurried him, had not the frightful convulsions into which his victim fell on beholding him approach for awhile proved her protection. Calling to some of the female attendants of Ethra, he ordered them to bear her to a chamber remote from the apartment of his wife, from whom, on peril of his wrath, they were to conceal the knowledge of her being in the castle.

Ralph de Gael knew how much he was detested, not only by the Saxon franklins and nobles whom he had oppressed, but by the inhabitants of the city generally, whom his exactions had on more than one occasion driven into unsuccessful outbreaks against his authority, the suppression of which had served as pretexts for fresh spoliation. But the present danger was of unusual gravity. Nobles and serfs, peasants and artisans, all seemed leagued against him. In his arrogance he had so offended the neighbouring Norman nobles that even from them he could count on faint support. He despatched, therefore, that very night, a message to the king, then holding his Parliament at Bury St. Edmund's, to demand prompt succour, at the same time informing him that the exiled traitor, Ulrick of Stanfield, was his prisoner. A council of war was afterwards called, and means debated to best provide against the threatened attack ; for the Norman, whatever might have been his crimes, was no carpet knight, but as prompt in battle as in evil deeds.

Ethra—the neglected, the heartbroken, but still loving Ethra—had on this eventful night remained long after the vesper hymn had ceased, praying in the castle chapel, unheeded and alone ; an unusual depression weighed upon her soul, a secret warning of the realisation of those undefined terrors which haunt the predestined and foredoomed. The only light within the sacred place proceeded from the ever-burning lamps before Our Lady's shrine, and as their reflection fell upon the pale but still beautiful features of the penitent, they lit up a picture which a painter might have copied with advantage.

"Peace !" whispered the suppliant. "Holy Mother, pray that my heart finds peace ! Pour thou the balm of kind oblivion on its bleeding sorrows ! Save me from madness ! save me from myself !"

[ULRICK BLESSING HIS DAUGHTER ETHRA]

"Thy prayer will soon be heard," exclaimed a voice near to her ; indeed, so near that the breath of the speaker bore the words to her very ear. " Soon will my prediction be accomplished."

Ethra started, and beheld the woman whom ten years before she had saved from the fury of her two hounds on the fatal morning when she first beheld Ralph de Gael. Although so long a period had elapsed, she had not forgotten either the adventure or the strange prediction.

" It is accomplished, mother," she answered humbly ; " I am indeed outraged—scorned."

" But not avenged," sternly interrupted her strange visitor.

" What meanest thou ? "

" Art thou so poor in spirit," demanded the hag, " as to ask that question ? While thou art praying, wasting thy hours in solitary tears, thy husband—but no," she added, checking herself, " why should I tell the tale thou hast no wish to hear ?—what is't to thee with whom he wastes his hours, so thou canst weep and pray ? Thou hast thy Norman mother's blood, not the proud spirit of thy Saxon race."

" What meanest thou ? " replied Ethra, drawing herself up with fearful calmness. " Nay, torture me not with dark surmise or womanish conceits, to raise false jealousy within my heart ; but if thou knowest aught touching my husband's faith, I charge thee tell it me ! "

He hath a mistress in these very walls—young, beautiful, and good as thou wert once," said the hag. " Soon will thy lord become the slave of her caprice, and know no law but the fair idol's pleasure."

" Thanks ! " said the unhappy Ethra—" thanks ! Thy words have fallen like coals of fire upon my head ; but still I thank thee. Monster ! " she added, with a burst of grief apostrophising her destroyer, " here, in my very home, to trample on my heart ! As yet," she exclaimed, and a fearful expression passed over her excited features, " Ralph but little knows the nature he has wronged : he hath seen it only in the weakness of its love ; let him beware of the strength of its revenge ! "

" And thy fair rival ? " demanded the woman.

" Dies," whispered Ethra, sternly ; " this very night my sleeping rival dies. Then will despair rage high in my destroyer's breast— then will he feel, in agonising throes, a portion of that hell which rages here."

Drawing her veil around her, with a calm step the speaker left the chapel to return to her apartments in the castle. Her informant remained gazing after her a few moments in silence.

" Now," she exclaimed, " are my years of plotting turned to some account ; mischief is high afloat, and misery rears its pale, still standard o'er us. The jealous wife will not fail to recognise her sister—her sister to impart their father's danger ; remorse and jealousy will find a means to save them both. Ulrick once free, these blood-stained towers must fall ; and with them their destroying, heartless tyrant. Curse him !" she added, sinking on her knees ; "the widow's lonely curse rest on him ! Avenge me, Heaven, on the destroyer of my husband, the seducer of my child, and earth and I will then be quits."

The speaker, who had twice so strangely crossed the path of Ethra, had indeed no common cause of hatred to the Norman governor, for her husband had been murdered by Ralph de Gael for resisting his violence towards their only child, whom the tyrant, in a fit of caprice, had torn from her humble home ; it was, therefore, with a mother's and a widow's lacerated heart that the Saxon crone had cursed him.

On reaching her apartment Ethra dismissed her attendants, from whose confusion and evasive manners, when she demanded if any strangers had arrived within the castle, she read the confirmation of her fears. As soon as she was alone she removed the jewels from her neck and arms, and changed her dress for a dark mantle and veil, such as, in the long corridor through which she had to pass, were likely to be least observed. Opening a small cabinet, she drew from it a dagger of highly tempered steel. Despite her resolution a sickening sensation came over her as she grasped the weapon in her hand.

"What am I about to do ?" she murmured. "Stain my soul with blood ! Better to end my own wretched, blighted existence. 'Tis but a blow, and——No, no," she added, after a pause, "gladly as I would welcome death, mine must not be the hand. There still remains a task to be performed. The captive priest, whose dismal dungeon I discovered in my wanderings, assures me he is armed with the means to prove my father's innocence—to crush my vile betrayer. Ulrick !" she exclaimed, and a flood of tears followed the word, "thy guilty but repentant child shall vindicate thy name, and ask forgiveness only in the tomb."

In a chamber within the keep of Norwich Castle, worn with grief and terror, the innocent Myrra slept. The female attendants to whose care she had been consigned, knowing all escape to be impossible, had withdrawn to their apartments, situated in Bigod's tower : and thus the helpless girl was deprived of even the feeble protection which their presence would have afforded. The room would have been in utter darkness but for the stream of moonlight which entered through the large grated window and fell upon the couch, lighting the heavy crimson draperies with its silver light. Myrra had always entertained a deep love, and almost superstitious veneration, for the memory of her mother, whose spirit she devoutly believed still watched over the safety of her child with all a mother's affection, with all a guardian angel's care. In all her sorrows she was accustomed to address her prayers to her loved shade ; and her portrait, which she wore suspended from a pomander chain round her neck, was to her fond imagination a relic to which some strange influence was attached.

Perhaps there is no feeling of the human heart so pure, so unstained by selfishness or passion, as the love which children bear their mother. How often, in after life, when the grave has closed around that tender parent's form, will a word, a look, recall to mind that guardian of our infant years—that confidante of childhood's sorrows ! Again her eyes, beaming with affection, seem to dwell on ours. Again her voice breathes sweet reproof, or whispers consolation in our ears. A mother's name claims from the world respect, and from her children honour.

Myrra's was not that calm and peaceful sleep which rests upon the brow of those who slumber in the security of home and watchful friends. Her restless dreams were wild and troubled as her fortunes ; dark threatening shadows weighed upon her spirit, and her deep-drawn breathings were interrupted by sighs and moanings, such as might break from an imprisoned cherub's unquiet rest. Her long chestnut hair, nature's own screen to modesty, had escaped from the embroidered veil which bound it, and fell in curling masses over her innocent bosom, which rose and sank with every exhalation of her fragrant breath. Her right hand grasped the chain and portrait, as the protecting ægis beneath whose influence she slept ; and her left arm rested carelessly on her dark robe, contrasting like sculptured ivory upon an ebon ground. It was a picture an angel might have contemplated with pleasure, a fiend should have shuddered to approach.

Cautiously the arras which covered the entrance to thè apartment was drawn aside, and Ethra, bearing a lamp and the poniard she had taken from the cabinet, approached. Her step was slow and stealthy as the pace of the midnight murderer ; her breath escaped from her clenched teeth more like the faint hiss of a cautious snake than the free breathings of a human being. Perhaps the strong effort of self-control was more fearful in the still beautiful creature than even the wildest storm of passion would have been. Her cheek was pale with the horror of the resolution which her knit brow conveyed, and her dark eyes flashed with the electric sparks of her contending passions.

" She sleeps," she murmured to herself—" thank Heaven she sleeps ! Oh ! when shall I know rest ? Calmly she sleeps, as if watchful angels hovered o'er her couch to shield their charge from danger. 'Tis but a blow—a bubbling gush—a moment's struggle— and life's fitful dream is ended ! Let me look on her fair face," she added, " gaze on the charms whose fatal beauty has robbed me of the love bought with so many crimes ; the sight will steel my heart and nerve my hand."

Twice did the speaker flash the light of the small silver lamp she bore over the features of her sleeping rival. So many years had elapsed since they had met, or jealously had so blinded her, that not one trait recalled the infant sister, whom she had abandoned, to her memory.

"Young, too," she continued ; "perhaps innocent. No matter, she hath crossed my solitary path ; her fatal beauty disputes with me the only heart I ever prized. Away remorse, and weak blinding pity ! She dies ! "

The hand of the jealous woman was raised—another instant, and the sleep of the gentle, innocent Myrra would have been eternal, when Heaven, whose wisest purposes so oft seem accident, interposed to save her soul from crime. Despite her resolution, the doubt that her rival might be the victim, and not the accomplice, of her betrayer, shook her purpose. The chain and portrait which attracted her attention promised to confirm or dissipate her doubts. Gently releasing it from the sleeper's hand, she raised it to the lamp, and saw it was—her mother's ! Twice did she press her hand upon her care-worn brow, deeming that memory had deceived her, or conscience conjured the accusing shadow to her blasted sight. Her burning eyeballs, incapable of tears, were riveted on the unconscious ivory. Convinced that it was indeed her mother's portrait, her first impulse was to cover it with kisses ; but a blush of shame, which suffused her cheek at the recollection of her crime, restrained her.

"It is no mockery of my senses," she exclaimed, "but real—my mother, such as in life she looked and smiled upon her child. Who is this sleeper, then ? " she added, fixing her eyes with pitiable terror upon the couch. "Why does she wear my mother's portrait ? Can it be ?—no, no ! " she shudderingly continued, as the fearful suspicion of who Myrra really was flashed upon her ; "God is too merciful for that ; madness were bliss to such a damning thought —yet doubt is worse than madness."

Rushing to the bed, she grasped the sleeper frantically, calling upon her to awaken. Myrra started at the voice from her uneasy dreams, and beholding a female, whose agitated features were more like those of the inspired pythoness than cold humanity, called in her fear for mercy.

"Call not to Heaven !" exclaimed Ethra, "in idle adjurations, but answer me. Whose portrait is this ? "

"My mother's," replied the astonished girl. "Oh, give it back— it is my mother's ! "

Her request was alike unheard and unheeded, for at the words "my mother's," the unhappy woman fell to the ground with a shriek so piercing, so unearthly, that it sounded like the yell which the departing spirit gives when driven from this world hopeless of the next.

Despite her terror and astonishment, Myrra sufficiently mastered her emotions to assist the incomprehensible being who had so rudely broken upon her slumbers. Pouring water from the vase of flowers in the window of her chamber into her hands, she bathed her burning brow, and chafed her hands; but it was long ere life, with a deep-drawn sigh, recalled the insensible Ethra back to the sense of misery and guilt. Her first feeling was to end her blighted, lonely existence; shame and remorse bowed her crushed spirit to the dust, and she feared death less than she feared to meet her innocent sister's eye.

"Where," she exclaimed, wildly starting to her feet, "where is the poniard—misery's last friend, dishonour's sole resource?"

"What!" said Myrra, misconceiving her intention, "and wouldst thou take my life?"

"Thy life!" iterated Ethra, her feelings suddenly diverted from their fearful nature by the question.

"Am I then quite a monster? Thy life! Oh, I would give the wretched remnant of my days to save thy heart one pang—pour the blood freely from my guilty breast, ere harm approached to thee, my guileless, innocent sister!"

"Sister!" repeated Myrra in astonishment.

"Ay, sister! thy elder born! she who taught thy infant lips to utter its first prayer; whose last kiss within her father's ruined halls was pressed upon thy cheek! Let me, ere I die," she added, "taste the last happpiness my soul can know—a sister's fond embrace! Come to this heart, which throbs as it would burst to meet thee—this broken heart, which, crushed by guilt and sorrow, still can spring to thee!"

With passionate tenderness the speaker threw her arms around her long-lost sister, pressed her almost with a mother's love to her agitated bosom, and printed a thousand kisses upon her unsullied brow and cheeks. Encircled in the weeping Myrra's arms, she felt as if not quite abandoned by Heaven: it was the first ray of mercy which had fallen upon her soul. Nature had struck the rock, and melted it.

"Ethra! dear Ethra!" whispered her sister, "why this mystery? Why so long concealed the secret of your escape upon that fearful night, which gave our home to flames, our hearts to desolation?"

"Ask me not; there's crime, there's madness in the fearful tale."

"And shame?" added Myrra, mournfully, in an inquiring voice.

Her sister started from her at the word, and gazed with a haughty but not angry look upon her.

"No," she answered slowly; "those who loved me once may curse my memory, but never blush for it. Thinkst I had clasped thee, my pure and innocent sister, to my breast, had I been the polluted thing my cheek would burn to name? No, though it freeze thy ears to hear the damning truth, blister my lips to utter it, still it must be told that Ethra is a wife."

" Whose ? " demanded her sister, with a look in which terror and pity were mingled.

"His," she exclaimed, "whose sword left a desert where he found a paradise—who made thee motherless, and me a wretch— the wife of Ralph de Gael."

" Of Ralph de Gael ! " repeated Myrra, in a voice of horror, " of him who holds thy father captive, whose licentious passion threatens thy sister with far worse than death ! Save me from him," she continued, " for our mother's memory, for the honour of our name—save me, or kill me here."

The agony with which the speaker urged her request proved how deeply grounded were her terrors ; and despite the impulse of her better nature, her sister felt a pang of jealousy that another should be preferred by him for whom she had sacrificed her hope of heaven, the world, and self-esteem. The sentiment was but momentary. Throwing her arm around the fair girl, as if to protect her even from imaginary outrage, she reassured her that she possessed the will as well as power to release both her and her parent from their tyrant's hold, and that long ere morning's dawn they should be both at liberty.

"And thou too, Ethra ? " urged the trembling pleader ; " thou too wilt quit this scene of shame and crime ? "

" No," replied her sister, sternly ; " I know my fate, and will not shrink from its fulfilment. Fearful hath been my crime ; as fearful shall be my expiation. Let me but obtain my father's pardon ere I die, and I have done with life ; but see," she added, pointing to the evening star, which began to glitter faintly in the heavens, "time presses ; ere the glorious sun shall gladden earth, I have much to do. Come, Myrra, come ; banish all dread from thy pure, guiltless breast ; indulge that hope I never more must know."

The prison in which Ulrick was confined was a deep sub-terranean cell, lying between the inner and outward moat, and, from the rude, massive character of its architecture, as well as the absence of anything like ornament, was evidently of much older date than the castle itself, having most probably formed, with the winding passages which led to it, a part of the ancient fortress erected by Canute, who held his court in Norwich. It was one of those dungeons which tyranny alone could have conceived or the eye of cruelty could have gazed on without a shudder The green, fœtid lichen tapestried its unequal walls with its unwholesome vegetation ; and monstrous fungi—the undisturbed growth of years, the home of the bloated toad and slimy reptile—carpeted the cold damp floor. The thick greasy plants were crushed beneath the impatient tread of our hero as he paced the cell, and the scared inmates lazily crawled from his path, trailing their hideous forms to some undisturbed retreat.

At first his storm of passion had been fearful—perchance its violence had exhausted itself, or the cold heavy air reduced the raging fever of his blood ; for, after a few hours' pacing of his cell, he gradually became calm and collected, his thoughts reverted to the past, and if hope whispered him no promise for the future, it was that a secret monitor assured him that for him time had indeed no future.

On approaching one corner of his dungeon, he observed an indistinct heap thrown carelessly together, half-hid by the same rank vegetation which everywhere encroached around him ; the indistinct light of the solitary lamp suspended from the ceiling did not at first allow him to examine it distinctly, but as his eyes gradually became habituated to the place, he perceived the object of his attention to be a human skeleton ; doubtless the remains of some former inmate, left to moulder in the den where its last prayer had been raised to Heaven, its last sigh echoed unheeded in its flinty walls. As he reverently raised the skull, a serpent, which had found it a convenient hiding-place, glided through his fingers, and fell upon the ground. The faint hiss of the reptile lacked that acute sound peculiar in those of its species who dwell in sun and light ; it was weak and sickly as the atmosphere of its damp, cheerless home.

"And this," he mused, "is man ! The noblest temple Deity has reared becomes a reptile's hiding-place ! God-given thought ousted from its shrine, that the foul toad may dwell there ! What lofty thoughts, what noble purposes may have had birth within this hollow skull ! Perchance," he added, after a pause, "what fearful crimes engendered there ! Its dreams, like mine, may have been those of liberty, and this the end on't."

"The end of all on earth ! " exclaimed a deep-toned voice, which sounded at a distance.

Ulrick started, and looked eagerly around his prison. He was alone.

"Who spoke ? " he demanded, " or have my senses mocked me ? "

"One who hath counted ten long years of solitude, yet never for one moment doubted justice on earth, or Heaven's absolving mercy in a better world."

"I hear thee," said our hero, "and yet I see thee not. Where art thou, whose voice breathes hope and consolation when hope and consolation seem to fail ? "

"Art thou alone ? " continued the speaker.

"Alone, with solitude and death," was the reply.

"Wait, then, a moment till I get my tools," resumed the unknown. "I laboured years to forge them from a fragment of my broken chain—ground them with untiring patience upon my

dungeon stone, less hard than my obdurate tyrant's heart. Wonder
not, then, I prize them," he added, "and conceal them carefully
from my suspicious gaoler's curious eye."

In a few moments Ulrick heard a noise against the wall which
evidently divided the vast vault into two distinct prisons. One by
one the huge stones were removed, until an aperture sufficiently
large to admit the ingress of a human being was made in the solid
masonry.

"Can I assist you?" he demanded.

"No," replied the stranger; "I am used to the attempt, and
require no aid."

The next moment the speaker stood before him—a tall, emaciated
figure, whose beard, straggling and thin, descended to his girdle ;
whose haggard features, from long seclusion, were of that death-
like waxy hue we see upon the corpse. The tattered robe which
enshrouded him, and the torn scapulary, denoted that the wearer
was a member of some religious order ; but the fragments were too
ragged and too much soiled and worn by time to tell the gazer
which.

"Welcome, brother in affliction ! " exclaimed Ulrick, extending
his hand to the strange phantom ; " doubly welcome if I read aright
thy priestly office in these sullied robes. Religion's minister, in
such an hour, is more than welcome to the captive's heart."

" I am, indeed," replied the wretched being, "an unworthy priest
of the Most High."

"And what virtue made thee the prisoner of Ralph de Gael?"

" My weakness and his crimes. Like some midnight thief, he
stole upon my peaceful path, and tore me from the only shelter sin
and the world had left me. Long I refused compliance with his
will—refused to aid him in the vile scheme of vengeance he had
formed, to crush the foe he had too deeply injured. Torture was
used ; I yielded, and am punished."

" Torture—and a priest ! " repeated his hearer, with horror.

"Ay," said Father Onfroy; for our readers have doubtless
recognised in the captive thus singularly brought in contact with
our hero, the priest whose skill in caligraphy had been so successfully employed by Ralph de Gael to forge the documents which
justified his attack upon Stanfield, and established a charge of conspiracy against Ulrick ; " the torture, the burning pincers, and the
cruel rack. In my early days I had often gazed upon the victims
bound there—counted their groans and shrieks—looked coldly on
whilst every limb was stretched in mortal agony—each muscle
quivering with pain too exquisite for nature to support. I have
felt it since," he added, with a shudder ; "felt all that I saw—all
that I inflicted. My punishment hath not been more fearful than
my crimes."

"Who art thou ? " demanded Ulrick, struck by the tone of his voice, which aroused painful recollections in his soul. "We have met before ; for as I hear thee speak the memory of many a year gone by passes in shadowy visions o'er my mind. I know not where or when, but I could swear that we have met before."

Seizing his visitor by the arm, the speaker led, or rather dragged, him to the centre of the dungeon, directly beneath the lamp, which hung suspended by an iron chain above them. They recognised each other instantly. There was no mistaking, worn and preternaturally aged as long captivity had made him, the unearthly features, disfigured by a thousand minute scars, of the unhappy monk, who equally traced, amid the ravages of grief and change of clime, the noble countenance of the Saxon.

"Robert of Artois !" "Ulrick of Stanfield !" they mutually exclaimed, and remained gazing on each other, each, from different emotions, unable to pronounce another word.

The priest was indeed no other than that most unhappy man, who, on the departure of his son Gilbert with his bride for Normandy, had, by the advice and consent of Lanfranc, concealed his crimes and repentance within the cloister, where, under the name of Brother Onfroy, he became remarkable for that fatal skill in caligraphy which had made him the tool and victim of his unprincipled persecutor.

The monk was the first to recover from his surprise. Long suffering had extinguished in him the pride which had rendered his earlier penitence imperfect. The hand of Heaven seemed to have brought about their meeting. Sinking on his knees, he could only utter the indistinctly pronounced words, " Pardon—pardon ! "

"Rise ! " said our hero. "The knee devoted to the altar should not be bent to sinful man. Whatever thy crimes, long suffering has atoned them ; an angel while on earth pronounced forgiveness —fear not I shall revoke it."

"Ulrick," faltered the still kneeling suppliant, "in this dark hour I feel the bitterness, the shame of vice, the holiness of virtue. As yet thou knowest not half thy injuries : my first crime failed to deprive thee of thy love ; my second robbed thee of thine honour."

"What meanest thou ? " his astonished hearer demanded.

"The letters which Ralph de Gael doubtless produced before the king to justify his outrage ; the details of the Saxon plot to break the Norman yoke—to assassinate, cowardly assassinate each noble in his hold—which gave thy name to infamy, thy memory to scorn —were forged by this degraded hand."

"Horror ! " exclaimed his victim. "Did that blow come from thee ?"

"From me," continued the guilty man, " whose early crime thou hadst forgiven, whose deserted son thou hadst protected. Loathing existence, yet afraid to die, I yielded to the racks of sharp agony,

and stained my knightly honour and my priestly vow by forgery
—by a vile felon's weakness and a felon's act."

For a few moments there was a struggle in the generous Saxon's
breast ; but, fearfully as he had been wronged, he felt that Heaven
had sufficiently avenged him, and that man had nought to add to
its punishment. His own span of life he looked upon as counted,
and trembled to appear before the Judgment-seat with the sin of
unforgiveness on his soul.

"Rise ! " he said.   "Where Heaven hath punished man can only
pardon. As freely as the creature can forgive its fellow-creature,
so do I pardon thee."

"Thanks," murmured Robert of Artois ; "armed with thy forgiveness, I may present myself at Heaven's bar, trusting it will not
prove less merciful than thou hast. Oh ! " he added, passionately,
"but for one moment's liberty, to wash this foul dishonour from
my soul—to rend the mask from this detested tyrant—to atone the
wrong my unwilling hand hath done thee, and place thy honour,
in the minds of men, pure as the angels who record it see it ! "

"Dreams ! dreams ! " said our hero, mournfully shaking his
head ; "this dungeon is a tomb from whence life finds no egress.
Behold," he added, pointing to the skeleton, "my history and its
moral. Some future inmate of this cell will muse o'er my remains,
wondering whose nameless bones moulder here."

"I'll not believe it," replied his companion ; "such fate might
be mine. There would be justice in it ; but Heaven hath tried thy
virtues far too deeply not to reward at last ; its purposes are ne'er
so darkly veiled from human eye as when near their fulfilment.
It speaks in parables and strikes through clouds. Why," he added,
with increased confidence, "hath my worthless being been preserved ? Why do we both meet here, but that the crime of years
should be atoned, and truth made clear at last ? "

"Impossible ! " exclaimed Ulrick ; "who would heed thy
tale ? "

"All," answered Robert. "Were I but free, I'd find the means
to place thy innocence beyond suspicion's breath."

At this moment, through the grating of the iron door which
barred their path to freedom the rays of a distant light became
faintly visible. The monk was the first to observe it. Pointing it
out to his companion, he whispered :

"Have I not prophesied ? "

" 'Tis but the gaoler, or my executioner."

"Say rather thy deliverer, and mine ; the hour so long dreamt
and prayed for is at hand."

Hastening to the door, he applied his eyes to the grating, and
saw at a distance, in the long damp passage, a veiled female form
bearing a lamp—it was the same figure which had often visited
him in his dungeon, consoled his sorrows and lone captivity, and

alleviated his miseries. His heart beat high with hope and expectation.

"She comes!" he cried ; "the avenger comes at last. Farewell, I must retire within my cell : none must know of our communication. If I err not, soon wilt thou have another trial to thy generous heart ; but it will bear thee through it. Say not that we have met. Shouldst thou obtain thy liberty without me, lead on thy friends to the attack : living release, or dead avenge me. If I fall," he added, "dig in the corner of my dungeon nearest the iron ring to which for years my body was enchained, and thou wilt find a scrap of parchment concealed within the skull of some lone victim who preceded me ; guard it as thou wouldst thy life and honour, for it may serve to vindicate them both."

Scarcely had Robert of Artois time to regain his den, and replace the means of communication between the two cells, than the bar which fastened the iron door of Ulrick's prison on the outside was removed, and Ethra, the guilty and repentant Ethra, her features concealed beneath the long sable veil which enshrouded her trembling form, entered the dungeon.

For awhile parent and child remained gazing upon each other in silence—Ulrick from surprise, and Ethra from the deep emotion which consumed her. Years had elapsed since she last gazed upon that stately form—since his deep accents had fallen upon her ear ; and yet it seemed as they had met but yesterday—so true to memory are the first characters time traces on its tablets. She feared to speak, lest the cry of her bruised heart should reach her lips, and nature vindicate her rights in the sweet name of father.

"Who art thou ?" demanded the captive—"some spirit of consolation haunting these fearful cells, sent to prepare me for the parting hour, when life and grief are ended ; shrouding the ministry of Heaven in veils, that thy glad beauty break not too soon upon us ?"

"Not the bright being of another world," quickly answered his despairing visitant ; "but one upon whose brow misery hath set its burning seal, hath come to weep in pity o'er thy woes—to soothe and to relieve them—to open thy dungeon door, and bid thee forth to liberty and vengeance."

"To liberty !" exclaimed her astonished listener. "Is that word breathed in these dungeons, which for years have heard no sound but captives' groans and supplicating sighs ? Who, then, art thou ? Thy speech bespeaks thee Saxon, but thy words imply a power which none but damning crimes could purchase thee in Ralph de Gael's halls."

Although Ethra had addressed her father in the Norman tongue, the accent with which she spoke it to his practised ear betrayed her race. Ulrick's allusion to her country touched her heart—it seemed like the first step towards his recognition of his child ; she forgot that for ten years he had deemed her dead—dwelt upon her memory as on a seraph's early called from earth, not as a guilty living thing of shame and sorrow.

"Thou hast guessed rightly," she faltered; "I am of Saxon blood." Then hastily added, as if fearful of the consequences of her admission : "But years have passed since I beheld my home —years since the sound of kindred voice hath fallen on my ear, or kindred love gladdened the desolation of my heart. Wonder not, then, that I became its victim—wedded the man stained with a parent's blood—brought foul dishonour on a noble man, unsullied save by me."

"What!" interrupted the horror-stricken Saxon, "wedded with one whose hand was red with the same blood which flows within thy veins ?—perchance a father's or a brother's blood. O woman, woman! affrighted furies spread thy nuptial couch, and hell and terror drew its curtains round thee."

His reproving words and lofty indignation fell like a sentence upon her self-accusing soul, and had not a burst of tears relieved her heart, its agony had broken it.

"Hear me!" she cried; "judge not my crime unheard. No common snares were spread to catch my soul. With mercy and compassion listen to my tale; weigh my long years of agony and deep remorse, my blighted youth, and outraged heart against my crime. Hear ere thou condemn me."

Moved by her passionate grief, Ulrick pointed to the rude stone in the centre of his dungeon, on which his trembling visitor sank exhausted by the strength of her emotions. With one of those violent efforts which strong minds only can exert, she, after a few moments' pause, collected her wandering thoughts, and then commenced her tale of many sorrows.

CHAPTER XXIV.

"I LOVED!" said Ethra. "Knowest thou the power those words imply? They are the key to the soul's mysteries—the ciphers of its passions. I loved, not with the light feeling of a girlish heart, whose smiles and tears, like April's sun-lit showers, succeed; but with the strength of summer's ardent rage, whose smile consumes, whose burning kiss destroys. We met in secret, but not in sin," she added quickly, as she caught the expression of Ulrick's eye. "Fallen as I am, that stain at least was spared me. I am not of a race that could survive dishonour."

"So shall thy soul prove lighter by a crime," said her hearer; "but tell me, woman, why this concealment? Was thy father cold, insensible, or churlish in his love—one who ruled by fear, and not affection's ministry?"

"No," answered the unhappy Ethra, "my heart hath not even that mean excuse to ease its burden. Oh! he was good, affection's self, tender, considerate, generous, loving, wise in all but his weak love for his degenerate child."

"And thou abandoned him?—left him in his age, perchance, to pass in childless solitude the remnant of his days in his once happy home—fitting return for all his care and fond parental love!"

"Worse," added Ethra, with a violent effort at self-command; "I brought destruction on that happy home; these guilty hands unbarred the door to the triumphant foe—gave to the fury of the Norman sword parents, kindred, friends—brought desolation on my name and race, and misery on myself."

"Horror!" exclaimed our hero, starting from her, for her words brought to his mind the destruction of his own lordly halls, and he recoiled from her as from a loathsome thing. "I had a child—in tears of anguish oft I mourn her loss; I now thank Heaven she lives not such a wretch as thou art. But why," he added, "why this sad tale of grief and sin to me?"

"Thou art my father's friend," replied the penitent. "Chance has revealed to me that still he lives; therefore it is I ope thy prison door, that thou, in turn, mayst plead for my forgiveness."

"Avoid that father," sternly answered Ulrick; "never meet his sight, lest, recognising thee, his heart-strings break, and, dying, he should curse thee."

At these fearful words, which seemed like a sentence to her despairing soul, Ethra wrung her hands bitterly; and the convulsive sobs and deep-drawn sighs which shook her form showed how deep was the remorse and agony of her bruised heart. Little did the returned exile deem the trembling, guilty creature before him was his own child; the once happy, smiling girl, whose arm a hundred times had been entwined around his neck—whose innocent kisses had so often sealed the words of warning on his lips.

"I have lived," she at last sobbed forth, "till life has been a curse; lived to become the scorn of all I loved—of all who ever loved me. Wouldst thou, stern judge," she added, throwing herself upon her knees suddenly before him, "thus harshly judge thy child? Would not thy iron nature melt while thus in agony she sued to be forgiven—pleaded her girlish years, her fatal passion, her long remorse, and broken heart, for mercy? Wouldst thou bid her on to her great sacrifice——"

"Sacrifice!" repeated Ulrick, "what sacrifice?"

"One," said Ethra, rising proudly from her knees, "which shall give this blood-stained hold to the avenging Saxon's sword, and hurl the tyrant to the doom he merits—one that shall end this guilty life and the oppressor's reign together."

" Meanest thou," demanded Ulrick, gazing on her with a look of admiration as well as pity, " that——"

" I mean," interrupted Ethra, " that as this guilty hand unbarred the entrance to the Norman foe, and let the wolf upon the slumbering fold of my own kindred, it now shall ope the Norman gates to the avenger's hand. Methinks," she added, glancing wildly round, " the spirits of my slaughtered race are all assembled here, and, sternly pointing to these blood-stained towers, claim the great sacrifice to soothe their shades."

" This is indeed atonement," said Ulrick—" a deed to win a pardon for a crime like thine ; a deed to gain a father's forfeit love, and crown thy days with penitence and peace."

" What ! " exclaimed the unhappy woman ; " thinkest thou so meanly of me that I seek to live, to bear upon my faded brow the brand of double treason ? Oh ! never—never ! To avenge my country, my murdered kindred, and my outraged heart—to save thee, Ulrick, and thy innocent child from Ralph de Gael's rage, I yield him to the doom ; but think not," she added mournfully—" think not I will survive him."

" Thy country's gratitude, thy kindred's love——"

" Say rather their pity, their humiliating pity," interrupted Ethra. " I know man's ingrate nature, and will not trust it. Thinkst thou I could bear to meet the world's reproving gaze, or hear it whisper, ' Behold the being who betrayed father and husband, duty and country,' forgetful that no choice was left me in my sorrow—no loop-hole to escape in my despair ? No ; I can welcome death, slumber in peace within the quiet grave, where passion moves not and the heart is at rest, let but a father's pardon rest upon it."

" And if he have a heart," said Ulrick, " it will."

These words fell like balm upon the listener's soul : they were the first rays of hope which pierced through the dark night of her despair. Laying her trembling hand upon his arm, she answered :

" Thou art his friend ; no voice will touch his heart like thine, no reasoning reach his ear."

" His name ? " demanded Ulrick, with surprise.

" That," resumed the speaker, " thou wilt know hereafter ; this paper tells the rest of my sad history. Not now," she hastily added, as her father was about to unfold it ; " read it not now. Leading from these dungeons, a passage conducts us to the outer moat. I have secured the skiff—a boat is ready to convey thee on."

" And my child ? "

" Already awaits thee there," answered Ethra. " Thinkst thou I would leave thy innocent child within the tiger's fangs ? Once free, summon thy friends, and return by the same means. Like Sin guarding the gates of Death, I will remain and give them entrance. But swear," she added, " that the great sacrifice accomplished—my country freed—my kindred blood avenged —swear that my father's pardon shall reward the deed."

"You tax me past my power," answered the bewildered Ulrick, astonished at the vehemence of her words and the deep passion which shook her soul ; but if my prayers can win the boon, I promise it shall be yours."

"It can, it can," resumed the agitated Ethra, with a burst of tears which relieved her heart. "He will listen to thy pleading. If thou shouldst find him harsh, if the absolving words should linger on his lips, lead him," she added, "to my grave—paint to him my sorrows and remorse, my blighted years, life's withered hopes—bid him forget my sin in its atonement ; then will the voice of nature speak within him, and his heart melt in precious, dear forgiveness."

There was something so desolate, so heart-broken and despairing in the speaker's voice, that the firm nature of the soldier melted at its tone. In the agitation of the moment her veil had partially fallen aside, displaying her still beautiful though care-worn features. Perhaps it may be wondered that he failed to recognise them ; but ten years of womanhood and sorrow had so altered their expression from those of the wild, joyous girl his heart so long had mourned as with the dead, and the pale lamp's uncertain light so shadowed them, that the suspicion never crossed his brain. Had it, oh ! with what eager love his arms would have enfolded his lost treasure—with what absolving tears his yearning heart pronounced forgiveness of her crime, oblivion of the past ! But it was not to be ; the sacrifice to conscience was voluntary and accepted.

"Live," he exclaimed, "to hear the pardon thy repentance merits from a parent's lips ; to feel once more the joy of his paternal kiss ; to rest thy heart, after life's storms and shipwrecks, in the calm haven of a father's love."

"Never," said his daughter, with an expression of resolution, amounting almost to sternness, upon her brow ; "my heart would wither should I see the blush of shame suffuse my father's cheek if men but named his child. Thinkst thou I could bear the world's forgiveness, or, far more hateful, its insulting pity ? No," she added, "my life hath been the comet's fearful path—my death be like its end. Time presses : in my father's name, pronounce a blessing and forgiveness on me."

The speaker sank upon her knees as humbly as a child before the absolving priests ; and Ulrick, with an emotion of pity and admiration, exclaimed, as he raised his hands above her head :

"In His awful name, Parent of all, and in thy earthly parent's name, I bless and pardon thee ; this deed shall be, in after times, by poets sung, thy virtues only live in our remembrance. But stay," he added, as his visitor resumed the lamp, and pointed towards the door of the cell ; " I have a companion, one whose life hath for ten long years been wasted in these dungeons, one whose safety is necessary to clear my honour of the foul stain the tyrant cast upon it ! "

"The priest," said Ethra ; " I have not forgotten him ; he, too, shall be the companion of thy flight ; the path is open to ye both, for liberty and vengeance !"

At the summons of our hero the wretched Robert of Artois issued from his den, and gazed for a few moments, with inquiring eyes, upon his two companions. A sign from the female informed him that Ulrick knew not that it was to his repentant child he was about to owe his liberty ; as his own knowledge of the tie between them was obtained only in the confessional, he was bound to silence. The unhappy woman, it would seem, had often sought him in his dungeon to receive consolation from his ministry, as well as to alleviate the horrors of his lone captivity with the sweet solace of sympathy and pity.

Bearing the lamp, Ethra preceded the liberated captives through the long damp passages which led to a small ruined tower beyond the second moat, and not far distant from the water's edge. From the unequal nature of the ground, they progressed slowly ; in many parts the stone-work had partially fallen, and they had to climb over the obstructing masses. At length they reached a low iron door, firmly imbedded in the solid walls. A figure, wrapped in a dark, warm mantle, sprang impulsively to meet them ; it was Myrra, who had been long impatiently expecting them. Throwing herself into her sister's arms, she exclaimed :

" Arrived—arrived at last ! How fearfully the dreary hour hath passed ! "

"Silence," whispered Ethra ; "remember your promise. Till safe beyond these walls our father must not know his wretched daughter lives—wedded to him who caused his house's ruin."

The next moment the still trembling girl was folded to Ulrick's manly breast. A deep pang wrung the heart of the elder sister as she saw the fond paternal kiss—a kiss her blighted cheek was destined never more to feel—a kiss which would have been dearer to her heart than the first smile e'en of an angel's love.

Drawing from her vest the ponderous key, with a firm hand she applied it to the lock ; years had most probably elapsed since last the rusty door had groaned upon its hinges. Like some surly guardian, it seemed unwilling to give egress to the captives, resisting all her efforts to force back the ponderous bolt. It required the united strength of Ulrick and his companion to turn the key within the corroded wards. At last it slowly turned upon its axle, and the first breath of morning entered freshly the narrow passage.

"Free ! " exclaimed Robert of Artois, drinking with delight the pure air to which for ten long years he had been a stranger. "I have dreamt of this, prayed for this, and it hath come at last. Relenting Heaven hath heard the lonely captive's supplication, and sent him forth for vengeance and atonement!"

· "We shall meet again," said Myrra, in an under-tone, to her sister. "Promise me that we shall meet again."

"No tears," murmured Ethra, calmly—"no lamentation now! Yes, we shall meet again; if not on earth, at least in heaven, if penitence may win my forfeit place there. Ulrick of Stanfield," she added, in a loud, firm tone, "haste to thy friends; wait not for numbers, lest thy foe escape thee. Here will I station one to give thee ingress to the Norman's hold. Once there, thy sword must do the rest."

"The second night from this," replied our hero, "thou mayst expect me. On every hill the Saxon torch shall gleam, on every breeze the Saxon banner float. Yes, Ralph de Gael, a nation rises in its strength to crush thee. These towers, the scene of thy polluted sway. shall fall before the cry of liberty."

"Let it but sound," added his deliverer, "and fearfully my acts shall answer it. Away!" she exclaimed, impatiently; "each moment of delay is fraught with danger to thy safety."

Despite the entreaties of Ulrick and the silent pleadings of her sister, Ethra remained firm in her resolution not to accompany them; her soul was fixed on the accomplishment of her fearful destiny, and she resolved to meet it calmly and alone.

"'Tis past!" she said, as after repeated efforts she succeeded in rolling back the ponderous door which shut her from liberty and those she loved, for ever— "life's last weakness is past, and the few hours which remain are due to prayer, to penitence, and vengeance. My heart is lighter now that I feel a father's curse will not rest upon his poor girl's grave—armed with his forgiveness, I dare to hope for Heaven's. No weakness," she added, as with an impatient gesture she dashed aside the tears which, despite her resolution, chased each other down her burning cheek; "no vain regrets, no weak, relenting pity. Here will I wait, and watch the hour whose sound shall strike for freedom and for justice, shall calm the tempests of life's stormy passions, and bring this weary, long-worn, restless spirit peace."

Seating herself upon a rough fragment of the fallen arch, Ethra passed the first hour of her lonely watch in silent, fervent prayer.

As soon as the fugitives emerged from the ruined towers in which the secret passage terminated, Robert of Artois bade adieu to his companions, and directed his steps towards the convent, where, after much difficulty, he succeeded in obtaining an interview with the prior, and making himself known to him. The indignation of the monks was boundless at the outrage offered to their order in the person of their brother. In its first burst, they threatened nothing less than death and excommunication upon the Norman governor, whose tyranny and exactions they had frequently felt in common with their oppressed and insulted Saxon neighbours.

Despite the secrecy with which the arrest of Ulrick had been conducted, the news soon reached the ears of the insurgent leaders, and spread dismay amongst them. It required all the influence of Arad and his son Edward to prevent many of the lesser franklins and chiefs from returning to their homes. Without Ulrick to conduct them, they looked upon their cause as hopeless ; so well they knew, not only his skill in war, but the influence his name exercised with the serfs and people. His sudden appearance amongst them, therefore, the morning after his escape, decided their deliberations ; the shout of joy which welcomed him was as sincere as the relief from their uncertainty was great. In an instant Edward was by the side of his loved Myrra, whispering those thousand tender consolations which love so well can utter.

"Welcome !" cried Arad, grasping the hand of his recovered friend ; "think not we have been idle in your cause ; this very day we marched to share your fate, or tear you from the tyrant's cruel power ; but say," he added, "how fell you into his hands ? "

"By Saxon treachery," replied Ulrick ; "the cause so oft of England's weakness in the hour of trial. Ethwold, to revenge my refusal of his proffered union with my child, betrayed me to the Norman."

The name of his betrayer was received with a shout of execration by the assembled chiefs.

"And how escaped ? " they demanded.

"By the remorse of one who long hast lived a wretched victim to her wayward passions, but in whose heart all trace of Eden is not yet extinguished. Despite her thrall, she feels her country's wrongs—despite the tie which binds her to its tyrant, will avenge them."

"Her name ? her name ? " was demanded on all sides.

"That," resumed our hero, "have I still to learn ; this packet tells the rest of her sad history."

Ulrick hastily broke the silken thread which bound the parchment Ethra had given to him ere he left the dungeon. It contained a ring, and a tress of her long, dark hair. For a few seconds he gazed upon the trinket with mute surprise, deeming that memory had played him false, or that he had seen the gem before.

"Surely," he murmured, "I have seen this glittering toy in happier days ! It was Matilda's ! given on the morning that I called her bride. Thou precious bauble, in whose magic circle recollection, with enchanter's power, recalls to mind past scenes of happiness and joys long fled ! Something," he added wildly, " she told me of her home destroyed—her father, long thought dead. Could it ?——No, no—I should have known my child ; and yet this ring, once the fond pledge of chaste, connubial love, gives token of a dreadful tale to come. Read, Myrra, read, and save me from the rack."

With a trembling hand he passed the parchment to his equally agitated child, whose eyes could scarcely decipher the few characters, so blinded were their orbs by tears. In a voice broken by sobs and sighs she read :

" Father, mourn not for Ethra ; in freedom's cause she dies—happy at last if thy forgiveness rest upon her grave."

The writing fell from her hand as she concluded, and with a burst of grief she threw herself into her father's arms, who remained for several moments as if transfixed to stone—his misery so vast that at first he neither felt nor comprehended its extent. As it gradually broke upon him, the tempest of his soul became terrible, his hand wandered over his burning brow, as if to reseat reason on her tottering throne ; and when at last his words broke forth, they but faintly indicated the agony of his tortured mind.

" My child," he murmured ; " my lost, suffering child ! left by her father in that den of crime ! Nature, that now canst struggle with convulsive throes, why wert thou silent when in agony she cried to be forgiven ? Earth should have shook, the heavens sent forth portentous and prodigious signs, to see a father murder l is own child ! Yes, chieftains," he added, gazing wildly on the assembled Saxons round him, " unknowing whom 1 judged, I, sternly zealous for my country's good, praised her resolve, and let her stay to die."

" Horror !" said Arad ; " thy child ? "

" Ay," continued the agitated parent, with a burst of passionate love ; " my elder born—the first fond pledge of my connubial bliss, is by her father doomed and sacrificed. Friends, these tears I am not used to shed flow from me like a girl's. Bear with me ; Nature will claim her rights, despite the heart's resolve, or cold philosophy's stern reasoning. The weakness past, I am once more my country's."

Drawing his mantle over his visage, the speaker retreated to a short distance from the assembly to commune with his heart, and seek consolation where, in life's shipwrecks and the storms of passion, weak, erring man alone can find it—in prayer. Although the blow had been terrible, it had wounded but not crushed his soul ; it rose with the elasticity of faith to meet the last trial Heaven had reserved to test his fortitude and patience. In a short time he returned to his silent, sympathising friends, pale with the fearful struggle he had passed, but calm and self-possessed. Many thought, as they beheld him, they saw the stamp of death upon his face—so cold and colourless, so worn and rigid, his agony of soul had made it. His was indeed the majesty of sorrow. The first burst of natural weakness past, and it became far too deep for words, too proud for tears ; like death, it veiled its dignity in silence, and only spoke its presence in its impress.

Calmly he proceeded to give his orders to the different leaders : some were despatched to raise the country round ; others sent into the city to urge the discontented citizens to join them—a task more than half-accomplished to their hands ; as, on their arrival, they found the indignant monks preaching not only in the market-place, but in every spot where a group could be collected, detailing to their horror-stricken hearers the imprisonment and sufferings of the tortured and persecuted Father Onfroy. The vast piles of wood collected for the purpose on St. James's Hill and the neighbouring heights, at the first stroke of midnight, were ordered to be fired, as signals for the coming onslaught, which Ulrick, in person, undertook to direct. To Edward and a party of his own retainers, who, on the first news of his return, had marched to the place of meeting, our hero confided the entrance of the secret passage, which Ethra had promised should be opened to their ingress. Had he dreamt that his child would have unbarred the door, her anxious father would himself have conducted the enterprise, and resigned to another the more dangerous post of leading the assault without the walls—but it was not to be ; their last words on earth were spoken. In life the heart-broken parent and his repentant child were doomed never to meet again. When all was arranged, and not till then, Ulrick and the weeping Myrra retired to mourn together.

Our readers may well imagine the rage and terror of Ralph de Gael when informed not only of the flight of his captives, but of the absence of his scorned and long-neglected wife, whose remorse and jealousy he doubted not had opened their dungeon doors. Fortunately, the men who searched the prisons proceeded no farther than the empty cells ; had they done so, they would have found the patient Ethra watching the arrival of the foe, praying for the hour to strike—the signal of her triumph and her death. The tyrant knew too well the energy of his enemy and the danger which threatened him not to prepare to meet it. The garrison were all recalled within the walls of the castle, every tower was manned, the furnaces for heating the boiling lead and oil to pour upon the assailants were got ready ; but his chief reliance was on the arrival of the king, to whom our readers will remember, on the first news of the intended outbreak, he had despatched a trusty messenger.

"Let but Henry come," he exclaimed, "within three days, and I will crush this nest of hornets—trample them like mire beneath my feet. Our walls," he added, as he cast a glance around the lofty battlements, and surveyed the preparations for the siege, "may hold the Saxon scum at bay and mock their idle efforts."

The boaster either forgot in his pride, or was ignorant of, the passages which conducted, one to the lonely tower where outraged woman's vengeance watched ; the other to the cloisters of the cathedral, by which, on a previous occasion, Ulrick, guided by Father Oswald, had escaped.

As the day rolled on, parties of men, variously armed, might be seen entering the city at every gate. The place of rendezvous was the vast plain which surrounded the castle—not as now, partially built upon and occupied by narrow dirty streets, but open and level to the river's edge. Crowds of citizens gradually joined them ; and even before the arrival of the more regular forces of the Saxon chiefs, the insurgents presented a formidable array of undisciplined numbers.

The inhabitants of Norwich had long been dissatisfied with the tyranny and grinding exactions of their worthless governor, whose interest had twice defeated them in their attempts to obtain a charter for their city—a boon frequently promised and as frequently withheld by their vacillating monarch.

Ralph de Gael was far too experienced a commander to waste the energies of his men before the moment of attack. He permitted, therefore, the assembling of the insurgents without attempting to disperse them. His policy was to rest on the defensive until the arrival of the royal forces which Henry, he doubted not, would despatch to his assistance on the first news of the intended outbreak. Doubly did he applaud his own prudence and foresight in sending a messenger to the king when banner after banner of the Saxon nobles appeared upon the ground. He saw that it was no petty feud he had to encounter, but the strength of the Angles arrayed against him. Once, and once only, did his cheek turn pale, as the crane-emblazoned pennon of the lord of Stanfield was planted, amidst the enthusiastic cheers of the enemy, upon a small rising mound almost within bowshot of the walls. Conscience whispered him the contest about to commence was to be one of life and death ; and secretly the tyrant prayed that Henry might arrive in time to his assistance. The day rolled on, and still he saw no symptoms of an attack from the tents and huts which the Saxons erected. It was evident that they contemplated reducing him by siege rather than assault.

"Good !" he murmured ; "the fools fall in the snare. Do they think to starve the lion in his den ? Soon shall they find that Norman swords are sharper than their wits !"

Turning upon his heel with a shrug of disdain to those about him, to indicate his contempt of the foe, he left the battlements and descended to the banquet-hall, where the evening repast was spread.

At the midnight hour the assailants divided their forces into three equal parties. The first, under the conduct of Ulrick, advanced towards the drawbridge, where a strong body of archers and billmen were stationed to protect the only approach to the elevated mound on which the castle stood. Their position was further strengthened by a numerous body of men-at-arms, who, from the summit of the lofty tower which formed the principal entrance to the fortress, were ready to pour down boiling lead, oil, stones, and missiles on all who should approach the gates. So that, in the event of the first attack upon the bridge proving successful, the retreat of the defenders into the interior would be effectually covered.

The second party, guided by the indignant monks, were conducted, under the command of Arad, to the secret passage which our readers will remember connected the cathedral with the castle chapel, and which would enable the Saxons to attack the building in the rear, where perhaps it was the most assailable.

The third, guided by Edward, proceeded to the lone, round watch-tower by the water's edge. This was the most dangerous of all to the safety of the garrison, for it conducted to the very heart of the stronghold. Its existence, either forgotten or unsuspected by Ralph de Gael, baffled alike his calculation and his courage. Little did the heartless voluptuary imagine, whilst he gave the necessary orders for the defence, and smiled in the fancied security of his position, that the hand of a weak woman would render his precautions unavailing. In his pride and wantonness he had sown the seed of desolation ; the hour had struck when he must reap the harvest of the whirlwind and the storm.

At the first signal of the Saxons the ponderous iron door rolled slowly upon its hinges, and Ethra, pale as her destiny, appeared before them. The first glance assured her that Ulrick was not the leader of the host, and her heart beat lighter. In the long lonely hours of her silent watch her fear had been to meet her father's eye—to listen to his voice again—to expose her stern resolve, to perish in the ruins she had caused, to the entreaties of paternal love, or the weak pleadings of her woman's nature.

"Ascend the passage branching to the left !" she exclaimed to the foremost of the band ; "it will conduct ye to your victims. I need not tell you, let your hearts be firm and your good weapons strong."

A shout from the eager Saxons proved that she was understood. Despite her worn appearance—for she had neither quitted her post nor tasted food since Ulrick's departure—and the simplicity of her dark robe and veil, there was a commanding dignity in her manner which enabled Edward to recognise the unhappy wife of Ralph de Gael. Eager for her safety, he entreated her to allow him to send her, under escort, to the camp, urging that the terrors of so fearful a night were ill suited to a woman's presence.

"I will not keep one soldier," she impatiently interrupted,

"from the work of vengeance. ' Is this an hour to think of women's safety, when knightly blows are to be struck, and freedom to be won ? Away, and leave me here." Turning to the men, she added, with a voice and gesture such as Boadicea might have used when urging her subjects against the Romans, " As ye rush on triumphant through the halls, think of the homes your foes have made a desert !—the blood they shed in mockery and scorn ! Let the remembrance of your country's wrongs nerve well each arm to strike the oppressor dead ! "

With an eager shout, the Saxons, excited by her words, sprang forward, and Edward, despite his reluctance to leave her unprotected, was compelled to follow in the stream.

" 'Tis well," she exclaimed, as the last flash of their torches disappeared in the windings of the low subterranean passage ; " once more I am alone, and mistress of myself. Triumph, my soul !—exult, and taste of joy ! My genius rises o'er my foe victorious : and this great deed satiates at once my hate and my revenge. 'Tis worth long years of suffering to live for such an hour as this. Yes, Ralph de Gael," she added, bitterly, " I pay thee now for heartless scorn. neglect, insulted love. The Saxon wife hath set the Saxon bloodhounds on thy track—the outraged child avenged her murdered mother."

In the excitement of the moment, which partook more of madness than of passion, Ethra continued to pace, with hurried step, the entrance of the vault, muttering alternately words of reproach, or giving vent to the insane expression of her triumph. Soon the shouts of the Saxons, as they burst upon their astonished foe, reached her, and her pale lips quivered, her dark eyes flashed with redoubled brilliancy at the signal which told her fearful vengeance was accomplished. Catching up a torch which one of the followers of Edward had dropped in his haste, she began to trace her way to the scene of blood and slaughter.

" The conflict is begun," she cried ; " I go to perish in the storm my breath hath raised."

Despite the impetuosity with which Ulrick commenced his attack upon the bridge, it would have proved unsuccessful against the compact body of archers stationed there had not the party of Saxons under Edda, whom the monks had guided, burst from the chapel and attacked them in the rear. The Normans, thus doubly assailed, seeing all hope of retreat into the interior of the castle cut off, fought with desperate courage, but in vain ; the conflict became too close to permit them to use their bows, and the missiles which the men-at-arms stationed on the tower continued to hurl down were not more destructive to their enemies than to themselves. Their light steel barrets proved but an inefficient protection against the heavy clubs with which the Saxon serfs were armed ; heads and helmets were alike crushed beneath their blows, and many chose death by plunging into the deep moat beneath, which soon ran purple with their blood, rather than meet it from the desperate Saxons' hands.

After an hour's hard fighting the bridge was cleared, and the assailants remained masters of the position, which, however, advanced them but little in their general attack, for the iron-studded gates resisted all their efforts, while from the lofty battlements directly over them the besieged kept raining down showers of boiling oil and melted lead, and ponderous beams of wood, which crushed by dozens the unhappy mutilated wretches upon whom they fell.

Ralph de Gael, who directed the defence, beheld with pleasure the foe recoil before the destructive missiles. In the insolence of his triumph he addressed their leader with every taunt and insult his malice could suggest.

"What ! " he exclaimed, ironically, "retreat so soon ! Strike one blow more ! Or is Saxon courage cooled with its first check ? For the future, women and girls shall guard our walls, and hold them, too, 'gainst such assailants. Ulrick," he added, "had Stanfield towers been kept like mine, my sword had found its task less easy. I almost blush to have crushed so poor an enemy."

"Coward !—cool, insulting coward ! " replied our hero, his eyes flashing fire at the allusion to his once happy home, "descend from thy stronghold, and let the sword decide between us. I'll stake my country's wrongs and rights upon the issue."

"Thinkst thou I am so poor a gamester ? " shouted the tyrant, with an insulting laugh, "to risk that which is mine already ? The gibbet, knave, and not a noble's sword, is the fit doom thy rash presumption merits. Slaves," he continued, addressing the Saxons, who had retreated beyond the reach of the burning shower, "Henry will soon be here ; long ere this the royal banner floats upon the breeze. To your homes—your homes ; wait not the lion's wrath, lest it consume ye."

The assertion of the expected arrival of the king, who was known to be at a day's march from the city, struck a damp on the hearts of many, and might have produced the effect the speaker artfully intended, had not the shouts and cries within the walls informed them that one part at least of their attack had been successful—that Edward and his troop had obtained an entrance to the castle.

The tyrant's flushed cheek turned pale as the war-cry of the victorious Saxons fell upon his ear.

The next moment Richard de Montmar, the seneschal, his sword broken, and his gashed brow streaming with blood, appeared upon the walls before his terror-stricken master.

"What meant that cry ? " he faltered.

"The foe are in our walls ; like Cadmus' sons, they rise from earth. Our men, discouraged, murmur treason, and demand their leader. To the hall, or all is lost."

For a few moments his chief stood as if struck by the destroying angel's hand, so wild, so improbable did the intelligence appear; nor was it till the renewed cries of the combatants burst upon the air that he started from his mental palsy. Calling to his men, he rushed from the walls, to stem the tide which Heaven had so mysteriously turned against him. In a few minutes the battlements were deserted, except by the wounded and the dying who had fallen beneath the arrows of the Saxons.

Ulrick, who judged the cause of the confusion, suffered not the advantage to be lost; but redoubled his efforts against the no longer well-defended gates, which, from their massive strength, for a time continued to defy his utmost efforts. While the assailants, with renewed vigour, are continuing the attack, let us follow the dismayed Norman to the scene which met his gaze within his hitherto deemed impregnable stronghold.

A large portion of the garrison were assembled in the great hall of the castle fighting desperately with the Saxons, who, under the conduct of Edward, occupied the low arched galleries which ran round the apartment, and from which their arrows did fearful execution upon their enemies; the floor was strewed with the dead and dying, whose mingled groans, yells of agony, and execrations added to the horrors of the scene. In the centre of the hall stood the excited Ethra: her right hand holding a torch; her long dark hair, freed from the veil which she had lost in the tumult, streaming like a meteor in the wind. Regardless of her own safety, she urged on her countrymen to the attack, her shrill voice rising above the din of arms as she reminded them of the wrongs and shames their Norman tyrants had inflicted on their hearths and homes.

"Traitress!" exclaimed Ralph, as he confronted her, "it is to thee I owe this desolation, this ruin of my hopes. Thine was the accursed hand to release my deadly foes, and bring the Saxon hound upon my track."

Ethra surveyed him with a look of withering scorn and an unblanched cheek; the haughty spirit of her race was on her, and though a secret instinct told her that the dark thread of her existence in a few moments would be severed, her heart trembled not, neither did her voice falter as she answered him:

"Monster! thinkst thou I would leave my gallant father in thy grasp, and have the power to save him? Is't not enough thou hast lured me to foul perdition's brink, but thou wouldst plunge my guileless sister in the dread abyss? Hark to that shout!" she added, as the triumphant voices of the assailants, who had just broken in the outward gates, burst upon her ear; "'tis the victorious cry of Liberty rejoicing to behold her children free. The Saxon,

the despised Saxon, hunts thee now ; the spirits of my slaughtered
kindred ride upon the storm ; the furies claim thee as their destined
prey. Soon shall they be avenged."

The passion of her tyrant was too intense for words ; surprise,
too, held him chained. His hitherto submissive victim, whose
heart he had trampled on, whose feelings wantonly sported with,
had turned like a lioness to rend him. With a look of concentrated
hatred, he twice passed his sword through her defenceless body,
and the betrayed, unhappy Ethra fell, without one groan or sigh, a
corpse at her destroyer's feet. She had met the fate she sought.
Love, honour, happiness were lost ; and as freely as the sea-bird
dashed the spray from its soiled wing, she cast her life away, a cold
smile of triumph lighting her features even in death.

The murderer had not long to exult over his revenge, for the
voice of Ulrick urging on his followers, or calling with passionate
vehemence upon his child, alarmed him for his own worthless
safety. Calling on his esquire and a party of the most determined
of his men to follow him, he made his way over the mangled and
the dying to a corner of the hall, where a narrow staircase led to a
solitary turret, the flat roof of which was large enough, perhaps, to
hold fifty men, and which one determined sword might defend
against a host of enemies.

"Turn, craven hound !" shouted our hero to him, as he ascended
the steps. The defiance which would have followed was cut short
by a pang such as a father's heart alone could feel. His child—his
deeply loved, long-mourned, repentant child—lay weltering in her
life's blood e'en at his very feet. With a cry like that a breaking
heart sends forth, he sank upon his knee beside her. The warrior
was extinct—the parent only lived within his breast.

"Wake !" he sobbed, as he pressed his lips with passionate
tenderness to her cold brow ; "wake to hear the pardon thou hast
so dearly won. Ethra—child of my love, first-born of my hope—
one look, one little pressure of thy hand ! Dead, dead !" he murmured. "God, my brain is on fire—my heart is broken !"

So majestic was the grief of the bereaved parent that even his
enemies respected it. These, however, were soon driven from the
hall by the arrival of Arad and the party under his command.
The slaughter on both sides had been fearful, for Norman and
Saxon fought with all the bitterness of long-garnered hate. The
castle, with the exception of the solitary tower into which Ralph
and his party had retreated, was in possession of the assailants,
when an unexpected event entirely changed the fortunes of the
night.

Henry, who had been holding his Parliament at Bury St.
Edmund's, was in council when the missive of the governor of
the East Angles was presented to him. His indignation, as well
as that of his nobles, was extreme. That the man whom he had

snatched from justice should so ungratefully repay his mercy stung him to the quick ; and he swore, by the oath of his race, to proceed at once to Norwich, and execute strict justice on the offenders. Despite the haste of his march, the battle was fought ere he arrived. But the overwhelming force which accompanied him rendered all resistance on the part of the victorious Saxons unavailing ; and they saw the fruits of victory snatched from them even in the moment of success. The larger body of them retired to their homes ; and Ulrick, Arad, Edward, and most of the chiefs remained prisoners in the hands of the Normans.

At an early hour on the following morning a council was held in the chapter-house of the cathedral, at which the king presided in person. Ralph de Gael, Salisbury, De Warrenne, De Vere of Oxford, and many barons of less note, were seated at the board. When the chancellor, our hero's old enemy, took his seat, the forgeries, upon which on a previous occasion the lord of Stanfield had been condemned, lay open on the table. At a signal from Henry, Ulrick and his companions in misfortune were introduced. His cheek was pale from loss of blood and the fierce emotions which had so lately wrung his soul. But if his step faltered from weakness, his eye was bright and proud as ever ; it shrank not from the stern gaze of his judges, nor quailed beneath the triumphant sneer of his oppressor. Henry was the first to speak.

"My lords," he exclaimed, "we are here to judge an ingrate and a traitor, whom I confess that, with a weakness unworthy of a king, yielding to an angel's prayer, I saved from your resentment. Of Ralph de Gael's administration, and the oppressions of which he is accused, we will decide hereafter. But however they may palliate," he added, pointing to the other Saxon chiefs, " the outbreak of these misguided men, they excuse not the lord of Stanfield—the plotter, the assassin."

" The wronged, the slandered !" exclaimed a deep-toned voice, at whose sound all present started.

The doors of the chapter-house were thrown open, and Robert of Artois, dressed in his priestly rags, just as Ethra had released him from his dungeon, stood before them.

"Wretch ! " he cried, fixing a glance of scorn upon the man who had so long held him captive ; "here, within these holy walls— here, in the presence of Heaven and of man, avow your treachery and Ulrick's wrongs, detested, grovelling, most unknightly villain ! "

" Who art thou ? " demanded the chancellor.

"Ask of yon monster," resumed the speaker, pointing to the astonished Ralph de Gael—"of him who for ten years hath held me captive in a loathsome cell, till of humanity its memory only rests—of him who, to conceal his murders, outrages, and crimes, forced me, an unworthy priest of the Most High—by tortures forced me to forge the proofs on which you would condemn the preserver of your monarch's life, and crush the noblest heart that tyranny e'er reached."

"Liar!" faltered the detected but unabashed miscreant—"what proof?"

"What proof!" iterated his accuser, with a cold smile, whose serpent-like expression was far more terrible than even his impassioned scorn. "Fear not, thou shalt hear proof enough to satisfy the doubt of incredulity itself—to brand the festering lie upon thy brow—to show thee to the world the monster that thou art, and strip thee of the last defence falsehood and infamy have left thee."

"Assertion is not evidence," interrupted the chancellor, rising uneasily from his seat.

"True," said the repentant man; "and an angel's oath would lack conviction to a heart like thine, seared in the subtle trickeries of office, and dead to every generous, natural impulse. Behold the proof!"

Hastily taking up the forged letters one by one, he laid them before the king. Passing over them, at the same time, a sponge dipped in some aromatic essence which he drew from his breast, to the surprise of the monarch and his councillors and the confusion of Ralph, a second inscription appeared beneath the first.

Henry seized the paper, and eagerly read as follows:

"I, Onfroy, caligrapher, and priest of the cathedral church of Norwich, trusting that Heaven will one day bring my weakness and the cruelty of Ralph de Gael to light, declare that, having been twice put to the torture, I have reluctantly consented to forge these letters, being prisoner the while to the aforesaid Ralph de Gael."

Our readers need scarcely be reminded that the composition of the sympathetic ink was, in the age of which we write, a secret confined chiefly to the cloister.

"Monster! unknightly felon!" exclaimed the king, as the last letter fell from his indignant hand, "what answer for thy worthless life—what subterfuge or subtle turn can serve thee now?"

"Sorcery," replied Ralph, desperately resolved to brave it to the last. "Relying on my innocence and Heaven's assistance, I demand the knightly combat."

Henry, surnamed "Beauclerk," was not to be deceived by an excuse which the more superstitious of his council took into their serious consideration. Whilst they clustered round the council-table to consult on the demand, the king approached the prisoner, whose cheek had proudly flushed on hearing the proofs of his innocence, but in a few seconds became paler than before.

"Lord of Stanfield," demanded the agitated monarch, "canst thou forgive the involuntary wrong I most unwittingly have done thee?"

"Protect my child—redress my country's wrongs," sighed our hero, "and all is well."

"Heaven!" exclaimed the king, "he is dying!"

His fears were but too true. Worn by loss of blood, and the many bitter trials he had undergone, the tired spirit of our hero was rapidly passing away to rejoin those he had loved, but failed to avenge, on earth. His eye-lids were half-closed in death when the voice of the chancellor for a few moments recalled him to the world.

"The battle is accorded," he coldly pronounced; "let the sword decide between the accused and the accuser."

The usages of chivalry with the Normans were sacred. Monarchs and nobles alike were bound by them; and the chancellor and his party thought by their decision to avoid the odium of so foul an accusation being proved against a member of their own order. Henry heard their decision with indignation, anger, and contempt.

"The combat!" he repeated; "and with a dying man!"

"I am ready!" faintly exclaimed Ulrick, like some wounded lion rearing his form erect to meet the hunter's last attack; "where is my sword?" and weakened by the effort, he fell back into the arms of Arad. Henry pointed to his feeble state in silence.

"Let him appear by champion!" exclaimed the council, in answer to his mute appeal.

"Be it so!" said Henry, with a burst of wrath, which told the presuming barons they had gone too far. "I'll be his champion. Ulrick of Stanfield," he continued, taking the dying hero's hand. "I here proclaim thee innocent—the soul of honour and the light of truth. Most foully hath thy vile accuser lied. There lies my glove—a monarch's glove shall be thy gage of battle."

Suiting the action to the word, the excited king threw his embroidered glove upon the ground. None presumed to raise it. The Norman nobles would have gone far to save one of their order, but not one felt disposed to brave a wrath which, once roused, might consume them. Even the chancellor was silenced, for he knew that Henry, when really excited, was capable of daring everything. There was a solemn silence in the hall, which the monarch was the first to break.

"No answer!" he exclaimed. "Away with him, then! De Vere, you act as marshal. In ten minutes let the trumpet's breath proclaim that he hath met a felon's doom."

Despite his protestations, Ralph de Gael was dragged from the assembly, and in a less space of time than even the king had announced, the fearful signal was heard, and his last sigh passed from him on the gibbet.

"Ulrick," said his champion, "preserver of my life, I have avenged thee."

"More," answered our hero, with a last effort; "thou hast preserved my honour. All is over, and the prediction of the prophet priest of Croydon is accomplished."

"I remember," added Henry; "a life of honour, a soldier's triumph, but a broken heart."

A smile of gratitude passed over the features of the dying man, as he fixed his last look upon the speaker. That smile remained after the spirit of Ulrick had passed away.

Most of the Saxon chiefs were pardoned. Henry kept his Christmas at Norwich, and granted the citizens their first charter, in compensation for the exactions which they had suffered from their unprincipled governor, who was found to have amassed enormous wealth by his oppression. Before the monarch left the city, the marriage of Myrra and Edward was solemnised in the presence of the Court by Robert of Artois, who did not long survive his restoration to liberty, but was found dead at the tomb of Ulrick, whither he went daily to offer up his prayers.

END OF VOL. I.